This may look like just a book, but NOVUS MONSTRUM could infect your brain, shake your sense of what's real, *change you forever*. This is twenty-two all-original new monster tales from the greats: Jonathan Maberry, Joe R. Lansdale, Gabino Iglesias, Gemma Files, Gaby Triana, Ramsey Campbell, Jeffrey Thomas, Gwendolyn Kiste, and Lucy A. Snyder, plus thirteen stories from *new* names (see below) destined to become some of your favorite authors.

These monsters are never-before-seen. These monsters bite, and don't let go. These monsters aren't your grandparents' boogeymen, but they are not tame, and they want to climb right down into your nightmares and *make you their own*.

Welcome to the new anthology series *The Midnight Zone*.

Ken MacGregor, editor of the Shirley-Jackson-Award-nominated anthology *Stitched Lips* and the uproarious *Burnt Fur,* teamed up with Bram-Stoker-Award-nominated short story author Douglas Gwilym, editor of *Appetites* and *Harmony & Dissonance*, to take you to strange and dark new places. They'll ask you to go deeper and weirder than *The Twilight Zone*, to a place (like the real-world *midnight zone,* a mile beneath the ocean's surface) where *no sunlight penetrates.* Join us as we explore the inhospitable, surprising, uncomfortable, bizarre, and otherworldly.

Go on. Dive in. Lose yourself to *The Midnight Zone.*

> Also Featuring:
> Amanda M. Blake
> Joshua Bartolome
> Matt Brandenburg
> R.A. Busby
> Marco Cultrera
> E.C. Dorgan
> Douglas Ford
> Sarah Hans
> Jamie Lackey
> Donna J.W. Munro
> Frank Oreto
> Tim Pieraccini
> Pris Sears

With an introduction by the amazing Jamie Flanagan, screenwriter for *Haunting of Bly Manor, Midnight Mass, Creepshow,* and *Fall of the House of Usher,* and original cover art by the astonishing Trevor Henderson, internet cult phenomenon, creator *of Siren Head,* and weaver of monsters!

Praise for Novus Monstrum

"Mysterious, merciless, mirthful. New favorites await you in this superb anthology."

— Johnny Compton author of *Spite House*
(esquire best horror book of 2023)

NOVUS MONSTRUM

Novus Monstrum

The Midnight Zone
Book One

Douglas Gwilym

Ken MacGregor

Dragon's Roost Press

Printed in the United States of America

Ingram ISBN: 978-1-956824-40-7

Print ISBN 978-1-956824-18-6

Digital ISBN 978-1-956824-19-3

Dragon's Roost Press

2470 Hunter Rd

Brighton, MI 48114

DEDICATIONS

Douglas Gwilym:
For my fourth grade teacher, Mrs. Mills, who first believed in me as a
storyteller, and Bill Riggs, my best friend at the time, who convinced me
the greatest stories have monsters.
Also, for Alan Moore.

Ken MacGregor:
To Mom, who instilled in me a deep and abiding love of the written word.
And to Dad, who was the first person to show me that one can look at a
story drawkcab as well as forward. I'm well-aware monster stories aren't
really your thing, either one of you, but I wanted you to know how much I
appreciate you both.

Contents

Introduction

I am not an expert on the subject of monsters.

I am simply someone who understands—as you do—what it is to be afraid.

Fears, general and specific, large and small, form the anatomy of monsters. Some fears—primal, universally understood—congeal into monsters that become eternal. Vampires. Werewolves. Ghosts. Cannibalistic spirits known to Indigenous Americans, whose names should not be written nor uttered. Familiar stories retold, reshaped, reimagined.

Here, fresh terrors lurk. New nightmares, new monstrosities. Made. Hatched. Conjured. Spawned from the celestial unknown to descend upon us, awe inspiring and inscrutable. Risen from the abyssal depths of the sea, ready to devour. Or born of the mundane, in places as innocuous as amusement parks or dating apps. Or the dining room of a newly purchased home.

Here, the familiar is swallowed by the unfamiliar and unsettling. Here, there be not dragons, but legions of space lizards with translucent stomach sacs.

There's a monster at the end of this book. And at the beginning. And many more throughout, shaped by authors and editors who know what it is to stay awake in late hours, staring deeply into shadows. People who—like you—know fear. At its most intimate and disarming.

The grotesqueries they've imagined claw for vulnerable places on which to latch. Fertile ground to sink a claw or tooth.

So read on. But be warned: as you stare into these pages, many eyes stare back. Hungry. Waiting. Eager to follow you home, where they may become—as their predecessors—eternal.

Jamie Flanagan
July 11, 2023

Brother Bone

Donna J. W. Munro

Ozark born and Ozark bred. Not these carpet-bagging lake refugees building all the strip malls and fancy sit-down restaurants. No.

Me and mine live in the old hills below the electric dam and lake where there's still a river and thick stands of trees. Takes courage to leave the highway and the two-lane black ribbon of road to turn up into the drive. The old wagon ruts cut in limestone barely hold the gravel when Micah, the town manager, tries to come fix up things.

He used to live with us in the old lean-tos circling the only clearing on the whole hill. He knows what guards us and that he ought to come on home and live next to his Daddy and Ma's bones.

We tell him that.

"No," he says, pulling back his shoulders real proper like. "I got a degree and a decent job. No need for me to live up here, folk. It's not fit for man nor beast."

"Was good enough for your Daddy and kin all the way back. Bone calls to bone," I told him.

He never stays 'til dark.

His ma didn't raise no fool.

"He ought to bring home a gal or two, you know you can't 'spect Brother Bone to wait forever."

All the old ones nod sagely. I knew that for my own. I'd done the same as Micah back when I was young. Thought I could put the dust of this place behind me. Ran myself into the army to fight in the trenches. Wasn't anything but horror and hate and every letter I got begged me to come on home and bring a gal for Brother Bone. Since Ma didn't write no letters, she didn't know how, the pages she sent were smudged with the black dirt of the hill and her tears, but I understood just the same.

When one came covered with blood, I knew I couldn't live with the guilt. I skinned off my uniform and worked my way back through the frontline, up into the north, and hopped a freighter ship. The damned thing got torpedoed out in the big ocean. The Atlantic. An ocean my kin hadn't seen for a thousand years and there I was swimming in it.

Took forever.

Sometimes a fish would nibble. They spit me out quick once they tasted my blood.

I swam forever until I got to Florida. All swamp and crocs and nothing, but it reminded me of home. I rode the rail and hitched on the rattle trap Fords some folks drove back then. Walked when I had to. By the time I got home, all that was left of Ma was her body from hip to chin, her head, and one arm. Daddy had been put into the ground already by Brother Bone.

"Get you a gal, son," Ma said. "A gal will save you even if she don't save me."

Brother Bone took the rest of her that night when I was laying up in my narrow childhood pallet in the rafters. I heard the clacking and the screaming and the chewing that ripped and tore and then the licking and I was a child again, covering my ears with the thin pillow and whimpering a prayer that he wouldn't find me in the rafters.

I got a gal the next day.

Purdy thing. Got her and took her back to the hill with promises of money.

Left her chained next to the boy that Sal brought home from the tent revival.

Nothing there the next morning but our rations.

Nothing but life.

I drive down into town, a real town now with a main street, a diner, a gas station, and a little museum to the criminals Jesse and Frank James. Folks turn away from us hill folk when we come to town. Somehow, they know that we are hunting when we roll up, even if it's so deep in their bones they can't put words or names to their feelings.

I head into Micah's office on the second floor of the brick city hall I helped build back when my wife Sal still had my little ones tucked away in their chamber, dreaming of legs and bones.

He glances up when he recognizes the smell of kin.

"Daddy, I can't come back. Not unless you want Brother Bone to take me. I'm in love with a gal so sweet I won't give her up."

I shake my head.

I know the gal. She's a spitfire. Raised on the river with Ozark in her blood. She's a beauty. Full of herself 'cause she's got money. A lawyer or some such. And she does love my boy. I smell it on him. A good woman's touch. Laughs that shine like blue armor in his life light.

Makes me sad to take her when she leaves her office that night. I plunge the needle into her neck and put her under, then carry her over to the car. Her limp body sags in the bucket seat of my old Ford, but it's better that way. Letting her sleep and dream of love was a kindness I could afford. She'd be strapped to the offering post soon enough and Micah would see the writing on the wall.

Your bones don't bend.

They don't lie.

They don't forgive.

I got her up the hill as the others laid out their offerings. Past a certain age, 'possum will do it. Rabbit and deer satisfies the *geas* once you marry and have youngins' to carry on for you. Even a dog will do on the rare occasion. But if you want a long life, you gotta give up youth to Brother Bone. And this gal of Micah's was full of that bright light only the young had to give him.

An hour passed as we prayed and sang the old songs to draw him. She came to and I'm sorry to say, she screamed and wet herself when she saw us covered in the gore of our offerings staining the white of our robes. I'd need to think about something more potent to keep the next one asleep. I'm not a monster that I'll let 'em suffer so. Least not if I can help it.

She writhed and begged. Promised so many things that made the oldsters leer and the gals blush. She threatened violence. She tried to negotiate for her life. Anything, she said. Anything.

They all say those things.

Light cones flashed up the hill and tires crunched against the ruts in our old road. It was Micah, sure as shit. I'd be disappointed in him if her life was so cheap that he didn't come to the end of it.

He leaped out of the car and ran to her.

She blubbered and called to him when she saw him comin'. Poor gal must'a thought he could save her.

Love can't cut through chains.

"Daddy, please!" Micah begged. "She's pregnant. We're getting married."

He knew better than that. He knew the stories. He'd felt the ground shake when Brother Bone danced. He'd tasted immortality along with us.

The elders hissed with disapproval.

"You done this to yourself, young one. Step aside or face Brother Bone," I said, though some of the words caught in my throat. I still loved him, even with all his hubris and high-falutin' ways. The worst lessons come soaked in blood and crunched between the teeth of those you serve.

She screamed when she saw Brother Bone coming up from behind us, rising up from the hill itself. Thin and tall, white as the freshest snow. He filled the sky as he got up all spindly and dry bones clacking.

We all dropped our eyes as we'd been taught. Brother Bone doesn't like eyes. He doesn't have them himself.

Micah fell to the ground, groveling, begging for Brother Bone to leave the lovely morsel he'd found alone. His words weren't new. We'd all said them once or twice, only Micah didn't scramble away as the spikes of our brother's arms pierced the ground beside him.

He shook and cried and kept begging.

"Please, Brother Bone, let me find you another. Please!" He begged with folded hands and such love in his words, it near broke my heart.

Brother Bone touched him for a second with that white, dry bone appendage. Pity from the bones of us.

But my boy, my idiot son, looked up into the pits of Brother Bone's face—the dark pits where eyes should be. And Brother Bone roared his disappointment so loud, so long, all the folk fell to their knees and covered their ears, mewling.

I admit I did the same.

One of Brother Bone's limbs skewered my boy right through the chest and I swear I felt it like it was in my own body.

He held Micah there to watch as he pulled apart the gal, ripping out every bone as Micah wept. Licking the pink and velvety red leavings off the sockets of her shoulders and flats of her leg bones. The slithering white of Brother Bone's tongue and his clacks and grunts filled all my senses and how my boy howled as his gal stopped moving. She was just a skin suit. A pile of meat by the time Brother Bone turned from her. He chewed up what he took and spit the white paste onto the ends of his spiked limbs, thickening them.

He purred as he filled in the little holes in his bones as he always did.

Micah moaned in the puddle of his and her blood that gathered under him. He knew what came next.

Brother Bone took Micah's leg bones so he wouldn't run away, then he picked a morsel of the cooling gal's body from her flapped open chest —a bit of her heart mayhap—and shoved it into Micah's mouth.

The magic of her meat closed his wounds and left him healing when Brother Bone yanked out his spiked finger and ambled away. He'd fed and healed enough for now.

The elders set to work, scraping out the meat of the girl and Micah's meat leg flaps, slicing and salting each strip for us to eat later, praising Brother Bone for the gifts.

"I... I loved her," Micah said, blood tears running from his eyes.

"I know. But it's not our way, son. You knew that."

"I don't want to live forever, Daddy. I don't want to eat people and feed bones to that monster," he wheezed as his body took in the magic of the heart meat, healing the damage in his chest from within.

I shushed him. He'd settle into it. Without his legs and a reason to leave, he'd settle in. Maybe marry his cousin Lucy and give me a grandbaby.

He'd settle in.

WONCE WAS A WOMAN

DOUGLAS FORD

FOR MARGE PIERCY, author of "The Secretary Chant"

IT TURNED out that they all had not only heard of the poem, but they'd read it, each one of them. While leaning against the sink and chuffing a cigarette, one of the older secretaries even recited the opening line from memory. When she finished, she said, "Your hips really will feel like a desk some days, what with the way they run you off your feet."

Carla pretended to laugh. She still found herself trying to remember all their names, but she knew this one went by Alberta. On the mirror's surface, just above Alberta's silver-streaked hair, she saw a "Good Luck Jerry" bumper sticker, but someone had used lipstick to cross out *Good* and scrawl *Rotten* instead.

Another secretary (*Trish*, Carla now recalled) saw Carla's eyes and gestured toward it. "Hope that doesn't offend you. We're all voting for Carter. We have to get that ERA passed."

"Amen to that," said Alberta. "The head honchos would have a conniption if they saw our non-endorsement up there. They're assuming we're all pulling the lever for Ford. If they ever came in here, they'd probably fire all of us."

"Or worse," said Trish, without elaborating.

Everyone nodded. But Carla didn't want to talk about presidential politics. Instead, she wanted to talk about the poem. These women knew something they wouldn't say out loud.

"But it's not just metaphor, right?" Carla asked.

They all looked at her quizzically, their ignorance clearly a put-on. Julie, the one who hardly ever spoke, asked, "The Equal Rights Amendment, or our political preferences?"

"No," said Carla. "I mean the business about the hips. Likening the hips to a desk."

They continued to gaze at her in a clueless way, until Alberta, the cigarette dangling from her lips, looked at her watch and said, "Shit. We need to get back to work, ladies—or we'll give those bald Vikings a reason to storm our sanctuary."

The other two nodded and stubbed out their cigarettes, waving away the smoke as they left the bathroom in single file. Carla trailed behind them, trying to stifle a cough.

Maybe she simply needed to better discipline herself, not make it too obvious what she sought by asking such direct questions. At least not so soon after starting as one of the many secretaries at Peabody Brokerage.

Not that she found it easy to land her new job, even with a resume full of embellishments, distortions, and outright lies. Fortunately, before he bit down on the wrong end of a gun barrel, her father worked for Decker Wetherell. Well into his nineties now and quite senile, Decker had met a much younger version of her when she visited her father at work, and he maintained enough of a blurry memory of her that he recognized her when she visited him at the Gray Oaks Retirement Facility. He nodded enthusiastically when she reminded him how she served as his personal secretary for five years. Not at all true, but by the time he started eating the chocolates she brought for him as a gift, he reminisced right along with her and eventually used a shaky hand to sign the reference letter she'd already written for him. The letter praised her diligence and work ethic, though she tried not to overdo it. When she got up to leave, he actually managed to get that shaky hand up her skirt and use it to squeeze her ass before she could bid him a good day. When the letter did the trick, she could almost, but not quite, forgive him for groping her. In this world, they all did that. If only she could bring the wrath of Eris down on them all, starting with him.

Eris. Who knew what name she really went by, or if she had a name at all. Absent one, Carla thought of her as Eris, named for the goddess of destruction.

The women returned to their desks and their typewriters, but Julie slowed her progress and pretended to extract a troubling piece of lint from her sweater. She whispered something Carla couldn't hear. When Carla asked her to repeat herself, Julie shushed her.

"I know what you meant," Julie said, indicating they needed to keep their volume low. She gestured toward the coffee machine. "Help me make some more. They'll want their afternoon fix soon."

Carla nodded. As Julie measured grounds, she said, "That goddamned poem about the woman turning into office material—that's the only reason you're here, isn't it?"

Julie's expression nearly made Carla wither and give up the ruse. As the youngest of the secretaries, Julie originally struck her as innocent and naïve, but she now realized her error. A façade, and more effective than her own. Maybe they all needed one to endure.

"It's not just a poem full of metaphor, is it?" asked Carla as she helped Julie arrange coffee cups on saucers. "She's *real.*"

Julie let her pursed lips answer for her, and Carla pressed on.

"I want to see her. Where is she? Where does she hide? When does she come out?"

"What makes you think she gets to come out? If she does, you wouldn't want to be around her. Trust me."

"But why?"

"*Why?*"

By that point, they'd failed to keep their volume low enough for the others not to notice. Alberta arched an eyebrow in their direction, causing Carla to bump one of the cups out of Julie's hand. It fell to the floor and shattered.

A string of profanities flew from Julie's mouth. It shocked Carla how incorrectly she'd read this woman. Perhaps she'd found the high priestess of this little group.

She knelt next to Julie and helped pick up broken shards of porcelain. "Please, I *need* to see her."

"Well, you can't. None of us see her. But we know if she's been let loose, and *oboy*, that usually spells trouble."

"Girls?"

They both froze as a bald head appeared from around a half-opened door. The head might have belonged to Hidey Fish, one of the senior executives, but they all looked alike to Carla with their spotted, hairless scalps. "Trouble out here?" asked the bald head.

Carla and Julie used their happy voices in unison. "No, sir."

"Well," said Hidey Fish, "get that cleaned up. We're awaiting our coffee. And Julie?"

Julie looked up with a smile so false that Carla wondered how Hidey couldn't see it.

"A little something extra in mine." He winked at her.

"Of course, Mr. Fish."

The bald head started to disappear, but it paused. "You know I always like something extra."

Julie's false smile widened. "I know you do. I'm here to please, sir."

"You certainly do," said Hidey Fish. As he withdrew his head like a fed eel, the man's gaze lingered a bit in Carla's direction. Her skin crawling, she tugged at the hem of her skirt as she stood up.

She tried to engage Julie further, but the appearance of the bald executive caused everyone's lips to tighten. Everyone now seemed hyper-focused and even a little scared. Alberta typed furiously while Trish went to a file cabinet she kept guarded behind her desk. Opening a drawer, she withdrew a bottle of bourbon and handed it without comment to Julie. Everyone instantly became a cog in the machine, fearful of appearing anything more.

Carla wanted to scream at them. Didn't they know that the poem warned them not to act this way? Not to allow themselves to become absorbed into the soulless environment of the office, becoming just another piece of furniture or office equipment? But the poem didn't just speak in metaphor. Julie believed that more than ever now. The woman in the poem composed of office parts was a messiah, a beacon of resistance. Her transformed body functioned as a weapon, and if they chose to follow her, the men would find themselves cowering for a change. She more than believed this—she *knew.*

After her father's suicide, her mother tried to survive on a job like this one, and Carla watched as it took her to her own early grave. It was one of her mother's co-workers who gave Carla a tattered copy of the poem at the funeral, saying "This is who could have saved her. Who could have delivered her and saved her from dying."

Puzzled, Carla read the poem and struggled to understand it. A chant for secretaries, one that described a woman whose body bore the features of office equipment, culminating in the birth of a Xerox machine. It struck her as absurd at first. But its images persisted in her consciousness, and during a brief stint of homelessness, she wandered the city, reciting it quietly to herself. Soon, she began noticing echoes of its lines in unexpected places—often as graffiti in subways and bathroom walls, perhaps scrawled there by despondent secretaries trying to summon the being to rescue them from their suffering. Carla came to understand it as not so much a shapeshifting entity like a werewolf, but something more like a golem, charged with championing an underclass of sorts.

Later, as her searches for it became more focused, she found that she could pry more information by offering booze, drugs, even sex on a few occasions, once she found the right people. In bed, one woman told her that she had actually seen it. "It comes out at night." Though Carla had never thought of herself as gay, she enjoyed letting the woman stroke her hair as they spent a post-coital moment together. "The time has to be right for it to be summoned."

"How do you summon it?" Carla asked.

"Anger? Sadness? Hurt?" The woman said she didn't know as she went on stroking Carla's hair, but she told her where she'd seen it.

The Offices of Peabody Brokerage.

———

IT TURNED out that Hidey Fish, the firm's most senior executive, did in fact take note of Carla. He closely scrutinized her work as the day slogged along, finding flaws in her typing that needed innumerable corrections as well as missing data that required her to thumb through files as ancient as himself. When Trish, Alberta, and Julie began gathering their things to leave for the day, Carla tried to do the same, but before she could grab her purse, the bald head of Hidey Fish appeared once more, his brow furrowing at the document in his hand.

"I can fix it in the morning, Mr. Fish," Alberta tried to say, but he waved her off. Alberta regarded Carla, not with disapproval but with genuine concern.

"It needs to be corrected right away." He meant these words for Carla. She accepted the document, her eyes fluttering over it, trying to puzzle out the errors. Judging by the looks she received from the three other secretaries, she suspected there weren't any.

"It's okay." She smiled at them as they stood near the door, their coats already snug around their shoulders. "I've got this."

"You don't," Alberta quietly said. "Trust me."

"It's alright. Really."

Nodding ruefully, they filed out the door, though the last one, Julie, lingered a moment longer. "Don't let him tell you about his name."

"What?"

"Just look away when he does that thing." But Hidey Fish appeared again, and Julie shuffled away without elaborating.

In truth, Carla approved of her situation. Without the other women watching her, she could explore the office a bit more deeply, including a rather imposing looking file cabinet snugged behind Trish's desk. Aside from booze, Carla didn't know what they kept in there, but she sensed that they kept it largely inaccessible for a reason. It held the air of something forbidden, and she felt herself drawn to it.

But at the moment she could sense Hidey Fish leering at her.

"Would you like me to go over the errors with you?" she heard him say. "Are my notations clear?"

She shook her head and affirmed he had made them quite clear. She just needed to freshen up a bit, she said, indicating the restroom.

"You all go in there so often together. Are you afraid to go alone? I could accompany you."

"No," she said, smiling with the same fakeness she'd learned from the others.

"Female bodies are amazing in how they all seem to work in sync. Your bladders, colons, menstrual cycles."

She continued to smile, waiting for him to leave.

"You're not experiencing a menstrual cycle, are you?"

"No, sir," she said.

Their stand-off continued until Hidey seemed to understand that she wouldn't enter the restroom until he returned to his office. When he finally did so, Carla exhaled the breath she'd been holding.

Instead of the restroom, she turned toward the file cabinet. All day, her intuition had whispered to her that it held something special, something that involved the poem and the being it described. No telling how much time she had before Hidey reappeared. Her eyes scanned the markings of the drawers, each one corresponding to the letters of the alphabet. She finally decided to start with the one marked with "E"—for *Eris*, even though she'd conjured that name on her own.

Sadly, she found it full of documents that looked mundane and ordinary. Quickly, she tried another drawer: "S" for *Secretary*. The results mirrored her first attempt.

She paused, remembering the poem.

"*File me under W*," she recited to herself, quoting the last line, "*because I wonce was a woman.*"

On her haunches now, she opened the last drawer.

At first a musty scent filled her senses, as well as faint traces of perfume. Then came the odor that the perfume was meant to mask. Not a pleasant one at all, but cloyingly organic, like wet straw and rotting leaves. She coughed and shielded her nose, but her spirits rose when instead of files she found wads of tissue and the kind of muslin one might use to create a funeral veil. Waving the air around her with one hand, she used the other to poke through the mess. Hidden underneath these layers, she felt something solid. She pulled it out to investigate.

A cigar box, likely owned by Hidey Fish or one of his associates. She opened it.

And recoiled.

Nested within, she found four human fingers, their skin wrinkled and parchment gray. Blackened fingernails with hints of red polish on one end, a fragment of bone on the other.

Somehow, she managed to not spill the box's contents.

Instead, she found the poise she needed to set it aside and continue digging through the drawer.

Which led to finding the book.

Ragged in appearance, it sported an ancient-looking leather cover and crinkled yellow pages. She thumbed through it and encountered a curious script as well as the occasional artfully conceived illustrations. Unable to read the script, she at first took it for someone's eccentric cursive. Closer scrutiny led her to a series of different conclusions, first that it constituted some kind of shorthand, then that it was a different kind of alphabet altogether. At times, the script devolved into confusing sequences of lines, crosses, and circles. She couldn't make heads or tails of it.

Just before giving in to complete frustration, she finally came across a word she recognized, spelled in all-capital letters:

BASEMENT

Underneath the word appeared what looked like a floor plan.

If someone meant to beckon her, that did the trick.

Anticipating that Hidey Fish might reappear at any moment, she quickly closed the cabinet drawer and, book in hand, made her way to the elevator. What she sought, she now believed, lay in the basement of this very building.

Thanks to the late hour, she had the elevator to herself—at least until it made one stop before descending all the way to the basement. On the third floor, a woman stumbled through the door, crying, her glasses askew. She glanced at Carla as she struggled to find something in her purse.

"Run while you can," the woman said. "This place'll chew you up and spit you out."

Carla clutched the leather book against her chest and watched the woman extract a tissue from her purse and use it to dab her eyes.

"I showed the fucker though," said the woman, as if Carla had asked a question. "I got him good in the balls. With my knee. Then I ran. They don't expect us to fight back. The balls—that's supposed to be their weak area, but he just looked surprised for a moment, and then he laughed. Sometimes I wonder if they're even human."

She watched Carla for a response as the elevator door opened on the ground floor. She paused when it became evident that Carla didn't intend to follow her out.

"Seriously, don't stay here a second longer. They're all monsters. I mean it—literally."

She stepped out and maintained eye contact as the door closed, leaving Carla with a pang of regret. She could have shown the suffering woman the book in her hands. She could have told her what she suspected—that it held the key to summoning the one who would bring down justice and revenge upon a sick system. Eris: the one who would bring retribution so fierce that a kick in the balls would seem like nothing. Carla truly believed it. In the basement she would decipher the key to bringing down a holy wrath upon them all.

Darkness met her eyes when the elevator finished its descent, and she regretted not having the foresight to take a flashlight. She stumbled about, willing her eyes to adjust, and she wondered if she would ever find her way back to the elevator, until finally her fingers brushed across a light switch. It powered a dull yellow light, barely enough to illuminate a partial area of the basement consisting of an uneven floor and overturned furniture. Beyond the circle of light lay a well of darkness too thick for her eyes to penetrate.

Standing still, she heard sounds though, what reminded her of a desk leg scraping a rough surface, the squeak of a wheel.

"Hello?" she called out.

As if frightened by the sound of her voice, whatever made the sounds went quiet. Mice perhaps? The single bulb hanging from the low ceiling cast enough light for her to see scratches and smudges on the floor, evidently made with chalk. Some of them suggested a sort of design, a notion she confirmed by comparing the markings to what she found in the pages of the book. More than ever, she believed she'd found a grimoire of some kind. She shuffled through the pages and found one that roughly matched the design on the floor.

She studied the two and determined that the markings on the floor only needed a few touches for completion. Amongst the refuse she found an ancient chalk tablet with a nub of chalk tied to it. Falling to her knees, she set about completing the diagram on the floor. Her intuition hadn't failed her yet, so she continued to trust it. She noticed more scurrying as she set about her work.

But she failed to notice the ding of the elevator.

"Well, this is where you went," said Hidey Fish.

She looked over her shoulder to see him smiling at her rump. Next to him stood a younger, larger, more brutish-looking man. Her intuition spoke to her again, telling her that he might be the owner of the steel balls. Carla hated him instantly.

"You didn't give me a chance to show you how I got my name," Hidey Fish said.

As he approached, he held his hands over his face, peek-a-boo style, opening and closing them to reveal comically wide, unblinking eyes as well as puckered lips, like those of a fish. He repeated the movement over and over as he walked closer. The effect proved not only grotesque and childish, but also hypnotic.

As if by some magic, the spectacle held Carla stunned and motionless. By the time he and the other man came close enough to grab her, she had to wonder if he *had* hypnotized her.

She struggled as their hands grappled for her, and she dropped the book. It drew their attention long enough for Carla to kick, and she landed her foot in the crotch of the younger man.

He grimaced. "Why do they keep doing that?" he said.

"They're told it's our only weakness," Hidey Fish said. He picked up the book while the other man secured her in a headlock. "No pain at all?"

The younger man shook his head. "Scar tissue."

"I thought it was impotence."

Instead of arguing, the man grunted from the effort needed to keep Carla still. She fought, reaching for his eyes with her fingernails, but before she could cause any damage, he lifted her from the ground and slammed her down onto the top of a dilapidated desk, which collapsed from the impact. She lay atop the fragments, struggling to recapture the air that escaped her lungs.

Hidey leaned over her with the book, tsking her. "You've been naughty. And this basement is full of naughty girls like you."

Once more she detected the scurrying noises. Something appeared at the edge of the light. Her vision blurred by pain, Carla caught a glimpse of it.

The pale face of a woman. Instead of eyes, two large, round objects protruded from her skull. They looked like chair wheels. The mouth consisted of a small table drawer, stuffed into a broken, unworking jaw.

Hidey turned in the thing's direction. Quickly, it scurried back into the darkness.

"You see that one?" he asked. "Always hungry. It eats paper."

"Whole reams," said the other man. "Can't get enough." With Carla subdued, he looked at Hidey. "Where should we start with this one? Hands? Feet?"

"You, always keen to use surgery. I like more nuanced methods." He gestured with the book.

Yet the other man seemed unpersuaded. "How about the arms? What should we replace them with?"

They both looked about the basement as Carla continued to gasp. Something else appeared at the edge of the light—another figure hobbled by a gruesome modification. This one had a face studded with typewriter keys. Naked and emaciated, a thick, black ichor leaked from its pale nipples. She opened her mouth as if to speak, but no sound came forth. Instead of teeth, bent paperclips lined her gums.

"Get back," Hidey said, waving the book at it.

This one hesitated, but after Hidey took a threatening step forward, it retreated.

As she felt her strength ebbing, Carla thought again of the poem. She uttered a line out loud. "My breasts are wells of mimeograph ink."

"Did she say something?" Hidey asked. "Is she trying to perform a spell?"

The other one twisted her wrist. "We perform the operations around here." He looked around. "Give me something to cut off her leg."

"We need to do the ritual first," said Hidey, "or she'll just die."

Not a spell, thought Carla. *A summoning.* She knew in her heart that the poem functioned as a chant of defiance. A call for deliverance from the curses cast by these men. "Eris," she said, "come to me! Mother of us all!"

She only had a poem and an assumed name. No liturgy. So she began making one up, reciting lines from the poem, adding her own flourishes, her own metaphors. But even to her ears it sounded contrived, inauthentic.

Even worse, Hidey and his cohort laughed at the effort.

"Listen to that," said the brutish one.

"It's pathetic," Hidey said.

"Where's... the thing? The one that cuts paper. The one like a machete attached to a steel board." The big man held Carla down with one hand while he used his free arm to make a cutting motion. "Let's use that and start carving."

Hidey surveyed the clutter around him. Carla noticed that as much as those creatures didn't want to come into the light, Hidey and the other man didn't want to go into their domain—the darkness.

"Eris," she said, pleading, "don't forsake me."

No comment this time from the men. Instead, a disturbance from elsewhere drew their attention. Something grated along the floor in the shadows, the sound coming from several directions at once.

"You know the thing I mean," said the big one, clearly flustered. "You see it?"

"I have it. I have it in my hand now." Did Hidey sound nervous now? He held nothing but the book, nothing like the tool the other one sought. Maybe he misunderstood.

But Carla sensed it: a presence stirring in the shadows. Listening to her pleas. Responding to her needs.

Two more malformations appeared at the edge of the light, the one with oozing breasts, and a different one. The new one that appeared looked smaller and more machine than any other. A Xerox machine with a baby's face, glistening with fluid as if recently birthed. It pulled itself forward with an appendage made of wires. This time, instead of stepping away at Hidey's command, they continued their slow advance.

"Smack the small one for me," said Hidey's companion. "It's been disobedient lately."

But Hidey only shouted for them to get back. Carla saw why. More of them began appearing, each with a uniquely modified, grafted body. The torso of one consisted of a water cooler, its sloshing organs visible through clear plastic. Another wobbled forth with a belly distended with protruding wires and gadgets, its thin arms ending in staplers rather than hands and fingers, making Carla think of the fingers she found earlier. All of them, nearly a dozen or so, moved slowly, hampered by disfigurements. Carla's captors appeared increasingly unnerved.

"Use the book," said the one holding her down.

Hidey shuffled through the pages before he settled on the correct one. He began reading aloud, enunciating speech that sounded to Carla garbled and unnatural. Eventually, the other man began repeating the same speech in a kind of call and response. At the same time, his grip on Carla loosened a bit.

She managed to lift herself slightly and realized that the shattered wood under her back concealed something metallic. And sharp.

What they couldn't find before, the object they couldn't name. Arching her back, she managed to touch it with her hand.

Carla had used one before, usually to make even cuts in big stacks of paper. She found the handle of the blade and gripped it, realizing it had come unfastened from the board used to line up straight edges.

She exhaled, summoning all the strength she had left. She used it to push the man off of her. Then she swung the blade as hard as she could toward his neck. She realized the truth in his words. It did remind one of a machete.

It didn't sever his head as she hoped it would, but it cut deeply. The look of surprise on his face filled her with satisfaction. It made her feel like a goddess of destruction.

Hidey Fish still chanted away, but his words failed to slow the slouching approach of his creations. They now poured from the shadows, all of them bearing unique disfigurements. One of them looked like an amalgamation of office parts, its whole head made up of a tangle of rubber bands. All of them *wonce women*, doomed to this existence by the arcane magic and cruel surgery of men like Hidey Fish.

The bald man continued to hold the book and chant. He failed to see Carla standing behind him, her clothes and face streaked with fresh blood.

He finally did notice her in time to see the blade in her hand fall. It sliced cleanly through the top of his skull. As he died, his lips puckered and his eyes grew wide, resuming the expression he used in his peek-a-boo routine.

"It's called a *guillotine trimmer*," Carla said to his corpse. "Learn the proper fucking name."

She gripped the bloody blade. It had fused to her body, a permanent part of her now. Even if she wanted to let it go, she couldn't. But that seemed just fine to her.

She looked upon the slouching forms around her, some of them shaking visibly, perhaps from pain, perhaps from excitement at her conquest, the prospect of revenge. Knowing they would follow, she turned to the elevator. She would lead them to the light of the upper floors, where they would eventually complete their liberation. She had found Eris. Herself. For them all, wonce and for all.

Lizard War

Joe R. Lansdale

They had only been on the planet a few twenty-eight-hour days. It seemed like centuries.

This unnamed planet was not part of the astronauts' mission. They had another place to go, but then something went wrong and they lost their course and had come down into the blue of the world's atmosphere with a roaring engine noise. The ship plowed into the jungle and parted the trees like a sharp knife through butter.

The impact killed all the officers and left Eliza, the head cook, in charge. She was the senior.

The ship was split open on one side by the trees. That's how they discovered the air was breathable, the gravity close to that of Earth.

Even with the ship ripped badly, they thought to stay there at first, make it their base. The communication device inside the ship didn't work. The ones they carried were full of crackles and hisses, no messages. A homing pigeon in a space suit could have done as well. There was food in the ship and weapons, but the water had leaked out when the trees tore through the side.

They hoped the mayday that was sent before they crashed had been heard by another cruiser ship, or had possibly reached one of the worlds inhabited by humans.

It was about the only hope they had, and it was as thin as the edge of a cracker.

First night, the lizards showed up. The largest ones were eight-foot high, twelve feet long, with extended jaws. Most were closer to seven feet long and five feet high. They were agile, not strong, but they were tooth-packed eating machines. Eliza remembered the shock when she first discovered that in the bright moonlight, she could see through them. See bones and organs, digestion taking place, glimpses of odd creatures struggling in stomach sacks, red acid flowing onto them, dissolving them into liquid.

The rip in the wall of the ship was large enough for the beasts to enter. They came in small numbers at first, testing it out. Only one astronaut was lost; surprised and eaten as fast as a dog might eat a greasy meat treat.

The astronauts managed to kill a horde of lizards, as they were easy to kill. The lizard's power was in their numbers. But the ship was impossible to defend well, so Eliza decided they had to find a better place. More importantly, they needed water.

When the day showed up, the lizards went away. Opposite of what one might think about lizards preferring sunlight, this didn't prove to be the case on this world. They liked the night, sometimes early morning, but as the day stoked with heat, they disappeared. Perhaps the heat burned their thin skin.

Carrying weapons and food into the lemon-yellow sunlight the astronauts trudged along, but the open spaces were quickly filled with trees and humidity. They were immediately uncomfortable and sweat-drenched. The planet's sun seemed enormous compared to the Earth's sun. It was a rolling ball of lemony fire. They stuffed their collapsible suits into their packs, shifted the packs on their backs, found an animal trail, and went in search of water.

Day came, and they walked along the narrow forest trail, Eliza in the lead, nervous as a long-tailed cat in a room full of rocking chairs. They discovered the miniature fortress. The door was partially open. There were no lizards inside.

———

THEY FOUND long bars that fit naturally across the door when closed, and served to secure it. Working together, they slipped the heavy bars in place.

The walls had steps that led to a runner at the top of the compound. Eliza stood on the runner and looked out. The walls were tall, slick with oil, and the lizards couldn't climb them quickly as long as the oil stayed fresh and slippery. Setting the oil on fire as they climbed was another plus. The fires licked loose the lizards' flesh and devoured their bones.

Using the oil was what the former non-human residents of the compound had done. The charred stains on the wall had explained it to Eliza at little more than a glance.

Cheryl, the mechanic chief, had figured out a strange device they had discovered inside the compound. It was tractor size, open all around, and had a swinging bucket on a long metal arm. It was easy to see that whatever had made and commandeered it was of a different anatomy than humans.

Fortunately, it could be worked by human hands, though it was necessary to reach wide to grasp gears, use two hands to turn knobs, and buttons had to be punched with a fist. It was amazing Cheryl had figured it out.

It could dip silvery oil out of the pit near the back wall, near a mound of smooth, white boulders. It could swing its long arm with the bucket completely about, and dump oil against the outside walls with surprising speed and accuracy.

How the former residents had managed to put up a wall and build the bucket machine was beyond Eliza. There were what looked like hardened bubbles in the wall, and the machine as well. Eliza had the impression that the wall and machine had been foamed out of some sort of device, and in moments hardened. Same for the dome at the back of the compound. It had one large open doorway and inside was a pool of sweet drinking water.

Eliza could see over the back wall as well. The land sloped deep and was free of jungle. There was a large expanse of blackened ground, perhaps a lightning fire, but it was impossible to say. There were more white boulders down there, and a small pool of blue water could be seen.

She had to wonder, had the aliens been here to take the oil? Had they had to abandon the wall and go home, or had they been overrun?

Night began to slide in. There was a mist in the jungle, low down and floating, tinted purple by night's oncoming shadows. Then came an explosion of strange birds, some with two sets of wings. They came before the lizards like heralds of destruction. They filled the air with bright, fluttering colors. Odd animals, with too many legs and too many heads, hopped and ran, divided at the wall and darted to who knows where. If they stopped to look back or so much as scratch their ass with a hind paw, they were caught and devoured in a shark-like frenzy.

The sun, now a pink glow above the jungle, dripped all the way down and the three moons came up. The big moon moved swiftly across the sky and the other moons followed, as if pulled behind the larger moon on a string.

On the lizards came. Hissing and growling, defecating as they ran, endless as the stretch of time.

The stench of lizard shit filled the air.

————

IT WAS AN ALL-NIGHT FIGHT. Up the walls the lizards came. Inside the walls the astronauts leaned over and lit the oil and there were flares of fire. The lizards burst into flames and dropped screeching to the ground. The lizards that could scream were eaten by their comrades. The charred dead ones were neglected. For whatever reason, they only ate living things, or finished eating whatever they had started to eat.

There seemed to be more lizards than planet. They came on endlessly, some giving birth as they ran, shooting out lizards like mortar shots. The babies came out in a ball and rolled over the ground. When they stopped rolling, they uncoiled and were already five feet in length. Without so much as motherly instruction, they came on hungry and angry, adding to the mayhem.

A couple of lizards managed to breach the walls. After a moment of panic, they were dispatched. By the time the sun came up and coated the jungle gold, the creatures were gone. The astronauts were exhausted. They chopped up the lizards in the compound with lasers and dragged their remains out of the metal door and let them roll down the rocky rise. The lizards were surprisingly light and fragile.

Another night of triumph for the astronauts, but it would have to be repeated time and again. In the end, no one doubted there would be unhappy results.

———

THE ASTRONAUTS RESTED and slept by day. One guard was set, and was replaced in four hours by another.

After some days had passed, the day guard was dropped. The lizards didn't come out in the heat. It gave the astronauts better rest, but still there was the night, and then they came.

The astronauts slept in a circle around the pool of drinkable water that was in the center of the dome. The dome was lit by a long light rod that was placed in a support at the back of the dome.

As Eliza slipped into sleep, she remembered her time on a massive exploratory ship, her first mission out. The ship was as much like a city as it was a spacecraft. It was stuffed full of would-be settlers, astronauts, and scientists.

The spaceship had its own forest and waterfall, shopping spots and restaurants. The portholes and long lengths of view shields that ran along the sides of the ship were designed for a view of space and were built to withstand reasonable impact from space debris. Reasonable was a matter of personal definition.

Eliza was the cook for the massive crew. It was a big, beaver-busy job. She and her lover, and second head cook, Joan, lived together in a small cabin with a small bed and a big porthole. You could look out of it while lying in bed. The view was crazy. The porthole was like a hole in space. Blackness. Stars.

But the tightness of the cabin and their time spent in space strained things between her and Joan. Even while making love Eliza found that she was barely holding herself together. And once, in a moment of passion, Eliza pushed up on her hands, her groin pressed against Joan's, and it was in that moment of near climax that she turned her head and saw through the porthole the vastness of space, the scattering of stars, and she was struck numb with what old-timers called the Moment of Unimportance—a sudden realization of how endlessly vast space was and how small and unimportant we humans were. In that instant, nothing seemed glorious or worthwhile. Life was empty and pointless.

Eliza, already stressed from years in space, felt herself tumble apart.

"You should be looking at me," Joan said.

It was just that simple. Next thing they knew, words were exchanged, and Joan demanded Eliza leave, and Eliza demanded Joan leave.

Due to emotional attrition, that lingering feeling of worthlessness and insignificance, Eliza was the one that hastily dressed and left. She stepped out into the corridor, bordered on one side by great lengths of the transparent space shields.

No sooner had the door closed behind her and the lock snicked, than the ship shook and she fell to the floor. Lights flashed. Buzzers and alarms went off.

It really wasn't much of an impact for a ship that size, but Eliza knew that the strike had been in line with the room she shared with Joan. She attempted to open the door. The lock held.

Glancing through the corridor glass, she realized that the porthole that had caused their argument had been breached. Joan, little more than rags of flesh, her blood hanging in drops around her like falling rose petals, her hair fanned out like a peacock's tail, floated by. Debris from their room drifted with her. She had been sucked through the broken porthole. The spacecraft moved away, and what had been Joan was no longer in view. The view was now as before, blackness, punctuated by spots of stars.

Later, it was discovered a meteorite, smaller than a pebble, had slammed through the porthole glass. Instantly, Joan and the room's contents had been sucked through and broken up, vacuumed out of the porthole like so much dust.

It was a one in a zillion kind of accident. But it had happened.

———

SHAKING SLIGHTLY, Eliza awoke, went to the doorway, and looked out. The rest of the crew were up already, gathered near the edge of the wall by the big white boulders that gleamed in the sunlight.

Eliza walked over. One of the boulders had been turned over. It had large eye sockets and a long mouth full of large, flat teeth. It looked almost like a silly snowman head made by children. Then she noticed that amongst the boulders were other pieces that appeared to be white sticks and withered tentacles. She realized the big boulders were skulls, and the sticks were bones and the tentacles were... tentacles.

One of the astronauts, Carol, said, "Now we know what happened to the previous owners of this place."

"I think they committed suicide," said another, Mary. "All lined up, all of them with holes in their skulls. "Looks like a ritual suicide to me. Being trapped in here I can sympathize. I think before they killed themselves, they opened the door to the compound."

"Perhaps there was a survivor who decided suicide was not the way," Cheryl said. "That one opened the door and went out. By nightfall that didn't turn out well."

"And there are these," Carol said.

There were odd shaped devices, red and black in color. They had been beneath the boulder-sized skulls. Eliza concluded they were weapons that the former occupants had used to do just what Mary suggested. The weapons looked to be in rough condition and beyond use.

———

MIDDAY, Eliza stood on the ramparts and looked in all directions. Her gaze rested on the blackened earth at the back of the compound and on the white boulders and the pool of blue water.

As she watched, the light shifted and she saw a glint of something in the trees that she couldn't identify.

She studied it for a while. She shaded her eyes with her hand and looked at the sun. There was still a lot of daylight left.

"Cheryl," she called down. "Arm up. You and me. We're going out. Mary, you're in charge."

———

DOWN THE HILL THEY WENT, pausing at the waterhole, tentatively tasting the water. The boulders around the waterhole were, as she suspected, just boulders.

"This must be running down from our water supply. A spring up there, a waterhole here," Cheryl said.

Eliza dropped to her knees, took a deep breath, stuck her head under the water. She could see a few feet into the tunnel that supplied it, then there was darkness.

Eliza jerked her head up, spitting water.

"What the hell?" Cheryl said.

"Just curious," Eliza said. "The mouth of the opening here is wide. Could be that way all the way up."

"For all it matters to us," Cheryl said.

"Satisfied my curiosity."

Eliza stood up and pointed toward the jungle.

"Do you see it?"

There was sparkle in the trees.

"I do," Cheryl said.

Not too deep in among the trees, a path had been plowed, and what had plowed it was a spacecraft. An immense shiny orb with a glass view port. In the side of the orb was an open, wide door with a kind of drawbridge ramp.

Weapons ready, they cautiously walked around it, looking it over, then went up the ramp and slipped inside.

The only light was through the view shield until they had been inside a moment, then lights automatically came on.

And there was something else.

Positioned in front of a control panel in a wide cushioned chair was a creature with an enormous head, odd twists of torso, withered tentacles as well as long arms, hands the size of catcher's mitts. There wasn't much left of the corpse. The loss of flesh was due to rot, not ravenous mouths. The tentacles were dry and mummified. The body was odorless.

"The survivor from the compound," Cheryl said. But why come here if this thing doesn't fly?"

"Maybe it was a desperate attempt to make it fly," Eliza said. "Or it thought it would be safer here. Hard for one individual to fight off those monsters at the compound."

"I assume the orb had technical problems. But why go to the hill and build the compound? They would have been better off holing up here."

"They had no idea what they were going to be up against," Eliza said. "Main reason I think they ended up on top of the rise, is they needed water. Up there was a perfect place to build, maintain until they could do otherwise. Repair the ship. But they didn't."

"I figured out the bucket machine, so maybe I can figure this thing out," Cheryl said.

Eliza felt a strange tinge, not exactly of joy. Was that a real possibility? Once they left this planet, found safety, she was no longer head of an expedition. She was just the cook again, with more free time to contemplate the loss of Joan.

———

CHERYL LOOKED OVER THE ORB. She didn't manage anything spectacular, but she did remove the control board. There were no wires inside, just little bumps and strips of color.

Cheryl stopped poking inside the control board and began pushing at the walls, finding that in spots the walls would slide open and reveal little cubbies. There were things inside. Neither Eliza nor Rachel knew what the things were, but one item caught Cheryl's attention. A thick golden rod snapped into a slot.

Cheryl looked it over. "It has designs on it? Figure them out, maybe the control board will make more sense."

Under the chair, most likely dropped after the poor creature climbed into it and died, was a shiny, round device with marks on it. Cheryl picked it up. She touched one of the marks.

The ramp lifted and closed with a tight snick.

Cheryl tried the same mark for the reverse, but it didn't work that way. She tried another mark. Nothing. Then another, and the ramp dropped.

"I'll take this too," Cheryl said.

They pulled the alien's remains from the seat, carried it out of the craft and placed it on the ground.

"Sorry, odd guy," Cheryl said. "We may need your chair. Rest in peace."

They started back to the compound.

When Eliza told the others what they had found, she could see a faint glow of hope on their faces.

"I don't want to say too quickly that all will be well, but it's something to think about, and if anyone can figure that craft out, it's Cheryl."

———

THERE WAS something different that night. It started to rain, blocking out the moons. Lightning sizzled and stitched across the sky in a way Eliza had never seen anywhere else. The lightning gave illumination in flashes. Eliza had glow strips placed at spots along the wall, some shining inside the compound, other shining out.

The illumination from the strips wasn't strong enough to allow them to see the jungle. Only the lightning did that, but it was not a constant light.

That night, when they came, they could only see the lizards when they were close. Much of the oil was washed away by the rain as they and the bucket poured. But if lit in time, the oil still burned and the water couldn't put it out.

The lizards got Mary that night. She leaned over the wall to take a shot, and a monster jumped out of the dark, as if leaping from a hole in space and time, and snapped its jaws around her head.

Without so much as a scream, Mary was headless and squirting blood. Her head was visible inside the lizard when the lightning flashed. The rest of her body joined the head in three or four quick bites.

The lizard was immediately dispatched with shots from several guns, including Eliza's. By then, other lizards had made it over the barrier.

It was assholes-and-elbows for a time, but they couldn't stop the creatures from clamoring over the wall. The astronauts fled from the wall and holed up in the dome, standing at the open doorway, taking shifts defending, firing weapons. There was only enough room for two of them to stand in the doorway at a time.

It was a horrible night.

In the morning, the rain had turned into a mist and the sun shone through it, weakly.

In the far distance, dark clouds were knotted against the sky. They were slowly moving toward the compound. Eliza figured that when the cloud arrived, it would be dark enough and cool enough for the lizards to come out again. A day of fighting them, followed by a night of the same, might be the end of them. And if the rain lasted a couple of days, most certainly.

Standing on the rampart, looking out at the jungle, Eliza was sickened to see the lizards were visible, crouching among the jungle shadows, waiting; they sensed the change to come.

All the astronauts were on the rampart with her. Cheryl came up beside Eliza, said, "I don't think I'm going to get a crack at repairing that orb."

"Could you, you if you had time?" Eliza asked.

"I studied the rod I brought back. It's a sort of manual for their ship. If I close my eyes, run my fingertips over it, it gives me sensory information, the schematics for the ship. I think I can figure out how to repair it, but I need to be there with my tools to know for sure. I have all manner of things in my kit. Tools, flares, a knife. The only thing missing is a toilet. But getting there doesn't seem likely."

"Maybe there is a way," Eliza said.

———

ELIZA GATHERED ALL THE ASTRONAUTS, except for one lookout on the runner, into the dome, next to the pool of drinking water. She asked Cheryl to move the bucket machine in front of the dome doorway. It wasn't much of a protection, as the lizards could come over it and still weasel into the doorway, but it might slow them down a few seconds; seconds could matter.

"If we have a chance, it's here," Eliza said.

"Think I'd rather die in the open," one of the astronauts, Sharon, said, "not like a cornered rat."

"The water pool comes out in another pool by the rocks," Eliza said. "It's not right on top of the orb, but it's considerably closer than here. If the pool's tunnel is wide enough, Cheryl might be able to swim to the other pool, run for the orb with her tools, use the door device, and if we're lucky, repair the ship. We hold the fort here until Cheryl can bring the orb to us. It's small enough to land inside."

"Of course, that's if she can fly it," another of the astronauts, Carol, said.

"I'd still rather go out the gate and run for this orb," Sharon said. "I say we do it right now."

"Time for that has passed," Eliza said, turning her head toward the door and the rising shadows. "The day is lost to us now. We could all go down the water tunnel, but if the craft can't be flown, it would be worse than here. It's small. All of us in would be tight. And if there's water in that orb, it's not enough to last us for long. The orb only matters to us if it flies."

"What if the water tunnel is too narrow?" Sharon asked. "And if Cheryl gets through, she still has to run from the pool to the jungle with the lizards out there."

"It's too narrow, guess I'll be stuck like a turd in a sewer pipe," Cheryl said, stripping down to her skivvies. She strapped on her weapon, picked up her tool kit. "Or I get through and the lizards eat me. I was on the track team, so I have a chance."

"I'm going with her," Eliza said, stripping to her underwear, strapping on her weapon and supply pouch. "I'll watch her back. That's the job for me. I wasn't on a track team. But I can give cover fire. I don't, she definitely won't make it."

"If you don't come back," Sharon said, "we're two more down. How in hell can we hold out?"

The guard from the wall climbed over the bucket machine and dropped inside. "They're starting to move."

"You defend this doorway," Eliza said. "For now, that's all that can be done. I'll be back."

Cheryl dropped into the pool and Eliza followed.

———

THE WATER WAS cool and the tunnel was tight. It scraped against Eliza's skin. She could feel water being pushed back against her from the flutter of Cheryl's feet.

The light from the drinking pool ceased to exist. Eliza was in utter darkness. She let the downhill flow of the water carry her along, kicking her feet to assist.

Dead dark. Very tight. Then she was hung up.

But Cheryl had swam through, so it was doable. Eliza's weapon was what was keeping her from going through. It had caught on a projection from the wall.

Eliza rearranged the gun, and pushed on. She slipped through this time.

Fear and panic crept over her. She thought, *what a horrible way to die.* Wedged in and drowning. But there was no turning back now; she couldn't have turned around in there if she'd wanted. Not enough room. It was all or nothing.

The tunnel widened and Eliza could move her arms more easily, kick her feet more freely. Her lungs felt as if they were about to explode. She was starting to feel lightheaded.

And then there was light. It wasn't a bright light. Just brighter than the tunnel provided.

Eliza's head and shoulders burst out of the water. As she drew breath, her lungs burned and felt as if they were full of broken glass.

Cheryl was crouched at the edge of the pool. She stuck out a hand and helped pull Eliza out.

Even as Eliza gathered herself, took some deep, smooth breaths, the clouds rolled in more fully, shadowing the land.

Eliza and Cheryl glanced at one another, then made a hard run for it.

The air was cool and damp and the trees held shadows. Some of the shadows moved. They could see the craft through the trees. They were almost there.

They heard gunfire from the compound. There was a flash of lightning. In its temporary glow they could see the lizards practically oozing out of the jungle.

Eliza and Cheryl let loose with their weapons. The guns bucked in their hands and the lizards splattered and piled, but still they came.

Inching forward, they were almost to the orb. But there were so many of the creatures. And then the world lit white-hot bright and there were specks of fire in the air.

Cheryl grabbed Eliza's hand. "Run!"

As Cheryl pulled her through a thin path between the lizards, Eliza realized Cheryl had let off one of her flares, startling the lizards. Within an instant, the glow died.

Cheryl thumbed the door device. A moment later they were on the ramp. Eliza turned to face the lizards, to hold them at bay. Two large lizards tried to cram their way into the gap.

Gunfire stopped the monsters, but the dead lizards collapsed on the ramp. Eliza grabbed at the legs of the beasts and pulled and pushed them off of it while Cheryl kept up a rocking gunfire as cover. Cheryl used the device and the ramp came up. Then they were inside and the light came on.

———

INSIDE THE SHIP, trembling in the cool air, made worse by the fact they were damp and wearing only their underwear, they took a moment to breathe. They could see lizards running before the windscreen, in the direction of the compound.

They could hear gunfire from the compound.

Cheryl prowled about inside the control board. She began to look frustrated. She scouted around the orb, found a triangular pull up in the floor at the back of the ship.

The trap door was heavy. It took both Eliza and Cheryl to lift it. Inside was a crawl space. There was a thin orange light. Cheryl dropped into it, moved about on her knees. Eliza, crouched by the gap, stuck her head inside to watch. She could see all manner of gadgets and shapes.

"There's something taken apart in here," Cheryl called out. "They were working on it. They just couldn't repair it."

"And you can?"

"I didn't say that. But I'm going to try."

————

A LITTLE LATER, Cheryl pulled herself out of the crawl space.

"I can fix it, but there's nothing here to fix it with. There's a piece of some kind of material in there that's shattered. I'm not sure how it shattered, but it is. For whatever reason, they didn't have a replacement. And neither do we."

"Then we're fucked," Eliza said.

"Maybe not. A long rod or length of glass with connecting fibers would do it. I think that could replace what's broken. It would have to be rigged, but it could work. Problem is, we don't have that either. Not here."

"The compound?"

"That's right. The light rod. It might work, but we'd have to get it and bring it back."

"No. I have to go get it. You're the only one that can fix this thing, if it can be fixed. It's up to me."

————

THE POOL WASN'T that far away, but when you thought about the lizards, it might as well have been a trip back to Earth.

Cheryl gave Eliza a couple flares from her tool kit. Eliza stuffed them into the weapon pouch. Eliza pulled out a sheet of flat bullet tabs and slipped them into her weapon. "Fully loaded," she said.

They stood inside at the rampway as Cheryl prepared to lower the ramp.

"I can only wish you luck," Cheryl said.

"Luck has nothing to do with it," Eliza said.

Chery nodded, lowered the ramp.

It was eerie. The lizards were like running silhouettes. They had yet to realize new snacks had been exposed.

Eliza saw a gap in their midst, took a deep breath, and ran.

Cheryl crouched at the base of the ramp, the door device on the floor next to her. She noted Eliza could run faster than she said she could. Then again, those lizards gave one athletic inspiration.

Eliza was halfway to the pool before the lizards noticed her. Cheryl opened up with her weapon. The lizards ran behind Eliza, blocking her from view. Cheryl kept trying to clear them without shooting Eliza in the process.

She could hear Eliza's gun bursts as she ran. See red streamers of fire.

And then there was a gap in the lizards and she could see Eliza. Cheryl's heart was in her throat. Eliza was almost to the pool. So were the lizards.

The lizards had taken note of Cheryl kneeling in the orb doorway. She fired a clearing blast, touched the ramp device. Her last sight before the ramp lifted and snapped shut, was Eliza, diving into the pool.

———

The water seemed colder, and Eliza had to swim against gravity, the water flowing hard against her. She was certain she wasn't going to make it, and just as certain she would die trying.

By the time she swam to the spot where she had temporarily been stuck, she was exhausted. She clung to the walls there for a moment and let the water flow hard against her. Finally, she pushed off again. The water shoved her back. She gave it all she had, cupping the water in her palms, moving her legs as much as the narrow tunnel would allow.

She was able to find spots she could grab at in the tunnel walls, use them to help gain traction, pull herself along. It felt as if the swim was twice as long as before, and her lungs were worse than before, and for a moment, she did indeed black out.

And then Eliza was out of the pool, lying on her back, gasping for air.

There was the sound of rapid gunfire, the shrieks of dying lizards.

Eliza realized she had blacked out the moment she broke from the tunnel into the drinking pool. Thank goodness Sharon had seen her and pulled her out.

The light in the dome brought her back to her mission, their last and final chance.

Staggering to her feet, she saw two of the astronauts at the door. The door was filling with the shapes of lizards. They dangled dead over the bucket machine, were starting to clog the doorway. That only lasted a moment, then they were clawed aside by other lizards trying to enter.

One of the astronauts, Carol, was missing. Eliza didn't need to ask what had happened.

"Listen," Eliza said. "Change of plans. The light rod. Cheryl thinks she can use it to fix the orb. In space, maybe she can contact one of our vessels, or find a safe place to land. Take the rod, go through the pool, and give it to Cheryl. All of you swim from pool to pool, then run and shoot like hell. Cheryl will hear the gunfire and open the orb for you. It's straight up from the pool, just in the jungle."

Sharon turned her attention to the two astronauts in the doorway. "They step back, they'll never make the pool."

"Yeah, they will," Eliza said. "Because I'm going to take their place."

———

ELIZA TOOK A DEEP BREATH, said, "Now everyone strip off and hit the water."

Eliza stepped to the doorway, and ordered the two defenders to step back. They left her a spare weapon on the ground. The light went out behind her. They had taken the rod. Susan touched Eliza's shoulder even as Eliza fired and a lizard shrieked. "We are gone," Susan said.

"Good. Go."

Eliza fired the gun so long it became hot to the touch. She leaned down, and while firing with one hand, picked up the spare weapon they had left her. She dropped the heated gun and used the other.

She had no idea how long she fired and exchanged weapons, but it was some time. She knew even with the great loads of ammunition the weapons held they were not inexhaustible. Her minutes were numbered.

And then from the doorway, through a break in the snapping, growling lizards, she saw a burst of fire tearing across the dark sky.

The orb.

Cheryl had done it. At least one of the women had survived from pool to orb, and was on board, because Cheryl had the light rod and had been able to repair the craft.

I hope you all made it, Eliza thought.

The lizards began to edge in. One person could defend the doorway only for so long. Eliza backed toward the water pool. She felt weak, as if all her muscles were slowly dissolving into soup.

And now she realized she had been bitten on the hip and was losing a lot of blood. She hadn't felt it when it happened. Too much adrenaline. Her legs were rubbery. She could hear her heart pounding so hard she thought it might break her ribs. Blood beat at her temples like blows from a blackjack.

She backed until she was on the edge of the pool. The lizards entered the dome in a rush. Eliza stepped backwards into the water, went under.

Eliza looked up. She could see through the water, see the shadow-face of a lizard up there. She had lost her weapon, but she opened her pouch and took out one of the flares Cheryl had given her. She fired it underwater and the hot, glowing load hit the lizard in the face. Its head caught fire. It nodded forward into the pool, and then the rest of it tried to slip in afterward. The lizard was too big. It lodged there. The water was dark with blood.

Eliza smiled.

She drifted down. She could feel her hair waving around her head and over her face, then spreading out the way Joan's hair had in space, fanning out like a peacock's tail.

Joan. Beneath her in the bed. She was looking down at her face. *I will not turn my head this time,* Eliza thought. *I will not.*

I'm looking at you, Joan. I'm looking at you, baby.

Dark.

Like the space between the stars.

First Day Jitters at Slappy's

Matt Brandenburg

When I saw Slappy's Magical Forest was hiring, I dared to dream. Then, when I had my phone interview, and they hired me on the spot, I cried. Never in a million years did I think I'd ever get to be here, let alone work here. We never went when I was younger; why would my parents want to take me somewhere happy? Instead, I'd hide in my room and study pictures, books, and videos about the theme park, imagining what it'd be like to visit. As I weave through families and sticky children towards the back area, or as the interviewer referred to it—*The Underdwelling*—for my first day, I keep reminding myself this is real. That I'm actually here.

Massive fantastical plants and trees made of fiberglass line the midway. Squat mushrooms from *Slappy's Fun Time Hour* contain souvenir stores and restaurants. As much as I want to buy a stuffed animal and shirt, I know I need to wait until after I put a down payment on an apartment and sign up for college. It's hard to focus on getting an education, so I can get a *real* job and I don't have to ever rely on my parents, when I'm walking through this fantasy. *Imagine living here, how amazing that would be.* The old daydream lingers as I float further into the Froggy Glade. Giant insects race down roller coaster tracks while unicorns on poles trot in a circle. A delicious aroma of fried food and burnt sugar washes over me and a grin cuts across my face. I ignore the mass of people shuffling from place to place, living their fantasies. Soon, it'll be my time to enjoy the dream. Soon, I can move away from that house and all its nightmares. An overwhelming sense of joy replaces the pain rearing its ugly head and I take a deep breath to focus on not being late on my first day.

A wall of cheering and laughing people block my path. *Maybe it's one of their parades?* I've only dreamt what they'd be like in real life. But then I remember from what I've read they usually go down the fairy trail. Excitement courses through me and I squeeze my way into the crowd. Whatever is here must be new and I have to see.

"Slappy!"

A few men and women glance my way. All the bad days at home seem small and less important compared to witnessing him in person.

The mascot is a plump mixture of a frog, rabbit, and squirrel. He bounces around with a broad rubbery smile revealing large buck teeth, his ears flopping above his head. A long green poofy tail curls out of the back of his overalls, swaying to the music. Some children dance with him, holding his furry webbed hands, laughing as Slappy gurgles and croaks. *They must have updated the outfit, it looks great!* Wearing one of those costumes and making everyone happy, maybe even helping someone forget the talks with cops and counselors, must be the best thing in the world. I pinch myself to remember I'm still doing something that's important here. Maintenance is what keeps the magic happening. *Besides, the hours will allow you to go to classes.* As the thoughts coil around my insides, I keep Slappy in my sights to lift my spirits. Its bulging black eyes are unfocused, yet there's a slick shine floating on the pupils, as if there's an intelligence in there. Is its chest moving like it's breathing? How can it look so thin with someone in there?

Slappy bows to the crowd, and I realize I need to go.

My nerves are all over the place when I arrive at the *Whimsical Cove* and find the huge red and white mushroom leading to *The Underdwelling*. A wet phlegm-filled groan behind me stops me mid knock.

"Shit!" The hairs on my arms go rigid as I jump. Whirling, I crane my neck to stare up into massive orange eyes. "Oh my god, I'm so sorry Wizzle. You just scared me."

The brown and green feathers covering his turtle-like head ruffle as he studies me. The fear on my face reflects in his glassy eyes. He opens his orange beak, revealing a wriggling wet pointed tongue. A rotten meat stench wafts over me and I swallow down a gag. Another groan gurgles out. I swear it sounds sad, but how can anyone feel sad when they're dressed as the smartest member of the gang? As much as I enjoy being in Wizzle's presence, annoyance prickles me the longer we stand here. He's not saying anything with his classic British voice, giving me any of his famous wisdom about the woods or staying true to yourself, and I'm running late.

"So, uh yeah, today's my first day. I'm sure we will be working together. I'm in maintenance. But I should probably go."

Wizzle jerks forward and slams a thick scaly arm on my shoulder. Old memories and bruises scuttle through my mind. Stubby owl claws dig into my skin. He tilts his head to the right, his forehead wrinkles tight around his eyes, then lets out a painful grunt. *They must have updated the faces of the costumes and I missed that news.* I do appreciate the work the engineers put into making them more realistic, even if it is a little unsettling thinking of him as a living thing. Which brings me back to the fact that it feels like he is trying to say something. The original mascot costumes were made to allow the characters to speak. Squeezing my arm tighter, he shakes his head in frustration. I yelp and try pulling away from him. Water drips from his tear ducts and for a moment concern creeps into those big eyes. A tremor ripples through him as he tenses, then he pushes out a long-strained moan.

"Are you okay?"

He gives his head a violent shake. A loud grating screech freezes him.

"You made it!" The husky voice full of cheer startles me. The owl turtle's eyes become as wide as hubcaps as they focus on the speaker over my shoulder. "Oh, I see you met Wizzle. Which is surprising. Wizzle, my dear friend, why are you here and not with the children?"

Wizzle removes his hand from my shoulder and shuffles back. Part of me worries I got him in trouble, the other part becomes a bundle of jittery mice in an old mattress. *What if they are someone important?*

Taking a deep breath, I turn. A woman in a crisp white lab coat with thick black goggles above her eyebrows stands in front of the open door. Behind her is a faint yellow glow, and what appears to be a stairwell of dirty cinder block walls leading down into shadows. She pulls her ruby red lips back in a giant smile, revealing shocking white teeth, while she stares at the mascot.

"Maybe you should take a trip to the relaxation area?" She cocks her head and nods. "You look tired, and you know Slappy wouldn't want you sad or not feeling well while spreading your wisdom with our magical citizens."

Wizzle bows and lays a pitiful expression on me that almost breaks my heart. At least the woman is concerned for the person in the costume. I'm sure it's hard tearing yourself away from the park. Knowing they are giving the crowds an experience of a lifetime has gotta be such a high for the actors.

"I hope you feel better, Wizzle," I tell his feather-covered shell as he slinks away.

"Now, where were we? Ah yes, welcome to our little slice of fantasy, Garrett."

With the mascot gone, it's just me and the woman in the white lab coat. All my focus has been on getting here and I didn't think about what would make a good first impression. Her voice doesn't sound like the person I talked to on the phone, so I'm not sure who this is. Maybe my supervisor? She doesn't move, just stares at me, her face never changing.

"Uh, yeah. Thank you." I nod toward the Magical Forest. "It's so beautiful here, and wonderful to see all the families having fun."

She claps her gloved hands together, the sound reminding me of popping balloons on a lonely birthday. "Oh yes, we are excited to have everyone in our kingdom! Please, let's get you started."

Before I can respond, she whirls and descends the stairs.

"Mr. Kline, I wanted to thank you for coming. We were quite thrilled with your interview. We could tell right away how much you loved Slappy and our land. I think you'll find we are the perfect fit for you, yes."

I follow the sway of her ponytail down the long decline. Fluorescent bulbs buzz above through yellowed plastic, highlighting the gray cement stairwell. My heart thunders. "I can't tell you how excited I am to finally be here Mrs....?"

"You can call me Mrs. Coen."

When we reach the bottom of the stairs, I wave my arms to dry out my sweaty armpits. Mrs. Coen motions with an outstretched hand toward the corridor of beige walls and shiny cement floor in front of us. Water drips somewhere and a fan hums. *How could this boring, regular, dumb place be below the wonders above?* I assumed the colors, the fantasy, the happiness would be even stronger down here, like this would be the unhindered epicenter of what goes on in the park. The disappointment only lasts for a moment as I tell myself I'm just trying to look for problems. My mom and dad always hid the truth behind a smile, a laugh. That doesn't mean everyone, and *everything* is wearing a mask.

As we walk through the tunnel, I try to picture how big *The Underdwelling* is. It's the one thing no one's ever put in a book or video. Could it be bigger than the park? At random intersections she guides me left or right until my sense of direction is useless. Every wall has the same boring look, no signs or posters to help me keep my bearings. Maybe it'll become second nature to me after a while. I assume the maintenance crew will be down here a lot, so eventually I'll know it as well as Mrs. Coen does. Every once in a while, I notice deep scratches or wide indentations in the drywall. I catch a whiff of wet animal fur and dung. *I don't remember reading about live animals here.* What surprises me most is we don't pass anyone as we walk. I always figured it would be a swarm of people making sure the park is running the best it can for everyone.

The clicking of our shoes on the floor and the silence from Mrs. Coen becomes too much for me. "So, I can't wait to get started. The chance to work maintenance on the rides is awesome. It's a small thing, but the hours were perfect for me and going to college."

"Well, I actually want to talk to you about that, but we're here." She points toward an opening. "Please enter and we'll get started."

Any further conversation disappears as I blink back tears. Bright lights in the sky-blue ceiling shine down on a floor of green turf. Huge painted murals of a fantastical forest and magical glade cover the walls.

On my left is a golden door with rainbow trim, on the right is a painting of a cave with a black door. An uplifting melody plays in the background. *Here's where they're hiding all the magic!* At the center of the room is a chair. I'm sure I'm practically glowing standing here.

Mrs. Coen motions for me to sit.

"Mr. Kline, again, we are so happy you have accepted our offer to work with the Slappy family. It's always a pleasure to find someone like you willing to chip in to make this the most magical place."

The music sounds familiar, and I find my thoughts drifting into the melody.

"... and we want a new member of Slappy's Gang."

"Wait, what's going on?" Why is she telling me about a new mascot right now? It is exciting to learn this insider information, but I curse myself for not paying attention.

The fake sunlight flashes across the goggles squeezing her forehead. "I know it's not what we hired you for, and you sound very excited about being in maintenance, which we appreciate: every member of the land is important."

Is she saying what I think she is saying? My stomach fills with butterflies.

"But, we find ourselves in the wonderful position to offer you something else. And to help me with this announcement...."

The door to the cave opens. Slappy's pal Cuddles stomps into the room. My heart leaps into my throat. I jab a fingernail into my palm as the giant lion bear stoops to keep his head from hitting the ceiling. Its golden eyes gleam with years of experience. A musky odor fills the room. I stifle a laugh of delight when its lip curls, revealing large dingy teeth. *They must be bringing him back, and he looks so good!* The time put into its twitching whiskers, the way his wet nose moves, the slight drool hanging off black lips floors me. Mrs. Coen pats the mascot's fur as it wraps her in one of its paws.

"So, what do you say, want to join the gang and be Cuddles' new nephew?"

"You mean you want *me* to be one of Slappy's friends?" *Yes, this would be a dream come true!* Then a nagging voice reminds me that even though I was willing to take any job here, the maintenance one allowed me time to go to community college. Would being a mascot take up my whole week?

I gnaw on my finger, a torrent of emotions pounding at my skull. Staring at Cuddles, the years of dreaming about being here, of being a part of this happy family, flood my brain. A giddy calm soothes me, and I push away the worry. *Maybe I can go to college later.* "Ever since I was young, I've always thought this place was special. The chance to work on the rides seemed like the best thing in the world. But now? Yes, of course I want to put on one of the costumes and join the gang!"

Mrs. Coen's gloved hands squeak as they ball into fists, her eye twitches. Cuddles rubs her arm, and she relaxes. The smile comes back. "I'm so glad to hear it! I think you'll be very happy this way. Once you hear the laughter and see all the fun you are giving the children, you'll totally forget all about the maintenance job."

She puts up a finger, "One thing. We don't call them costumes here. Especially now that Slappy's friends are the best-looking characters in any theme park in the world. No *mouse* can compare to what we have here."

Heat burns up my cheeks. "Oh sorry, I didn't mean any-"

"It's okay. Water under the bridge." Mrs. Coen produces a large golden key from her pocket. "On to brighter things! I think you're going to be a great addition. You have the joy and spirit we need."

Excitement buzzes through me.

"Well, then the only thing left is to send you through the magical forest." She slips the key into the gold door. "On the other side you'll find everything you need."

Before I can ask what my hours will be, where I'll be performing, Cuddles grips me with his massive paws and lifts me out of the chair like I'm a child. He sets me on my feet, then pushes me to the doorway.

As I pass the threshold, I'm overcome with happiness. Pink, purple, and red trees twisted in whimsical shapes reach up and block out my view of the ceiling. A candy cane striped lane lay before me. The scent of chocolate chip cookies fills the air. When I turn to thank her, the door slams with a thud. Then a staticky voice comes from above.

"Please follow the path. Your journey to becoming one of the gang is through the woods."

Exhilarated and just a little nervous, I begin walking down the trail.

After some time of passing the same fairytale style trees I saw when I entered the room, I wonder if I'm lost. I scan the fake forest and notice a break in the branches above me. A few black bubbles mark the sky-blue ceiling, along with big metal vents. *Are they watching me, is this a test?*

The path guides me to the left and I slow. Large tufts of cotton float and dance in the air. *It's like snow!* Laughing, I twirl amongst the fluffy white bunches, forgetting how long I've been here. I imagine living in this winter wonderland, this real-life dream.

Taking my time to appreciate how lucky I am, I watch the fake snow fall and collect in big comfy piles. Pieces cling to my clothes while I stroll deeper into the forest. The cotton sneaks in through my collar, sticks to my hair; my pants grow heavy with the stuff. More and more cotton fills the air. My hands and neck feel like they are on fire. The pain doesn't go away when I scratch at the skin. A tremor of panic slinks through me. When my focus goes back to the path, I can't see it anymore.

Everything is white.

Fear creeps up as I try wiping the fluff off. No matter what I do, it clings to every part of me. The inside of my arms feels like they are stuffed with barbed wire. More fluff sticks to my head, burning my scalp. Tears stream down my cheeks until the fake snow starts absorbing the wetness. Cotton fills my mouth and smothers my attempt to scream. I hack and cough, yet the stuff clogs my lungs. My vision spins and I stagger to a tree.

That's when I see the red dripping down my hands.

The scream finally pushes through the cotton in my mouth, and I stumble off the tree. After a few steps, I feel a pulsing in my thighs. Through watery eyes I see strange growths bubbling on my legs. The sight causes me to fall. Piles of stuffing catch me, yet my tailbone cracks on the ground. My spine pops and grinds, pain becomes lightning streaking across my skull. Gritting my teeth, my body contorts and jerks. A dry yelp sneaks out as I feel the skin on my back tearing, my bones stretching with each new contortion. The agonizing torment stabs and pounds its way through me, jolting my nerve endings. An intense pressure builds against the back of my eyeballs. My perspective warps as I feel my eyes bulge. Something pushes out from the sensitive meat under my nails, sending waves of agony through my arms. As I writhe on the ground, my skin feels like it's shrinking, like I'm in a prison.

Time blinks out, my mind in some gray place.

———

Sunlight welcomes me. There's a clopping with every step I take. My head is off balance. At the top of my vision, I can see two bony, twisted, protrusions that seem to be coming from my skull. There's something long where my nose should be, and I can pick up a million scents. When I glance at my arms, they're covered in white fur, three hard black fingers where my hands should be. Then I look up and Cuddles, Slappy, and a ton of children are looking at me, smiling at me.

A loud voice booms over the crowd. "We are so excited to introduce our newest member of Slappy's Gang and Cuddle's nephew: Spottie the Canine Goat!"

Some small part of me screams, *I'm not in a costume, I'm a human like you!* But the longer I stand here, the more the children clapping and laughing wash it away. Lingering memories of home, two adults with painful hands, anger barely hiding behind fleshy masks, a dank basement with a sad mattress, disappear into the urge to spread cheer. A silly worry about hours sitting in class so I can get something called a job flit about like an annoying gnat. Pesky thoughts about a world outside the Magical Forest bother me for a moment, then I remember: Slappy protects us, as long as we dance and make the visiting children's dreams come true. Testing my new muscles, I force my muzzle to spread wide and begin prancing, living my new magical life.

God Damn You To Hell, John Glenn!

Frank J. Oreto

PETEY BURST through the front door like an eight-year-old ball of lightning. "Mom, mom, wait 'til you hear! Wait 'til you hear!"

Suzanne looked from the stack of ungraded trigonometry tests to the Cheshire Cat wall clock. Two-thirty. Gerald had promised 5 p.m. She put down her red pen and tried to force all annoyance from her face.

"I saw a launch. A real live rocket launch. Dad and me got up at four goddamn a.m."

Suzanne took her boy in her arms. "That's not appropriate language."

Petey's face clouded for a moment. "It's okay between us men. Dad said so."

"Well, don't say it around us moms. How was the rocket?"

"SOOO loud!" Petey let loose his best rocket roar.

"Oh, my gosh. Sooo loud!"

"And I met an astronaut."

"I bet you did." Petey's father, Gerald, liked astronauts. He liked to go out to bars with them and hit on the women they drew like flies. Astronauts were one reason Gerald was Suzanne's ex-husband.

"And you know what, Mom? You know what?"

Gerald pushed through the front door. In his arms, he carried Petey's overnight bag along with a large glass box.

"The Astronaut gave me space monkeys. I gotta clear a spot. I'm clearing the spot, Dad!" Petey wiggled out of his mother's embrace and raced to his room, leaving the two adults staring at each other.

"Hey Suzie. I just said hi to Harry and Eugenia next door. You know, I actually kind of miss them."

"You said you'd keep Petey until goddamn five o'clock."

"Oh, come on, Suze. There's no need to—"

"Don't worry, it's okay to talk that way between us men. Petey said so."

"The launch *was* pretty damned early. But he was so excited."

"*You're* pretty damned early. I plan my work around the times we agree on."

"I know. I'm sorry. I have to get back to the cape. There's a press junket thing."

"Sure, I get it. Dinner, drinks, the grind never ceases."

"Dad, I cleared the spot. Where are you?!" Petey's excitement verged on hysteria.

"Duty calls."

"Wait a second, is that an aquarium? You can't just bring pets—" But Gerald was already past her and stepping into Petey's room.

Gerald worked for NASA in media relations. A job you rarely associate with the space program. But it *was* a job that let you give the son you only saw one weekend a month every official NASA themed hat, t-shirt, toy, and now... space monkeys?

I earn a masters in mathematics and teach tenth grade trig. He barely scrapes a BS in communications and works for the space program. "The world is a stupid place."

And now, if I go in that bedroom and say, "Petey, you can't just have a new pet without asking," I am the giant monster bitch versus his superhero, rocket-launching, astronaut-befriending dad.

Voices came from Petey's room. "We can fill it up in the bathtub."

"Okay, monster bitch it is," she muttered. Suzanne was waiting when father and son came back into Petey's room carrying the half-filled aquarium. "Wait. No one asked me if you could have an aquarium in your room."

"Dad said it was okay." Petey said, as if this settled things.

"Your dad doesn't live here anymore." Her words were like a slap. Petey's excitement evaporated, replaced with barely held back tears.

Monster bitch.

Suzanne kneeled, so she was face-to-face with her son. "Sweetheart, I need to talk to Daddy alone for a few minutes. Go in the kitchen and have some Tang, okay?" Of course, Petey looked to his father.

"Do what your mother says, son."

The boy sniffled and walked out of the room. "But... space monkeys," he said in a sad, barely audible voice.

Suzanne turned on her husband. "You can't make decisions like this without talking to me first."

Gerald put the aquarium on top of the chest of drawers Petey had cleared off, then sat down on his son's bed. He patted a spot beside him.

Suzanne didn't move.

"Fine, I know you don't like me getting him things."

"Oh, screw you, Gerald." Suzanne hissed the words in a stage whisper she hoped didn't carry to the kitchen. "That is so unfair." She gestured around the room. A poster of the Apollo moon landing crew hung on the wall. Signed by all three crew members. In the corner by the closet, a four-foot-tall Apollo 6 replica stood poised for takeoff. "Yes, I don't appreciate always being the Grinch to your Santa Claus, but pets are different. Are you planning to drop off a surprise pony next time?"

Gerald spread his palms in a calming gesture that made Suzanne want to kick him in his khaki-covered shin. "I get you. I've been trying to cut down on the presents. You know, let spending time with Petey *be* the present. That's why we went to the launch. Even got a look into ground control."

Suzanne felt the anger fade a bit. Maybe Gerald had listened a little over their last half dozen arguments.

"This whole space monkey thing wasn't my fault. It was John. You know, John Glenn."

Suzanne knew John. She'd met him a few times in the last days of her marriage. "So, John was the astronaut Petey met?"

"Yeah. It's really not a big deal. They'll all be dead in a month... Jeez, I'm not explaining this well. You ever heard of sea monkeys?"

Suzanne shook her head.

"Wait, a second." Gerald grabbed a *Fantastic Four* comic from a stack on Petey's nightstand and flipped through the pages. "Here." He held up a full-page advertisement showing a family of pink cartoon fish people complete with webbed hands and stubby antenna. Above them the ad proclaimed "Enter the Wonderful World of Amazing Live Sea-Monkeys, Own a Bowl Full of Happiness."

"I think I need a little more explanation."

"This is what John gave him. They're brine shrimp. So small you can barely see them even when they're full grown. You pour the brine shrimp eggs in some water along with a little food and in a couple of days, you got your sea monkeys swimming around. Feed them once a week and they last for a couple of months."

"Petey called them space monkeys."

"Well, yeah. The eggs are good for experiments. So, they took some on a few Apollo flights. Let them get frizzled by cosmic rays to see what happened."

"They aren't radioactive or anything?"

"No, nothing like that. The scientists hatched a bunch of them when they got back to earth. They turned out just regular old brine shrimp, maybe an extra set of legs or two. So, John got permission to give a few batches of the unhatched eggs to kids. Calls them space monkeys, because he's John. What was I supposed to do?"

Suzanne sat down on the bed next to her ex-husband. "I know you have a hard time saying no. They last a couple of months, that's it?"

"If you're lucky. Once they're gone, you can throw out the aquarium. Better yet, get the kid a goldfish."

Suzanne looked at the aquarium sitting on the dresser. She tried not to imagine a badly thrown baseball crashing through the glass and water cascading over Petey's clothes. "All right. He did get them from a real live astronaut. Let's give boyo the good news."

They made a deal. The space monkeys were Petey and Gerald's project. If Petey had an issue that didn't involve a waterfall in his room, he called his dad. "If I have to deal with your space monkeys, they go to your dad's on his next weekend."

And for the most part, Petey's word was his bond. Once, he complained he couldn't find his space monkey food. But quickly followed up with, "Don't worry, mom. I'll take care of it." There was also a tense thirty minutes when Petey ran back and forth from his room to their backyard carrying a large plastic cup.

Suzanne took a peek in his room. No broken glass or soaked carpet. She went back to folding clothes and threw out a casual. "Everything okay, Champ?" on Petey's next lap. "You watching out for alligators?" There was a small stream just past their lawn that turned the backyard swampy on the rare occasions it rained. 'Watch out for gators' was a family joke.

This time, Petey didn't crack a smile. He just frowned into the cup for a moment. "There's not really any alligators outside. Right, Mom?"

"No sweetie. Not enough water."

"Okay, then everything's fine."

By the time Gerald's weekend came around again, Suzanne had to admit the space monkeys weren't a problem after all. She'd arranged for Gerald to pick Petey up from Hank's Dog Shoppe, Petey's favorite watering hole. The eight-year-old had already polished off a chili dog and was half-way through his strawberry milk shake.

"Don't eat too much. You might get sick in your dad's convertible." Suzanne reconsidered. "Eat as much as you like." It was nice to be the one spoiling Petey for a change.

The boy took a deep slurp of milkshake and sighed with satisfaction. "Mom, can you do me a favor? It's about Rudy, my space monkey. I know you don't want to take care of him, but I'll be at Dad's and...."

"You've done a great job with them. Wait. There's only one?"

"Yeah, but he's doing really good."

They must be dying off even quicker than Gerald said. Suzanne almost felt guilty. Maybe she would get Petey that goldfish. "What do you need?"

"He's fed and everything, but could you just check on him? Make sure he's okay?"

"Of course, sweetheart."

"And I won't have to take him to Dad's for that?"

"No, I'm happy to do it."

With Petey safely on his way to the Cape, Suzanne took her time driving home. Her neighbor Harry was out watering his grass next door. When Suzanne pulled in, he waved her over.

"So, is this Petey's weekend with Gerald?" Harry was in his late forties and had a penchant for beachcomber style straw hats and keeping his ever-present Hawaiian shirts unbuttoned down to his pot belly. Despite his fashion sense, Harry was a good neighbor, always ready to lend a hand or loan out a tool or two.

"Yep. Got the place to myself." *Just me and Rudy, the lone space monkey.*

"Well, we're having a few friends over later, if you get bored and want something to do. Eugenia's always saying we should have you over for a drink."

"Sweet of you to offer, Harry. I think I'll probably just bask in the solitude tonight, but If I change my mind, I'll give you a call."

"I'll tell Eugenia you're a firm maybe," said Harry and gave her an exaggerated wink.

Two hours later, Suzanne still didn't feel like partying with her neighbors. But she decided a drink was a fine idea and maybe some Chinese delivery. She opened a bottle of chardonnay when the food arrived. *White wine goes with fried rice, right?*

She woke up snug in her bed. With dim memories of corking the half-empty chard and putting the leftover Chinese food in the fridge. *You sure know how to party.* Thoughts of coffee and some aspirin were enough to get her out of bed. *Oh, and don't forget your space-monkey sitting. Better take a peek in Petey's room.*

The carpet outside Pete's half-open door squelched under Suzanne's bare feet. *Oh no.* And things had been going so well. Sure enough, the side panel of the aquarium was shattered, and water covered both the dresser and floor. *What the hell could have happened? Petey's at the cape. And a few glasses of wine do not send me into an aquarium-smashing frenzy.*

She didn't see a brine shrimp flopping on the carpet. Gerald said they were tiny. Well, time for towels and a pair of shoes. Suzanne didn't feel like bleeding this morning.

A crash sounded in the kitchen. "Oh, what now?" Could an animal have gotten in? A cat maybe. "Watch out for gators." But the family joke didn't sound so funny just now. "A cat," she said in her no-nonsense teacher's voice. "Or maybe a possum."

It wasn't a possum or even an alligator. The door to the refrigerator hung open. The thing inside was about three feet long. Sickly green horizontal bands covered the length of the creature. The bands looked hard, like tortoise shell polished to a glimmering sheen. At least a dozen legs poked out from the thing's sides. Each limb looked meaty and muscular and ended in three long talon-tipped digits.

Oh Jesus. The house was locked up, windows closed, nothing that big could have gotten inside. Suzanne thought she knew what broke the aquarium.

"There's only one," Petey had said, "but he's doing really well."

Rudy, her son's last remaining space monkey, pulled its—what? head section?—from the plastic drawer, the smell of leftover fried rice and Oscar Mayer bologna filled the room. Two long antennae—arms? mandibles?—locked onto a half-full gallon of milk and pulled the jug to the thing's head. The space monkey made a sound like Petey finishing off his strawberry milkshake. The jug imploded.

Rudy's body gave a full-length shudder and grew. Broadening and lengthening by a good four inches. A blue ooze flowed out from between the bands of shell. The ooze coated the freshly-grown flesh, hardening into new layers of protection.

Suzanne took a cautious step back, angling for the front door. She held her breath, but the space monkey somehow sensed her. Rudy's head section rotated on its body. A long, segmented tube, wet with milk, extended tentatively in Suzanne's direction. The lip of the tube was red and wet. Black triangular teeth pushed through the red flesh and came together with an almost musical clink.

The space monkey's body spun, its many legs breaking into a galloping scurry toward Suzanne. She turned and ran flat out for the door.

She made it three steps before her foot came down on the Mattel

Lunar Lander model Gerald and Petey had put together three months before. Suzanne cursed and fell hard on her shoulder. The fall saved her life. Rudy was practically airborne when it ran right over her. A few claws tried to gain purchase. But they only snagged for a moment on her terry-cloth robe as the creature passed over.

The space monkey rammed the flowered wallpaper with a thud. Its mouth tube brayed a sound that was half bellow, half kazoo. Suzanne let out an involuntary bark of hysterical laughter. She kept seeing the milk jug collapsing in on itself as Rudy sucked out the contents.

Fear gave Suzanne speed and the fortitude to ignore the pain in her shoulder. She rolled to her feet and dashed to the door, slamming it behind her before the space monkey gave chase.

A jolt of panic ripped through her as she realized she hadn't pressed the button on the knob so it would lock when closed. Maybe it wouldn't matter. Could the thing turn a doorknob? As if in answer, the door bulged outward as something strong and pissed off slammed against it.

Suzanne looked around the neighborhood. No one was stirring yet on this quiet Saturday morning. *I have to get to a phone.* Another thud shook the door. Suzanne stopped trying to plan and ran for Harry and Eugenia's sea-foam green bungalow.

The front door gave way with a crash. Rudy let out another of its strange kazoo-colored bellows. Suzanne didn't look back. She didn't want to see the black teeth of the space monkey's mouth tube snapping open and closed.

Her hand reached Harry and Eugenia's doorknob. *Not locked. Thank God, it's not locked.* Suzanne pushed inside, then slammed and locked the door. She stared at the white wood, waiting for the thud.

"Well Suzanne, I know Harry invited you to come by, but you really should have called first or at least knocked."

Suzanne turned to her neighbor. "I'm so sorry, we have to call the police—uh..." Suzanne would not have believed it possible, but for the moment she had completely forgotten why she came over.

Eugenia Price, Suzanne's neighbor for the last five years, and vice president of the Caderro County historical society, stood naked in her living room but for a complex arrangement of black leather straps that supported the foot long, bright red phallus protruding at a jaunty angle from about crotch level.

"Now hold on, Suzanne. There is no need to call any police. We're all consenting adults here." Eugenia gestured to a naked man sound asleep on the flower-print sofa. "It's just a lifestyle choice. Nobody's getting hurt."

The door burst inward with a bang and a shower of splintered wood.

The space monkey reared up its top half, mouth tube thrust forward as if tasting the air. Eugenia screamed and ran through a beaded door curtain into the dining room. "Harrrrrry!"

Suzanne spotted a black club on the floor and snatched it up. It wasn't a club, but it was the closest thing to a weapon in the room.

The Space monkey ignored Suzanne and Eugenia. The naked man, now sitting up and blinking dazedly, was not so lucky. Rudy's multiple legs flexed, and he leaped across the room. The man never even screamed. The space monkey's fanged mouth tube plunged into his narrow chest while dozens of legs held him immobile. Blood bubbled from the man's open mouth, then reversed course as the space monkey sucked in its meal.

"Get down, Suzanne." A rapid series of explosions filled the room. Suzanne dove to the floor. Harry and Eugenia stood in the door to the dining room. Harry wore his signature beachcomber straw hat along with a rhinestone studded cod piece and nipple clips. He held a pistol in each hand. Eugenia had a rifle pressed into her shoulder.

Bullets struck the space monkey shell, ricocheting away with shrill whistling sounds.

"Get out, Suze," yelled Harry over the cacophony. "We got this."

Suzanne wasn't too sure about that. The space monkey rocked under the onslaught of bullets, but even where a stray shot got past its shell armor, blue ooze bubbled out of the wound, sealing it.

The crawl toward the front door seemed to take hours. Any moment, Suzanne expected to feel Rudy's mouth tube plunge into her back. Harry and Eugenia were still firing as Suzanne crossed the threshold. *Where did they keep the extra rounds?*

A dry click sounded as Suzanne stood and pulled the door, still hanging by one hinge, as close to closed as she could manage. A few more sporadic shots sounded, and then the house was silent.

Suzanne stood in the cul-de-sac praying that her gun-toting, swinger neighbors had killed Petey's pet. She didn't even notice the two police cruisers until they'd stopped their engines and one of the policemen yelled to her.

"Ma'am, put down the... um, the object." The man speaking was tall and thin, his face dominated by a bushy mustache. The other officer, shorter, with broad shoulders, stood in the open door of the second cruiser. He had his gun drawn, but he was laughing too hard to point it anywhere.

"Shut up Hawkins," yelled Mustache. "Ma'am, put down the thing in your hand and approach me slowly."

Suzanne dropped the two-foot-long black dildo on to the asphalt. She hadn't even realized she still held it. "Harry and Eugenia." Suzanne pointed to her neighbor's house. "I think they're dead." *No, they killed the monster, they shot it to death, and Eugenia is probably having sex with it now. Please lord, let that be the way it happened.*

"We had reports of shots being fired." Mustache was talking again. It took a little while for the words to make sense to Suzanne. *I think I'm in shock.*

"Are you hurt, ma'am?"

"No." Suzanne didn't know if she said the word out loud. *I should be the one hurt. Not Harry and Eugenia. It was my monster. I could have stopped it.* She imagined Petey watching as his space monkey grew. *He would have told me about it. Would have asked me for help.* "Is it supposed to get so big, mommy?" *But I had to make him* take some responsibility *because my ex-husband pissed me off. Now people are dead. What if Petey had been home?* Suzanne let loose an involuntary groan.

"Ma'am, I need you to talk to me. Did you call the police?"

Suzanne looked back to mustache cop, then to Harry and Eugenia's door hanging from its single hinge. "Harry had guns, but I don't think it helped."

"Who has guns?"

Suzanne took a deep breath. "Harry, my neighbor." She pointed to the bungalow.

"All right. I want you to go to my cruiser. We're going to take care of this."

Harry and Eugenia's broken front door pushed open almost languidly. As if the creature coming out had nothing to fear.

"What the hell is that?"

Rudy was now the size of a cow, maybe a hippo? *How big is a freaking hippo?* Suzanne shook her head hard. *Get it together, Suze.*

Hawkins, the wide-bodied cop, stood between the two cruisers, his pistol in a two-handed shooter's grip. Bullets struck the enormous space monkey, pinging off in random trajectories.

Suzanne had been here before. She ducked her head and ran.

Mustache cop added more bullets to the party.

Suzanne yelled. "It won't help. Get back in your cars. Drive!"

Maybe it was the bullets bouncing off the space monkey's shell, but mustache cop stopped firing. Suzanne could hear his feet striking the asphalt as he ran after her.

Shots still rang out from the second policeman's gun.

Suzanne reached the cruiser and threw herself into the front seat. She saw mustache cop in mid-stride, reaching out as if Suzanne could somehow pull him to safety. The space monkey's mouth tube burst through the man's chest. Blood and bone sprayed the cruiser's windshield.

Hawkins screamed and kept firing.

Suzanne screamed herself, just to cut through the panic filling her head. It helped. She pulled the cruiser door shut. Keys hung from the ignition. In front of her, the space monkey finished up with mustache cop. Another person who tried to help her, dead.

Suzanne started the cruiser. This had to end. She never wanted to be the monster bitch, but it was time. She shifted into drive and stood on the gas. The cruiser leaped forward with a shriek of tires chewing asphalt. But the only thing to go down beneath its wheels was the dead police officer. Rudy's first leap carried it to the hood of the cruiser. Its second sent it over the car altogether.

Hawkins had replaced his empty pistol with a shotgun. He got one shot off before the space monkey landed in front of him, stretched to its full height, and rammed its mouth tube straight down through the top of the man's skull.

Suzanne watched through the cruiser's rear view as the space monkey grew. "No." She shifted into reverse and punched the gas again.

Maybe the space monkey tried to jump, but the mouth tube was lodged too deep. That didn't matter. What mattered was the sound of shells cracking as the cruiser's rear fender pinned the space monkey against the other police car at twenty miles per hour. Blue goo gouted from the thing's wounds. It poured over the twisted metal of the cruisers, cementing monster and machine into a solid, immovable mass.

Suzanne picked up the shotgun, slick with Hawkins' blood. She'd never fired one, but she figured it out. The first squeeze of the trigger blew Rudy's mouth tube into fragments. Suzanne racked the slide and shoved the shotgun barrel in the crater the first shell had left. She pulled the trigger again and again. Shoving deeper into the space monkey's soft insides with each shot. "God damn you to hell, John Glenn!"

The sixth time Suzanne racked the slide and fired, the space monkey stopped moving. She pulled the shotgun from inside the carcass. Blue ooze stiffened and cracked on her forearms. The pieces fell to the asphalt.

Once she got past her missing front door, the house seemed strangely undisturbed. Suzanne picked up the phone and pressed it to her ear. The number she dialed was not the police. More of them were probably on the way. Instead, Suzanne called a two-bedroom condo in Cape Canaveral.

"Hello, Glenshaw residence." Petey's high voice articulated each word carefully.

The sound of her son's voice sent a thrill of fierce joy through Suzanne. Petey was safe in Cape Canaveral with Gerald. *And I killed the goddamned monster.* "Hey Sweetheart. Are you having a good time?" Suzanne's voice only cracked a little, but Petey noticed.

"You okay, Mom?"

Suzanne wiped tears from her eyes. "Yeah. Mommy just misses you, kiddo."

"I miss you too. Mom. Is Rudy okay?" The silence on the phone stretched as Suzanne thought about her answer. "Mom, I don't mind. I mean, if he's not okay. I don't like him much. He ate up his brothers and sisters."

Suzanne nodded silently. *Of course he did.*

"I saved the ones I could, but he ate most of them."

"What?" An ice-cold void opened in Suzanne's gut.

"Daddy says sometimes fishes do that."

"Honey. What do you mean, you saved them?" She replayed the memory of Petey running back and forth from his room to the backyard, a large red plastic cup clutched in his small hands.

"I put them in the stream. I was careful, Mom. I didn't get wet or anything. And no gators."

Suzanne wondered how many space monkeys Petey had saved? How many had been outside eating and growing for over a week? "Petey, guess what? You're going to stay with Daddy a few more days." Distant sirens grew nearer. "Tell your dad I'll call him soon."

The phone felt suddenly heavy and awkward in her hand. It took Suzanne three tries to get it on the cradle. She pulled her torn and stained terry-cloth robe tighter, though the day was already heating up. The police would be here soon with more shotguns. While she waited, Suzanne watched the backyard and prayed for alligators.

A Grace of Finer Form

Sarah Hans

WE WORRIED FIRST about the polar bears, my mother told me, but
nobody cared much about polar bears. Next, we worried about the bees,
which was much more pressing, for reasons I didn't completely
understand. And then, of course, finally, as the ice caps melted and the
seas rose and the freshwater lakes dried up, we worried about ourselves. I
asked her so many times how it was that people didn't see the end
coming, when they were warned for so many years, but my mother
would shrug and look away, in those days, when she would still talk
about it.

Later, I understood the guilt and shame that must have pressed on
her and driven her to silence, and, eventually, to a dark place where she
took her own life. I was so accustomed to her coldness and distance that
her death barely registered. I was alone for the first time in my life, but
I'd always been lonely, so it wasn't as great a change as you might expect.
I buried my mother down the hill from the spring, where her body
could nurture the trees. Out of the hardest wood I could find, I carved
for her a marker in the rough image of the naiad who blessed our spring,
whispering to myself the stories of gods and titans she had told me so
many nights around our fire.

I stayed at the spring where we had lived for so many years, the water a dangerous life-giving secret. I kept the same routines. Everything I did was for one purpose: to keep myself alive. My mother had, after all, clung to life for nearly twenty years in order to teach me how, abandoning the comforts of civilization for my benefit. Living was the only thing I could do to honor her memory.

There was little joy in it. My mother had taught me few of life's pleasures. I knew a few songs, though, and at night I raised my voice to the trees. Sometimes the creatures that lived in the forest sang with me, a harmonious echo of howls and chirps. Over many seasons, some of the animals grew closer to the spring, daring to drink the water while I watched from nearby. My mother's admonitions reverberated in my head when a six-legged doe, fat with the promise of fawns, nested in the thicket near my cave. Mother would have frightened her away, but I let her stay. It was better than being alone.

I had never understood mother's fear of the mutated forest creatures. She, of course, had remembered a time when the animals weren't the distorted versions we had now, with extra limbs, and eyes in the wrong places, and wings or tails that didn't belong. But, to me, the two-headed chipmunk-lizard hybrid that scrambled up my sleeve one afternoon to take a seed from my hand was as natural as any other thing in the forest. These twisted animals were all I had ever known.

Sometimes, at night, while I lay lonely on my lumpy cot, shivering beside the dying embers of my fire, I thought I heard the whisper of leaves and crack of branches, like something massive moving through the forest. But when I rose to investigate, there was no sign of anything. I began to wonder if I was losing my mind. Maybe I was just as warped as the other denizens of the forest, but my unnaturalness took a different form.

Two humans arrived one winter morning while I bathed in the hot springs. They were so covered in clothes—utility trousers and heavy jackets and handkerchiefs and hats—I couldn't even tell whether they were human. Every story my mother had instilled in me about men and the other dangerous creatures in the world raced through my mind, a jumble of terror. I imagined the chipmunk-lizard hybrid and what horrors would result from similar human distortions. Every cell in my body screamed that I should grab my gun to defend myself and my water. Instead, naked and vulnerable, I was paralyzed.

"Is that a hot spring?" One of them exclaimed, her voice high like my mother's.

The other removed her pack and pulled the bandana from her face. She was a woman. Her cheeks were red and her lips chapped, but her eyes were bright and silently begging a question. When I made no indication either way, she fearlessly stripped off all her supplies and clothing and lowered herself into the steaming water. The other woman did the same.

Fear coursed through me, my own blood pounding in my ears. My mother's disembodied voice scolded me for allowing them so close.

But they were filthy, exhausted, injured. Their ribs showed through their skin. One was covered in livid purple bruises and the other had a long gash down her arm bandaged with a dirty rag. Filth sloughed from their bodies, turning the spring water briefly gray, until both women were pink as baby mice. They were harmless.

No one is harmless, my mother's voice assured me. I thought of the chipmunk-lizard and the doe. None of the forest's creatures had ever harmed me. These women didn't seem very different. Mother had filled my ears with warnings about men and their depravity, but had never mentioned women and what dangers they might impose.

They introduced themselves to me as Amber and Kelly. When I asked how they had found my spring, Amber said they'd heard me singing at night and followed the sound of my song. Kelly called my voice beautiful, angelic, a beacon of hope in the darkness. No one had ever complimented me before. My heart felt as if it would swell too big for my chest.

I would do anything to hang onto the feeling those compliments inspired. Was it joy? Bliss? I had never felt something so divine.

I told them they could stay. There were plenty of resources for three, as long as they were willing to work, and as long as they swore to defend the spring as ruthlessly as my mother had taught me. They agreed to these terms.

I taught them how to properly care for a wound, how to start and tend a fire, how to clean and use the guns in my cache, how to tend the spring, how to make offerings to the naiad, and how to dry herbs and preserve plants so we could feed ourselves over the winter. Our lives settled into a pleasant rhythm. I was shocked by how ignorant they were in the necessary tasks for survival. They were like children, at first, and I found myself channeling my mother's patient instructions as I taught them how to do everything, even simple tasks like digging a latrine pit far from the cave or boiling spring water so it would be safe to drink.

To their credit, both women learned quickly and neither shirked her responsibilities. With three to share the daily tasks, there was more time for joy, and while I taught Amber and Kelly to survive, they taught me to really live. We bathed together, slept together, gathered wood together, and performed the ritual offerings together. At night, we raised our voices to the stars together. For the first time in my life, I was happy.

Yes, sometimes I missed my solitude. Kelly talked too much--especially about men, an obsession I couldn't begin to understand--and Amber's laugh sometimes made my skin prickle. They complained about my aversion to killing animals that made us all vegetarians. They both acted as if the offerings to the naiad were silly, and rolled their eyes when I retold them the mythical tales of gods and heroes I had learned from my mother.

But it was still better than being alone. Sometimes, in the night, I still heard the rustling of leaves and snapping of branches that made me imagine something taller than any tree walking through the forest. I would nestle in closer to my friends and match my breathing to theirs until I returned to sleep.

Amber and Kelly told me stories about the world outside the forest. About how, while my mother took me into the trees and made a life for us around the spring, the rest of the world had tried to go on. Their families continued to send them to school even as water rations dwindled. The powerful hoarded the best of everything, leaving the dregs for everyone else. There were riots over food. Life in the cities became unbearable as the temperatures rose and electricity became less reliable. Heat stroke became a common way to die in the summer, while starvation and hypothermia took lives in the winter. It didn't all happen at once, the destruction of society. It happened in fits and starts, slowly, over many years, before things were so bad it was clear nothing was working like it should, and it was impossible to continue living in the city.

Their families tried to move to the country, but the countryside was already swarming with desperate people and dangerously mutated animals. I held my rifle close and was grateful for the lessons my mother had taught me. And I was grateful that my mother had taken her own life, instead of wasting away of thirst, being attacked by one of the deformed predators that lived in the forest, dying a long, lingering death from infection, or getting shot by other desperate water-seekers. Amber and Kelly made a long, tragic list of their dead. I had not known, before then, there were so many ways to die.

There were stories, they said, of a haven in the north, a place where water flowed freely and people lived in harmony. They were going there when they stumbled upon my singing. Their water rations were dangerously low, and the creatures that lurked in the forest had started coming too close. Finding me had likely saved their lives. They were so grateful.

I told them I was grateful for their company. I hadn't known how unhappy I was before they came. I confessed that it seemed like the fates had brought us together, to care for each other and be a family, forever.

They looked at each other awkwardly. Amber licked her lips. Kelly cleared her throat.

They were leaving, I knew then. They didn't have to say it. Hadn't we spent weeks together, months, the whole of winter? Didn't I know the meaning of every twitch and glare? They were still planning to go to this fabled haven, this imaginary place of endless freshwater and harmonious living. The naiad's spring and I were only a temporary way station. Now that their bodies were healthy and their canteens filled, they would be on the road again, as soon as it was clear of snow.

My heart felt like it was made of sharp glass, stabbing my chest every time I breathed.

"Come with us," Amber said. "You can't stay here forever. What kind of life would that be?"

If only they would stay, it would be a joyful life, I thought. A content life. No men, but few problems. All the water they could drink.

All the companionship they could ever need. I gazed at my mother's grave down the hillside and set my jaw.

That night, the earth trembled beneath me while I slept, and I dreamed of many arms holding me while I sobbed. The next morning the snow had melted. Amber and Kelly were gone, and the forest was silent, as if all the birds that chirped and insects that clicked had gone silent in deference to my grief.

I didn't know true sorrow when my mother died, but she had not held me skin-to-skin on the cold, dark nights while dogs howled outside our drafty home. She had not taught me songs about love, had not told me jokes from the world before, had not bathed with me in the spring and playfully splashed me. She had not made me laugh. She had not brought me joy.

But Amber and Kelly had, so now I knew sorrow, down to my bones. I knew the miserable keening of loss, because it forced its way from my throat. Grief burrowed its way into my chest, into my soul, and a dark veil was pulled across the world. The sky was the color of ash, and food tasted like dirt.

I tried to keep my routine. I tried to go through the motions, doing the things my mother had taught me to do, to preserve my life. But without Kelly and Amber, without love, I could see little reason to stay alive. Loneliness was worse, now that I had known its opposite.

All I wanted to do was sleep the day away, and that would lead to my death. The perimeter had to be maintained, the spring protected. Food had to be gathered and stored, water collected and boiled, offerings made to the naiad. There was too much to do to wallow, but I didn't want to do any of it.

As the first crocuses poked their heads from the frost-rimed earth, I gathered supplies, loaded my guns, and went north.

That first day, I walked the road alone. Eventually I came upon a recently-abandoned campsite. I didn't know to whom it belonged, but I piled wood on the embers and camped there, imagining that Amber and Kelly were just ahead, and I slept where they had slept.

I went on like this for days, moving north unerringly, following the long black snake of the road that disappeared on the horizon. My legs ached and my feet burned, my boots giving them new and exciting blisters. I lay awake in the darkness each night, terrified to be so far from my home, my feet throbbing and bleeding. I wanted to turn back so many times, but I didn't know if I could find my way back to the spring. My water rations ran low.

I encountered no one, not even the usual wild animals with their assortments of mismatched eyes, and the loneliness became oppressive. Out here, I couldn't even hear the voice of my mother. Death was close behind me. If I died so far from the spring, what would happen to my spirit? Would I wander the road alone eternally? This thought kept me going past the point of reason, limping northward long after I should have made myself rest and let myself heal.

On the distant horizon, something moved against the clouds. It was dusk, and my vision had never been good, so the image was hazy. It looked like an enormous person, tall as a mountain. Was I hallucinating? Was this what people saw before they died?

Laughter, as familiar to me as my own, rose up from the trees ahead, and I dried my face and managed to mince up to the campsite. The laughter faded when I stepped into the firelight. Amber and Kelly were there, but they looked different. Kelly's eyes were too shiny, and Amber's mouth was strangely slack. They held bottles of brown liquid in their hands and waved them about, crying my name and running to embrace me. I should have felt relieved, or excited, but I felt only dread when I saw their companions.

Men. They were just as my mother had described them: taller than women, broader across the shoulders, great hulking versions of us with square jaws and hair on their faces. They stank like wild animals and they radiated menace.

I begged for Amber and Kelly to come home with me. They couldn't see it, but these men were making them strange and wrong. They laughed and shooed me away. The men stood in threatening poses until I staggered away into the brush to make my own camp nearby.

All night I eavesdropped on their conversation. "We have to go before dawn. We don't want her following us," Amber half-whispered, her speech slurred.

A man's gruff voice: "I thought she shared her food with you and stitched you up and all that. Why are you so scared of her?"

"She's a nice enough kid. But... you ever have someone get way too attached to you? Like stalker-level attached?"

The man chortled. "Sure. She's harmless though."

"Nah," Kelly said. "I know her type. She seems harmless, but you gotta be careful. We should sleep in shifts, watching out. Otherwise she might shiv us in our sleep."

That prompted laughter from the group. I clapped my hands over my ears but I could still hear Amber's voice, cutting through the darkness like a knife.

"It's not like that. She just thought there was more between us than there was. We wanted to go north to find a haven and she was never going to leave her spring. So we just left. It was best for everyone, she just didn't know it. I can't believe she came after us! So stupid."

Her words burned like a wasp sting, pulsing in my chest, an open wound. I had mistakenly thought Amber and Kelly loved me as I loved them, but they'd brushed me away the moment they saw me. I had bandaged their wounds and fed them and kept them safe, and here I was with bleeding feet and empty canteens, going to sleep on the cold, wet forest floor only fifty feet from their campsite while they cavorted with men who had given them nothing but liquor. I wondered if I could find my way home to the spring before I died of dehydration. I held back my tears, mindful of wasting water on emotion.

In the morning, the massive thing on the horizon was closer, resolving itself into a towering titan's form, still hazy in the dawn light. It was a person, but with too many limbs, too many faces, pearlescent skin shimmering in the sunlight, horrible and wonderful to behold. It was so tall its faces were wreathed in clouds like a crown. Around the titan's head, winged creatures wheeled and dipped like a god's heralds. At its feet, a retinue followed, at this distance appearing like a seething mass.

This mountainous person wasn't a hallucination at all. I had to warn my friends. I limped to their campsite and it was abandoned, the remnants of the fire ring still smoking. I ran to the road barefoot, no longer able to pull my boots over my swollen feet, leaving behind me a trail of blood.

Amber and Kelly and their men were on the road, fully clothed and burdened with packs, but they were walking south.

I screamed at them. "Where are you going? Your mythical haven is to the north."

The men laughed with that same dismissive chortle. Amber and Kelly at least had the good sense to look ashamed. One of the men said, "Why go to the north when there's a spring and a cave a few days' walk to the south?"

When my heart broke, I swear it made a sound like stone cracking in two. I collapsed to my knees. The ground shook beneath me as if an earthquake were about to tear the earth apart, and I turned to find the titan moving toward us with great strides that ate the miles in moments. Its faces turned and turned so that each pair of eyes could behold me there, on the ground, the naiad too far from her spring, the trail of blood behind me. It stood over me, five-breasted and seven-armed, three phalluses dangling between its many legs. What I had taken for a pearlescent shimmer at a distance was actually the oscillation of the vegetation that sprouted from the titan's skin, long-stemmed mushrooms and coiling vines and bell-shaped flowers the size of a dog waving and juddering with each of the giant's steps. The creatures swarming the air, flying joyful loops around the titan's body, were the hybrid monsters I was used to seeing, only moreso: the wings of an eagle combined with the body of a lynx, but also the eyes of an insect, the paws of a raccoon, the tail of a snake. Horrifying and miraculous all at once.

Water sluiced from the titan's skin and over me like a torrential rainstorm, like a refreshing summer downpour. I swallowed what I could, letting the rest drench me down to my bones, knowing it would change me and longing for that change.

Hands lifted me up and they were the hands of the titan's worshippers, men and women who had once been human. They were so much more, now, with ten arms and twenty legs and countless faces. They were furred and feathered and scaled. They regarded me with yellow eyes with slitted pupils or the unnerving square pupils of a goat. When they kissed me, their lips tasted of nectar.

The titan's tears healed my injuries, those of the flesh and those of my spirit, until I felt as if I would burst into sunbeams. I had thought I knew true happiness in companionship, but it was nothing close to this divine feeling of completeness. I would never know loneliness again, and I wanted all of humanity to know this enlightenment.

The men fired weapons at the titan, ammunition from guns stolen from my cache. The titan ignored the bullets the way a man would ignore a mosquito. The mass of worshippers fell on them, ravening, filling the air with the scent of blood.

Amber and Kelly ran, screaming. I followed them, pursuing them doggedly into the trees. I was faster, now, the titan's tears making me an ideal version of myself, one that felt no pain, one that had no hesitation. I enclosed them in my embrace, my arms lengthening and my flesh stretching to encompass them wholly in the love of a goddess. They shrieked and struggled but I knew what was best for us. I knew how I could keep them safe and happy forever.

And we would never be alone again.

The titan's tears melted their skin and melded it with mine. Our bones snapped together into one skeleton, our hair braided itself into one wild tangle. Amber and Kelly and I became one creature with six legs and six arms and three faces, weeping with terrible joy. The warped creatures in the titan's parade caressed us with welcoming hands, cooed over our raw beauty, whispered appreciation for our sacrifice.

My mother told me the titans created man in their image. And now, with the seas risen and the lake beds dry, they had returned to remake us in their image once again.

We turned north and began to walk.

The Assembled

Ramsey Campbell

Each bite Justin took left the burger bun floppier. He used up a wad of paper napkins before he risked touching his phone to thumb Sandra's number. The only other customers in the motorway food court were a woman in a wheelchair and her equally wordless male companion, both apparently giving their paper cups of coffee ample time to grow lukewarm. In seconds he heard Sandra, but only in recorded form. No doubt she was asleep in bed by now. "Not even halfway yet," he said. "I'm going to the lorry park in case I can get another lift. I'll see you sometime tomorrow."

"Where are you going?"

He thought the woman was addressing her companion, who'd begun to stump his chair away from the table without standing up, until he saw she was gazing at him. Her face looked held firm by dogged determination, while the man's had grown flabby around a version of the same cramped set of features: small close eyes, token nose, mouth not much better than begrudged. Hers was barely able to contain her extravagantly uneven teeth. "Down to Bristol," Justin said.

"We can take you. Push me, son."

Her son towered over the wheelchair as he propelled it towards

Justin. "What lovely long fingers you've got," the woman cried as she reached him. "Lovely eyes as well. Give me your hands."

Her painful effort to let go of the arms of the chair made him wince. He supposed arthritis was the problem, which had distorted her fingers so much they looked unmatched. When she turned up her palms he felt bound to lay his hands on them, as flat as her infirmities permitted. "You'd think I was going to tell your fortune," she said.

Her son's voice was a sluggish bray far larger than his mouth seemed likely to emit. "Go on then, ma."

"I didn't say I would." Justin thought she was sending him a wink until he saw her left set of eyelashes had fallen askew. "Why didn't you say I was coming unstuck?" she demanded of her son. "Do you want me looking even more of a sight?"

"He doesn't think you do, ma. He'd have said."

She snatched the lashes off her wrinkled drooping eyelid and dropped them on Justin's plate. "Ready for your ride?"

"Don't you want your coffee first?"

"I've got enough to keep me awake. Push me to the car then, son." Despite her gaze, he thought this wasn't aimed at him until she said "Show us how strong you are."

No doubt she meant to give her son a brief respite. Justin had to fight to steer the chair straight as he inched it effortfully to the exit. "Glad you're stronger than you look," the woman said.

Shadows outnumbered the infrequent vehicles in the floodlit car park. As Justin guided the chair down a concrete ramp the woman used a fist to indicate the car skewed across the nearest disabled space. "Don't judge by appearances," she said. "If I can keep going it can."

It was a decrepit saloon with a grimy cracked rear window above a deeply dented bumper. The absence of a hubcap displayed how rusty the left-hand back wheel was. "Just put me by the front," the woman said. "He'll do what we need."

Her son hauled the door wide with a screech of the hinges, rousing a dim light under the roof, and lifted her out of the chair as if she weighed no more than a hollow plastic doll. "Gently," she cried, though with the delight of a child sent high on a swing. "Save your strength for later."

While her son deposited her on the seat beside the driver's, Justin tried the left rear door. Was it locked? He was bruising his fingers under the handle when the man caught his wrist. His light grip hinted at considerable force. "I'll do it," he said. "We don't want you messing your hand up."

"That's my boy," the woman said. "Always caring."

Her son wrenched the door open, releasing a squeal. As soon as Justin sidled past him onto the rear seat he slammed the door so hard it shook the car. "Just seeing you don't go tumbling out," his mother said.

"I expect the belt should stop me."

"That's it, you see you keep it on. Make yourself the comfiest you can." Less maternally she said "Somebody didn't. That's why the door's in such a state."

Justin strapped himself in behind her, since the rest of the rear seat was occupied by a suitcase with its muddy wheels turned towards him. "Don't you forget your belt either," she told her son as he clambered into the car and shook it with another slam. She dragged the belt across him and poked its tab into the slot between the seats, then groaned at flexing her fingers. "Let's go where we're going," she said.

Her son dug the key into the ignition, only to stare at it. "I know," he said as she took a breath like an inhalation of impatience. "Don't start telling me again."

"Turn it like the clock, not how we dance."

"I knew." As he gave the key a vicious twist the man stamped his foot, trampling a creak out of a pedal. "I said."

"Don't go getting yourself in one of your states. There's the way out where the arrow's pointing."

"I can see. I've got as many eyes as you."

Justin wondered why this should earn a giggle like a reminiscence of her girlhood. The depressed pedal had stalled the engine, and the driver screwed the key around so furiously Justin thought it might snap. The exhaust emitted a clogged splutter, and the car jerked forward. It was halfway across the car park before Justin felt compelled to say "Excuse me..."

The woman sent him an asymmetrical blink in the mirror. "Forgotten something, son?"

It made him feel too much like a child who'd neglected to visit the toilet. "I think you need to switch the headlights on."

"He can do that himself. Don't go thinking he's incapable."

"I wasn't saying that. I mean he needs to."

"He'll do it when we're past the lorries. He doesn't want to wake them up."

This sounded like a fancy meant for someone younger than the driver. The car coasted past the lorry park, where drivers dozed in their elevated cabins. Justin thought of asking to be let out of the car in the hope of hitching the kind of lift he'd planned to seek, but why should he assume anyone would take him? He ought to be grateful for the ride he had. The woman had taken pity on him, after all, however discomforting he found some of her dealings with her son. "What's the matter with the lorries?" he said.

"He doesn't like anything skulking behind him."

"I hope I don't seem to be."

"He can handle you," the woman said as the car gathered speed past a petrol station. "Put your lights on now like our new friend wants."

The car faltered while her son activated the headlamps. "Go faster now," she said. "Nothing's coming. You won't bump into anyone. Put your foot down like you do."

Each of her remarks left Justin feeling he should have chanced the lorry park. He was opening his mouth when the car raced onto the motorway, and he could only clamp his lips shut, hard enough to swell them into an ache. "Enough lights for you, son?" the woman said.

The driver flailed a hand at the oncoming beams across the motorway. "Don't want them."

"Not you, son. We know you don't like it much."

"So there won't be any more confusion," Justin said, "my name's Justin."

"We don't need to hear names," the woman said.

While he attempted not to feel dismissed, Justin was compelled to speak. "Do you mind if I ask if you have a licence?"

"I've got everything I need right now."

"I was asking your son."

"He's got me."

"It's only I don't know if you're supposed to take a learner on the motorway."

"Then it's a good job it's dark, isn't it? That's one good thing about it." She stared at him so fiercely he could feel it through the mirror. "Everybody's some use," she said. "What about you? Can you drive?"

"I'm only learning or I would."

"I wasn't asking you to. You wouldn't want him thinking he's no good to anyone. Better keep him occupied while you can." She gave her son a sidelong smile and then returned her scrutiny to Justin. "Let's see if I'm still good at guessing," she said. "I'll say you're another student."

Justin felt unable to avoid saying "Like your son, you mean."

"He won't be any of you." Her laugh implied Justin hadn't made much if any of a joke. "He could use your brains," she said, "but you can keep them."

"Like who, then?"

"Like all the rest of you we've seen offering their thumbs."

"I wasn't thumbing, was I? I mean, thank you very much, but I didn't even ask for a lift."

"We aren't complaining, nothing like. All I'm saying is we've seen a lot of you about. You'd think you could get yourselves a bit more together. Safety in numbers, isn't that what they say?" Before Justin could decide on a response she said "So what are you learning besides how to drive?"

"I'm reading English."

This earned a grunt like the start of a laugh from the driver. "I can."

"Well, good. I mean, well done."

The suitcase beside Justin broke a silence with a muffled thumping as the car sped over some unevenness. He thought his listeners had found his comments patronising until the woman said "He doesn't mean that, do you, son?"

"Sorry," Justin said without believing he had reason. "Who are you talking to now?"

"Only trying to make you feel part of the family. Tell me to shut my trap if it bothers you that much."

"I'd never be so rude." He felt bound to answer her first remark as well. "I do have people of my own, though."

"We heard her. She didn't have much to say for herself."

"If you mean my girlfriend, that was her answer message."

"I've got no time for all this electronic stuff. I hear there's even people putting bits of robots in themselves. I'll trust the old ways, thank you very much." As Justin tried to discern any relevance, the woman said "Is she another one like you?"

"We're both reading English. Studying its history."

"And what's that going to do for us?"

"I'm not sure what you'd expect it to."

"Not just me and him, the world. It sounds less use than him."

"I thought you believed everyone's some use."

"You will be."

He took this to mean she regretted dismissing his prospects. "We hope we'll teach our subject when we've finished university."

"What use is that to anyone? I wouldn't call it any of a life."

"You're doing it again, ma. Telling people's futures like you say you always can."

Justin's anger overcame the politeness he was striving to maintain. "So," he challenged the woman, "what have you done with your life?"

"Lived. Still do." The dark glint of her eyes in the mirror might have been providing evidence. "I won't be put down for a while yet," she said, "not while there's any left of me."

"If you're saying that's enough—"

"It is for me and him." As if she was proposing some notion of indulgence she said "Now it's time you helped."

The driver stared at her, allowing the car to veer sideways into the dark. "There's miles yet, ma."

"I just want something passed," she said and found Justin in the mirror. "Can you open my case."

Even with the intermittent fleeting aid of distant upraised headlights, he could barely distinguish the suitcase. A defiant pair of beams stayed level long enough to let him find the tag of a zipper. As the beams abased themselves he tugged the tag along its track and felt the suitcase grit its metal teeth. The case began to gape as if its contents were eager to emerge. Its lid flopped open, releasing a smell that put Justin in mind of the refrigerator at his student lodgings—of the time they hadn't realised it had failed until they'd scented evidence. "Find the tin for me," the woman said.

The road had reverted to unhelpful darkness. Justin groped for his phone and shone the flashlight into the case. Black shapes swarmed away as if they were seeking to hide: shadows of some of the contents—a stained lumpy bag choked by a drawstring, the handless wrist of a ragged sweater raised in an empty gesture, a round tin illustrated with images of wrapped sweets scuffed to crumbling. He managed not to touch anything except the tin as he lifted it out of the case. "This one?"

"Don't go expecting any treats, will you? You'd only rot your teeth."

A muffled tinny clatter suggested objects smaller than the sweets pictured on the lid. Justin crouched forward to pass the tin between the front seats. "In my lap will do," the woman said.

By straining as far as the belt would allow and stretching his arm to its fullest extent he succeeded in planting the tin on her thigh. Her jagged nails scraped the back of his hand as she seized her prize—the tin, not him. Having scrabbled at the lid to prise it off, she stood the tin on it. "Let me have your light," she said.

Why should he feel wary of illuminating the contents of the tin? When he hunched forward to train the beam between the seats he couldn't see what he'd lit up. "Not like that," the woman complained. "Give it here."

He might have refused if the belt hadn't been bruising his chest. As soon as he brought the phone within her reach it was snatched from his hand. "Sit back now," she said more maternally than ever, and fumbled at the mirror to angle it towards her face. It found her garishly illuminated mouth stretched so wide the wrinkled lips quivered, framing a variety of sizes of skewed teeth set in greyish gums, beyond which a tongue writhed like a snail emerging from its shell. "What do I look like?" she complained. "Those won't do."

She began to rummage in the tin, which uttered clatters like a multiplication of dice. Justin heard her choose items only to drop them back in. "Why did I bother with these?" she muttered as she abandoned yet another selection. "I knew how big a mouth she had. It made enough noise till it stopped."

Justin was restraining a question if not several when the flashlight beam fluttered across the splintered dashboard while the lid of the tin clanged into place. "They'll have to do for now," the woman said. "I'll be getting better soon. Here, put it back."

She inched the tin between the seats, and Justin had to struggle against the seatbelt to retrieve it. As he returned it to the suitcase she said "May as well leave that open."

Rather than ponder the reason he said "Can I have my phone?"

"We don't say can I, do we, son?"

Justin was wondering how much this was addressed to him when the driver brayed "May."

"That's what we say, and just you remember."

Justin had to force the words out, feeling like a rebuked child. "May I have my phone."

"He didn't say it nicely, ma."

As Justin tried to bring himself to make that effort too, the woman appeared to relent. "Let's have the light off first."

"It's not time yet, is it, ma?"

More nervously than he cared to understand Justin said "Why do you want it off?"

"We don't want you wasting your power, do we?"

He strained forward and thrust out his hand. "I'll do it, thanks."

"I can see how." In a moment the light was extinguished. "Here then, take it," the woman said, and Justin was reaching into the unproductive dark when he heard a thud. "Damn the wretched thing," she said. "Slipped out of my hand and no wonder."

"Can you find it?"

"You don't want me straining myself, do you? That's what's going to happen if you start me fumbling around."

"Can't your son?"

"Not unless you want us going off the road. Just try waiting till we've got some light and we can see what's what."

She must have seen the signboard ahead, proclaiming that the nearest services were a mile beyond it. Surely he could wait that long. The lit board sailed past, and the darkness closed in. How could he have been so thoughtless that he'd tried to distract the driver? The man was barely equal to his task as it was. The imminent halt began to feel not merely welcome but essential—an opportunity to bid goodbye to his hosts and find another ride, however long that might take.

Was it only a mile to the services, or had nervous eagerness caused him to misread the sign? He was quelling a compulsion to ask how much further, that most infantile of questions, by the time he saw the first marker beside the road. Three white stripes on the blue post signified that many hundred yards to salvation. The car sped past the sign, restoring the avid dark. "I think you're meant to indicate you're leaving the motorway," Justin said.

"Still learning, aren't you," the woman said.

"That's how I know what the rules are."

Her eyes glimmered with some emotion in the mirror she'd adjusted. "You'll learn."

Could he see her eyes because the car had grown a little less dim? The outlines of the front seats and the unkempt scalps that sprouted above them had taken on more detail, because headlights were catching up with the car. Suppose they belonged to one of the lorries the driver disliked having at his back? Perhaps it was best not to draw his attention to it, since Justin would be safe soon enough.

The car passed the second marker. Two hundred yards to go, but the driver wasn't indicating. A backwards glance showed Justin the approaching vehicle. It wasn't a lorry, it was a car, and not just any car. "I think you'd better put your indicator on," he said. "Here come the police."

"Don't worry about them," the woman said.

"I'm not, but maybe you should."

Her eyes glinted like knives in the mirror. "What do you think you know?"

"If they stop you they'll find out he doesn't have a licence."

"Nobody's going to give them a reason to stop us."

Was this a warning? Her son's grunt resembled one. If his negligence prompted the police to pull them over, that might be more welcome than Justin had let himself think. The possibility sustained him as far as the last marker. Even now the driver failed to indicate, but why should this alert the police? They couldn't know he meant to leave the motorway, if indeed he did. "We're coming off here, aren't we?" Justin urged.

"Why would we want to do that?" the woman said.

"So I can find my phone."

"What's the panic? Your lady friend must be well asleep. You don't want to go waking people up."

"They'll have got their eyes shut," the driver said, "them that's still got any."

"You said we'd stop where there was light," Justin told the woman as calmly as he could.

"There will be when we stop. You saw it come on in the car."

Though they were almost abreast of the entrance to the services, the car hadn't moved into the lane. "I could use the toilet while there's one," Justin pleaded.

"You all end up wanting that. You'll have your chance."

The car sped past the lane without slowing. Justin twisted against the restraint of the belt and began to thump the back window. "No call for that," the woman cried. "You know we don't want you spoiling your hands."

Had the police seen him? It seemed neither of them had. Their car veered into the entrance to the services without indicating even once. Justin slumped on the seat as the services receded, and then he caught sight of the police car along the lane that rejoined the motorway. They must have raced across the deserted service area, having observed his appeal for help after all. He was trying to relax so as not to tip off his captors when he saw the police had pulled in at a petrol station. In moments they were gone, and he was back in the dark. "Nearly there," the woman said.

She might have been placating a fretful child. Justin glimpsed the dim silhouette of the hand she raised to beckon to him. "Pass the strangle bag," she said.

He was nowhere near certain he wanted to learn "The what?"

"That's what he calls it," she said with audible pride. "The bag with the string round its neck."

"I can't see where it is without my phone."

"Just stick your hand in. You'll find it soon enough."

His protest had been partly a ruse. He'd noticed the bag while he was lighting up the contents of the suitcase. Surely if he did as he was asked his captors would eventually let him go. He peered into the case and managed to distinguish an object like a heart on the way to losing its shape. When he risked touching the soft lumpy item, he encountered a veinous tendril—the drawstring. He pinched it between a finger and thumb to swing the bag between the seats, trailing the stale smell. "There you are," he heard himself beg.

He hoped the discontented noise the woman made wasn't aimed at him. As she dragged the bag open she came close to poking her son in the face with an outflung elbow. Ducking her head, she began to delve in the bag. Was she rubbing her fingers together, perhaps inadvertently? Some such activity appeared to be involved, though in the dimness Justin could have fancied they were excessively numerous. Her disgusted groan wasn't much of a surprise, given how pronounced the stale stench had become. "It's a good job we've got you," she said. "They're no more use to me. They've all gone off."

She lowered the window to shy the bag out of the car. It landed on the hard shoulder like a specimen of roadkill. "That'll give them something to think about," she said and giggled. "Don't worry, son, they'll never find us."

Justin doubted this was meant for him, and found he hoped none of her recent comments had been. Might the sign for the next exit represent any kind of promise? It appeared to name places he'd never heard of, though the jittering of the light that crowned the board left him uncertain. "Go on then, son, put your light on," the woman said. "Keep him happy while you can."

Justin succeeded in hoping she meant to search for his phone until the driver set off the left-hand indicator as they passed the signboard. Surely the car would have to slow down at some point, giving Justin a chance to escape. He let his hand fall beside him on the seat, uncomfortably close to the suitcase and whatever it contained, and then he inched his fingers to cover the clasp of the seatbelt. As the car passed the first marker for the exit from the motorway he began to press the catch.

How rusty was the mechanism? The button felt determined not to release the belt. He edged his other hand across his waist to add more pressure and hide what he was desperate to do. The second marker swept by, and still the catch refused to yield. Why wasn't the car losing speed? As it reached the final marker all too soon Justin felt the snagged tab spring loose of the slot. The belt began to whip across his chest, and he barely managed to recapture the tab. He was afraid the woman or her son might have noticed his flurried activity, but they seemed intent on the road. The car slowed at last as it climbed a ramp to an unlit roundabout, where the headlamps found a sign for Flinders Forest. "There's a bit of history of language for you," the woman said. "They named it for the likes of me."

Justin had no time to ponder this, because the car had halted at the top of the ramp while a lorry drove around the roundabout at length. He released the seatbelt, which fled into its housing with a clang of the tab as he threw himself against the door and levered at the handle with both hands. It gave as much as the door—not a fraction of an inch. "Don't bother trying that," the woman said as if speaking wearied her. "Nobody can open it but him. He'll do it for you soon enough."

Justin saw the taillights of the lorry vanish around a bend, too far away for him to shout after the driver. "Let me out here, then. This is fine."

"It's nothing like. No use to anyone."

"I can walk. I don't mind walking. I like to walk."

"That's why you were asking for a lift, was it?"

"I said before, I never asked."

"You've got one, so try being thankful. We are."

As he searched for some way to persuade her, the car sped around the roundabout onto the Flinders Forest road. It was narrow and devious, walled in by hedges whose vicious thorns the headlights seemed to rouse. Some of the spikes clawed at the door beside him as though mocking his bid to escape. "Better be getting myself ready," the woman said.

However much of a question this invited, Justin preferred not to open his mouth. As the car raced around yet another unmarked blind bend, the woman lowered her window again. "Not too cold there in the back, are you?" she scarcely asked. "You won't be too much longer."

Surely this meant they would let him out soon, and then he would be able to escape, whatever he might be eluding. He had to think he could move faster than her son. He was trying to prepare himself while he bided his time when the car swerved off the road at a constricted bend and bumped across a ditch. He thought the driver had lost control until he saw they'd swung onto a forest track, if progressively less of one. As lit trees reared up ahead of the car the woman started singing in a high uneven voice. The nursery rhyme might have been intended to amuse a child, or perhaps the driver. "This little piggy went to market..."

She hadn't found much of a tune. It was more a chant suggestive of a childish rite. While she uttered the line she bent forward over a task, and a harsh groan of protest followed her words. Her arms flew apart as though achieving her objective had freed them, and her elbow almost jabbed her son. As she tossed a thin object out of the window Justin glimpsed her right hand, which looked depleted in a way he was anxious not to comprehend. "Join in if you want to help," she said. "This little piggy stayed at home..."

Her son lowed along with the line, though not with her approximation of a melody. The headlight beam set trees dancing with their shadows to greet the car as it lurched and swayed along its route, which no longer resembled anything Justin would have called a track. While the woman gave another wounded moan before jettisoning a second item, he clung to a notion as if it might shield him from any further thoughts: the rhyme was meant to be about toes, only toes. "You'll have to do the other ones for me," she told her son. "I'm sick of all this lot. This little piggy had roast beef..."

Justin didn't know why he was bracing himself, clenching his fists as if to keep them safe, until he recalled the last line of the rhyme. It was indeed even more dismaying than its predecessors. "Wee wee wee," the driver screeched as the car staggered deeper into the prancing forest. "All the way home," his mother cried, and his continued porcine squeals covered up whatever sound she made while performing the last of her task. "Nearly there," she told whoever needed to be assured of it, and flourished her right hand in anticipation if not celebration, though Justin saw the hand no longer warranted the name. Far too soon to let him feel prepared, the car juddered to a halt and the driver switched the headlamps off. "Here's our dark," the woman said. "I don't like seeing what we have to do."

The driver sprang his door open, triggering the light under the roof. Despite its feebleness, it seemed to offer Justin the pitiful hope that it would fend off enough of the darkness to forestall whatever the woman had said she disliked, at least until he succeeded in making his escape. As the driver tramped to loom outside the passenger door he poised himself to leap out of the car. The man wrenched at the handle and hauled the door open, then stood back. He retreated no more than a couple of feet, stretching his arms wide to block any bid to escape. There was no way to avoid him, and Justin could only launch himself at the man in a desperate attempt to knock him down. He was about to try when a phone began to ring.

It was his, on the floor in front of the woman. The driver turned towards the sound and stepped away from the passenger door, and Justin darted through the gap. "Sand," the phone just had time to announce before the woman trampled it into fragments. The grab the driver made missed Justin, who dashed away from the car, slipping on leaves treacherous with rain and rot, almost sprawling headlong. "Fetch him back," the woman cried as though she felt robbed of a prize. While she sounded by no means sufficiently distant, the glow from the car was already so remote that Justin barely glimpsed the people who crowded into his path.

It wasn't a crowd, he realised as he dodged them. It was just a few people huddled together—not so much huddled as heaped. Nor had they moved to hinder him. If they were capable of moving they would certainly have sought to ease the discomfort of their position and of their incompleteness. Justin was floundering out of their way, not least to avoid distinguishing any more details, when an outstretched leg tripped him. Whoever it belonged to, it was unreasonably aloof from them. As he scrabbled at the leaves in a frantic attempt to shove himself to his feet, a weight pressed him helplessly into the mud. The driver had knelt on his back. "Wee wee wee," the man enthused, and set about chanting the rhyme as he bent to his task.

CRITICAL MASS

JONATHAN MABERRY

-1-

CONNER BRIGHT WAS PISSING off the side of the boat when he died.

He was twenty-two, well-liked, just starting work on his graduate degree. Decent grades, a girlfriend who he thought was good in bed but could use a little more patience when it came to certain things. A mom who thought the sun rose and set specifically for him. A father who was grudgingly proud that he was the first of the Omaha Brights to go to college, though why in hell a Nebraska farm boy would ever want to make a career studying trash in the goddamn Pacific goddamn Ocean was beyond his understanding. And a professor who thought the kid might have an actual future.

The professor was wrong.

Potential did not guarantee either accomplishment or longevity.

As for Conner, he was leaning his belly against the pipe rail as he emptied his bladder of four long-neck bottles of Yuengling, and he had no thoughts at all about death, dying, illness, catastrophe, accidents, or anything else in which his demise played a role. He wasn't even thinking about his girlfriend and whether he should cut ties or ask her to move in. He'd been on the fence about that for weeks now. The part of him that was still an undergrad frat house lout wanted to say bye-bye because there were a lot more fish in the sea. The grad student part of him—creeping toward actual maturity—realized that by dating her he was punching far above his weight in both looks and overall intelligence and knew that he should cement all that in place.

He wasn't thinking about that, either.

His thoughts, in the moments before his death, were entirely focused on trying to understand why a large cluster of mixed microplastics was moving against the tide flow. Had he slammed fewer beers and a lot fewer shooters of mediocre tequila, he would have been worried about it. Had he been completely sober, he would have been interested enough to do something about it—call the professor or the captain, get a net and capture a sample, use his phone camera to record it. After all this was exactly what this project was all about. Anomalous drift patterns of trash and the various life forms that had turned the floating continent of garbage into a unique biosphere. Spotting it could lead to proving it, which would elevate him in the esteem of his professor and go a long way toward improving his grades and his potential as a scientist.

Instead, being more than a little shitfaced, he lifted his cock and pissed on the anomalous clump of sea-soaked garbage.

And then he died.

Just.

Like.

That.

-2-

"WHAT WAS THAT SPLASH?"

Carrie Wingate looked up from her laptop, peering at her graduate assistant, Todd, who was peering out of the portside window.

"What splash?" she asked.

"You didn't hear it?"

She pulled the earbuds out and dangled them. *"Gymnopédie No. 1.* Erik Satie."

Todd tapped the window with his forefinger. "There was a splash."

"In the middle of the Pacific Ocean?" murmured Carrie, turning back to the project budget spreadsheet she'd been fiddling with all evening. "I'm shocked. Shocked, I say."

"I'm going to take a look," Todd announced.

"My hero," said Carrie, screwing the earbuds back in place.

The R/V Desmond Perry—known affectionately at *S.S. Dumpster*—was a 125-foot modified Gulf Coast workboat converted for use by the UCSD Scripps Institution of Oceanography. It was old, cranky, smelled of engine oil, rotting fish, and garbage, but was comfortable in its own limited way. The 32-foot-wide beam gave it some room for labs, sample storage, crew quarters, and galley. The crew was Carrie, Todd and their newest recruit, Conner Bright, along with five other grad students. The captain and his four-person crew were contractors working for UCSD, and all of them were certified divers with thousands of underwater hours apiece.

The Dumpster rocked gently in a light swell in the Northern Pacific Subtropical Convergence Zone located a few hundred kilometers north of Hawaii. Warmth from the South Pacific mingled there with cooler water from the Arctic, acting like a highway that moves debris from one patch to another.

Around them, stretching far into the distance on every side, was the Great Pacific Garbage Patch. It was a wilderness of trash with a surface area of 1.6 million square kilometers, an area twice the size of Texas and three times the size of France. And the Dumpster was in the middle of it, which accounted for the biggest part of the stink. During the first weeks Carrie had tried to combat the stench with incense, but eventually gave it up as pointless.

Todd went out on deck, not looking for Conner in particular. Just looking. The moon was down, but the sky was bright with ten thousand stars and a handful of unwinking planets. The gentle pale wash of the Milky Way curved above, and Todd paused for a moment—as he always did—to take in that vista. Then he continued his search. No one was on deck that he could see, but he prowled around, one hand brushing lightly over the handrail.

"Yo," he called, but there was no answer. "Yo, dickhead. Where you at?"

He moved aft to the stern, where the rigid-hull inflatable workboat was snugged against the housing for the big propulsion motor. But he saw nothing but stars and trash. So, he reversed course and then made his way forward to the bow. That's when he saw it.

That's when he screamed.

For a big man, his scream was exceptionally shrill, rising three octaves.

Conner Bright stood there.

Most of him.

His legs, his torso.

Nothing above his sternum. No chest, no shoulders, no head.

What remained was held upright by the rail. Around his feet was a small pool of blood that looked like oil in the starlight.

He screamed his throat raw.

-3-

Dr. Carrie Wingate screamed, too.

Not as loud. Not as long, but with equal horror.

Everyone froze into a grotesque tableau. Even the captain, who had served in the navy during the Gulf War was locked into immobility. Death at sea was one thing. He'd seen his share, from dive accidents to sailors torn apart on land and sea.

Everyone there knew stories about sharks, box jellyfish, beaked sea snakes, Portuguese Man O'War, the Blue-ringed octopus, lionfish, Great whites and tigers and bull sharks. They knew about tsunamis and underwater earthquakes, volcanoes and icebergs. They had endured raging storms firsthand, and snorkeled the five hundred years' worth of shipwrecks.

But this....

Half of Conner was gone. Cut off with such speed that the body hadn't been thrown back or down, nor had it been pulled over the rail.

Then the ship moved as a heavy roller passed under the keel, and the corpse leaned back and fell, spilling the contents of the abdomen across the deck. Todd spun away to throw up, and did not manage to aim. Half of his bellyful of fish tacos, dirty rice, and beans splashed across the first mate's legs. Then the mate vomited, too.

That was when Carrie screamed. Somehow, on some level, that made it more real. The vomiting. The reaction *to* vomiting. The churning of her own stomach.

Real.

The ship lifted and fell again. And again.

Except for automatic shifting of weight for balance, no one moved. There was nothing in the ship's protocols or the guidelines for marine research that mapped out a plan for this.

Not a goddamn thing.

-4-

DR. WINGATE and her students were in the galley. Some of them had cups of coffee, Todd had a beer, Carrie had a cup of tea. Nobody was drinking. Eating was an alien concept.

The captain, a comprehensively tattooed man named Tunny, sat on a chair turned backward, his thick forearms crossed on the backrest.

"I called it in," he said.

Carrie looked at him. "The Coast Guard?"

"Yes. They said they'll be here at first light."

"Why so long?"

Tunny shook his head. "Storm on the Big Island. Can't put a chopper in the air, and too rough for boats."

"Storm?" asked Todd. "Sky's clear."

"Sky's clear here," said Tunny. "Hawaii's two hundred miles to the northwest. They have sustained winds of fifty, sixty miles. Not a hurricane, but big enough. Came at them from the west and it'll be here by one or two in the morning."

"I didn't see anything on the forecast," said Todd. "And there's hardly any wind at all out there."

The captain snorted. "Welcome to the Pacific Ocean, kid. If I had a dime for every storm or weather change that came out of nowhere, I could buy this boat ten times over. The weather's always unpredictable and the sea's fifty times worse."

"Sea's a treacherous bitch," agreed the first mate.

Todd looked away and stared out of the window at nothing.

"Did you tell them what...happened?" asked Carrie.

"Yeah, Doc," sighed Tunny. "I told them. Chunk took pictures with his camera, and I sent those, too."

Chunk was the first mate. A big Samoan with a shaved head and steel-rim glasses who'd spent his life on the water. He had changed his vomit-splashed pants for cargo shorts and deck shoes.

Carrie licked her lips. They had gone dry and felt oddly chapped. Her whole body felt desiccated, and she wondered if that was a symptom of shock.

"Do you have any idea what could have happened to Conner?" she asked. "I mean, was it a shark?"

Tunny shook his head. "That part of the bow's sixteen feet above the water. No shark's going to jump that high."

"You're sure?"

"Ask Chunk. He knows these waters better than I do."

Chunk pushed his glasses higher on the bridge of his nose and nodded. "No way a shark did that, Doc. Even a dolphin couldn't jump that high. I mean, a great white can swim at forty miles an hour and breach—jump—*maybe* ten feet. And if Conner was aft, where the freeboard is eight feet, then maybe. But the forward deck is, like the cap'n said, sixteen feet, and then you have a four-foot rail. Even if that kid was leaning out, it's too high."

"It's also too much," added Tunny. "Poor bastard was cut in half. Hard enough for a shark to do that much damage in the water. Besides... did you see the cut? Almost straight across him. A shark bite's curved. So...this isn't a sequel to *Jaws*."

"Then what *did* that to him?" begged Carrie.

The captain and his mate exchanged a look, then shook their heads.

"Fuck if I know," said Tunny. "This is a new one on me. And I have seen some weird shit."

"I've seen a *lot* of weird shit," agreed Chunk. "Saw an octopus pull a five-year-old kid off a belly board once. Didn't kill him, but even so. Oh, and I saw an orca—big old sumbitch—breach and belly flop onto a racing kayak. Smashed it all to hell. Damn near killed the guy in it. But this? Man, this is something I ain't never seen. Hell, it's nothing I ain't never heard about."

"Maybe it wasn't like that," said Todd, turning back to Carrie.

"What do you mean?"

"Maybe it was the trash."

There was a beat of silence.

"What's that now, son?" asked Tunny.

"What do you mean 'the trash'?" prompted Carrie.

"Look," said Todd, "over the last few months there have been all kinds of reports of trash islands. Bigger clumps of debris that stack up pretty high, with most of it underwater like an iceberg and other junk just piled up, all held together by stuff like fishing line, torn netting, lengths of nylon rope...."

"Okay," said Carrie, "and...?"

"And maybe one was big enough to—I don't know—go past the bow and clip Conner. We've been getting those heavy swells. Rollers. Whatever."

"Clip him?"

"Maybe there was some debris embedded in the trash island that was sharp."

Tunny half smiled. "Like what, exactly?"

"I don't know," protested Todd. "A piece of a boat hull." He looked around for support. "We've all heard about small fishing boats going missing out here. Maybe the reason they can't be found is that they got busted up. Storm damage or whatever. A lot of them are fiberglass, which is sharp as shit when it's broken. And with all that weight of water pushing it...."

Tunny began to laugh, but stopped himself. The others all stared at

Todd, each of them working through the logic—the likelihood, the physics, the anatomy.

"Is that even possible?" asked Carrie.

Tunny shrugged. "Forty minutes ago I'd have said no. But my list of what *is* possible is pretty fucking short, Doc. Been on the sea a long time, here and in the Persian Gulf. Seen a lot of accidents and war wounds. Nothing I ever saw makes this make sense. So...who knows, maybe Todd's got something."

But Chunk shook his head. "I don't know if I can buy that. Not to get gross and all, but even if a roller took a mound of trash and that's what hit Conner, seems to me more likely it would have cut him and then got hooked on bones—ribs and spine and shit—and pulled him over the rail. I can't see how a roller like we've been getting would have enough speed to slice through him."

He paused, removed his glasses, and mopped the sweat from his face by dragging his arm across. His color had been bad before he spoke, but his own words—and the images they conjured—had turned his skin a mix of beige, gray, and green.

Another roller—a heavier one than before—made the ship lift and pitch forward. Everyone grabbed for their cups or bottles, but the jolt was intense and tepid coffee and tea splashed the deck.

"Jesus," cried Carrie. "Is that the storm?"

Tunny got to his feet. "Too soon for that much swell. C'mon, Chunk, let's see what's what."

They left the cabin quickly, leaving Carrie with her students.

"What's going on?" asked Todd.

Carrie got up, too. "I don't know," she said, then she followed the sailors out of the room.

-5-

WHEN SHE REACHED THE BRIDGE, she could see the sky outside.

"It's clear out," she said, leaning close to the glass.

Tunny said nothing. He was bent over a computer screen that had the weather report. Chunk was at the wheel.

The Dumpster was anchored in a section of the Convergence Zone. There were more than fifty sensors that were also anchored, each of them at different depths and scanning for different things—salinity, microplastic particulates, and different versions of plastisphere ecosystems that had evolved to live in human-made plastics discarded at sea. Some of the sensors had traps attached, and those had captured items as wildly diverse as colonies of mutated barnacles attached to swim fins, an artificial heart valve, and a sea snail that had made a home out of a medium-sized athletic groin cup. On a previous trip, one of Carrie's colleagues had done some field work involving collecting anecdotal accounts of larger colonies of marine life that seemed to be thriving on the manmade materials out there, though so far few of those stories could be verified through direct analysis.

It was meticulous and painstaking work, but also important. Although the marine line that tended to cling to the trash—particularly the plastics—were small, they have been forming increasingly large colonies. Radiation from the Fukushima disaster farther south in the Pacific was a factor, and there were at least a dozen other research teams from Japan, Korea, Mexico, and the States studying the environmental impact of that on microorganisms like bacteria that infected all of the animals out here, and each step of the food chain increased the overall yield of radioactivity in the cells.

Trash, per se, was the least of the potential problems. Mutation was a far greater threat, especially as the food chain in question included fish that landed on dinner plates from Alaska to Okinawa.

Despite her grief and horror at what happened to Conner, Carrie was also concerned about what a tropical storm could do to the sensitive instruments seeded throughout this part of the sea of trash.

"Will we be okay?" she asked. "Will we have to move if the storm hits?"

"To be determined," said the captain.

Carrie felt conflicted. The *person* she was wanted to get the hell out of there, because she knew how frightened she was and how badly it was impacting her team. The *academic administrator* in her was bracing for what would almost certainly be negative press, withdrawing of grants, outrage, accusations, and lawsuits. The *scientist* part of her feared the loss of so much research and the abandonment of areas of study that had already yielded eight new or radically mutated species of crustaceans, a gigantic and previously unknown species of anemone with tentacles nearly twenty feet in length, and forty-three new bacterium. Her papers alone would likely have greatly advanced her career, and combining her research with her colleague back in San Diego, Dr. Allyn, a Nobel prize might finally be something more than a distant and unlikely dream. Their paper-in-development postulated that the Fukushima radiation and the chemicals in those plastics was creating a new *primordial soup* in which known species were mutating and new ones were developing at unbelievable rates. It was exciting. There were books and lecture tours and Nat Geo documentaries waiting to happen.

And now this.

Carrie fought against the guilt she felt for resenting Conner. She knew it wasn't really his fault, but his death, no matter what the cause, put everything in jeopardy.

Everything.

She was shaken out of her glum thoughts when she realized Tunny was talking.

"The storm's screwing with the Wi-Fi and the radio," he said. "Been trying to get through to the Coast Guard, but now all I get is static."

"Don't you have a satellite phone?"

Tunny glanced at her. "Yeah. Let me fiddle with this first, though. Probably just some atmospheric crap. It never lasts long."

The ship lifted again, very suddenly and sharply. It yawed as it settled, making everyone grab for something solid. Tunny and Chunk exchanged another look.

"What's wrong?" asked Carrie. "Are we in trouble?"

Chunk went outside, leaving the captain with Carrie.

"What is it?" she pressed.

"That last roller," he said.

"What about it?"

"It came from the wrong direction."

"What do you mean?"

Tunny pointed out the window. "The way I have the anchor set, we should be bow-on to the waves. That's what I came up here to check. We face into a storm, especially with seas like what we got running. And all the waves I can see are going west to east, almost straight. But we've had three waves take us side-on, and that doesn't make sense. These aren't cross-seas. The wind is calm."

"Maybe debris hit us?" she suggested.

"Maybe. I didn't hear a thump. But Chunk's checking that out right now anyway," said Tunny. After a pause, he added, "I don't like it, though. Not even a little. First there was what happened to that kid, and now the seas are confused with almost no wind."

"What should we do? Pull up the anchor and move somewhere safer?"

"That's what we might have to do," he said. He glanced at the door. "What the hell's taking him so long?"

He flipped a switch to turn on the big floodlights used to illuminate the forward deck for night work. Tunny leaned close to the glass, peering outside.

"Where is...?"

That was all he said.

Carrie stared, too.

The bow was empty. There was no Chunk outside to be seen.

"Maybe he went aft?" she said.

"Why would he do that?"

Instead of answering, the captain ran out on deck. Carrie followed behind him, though she lingered in the doorway. Tunny hurried along the rail, almost to the place where poor Conner had died. He stopped and looked around.

"Chunk!" he yelled. "Yo, where the hell are you, you lazy sack of shit?"

The only answer was the rustle of the countless tons of trash and the slap of water against the hull. There was a flash of distant lightning, but no boom of thunder. No clouds above yet, though they seemed to be blotting out the stars on the western horizon. The storm was coming.

Tunny glanced up at the sky and then down at something on the deck.

Carrie could see the exact moment when the captain went from being confused to being worried. He knelt suddenly and picked something up that sparkled like glass or metal.

"What is it?" she asked, stepping out onto the deck. When he didn't answer right away, she came over. The captain pivoted slowly on the balls of his feet and held the object up so she could see it.

It was a pair of steel-rim glasses. One lens was cracked, and the earpieces were twisted out of shape.

"I don't understand...," said the captain softly. He turned in a complete circle, looking for more, looking for answers.

A roller, the biggest yet, picked the Dumpster so high the anchor line went taut as a fiddle string. Carrie could hear it thrum, and then the ship dropped.

For a moment there was a feeling of weightlessness and Carrie saw the captain rushing toward her, arms wide as if to tackle. Then, just as he grabbed her, the ship smacked down into the trough gouged by the roller. Carrie fell backward very hard, crying out in pain as Tunny's weight smashed her against the deck. Her head snapped backward against the rubber-coated metal and instantly the stars above were obscured by fireworks.

Tunny rolled off her, wincing and hissing with pain, blood running over his lower lip and down his chin. He howled, and as he opened his mouth, she could see how deeply into his tongue the fall had made him bite. Tunny crawled away, gagging, spitting blood onto the deck.

But Carrie laid there. She felt like a swatted fly—flattened, hurting, trying to drag in a spoonful of air. Getting up was an impossibility. Even lifting a hand to probe the back of her head was like jacking up a truck.

Her fingers found warmth and wetness, and when she looked at them, they were bright red.

"No," she gasped in a choked little voice.

The pain really started then. Carrie had received a concussion once before, back when she was thirteen and her skateboard had hit a deep crack in the asphalt, sending her flying. That was bad, but this felt worse. Apart from the nausea and the lights dancing in her eyes, she knew this injury was serious. A bad cut for sure, and from the deep intensity of the ache, maybe a skull fracture.

"No," she said again.

More lightning. Closer, brighter, and a soft chuckle of thunder. Sneaky and low. There was a storm coming and the Coast Guard did not want to risk a helicopter or a rescue vessel in a storm. That's what Tunny had said.

She turned her head and saw Tunny sitting on the deck, his face white except where it was crimson. There was blood all down the front of his shirt. A lot of it. Way too much.

"No...."

Carrie fought to clear her eyes because there was something about Tunny that made no sense. He had been wearing a pale gray USCD sweatshirt and jeans. But now he seemed to have a belt around his waist. Very dark, very thick, and very lumpy. The lumps looked weird. Like... barnacles. They moved slightly... and Tunny was trying to pull at the belt.

"No," she said again.

Then she saw that the belt was also hooked around his thighs.

It was thicker there. She could see some kind of crustacean scuttling down his trouser leg. Or... was it a spider?

"No, no...."

Then Tunny stood up. All at once. It was almost comical to her dazed mind. He was sitting and then he was standing.

Then on his toes.

And... then his feet weren't touching the deck at all.

"No, no, no, no."

The lightning flashed again and this time its glow lit the contours of everything, throwing it all into sharp relief. Tunny, hanging in the air. The belt—which was not a belt—coiled around him and then curving up and up.

And up.

Carrie saw what it was attached to.

"No," she said. Quite reasonably, because this was not real, not possible, and she wanted—*needed*—to dismiss it with logic. A frank, flat, "No."

Lightning flashed and flashed now as the first breath of storm wind swept across the deck. Thunder was louder, angrier.

The thing that held Tunny was not the tentacle of some Jules Verne giant squid. It was not the rubbery arm of an octopus, either. In the blue-white glow of the lightning she could see the tangles of plastic netting, trash bags, fishing line, blue Tyvek tarps, drag lines, parts of milk jugs, single-use bottles, drinking straws, fast-food cutlery, toothbrushes, a child's toy guitar, parts of beach chairs, sections of rubber rafts and floats, food wrappers, microwave containers, thermal insulation, plastic sponges, cling-wrap, shower curtains, electric power cords, and ten thousand other pieces of trash.

Mixed in with the plastics were tens of thousands of snails, crabs of a dozen kinds, eels, anemones, chunks of bleached coral, fish—dead and decayed and still alive and thrashing—unidentifiable slime, seaweed, and other kinds of ocean life. Caught, mutated, diseased, conjoined.

Alive.

And angry.

It all rose above the Dumpster.

It rose.

It.

Carrie saw a mass of trash as large as an iceberg rise from the black waters. Larger than the ship. Larger than a house. Larger than the greatest cathedral. A mass at least as big as the Great Pyramid. And all of it alive.

Impossibly alive.

The lightning flashed and flashed, but between those bursts of celestial fire, Carrie saw that the thing had its own light. Bioluminescence and... something else. There was heat of a strange and awful kind. Dimly, in the recesses of her bruised brain, she knew what it was.

Radiation.

The thing kept rising, and as its mass lifted from the ocean, the displacement drew millions of gallons of water in. The Dumpster was tossed and rocked. The anchor ripped free of its purchase and the ship began to turn. Around counterclockwise, caught in a swirling whirlpool.

Carrie looked up at the creature. Her scientist mind wanted to ask questions. Was it alive, or was it a lot of living things caught together in a skin of discarded plastic? Was it angry? Could it see her?

Did it care?

That last question carried its own answer.

Yes. It cared.

And, also, yes, it was angry.

Very, very angry.

Carrie heard screams as the others came out to see what was happening. Such screams. High. Terrible. Wet.

And then... gone.

Gone.

Tunny was gone, too. She hadn't seen what the thing did to him. He was just *gone.*

Then it leaned over the deck of the ship and for a bizarre moment Carrie thought that it could actually see her. It had, after all, a million eyes.

There was a mouth, too. Vast. Filled with teeth made from a thousand shards of plastic.

"No," she said one last time.

But the ocean said yes.

Sight Unseen

Amanda M. Blake

The yard is a weedy, dirt-pile mess, the gutters and shingles need to be replaced, and she desperately needs to hire a contractor for that crack in the foundation. She packed up her apartment, quit her job to freelance until she finds her feet, and drove a thousand miles, all to get here—a ranch house on the verge of tumbling down its own hill. But it's hers, her home, bought in an online auction, sight unseen.

She strides up the uneven sidewalk stairs to the front door. The lock sticks, but she jiggles the knob, pushes, pulls, finally gives birth to her entrance.

Overgrown bushes block every window, leaving the rooms in ambient twilight, with dense shadows and dust motes in still air that she disturbs as she steps through her house. The online listing only showed a listless exterior and feral backyard, but what seduced her then was the price—an affordable down payment and a mortgage better than monthly rent.

A risk worth taking, she tells herself to raise her spirits and keep her stomach from sinking.

Stained carpets curling away from dusty or absent baseboards, a hole in the drywall of the living room, dust bunnies and ancient clumps of dog hair, cobwebs in corners with dead cockroaches caught suspended, frozen in another decade. But nothing a vacuum cleaner, soap, elbow grease, and a few trips to the trash bin won't fix. At least the cockroaches are dead—an improvement on her apartment.

A sunroom in the back in lieu of a lanai, with terrarium plants threatening to burst through the skylights and windows, and a sickly smell beneath ripe and overripe tomatoes. Then a kitchen sectioned off to the right, and behind it, vaguely in view, a formal dining room that, instead of a welcoming table, houses a monster.

It blends with shadow, dust-fuzzy belly heavy between its informal legs. At first, she thinks it's someone's idea of a joke or some forgotten stuffed decoration, but the cobwebs shiver with every slow, even, rattling breath, and although it doesn't blink, its eyes hold depth within pinpoint pupils. As she enters, the black ink expands in yellow traffic-lantern irises, glowing warning in the darkness, and beneath, an unwavering smile of butcher-knife teeth gleams in the faint gold glow of its unflinching stare.

Beyond blinking and breath, the monster doesn't move, although it can snatch her from the dining room entrance and stuff her into its cavernous mouth in a matter of seconds if it wants to.

But it just stares and breathes and smiles as though waiting, perhaps for her to climb into its lap, onto its belly, and into its mouth of her own volition.

Part of her wants to *nope* right out of the dilapidated house and back into her car with all her worldly possessions to find a nice hotel with room service and someone else to dust the corners, but she isn't sure she can afford the gas or another night anywhere else but home. Because this is her home, her house, her title, her deed, her sidewalk, her tomatoes, her mess, and there is nowhere else to go.

She tosses her keys in her hand, the jingle deafening in the stillness, but the monster doesn't change, doesn't move, doesn't flinch.

Her keys, her house.

She leaves the monster in the dining room and the keys in the kitchen as she heads back down to her car to bring all the boxes into her house.

———

NIGHT FINDS her in the main bedroom on a blow-up mattress. She stares at popcorn ceiling with glitter between the nubs and strains to hear creaking footsteps. But although the house settles around her like a blanket, nothing groans or whispers in the hall and no shadows shift under the door. Through to the morning with eyelids sinking, she remains alone, and when she can't hold back anymore, under the weight of warmth and a perpetually shadowed room, she wakes up undisturbed, uneaten.

When she comes out to get some breakfast from her box of protein bars, the monster is still sitting, staring, smiling, still unmoving except for its breathing.

"Okay," she says.

———

SHE CAN'T vacuum underneath it, but it lets her run the appliance up to its knees without protest, watches her edge the baseboards, then free the cobwebs and desiccated corpses from every corner, including its own where its massive body does not block her.

While she clatters in the kitchen and living room, its breathing remains as regular as a clock. While she snips at the indoor foliage to tame the tomato plants and find the basil, thyme, rosemary, and mint, its gaze follows her, not indifferent but without judgment on her presence or what she chooses to do in the house it occupies.

She wonders whether it chased off the previous tenants, if it convinced the bank to sell sight unseen rather than through an inviting open house. Or perhaps that was simply due to the number of repairs, the unprepossessing façade and interior, the mice in the walls that make her shriek when she finds them and that she swears makes the monster smile wider.

At least they're mice instead of rats.

Mouse traps and fly paper line the rooms until their yield equals her bank account.

———

"You know there's a monster in the dining room," the inspector says, white as a sheet with his pen poised over the checklist.

"I'm aware," she says, dreading not teeth but the cost of removal. "Am I required to get rid of it?"

The inspector checks his list, though hesitant to look away while standing so close to such a smile. "If you had a squatter, I'd recommend eviction proceedings, and with vermin, an exterminator. Nothing here about monsters."

"Then why mention it at all?" She's growing tomatoes on her bushes, not cash.

The inspector hurries into the kitchen to turn his attention to the more-straightforward plumbing.

———

After almost a year of air mattress, beanbag chair, phone hotspot, ramen, and a sanguine roommate, she saves enough for some furniture—a living-room couch, television console, coffee table, bed, a bench for the sunroom, and a dining room table.

The furniture store delivers, assembles, moves, pauses at the entrance to the dining room, and decides they're not paid enough to ask.

———

After a visit to the backyard jungle with a machete, she brings a vase into the dining room and arranges it with sunflower heads beaming in every direction.

"They match your eyes," she says.

She starts to leave, but a rustle whirls her back around.

The monster's smile has widened. It holds a sunflower to its cheek to set off the eyes that she called pretty.

Mother Ship

Joshua Bartolome

"She's pregnant," Kiyoko said. Her words hung heavy in the sterile air of the Cordova Station's briefing room. Only the whirring of the overhead filtration scrubbers could be heard.

"What?" Ravi asked at length, breaking the silence.

"I just got the results for the scan," Kiyoko replied. "That neoplasm we found growing in the hold? It's not cancerous. It's an embryo. The Undine is keeping it alive."

Kiyoko took a USB from her coat and plugged it into the nearest console.

"Could it be a parasite?" Ravi said as he waited for the upload to finish, its black-and-green interface swarming with lines of esoteric code. "Like the ones on the Melusine?"

"That's what I thought," Kiyoko replied. "But this thing seems to share the same genetic markers with its host, although I can't be absolutely certain until we take a sample."

The screen displayed a transparent, three-dimensional rendering of the Undine, its outer shell a bright-red crosshatch of vertices, while the interior glowed an eerie, greenish hue. Upon closer inspection, the ship's propulsion organs had been replaced by what appeared to be a clumsy replication of a mammalian uterus, flanked by two ovaries, fallopian tubes, and a narrow cervix.

Inside the womb floated a humanoid approximately seven meters tall, with no distinguishing features on its face besides a lipless mouth. Though the rendering itself was little better than a scanned ultrasound image, Kiyoko could still see the slight, jerking movements of the nameless symbiote, its head twitching spasmodically, as if experiencing REM sleep.

"How long has it been gestating?" Ravi asked, voice low, almost whispering.

"Judging from the time the Undine spent in the Orion Sector," Kiyoko answered, "probably two hundred standard years, at the very least. This modification doesn't happen overnight."

Kiyoko trailed off. When they hauled the derelict carrier from an asteroid cluster, Ravi had assured her that it would be a guaranteed payday. But they didn't expect to find this.

"What should we do?"

"I don't know," Ravi replied.

———

WHILE KIYOKO WAITED for Dock 13's gates to open, she glanced at the readings on her helmet's display: 1.7 degrees Kelvin, a tad warmer than the void of space but still cold enough to freeze a person to death. Without her EMU suit, the conditions would have killed her in seconds.

"Status?" Ravi's voice crackled through her transceiver.

"We've got her doped to the gills," Kiyoko said. "If we cryogen the Undine's veins, her code won't undergo binary sepsis. That'll give us enough time to complete the procedure."

Ravi walked beside her as they entered Dock 13. Like Kiyoko, he wore a bulky EMU, his face half-concealed by the reflections on the helmet's translucent LED surface.

"You mentioned anomalies," he said. "What kind?"

"Her immune system's going haywire," Kiyoko answered; she then took a data slate from her utility pocket and passed it over to Ravi. "I've been monitoring her vitals for the past 24 hours, and it looks like she's undergoing leukocytosis. Possibly a side-effect of the pregnancy."

"Are you expecting a reaction?" Ravi asked while scrolling through the slate's feed.

"Not if the sedatives hold."

Lifts and lattice cranes kept the Undine suspended fifteen feet above the floor inside the hangar. Cryogenic filters hummed as they pumped liquified hydrogen narcotics into the bioship.

Kiyoko and Ravi walked into the elevator to the maintenance dock's second level. While the lift ferried them upward, she stared at the Undine's slumbering form through the transparent plexiglass. Like most of her long-lost sisters, the bioship had a structure resembling a Balaenoptera musculus. Her pockmarked surface was covered with a chitinous material that protected its crew from interstellar radiation. Only the sides of her hull remained exposed, revealing gills that typically had a bright orange color but were now a lifeless, anemic gray.

Upon arriving at the second level, Kiyoko followed Ravi to the Undine's sealed entry hatch. Cordova's head of crisis management, Carnahan Santiago, stood near the access point, along with three other security personnel. All four of them carried standard-issue M230 pulse rifles, the kind used by shock troopers during a labor dispute on the factory world of Sultan Kudarat 210.

Carnahan gave Kiyoko a nod, one that she returned. This wasn't the first time they would perform a sanitation, and she had seen the surgical efficiency of Carnahan and his team. They had a knack for excising alien lifeforms while minimizing damage to corporate property.

"Listen up," Ravi addressed the salvage crew. "We're working with an extremely slim timetable here. The Undine's metabolizing our cryo-sedatives faster than we can pump them. That means we have approximately 180 minutes to achieve our objectives."

Ravi looked sideways at Kiyoko.

"You'll escort Doctor Fukada to the ship's cerebral cortex," Ravi continued. "Once she's severed the primary node, the Undine should enter a prolonged comatose state. This will hopefully give us enough time to extract the specimen and determine its genetic makeup."

Kiyoko could sense the apprehension from Carnahan and his

subordinates. Such a procedure had never been performed—especially on an organism as large as the Undine.

"Central expects the usual performance," Ravi said. "They want the xenoform tagged and shipped to Rajapalayam 115 in two solar cycles. There's a fat bonus if we pull this off right."

———

YELLOW FLOODLIGHTS SWIVELED across the Undine's first level, revealing arterial walls smeared with congealed slime. Kiyoko examined the semi-transparent substance. Although she wanted to extract samples for testing, she didn't have the proper equipment. Perhaps later, Ravi could give her authorization to study the Undine on a surgical level. Kiyoko wanted to learn more about the changes this vessel had endured during her voyage through the vast gulfs of uncharted space.

She glanced at the coordinates on her data slate.

"This way," Kiyoko told Carnahan and his group.

They walked alongside her, rifles held low. Hushed chatter filtered into her transceiver. Kiyoko could sympathize with the recovery team's confusion. Most of them had never seen the interior of a bioship without augmented reality cosmetics. It was like looking at the inner workings of an old freighter, except instead of seeing gears, bolts, and wires, they saw hallways of flesh the color of pulped mulberry. Above, ridges of bony, chitinous matter held the ceiling aloft.

"What do you think happened here?" Carnahan asked.

"Can't say," Kiyoko replied. "The last known records for the Undine were back in 250 SCE. She was supposed to deliver pharmaceuticals to an outer rim settlement. Never made it."

"Ships don't vanish just like that."

"This one did," Kiyoko said. "I want to know why."

Then, like a swarm of digital insects, a holographic projection of binary integers scuttled down the nearby walls. Startled, Carnahan and his men formed a circle around Kiyoko, creating a human barrier. Weapons held aloft, they scanned the surroundings, ready to fire.

"Stand down," Kiyoko said. "It's just the AR projectors booting up."

Gradually, the mass of floating numbers dissipated and transformed into a well-lit, steel-lined hallway, the kind seen in low-orbit ports. They no longer stood in the gullet of a sleeping behemoth. What was once flesh had been reshaped into a projected illusion of steel and glass.

"I thought you said she was asleep," Carnahan said, annoyed.

"The sedatives are wearing off faster than anticipated," she replied. Kiyoko had suggested a more potent dose, but Ravi shot down the idea. He didn't want to risk causing anesthetic toxicity, endangering the Undine, and prematurely terminating the specimen's gestation.

"How long before she wakes up?"

"An hour. Maybe less."

Carnahan looked at his men.

"You heard the lady," he barked. "Let's move."

It took thirty minutes for the salvage team to reach the annelid thorax housing the cerebral cortex. Carriers like the Undine had internal systems designed like earthworms, with neural matrixes in four sections. Thankfully, the reality augmentations provided an accessible reference, allowing them to traverse the unfamiliar hallways with relative ease.

"Don't you find it strange?" Carnahan asked while Kiyoko prepared her equipment. The other security personnel stood near the entrance and kept watch, focused, unspeaking, professionals through and through. She felt more confident, safe, with their presence.

"We haven't come across any bodies," Carnahan continued. "No uniforms, no equipment, not even a single bone fragment. Corpses don't usually decay in sub-zero temperatures."

Kiyoko knelt and took a scalpel from her EMU's utility toolkit. At first glance, the cortex looked like an unassuming processing device covered by a stainless aluminum sheet.

"This ship has nano-bacteria strains that convert biological waste into energy," Kiyoko answered. "The dead passengers would have been repurposed for their carbon molecules."

A sliver of blood flowed from the shallow cut as she sliced into its metallic surface. The hologram fizzled out and revealed a semi-spherical mass of pinkish meningeal tissue.

"Or food for that thing below," Carnahan pointed his rifle at the floor, in the direction of the Undine's womb. "I'd feel a hell of a lot safer if we just sanitize it. One less problem to deal with."

"Not our call," Kiyoko replied. "The suits will fry us if we torch the specimen."

She sliced off the corpus callosum that connected the core's hemispheres. Thin plumes of smoke rose from the membrane as she cauterized the incision using a diathermic electrode. Afterward, she pulled a cord from her data slate and injected its stainless, pointed tip into the core's frontal lobe. The spongiform matter gave a wet, sucking noise. Kiyoko inputted the reboot sequence on the compiler to initiate baseline functionality. However, a radar ping appeared on her HUD before she could complete the process, breaking her concentration.

"We've got incoming," Carnahan said. He marched over to the doorway to join his men. Kiyoko saw red beacons congregating like glowing sores on her visor's bottom left corner.

One of the security personnel shouted:

"Fifty—no—sixty marks! Closing in fast!"

"How much longer?" Carnahan asked Kiyoko.

"I need one minute," she answered. Now that the Undine was regaining awareness, rewiring the cortex took precedence over everything else. If she had to stay behind, then so be it.

"You've got thirty seconds," Carnahan replied.

Moments later, a controlled fusillade of rifle fire erupted, followed by the squelch of ruptured meat and the high-pitched death wail of some grotesque and unidentifiable creature. With mounting, unbearable dread, Kiyoko watched the progress bar on the compiler creep upward to almost one hundred percent completion. The urge to drop everything was overwhelming – but she managed to stifle the surging panic and stand her ground. To her horror, the data slate stuttered and transitioned into a blue screen filled with lines of unintelligible machine code.

Disbelieving, Kiyoko swore and nearly tossed the compiler in frustration.

"What's wrong?" Carnahan asked.

"The system's unresponsive. I have to start over."

"Are you crazy?"

"I can't leave until it's finished!"

Someone grabbed Kiyoko by the arm and dragged her away.

"We are getting the fuck outta here, right now!"

———

Gunshots thundered as Kiyoko ran down the hallway. Her bulky EMU suit was too cumbersome for prolonged sprinting. It took a mere ten seconds of running before her lungs started seizing up as if she were on the verge of cardiac arrest. "Control, do you copy?" Kiyoko blurted into her transceiver. "The ship is awake! We need extraction immediately!"

Carnahan and his men alternated between shooting and reloading. They covered each other while retreating—a tactic they had employed countless times. There was a rhythmic pattern to the barrage macerating its targets in a brutal staccato. Although she couldn't see the swarm that bore down upon them, Kiyoko could still hear their uncanny chittering. Her visor displayed wave upon wave of red beacons that inched closer to the five blue dots representing the salvage team.

"Stay focused," Carnahan ordered. "Don't stop or these things will cut us down!"

A gurgling scream startled Kiyoko.

She turned and saw a four-limbed creature sinking its feelers into a security personnel member's neck. The thing resembled a hybrid of a locust and a cuttlefish, frontal legs lined with jagged, tibial spines. It made a clicking noise while gorging on the blood spurting from the man's jugular using an elongated proboscis. Similar-looking creatures pounced on the flailing, shrieking victim, digging their claws into his torso, shredding armor and flesh with disgusting ease.

Disoriented words from multiple vox channels swarmed into Kiyoko's headset. One of the security officers tried to help her fallen comrade—only to be intercepted mid-stride and cut in half by scythe-like mandibles that belonged to a larger bio-form with a segmented, plated torso. Streaks of bright red blood splattered across the holographic walls, making them shimmer and flicker.

Carnahan emptied an entire clip into the writhing mass of mutated flesh that had vivisected his subordinate. The organism gave an obscene ululating noise as energized bullets shredded its body.

"Run," Carnahan shouted while slotting a fresh magazine into his rifle. The sheer panic in his voice snapped Kiyoko out of her involuntary stupor. She turned and fled down the tunnel as fast as her aching legs could go, cold sweat pouring down her brow, gasping for breath.

"Ravi, for fuck's sake, say something!" Kiyoko pleaded. Instead of receiving a reply, Kiyoko merely heard a monotone, mechanical drone, followed by a piercing noise that would've punctured her eardrums if she hadn't hurriedly cut off the vox-channel.

From behind, heavy footfalls accompanied a sporadic burst of electrified rounds.

"I'm not getting any response," she radioed Carnahan. "What do we do?"

When she didn't get an answer, Kiyoko glanced backward. She saw Carnahan clutching his stomach, right glove dripping with blood. A ragged gash extended across the left side of his EMU, just below the armored plating. Kiyoko winced when she noticed a sliver of bone jutting out from the oozing wound—possibly a broken fragment that had splintered off his ribcage.

"One of the fuckers clipped me," he said.

Before Kiyoko could approach, Carnahan tossed a modular pistol that she caught in mid-air.

"You know how to use that?"

She noticed flecks of reddish spittle staining his beard.

"Safety's on the left," Carnahan continued. "Just point and pull the trigger."

"I'm not leaving you here!"

Horrified, Kiyoko saw the silhouette of a gargantuan, mishappen xenoform emerging from the adjacent corridor, an organism composed of writhing tendrils and lamprey-like mouths, propelled onward by smaller limbs jutting from its sides like an overgrown millipede.

"Goddammit," she shouted. "Don't be an idiot!"

Instead of replying, Carnahan stumbled away, coughing, a soldier till the end.

Kiyoko felt pathetic. Helpless. But this was no time to wallow in self-pity. Teeth gritted, she resumed her flight through the labyrinthine hallways of the Undine. While fleeing, she saw the augmented reality projections fizzle out of existence, revealing ramparts of dripping gristle and twitching viscera, exposing the bio-ship in all its profane, blood-drenched nakedness.

Carnahan's last transmission was a litany of vulgar swearing almost muted by the retort of his pulse rifle. A series of metallic clicks, a trigger repeatedly pulled in frustration, preceded wet, gurgling screams, slithering noises, and the brittle crunch of teeth on bone. Afterward, there was only a constant, unceasing chirping, like a murmuration of alien starlings gathered at dusk.

———

ESCAPING that nest of chittering nightmares proved more strenuous than Kiyoko had anticipated. The breach point was already sealing shut. Once, it had been wide enough for three grown men to enter, but now she could barely squeeze through the crevice. Scar tissue was forming around the incision, its protein filaments twitching like bloodworms.

Kiyoko removed the armored chest plate covering the front of her suit. Grunting, she tried slipping out of the fissure sideways, staining the surface of her EMU with brownish grime and bits of loose gristle. The logistics personnel should have prevented their only entryway from scabbing over—unless they had to evacuate the area due to a mass casualty incident.

Upon crawling out of the bioship, Kiyoko glanced around the second-floor walkway and saw that the station's primary harbor, once a frigid area dangerous to unprotected human bodies, had been transformed into a seething, fetid jungle of flesh pulsing with an abhorrent and malignant vitality. Ropy vines of crude biomass crawled across every surface, on railings, on walls, slithering into ventilation shafts and unmanned maintenance bays, like the roots of a tree about to bear fruit.

How long had they been inside the Undine? This uncontrolled outburst of mutated tissue couldn't have been produced in such a short period, not with the current state of bioengineering technology. No wonder she couldn't raise Ravi on the vox channels. While Kiyoko and the salvage team fled for their lives, the support crew was dealing with this unprecedented catastrophe.

After seeing the temperature readings on her visor, Kiyoko realized, with escalating terror, that the bioship was terraforming Cordova, turning steel into meat, creating a humid, temperate landscape that could serve as a suitable birthing chamber for her spawn. They were no longer dealing with a manufactured, lab-grown organism possessing low-level intelligence, but a xenoformic matriarch, the first of her kind, hell-bent on protecting her unborn progeny.

"This is Doctor Fukada," Kiyoko spoke into her transceiver. "Can anyone hear me?"

To her surprise and almost tearful relief, someone replied.

"Kiyoko?" Ravi's voice came through.

"Where are you?"

"Fourth floor, east wing, observation hub," Ravi replied. "I'll keep the shutters unlocked for five minutes. Hurry up before those things spot you. They're everywhere now."

"What about the others?"

"Dead," he answered. "Absorbed. Does it even matter?"

Kiyoko's knees almost buckled. "Everyone?" she whispered.

"There might be survivors. But not for long. Not after the Undine gives birth to her son."

The transmission cut off abruptly; Kiyoko buzzed Ravi again but received no answer. She had no patience for her superior's cryptic nonsense, but his tone of voice—so monotone and defeated—suggested an already depersonalized state of mind. She had to reach him before something truly awful happened. Faint beeping alerted Kiyoko to her suit's dwindling oxygen supply. The EMU had three minutes' worth remaining. No wonder she felt drowsy.

Kiyoko thought about removing her helmet but decided against it—who knew what sort of pathogens lingered in the air? She would not risk exposure unless it was absolutely necessary.

Though Kiyoko's calves burned, the threat of asphyxiation bolstered her faltering limbs. Each step taken revealed more of the corruption consuming the station inch-by-inch, devouring everything it touched.

Fleshy growths resembling tumorous neoplasm clung to metal and glass like soft-shelled barnacles, expanding and contracting before discharging clouds of yellow spores.

This noxious blight had also spread throughout the corridor leading to the observation hub. Kiyoko couldn't fathom how Ravi managed to survive under such circumstances. Even a total lockdown would fail to quarantine the widespread contagion. Soon, she surmised, everything would be reshaped until only a bloated, writhing landscape of carcinogenic tissue remained.

Surely, there was still something they could do to halt this calamity. There had to be a way. Kiyoko didn't know if the Undine could be put back to sleep—and perhaps it was already too late.

But she had to try. If only to give Carnahan's death some meaning.

The doorway to the observation platform, as promised, remained unlocked. Kiyoko swiped her electronic pass on the card reader, and the shutters parted with a hydraulic hiss.

After crossing the threshold, she saw Ravi sitting near one of the consoles, still wearing an EMU but without a helmet protecting his head. "I know where it came from," he murmured.

Kiyoko didn't know if it was safe enough to breathe. Nevertheless, she unlatched the helmet's metallic clasps and lifted them off her shoulders. Then, she inhaled a mouthful of air, gasping as she filled her lungs with precious oxygen. She didn't know it could taste so sweet.

"We can exclude the possibility of spontaneous parthenogenesis," Ravi continued without rising. "A bio-ship undergoing asexual reproduction would, logically, produce another vessel similar in shape and function. A female clone. But this specimen—it's different."

"Have you contacted Central?" she replied. "Do they know what the hell is going on?"

"Something must have donated the genetic material necessary to create the embryo. Think of the old religions from Terra Prime, myths passed down through generations of pre-spaceborne civilizations. They all have one element in common: a young virgin, touched by a divine hand, gives birth to a demigod. Dionysus and Semele. Rama and Kausalya. Yeshua and Maryam."

"Did you hear what I just said?"

"Don't you understand?" Ravi, eyes wide, clasped both hands. "The Undine has already breached our firewalls. She has total control of our systems. We're all trapped in here. There's nothing else we can do, Doctor, nothing except to witness the inevitable."

"For fuck's sake, I don't have time for this bullshit!"

Judging from her supervisor's flat, expressionless affect, Ravi had most likely suffered a complete mental breakdown. If the chief engineer couldn't fulfill his leadership responsibilities, then she would have to take over. How, Kiyoko didn't know. *But there are other methods besides reasonable dialogue available,* she thought while reaching for Carnahan's pistol in her toolkit.

"I took a sample of the ship's blood and ran it through a protein cryptographer," Ravi continued. "It contained terabytes of data that recorded the conception period. The experience was traumatic enough to embed itself into the Undine's genetic code. That's when I saw it."

"Saw what?"

Ravi began to sob and laugh simultaneously.

"What the fuck did you see, Ravi?"

"The father," he answered, features contorting in a grimace of terror. "An unknown xenoform of immense size and anti-matter density. It emerged from *God knows where,* a dimension whose natural laws are utterly incompatible with our own. This being came to our universe looking for a mate, and soon found the perfect match: a biomechanical mutant capable of growing her own reproductive organs. It chose her as the vessel for its seed. And she accepted."

Kiyoko instinctively drew the pistol from her utility belt.

The hideous implications of Ravi's discovery stirred a deep, profoundly overwhelming sense of dread and existential despair. Whatever this creature was, wherever it came from, she couldn't allow it to be born. Its mother had already slaughtered almost every person inside Cordova. The thought of such a hideous abomination spreading madness and carnage across hundreds of neighboring interplanetary settlements strained Kiyoko's sanity to the point of buckling.

"It's not too late," she said. "If we overload the generators, we'll cause a chain reaction strong enough to vaporize the Undine. But I'm gonna need your security clearance."

Ravi shook his head.

"She won't let you," he answered.

Frustrated, Kiyoko pointed the pistol at Ravi.

"Just give me the access codes. Please."

Instead of responding, Ravi dislodged his EMU suit's front harness. Bewildered, Kiyoko could only watch, dumbstruck, as he pulled down the zipper tag on his collar, exposing his body.

"She did this to me," he said. "To all of us."

Bloated pustules as big as a man's fist throbbed across Ravi's chest, each connected by interlacing veins. Kiyoko understood why he wasn't wearing a helmet for protection. He had already been changed. "Jesus Christ," she said, bile rising up her throat like battery acid. She suppressed the nauseating urge to vomit and tightened her shaking grip on the pistol.

"Soon, she'll do it to you, too."

Ravi plodded onward, torso exposed, until he was only a few inches away from Kiyoko. A fissure appeared across his solar plexus, which expanded inch-by-inch, revealing rows of jagged, malformed teeth; strings of pinkish slime dripped from the orifice as an eel-like, purplish tongue poked out. Something broke in Kiyoko's brain. Shrieking, she fired the gun again and again as Ravi stumbled toward her. She didn't stop even after his lifeless corpse fell to the ground with a sickening, wet thud, like damp seaweed slapping against concrete. Viscous, yellowish blood seeped out of the exit wounds, forming an ochre-hued puddle on the floor.

———

KIYOKO FELL TO HER KNEES, crying in terror and exhaustion. She felt a burdensome weariness and a desire to just end it all—to sleep forever and not think and feel.

For what reason was she spared?

She had never been a believer in a higher power, in gods, saints, or angels, but the urge to visit the station's multi-faith chapel swelled within her chest. Perhaps, Kiyoko wondered, Cordova's resident pastor could give her a few words of sage advice in confronting the inevitable—

if he was still human and not a malformed mutation like the cadaver lying before her.

Fingers shaking, she raised the pistol until its still-smoking nozzle touched her temple.

Her mind was her own. Her body was her own. As long as she drew breath, she would not allow anything to turn her into a lump of corrupted biomass, a piece of unthinking flesh, like the rest of her colleagues. *My life,* she thought, *my death. Come and take it from me, you bitch.*

Closing her eyes, Kiyoko took a deep breath, held it in, and pulled the trigger.

Click.

She tried again.

Click.

This is a joke, she thought, giggling madly.

It had to be a joke.

Laughing, Kiyoko continued to pull the trigger, even as a horrendous, keening wail reverberated throughout the station; she pulled and pulled and pulled while listening to the cries of an alien god-thing emerging from its mother's birth canal. She begged for a merciful death that would not come while rivulets of blood seeped out of her nose, her ears, and even her eyes.

Please, please, please, just kill me, please, she screamed.

Anything but this.

Outside Cordova, the stars gleamed coldly, stark and uncaring.

Click.

Click.

Click.

The Corpse-Door

Gemma Files

Late one year I became ill with a fever that laid me low enough both Guthorm and my mother thought I would die, and it was Kellern the Christian monk who nursed me through it. When I woke at last I could no longer run and tussle, as I had been wont to in those days when I dreamed of being a famous shield-maiden like Lagertha, wife of Ragnar Lothbrok. Instead, I could now walk only with two sticks, forever pulling my newly slack and withered legs along behind me like Ragnar's son by Aslaug Sigurdsdottir, Ivar the Boneless... and as you see, things have improved but little, in the years between now and then.

My mother wept and Guthorm frowned, and while none of our neighbours said so I knew they believed I would never amount to much after that, for which I could not blame them. But of all those living near our farm in those days, it was only Kellern who made sure to remind me that no matter my present unluckiness, my life was not yet over.

"You have a strong mind, Aud," he said, "with great aptitude for what you heathens call women's magic, the reckoning of numbers and balance of household goods—and if you were to apply yourself I could easily teach you to write and read, not only in your own language but others as well, thus making you precious in the eyes of any suitor." Here I scoffed at him, but he continued: "Yet because you are such an intelligent person, you must also see that your mother and step-father's time will soon be over—the Christ is coming, even here, and all shall fall beneath His banner. You could go far if you chose, once things change for the better. You might join an order, profess as a nun...."

Which was foolish in every way as a suggestion, though I could see very well he truly did care for my welfare, which kept me from mocking at him outright.

"Don't be daft, priest," I told him, eventually. "Even a cripple like me can hope for better than to marry a dead man nailed to a tree." And he laughed at that as well, for all his great faith.

He was a good friend, and a better ally. We faced terrible things together, and triumphed. Yet he could never convert me to his ways, no more than I could have converted him to mine, or ever would have thought to.

I have learned far too much of the darkness which lies in wait underneath all things to ever share a faith such as his, much though I might have come to admire it.

———

"WHAT IS A *VOLVA*?" Kellern asked me, when the fire was dying down, the night my stepfather brought back what looked like a small lump of ice, somehow unmelted, from Asdis Witch-Face. "A sort of sorceress?"

I shook my head, looking up from where I lay, watching the shadows chase themselves across the roof. "A seer—one whose dreams fore-tell, one who speaks for the dead. Though she can certainly remove curses, Asdis, from what I've heard, and probably cast them as well. Some *volvas* also make sacrifices on behalf of others before battles and are employed to perform funerals, or even marriages."

"You have women here who serve as priests? That I didn't know."

"We have women who serve as everything." But I heard the boast in my own voice, and after a moment, amended my words; I did not wish to lie to Kellern, who had never lied to me. "Well... they may serve as they feel inclined to, *if* they're free-born, and can pay their way. You've seen yourself that our women farm, and trade, and make, and fight; should it surprise you that some vow themselves to the gods, too?"

"I suppose not. But why do they call her Witch-Face, if she is not one?"

I shrugged in my furs. "Because she is accounted a daughter of Loki, a by-blow of the *jotnar*; her size alone betrays it, so much so you will surely know her on sight if she passes this way, long before she tells you her name."

For Asdis Witch-Face stood taller by half a head than the tallest man any of us had ever seen, bearing a cat's flat nose and split upper lip, her eyes green as old ice. Her cheeks were tattooed with runes, her neck with a collar of snakes, and her hair hung knotted full of small bones that rustled as she walked instead of clattering, showing that they were hollow—those of birds, probably, boiled and cleaned. She was something more than human, or less; different, at any rate. Her very footsteps were enough to set one's teeth on edge.

(Such people have gone out of this world almost entirely now, you Christians like to say, along with our gods. But in this case, as in many others, you lie; perhaps without knowing, I suppose.

Or perhaps not.)

———

HOW SHE MADE her living none knew, but Asdis was often seen to cross back and forth to the sea-shore by way of a scree called Geirrid's Lip, which bridged a small river often swollen with meltwater. The next day, therefore, I took care to make sure Kellern was busy elsewhere before dragging myself down to the sand and crawling the last thirty feet, taking refuge behind a ridge topped with clumps of grass. There, I watched as Asdis harvested seaweed from the low tide and filled two large baskets with it, no doubt intending to dry it on racks outside her hut.

"Ho, Knife's-Priest's girl," she called out, without looking up from her work, her voice high and oddly sweet for such a creature. "Has your mother yet told you? I danced at both her weddings and sang her fortune each time too, for all she showed no interest."

I propped myself back up, using my sticks as leverage. "No, she never told me that," I answered. "Yet I have questions I would ask of you, if you will answer."

Asdis Witch-Face half-laughed, half-hissed, like rainwater falling. "I can promise you the first for certain, little Aud. The second I may have to think on, depending."

"Very well. Why did you give my mother's husband that stone?"

She shrugged, her huge hands still busy. "He complained of being ill-treated, having no money of his own; if he had only returned from viking with plunder, your mother might have welcomed him back into her bed. Being as she is akin to Gullveig, the woman for whom Hjeimdall opened the rainbow bridge's gate—a hard whore, who grows soft only for gold. Or so he said."

I spat. "Odin's eye! He is a pig, and one day—"

"—you'll slaughter him like one? Slide that knife you keep in your sleeve across his throat while he sleeps? Oh believe me, he fears that, much as he fears your mother and that Christian he dragged home would both gladly hold him down, to help you do it. He knows he is unloved in her house, and everywhere else."

I did not wish to think on this, having no desire to pity Guthorm.

"Yet you gave him the stone anyhow," I said. "Again, why?"

She smiled then, her teeth all different lengths, yet all filed to points. Replying, softly: "Why, to see what would happen, of course. That is the only reason I do anything, Aud. In honour of my sire, for whom the same is equally true."

Chaos and mischief, I remember thinking, as Loki Laufeyjarsson's image sprang up in my head, sketched on a wooden board soaked in blood-offerings each festival, with his *jotunn* wife on the one side and his Aesir wife on the other, while all their monstrous children sat around besides: the Fenris-wolf, the Midgard's-serpent, Death's-hall Hel with her slack corpse's half-face. Not to mention Nari and Vali his half-god twins, one cut open so Loki might be bound in his own son's guts, unbreakably, to suffer 'til world's end for the crime of Baldr's death. *A thousand faces has Loki Slip-skin, Aud,* my mother had often told me, *each flickering like flame... all equally false, and hungry.*

And there sat Asdis as yet one more of them, so tall and dreadful, smiling at how my fear had finally begun to show. Waiting for me to turn and flee at any moment, no doubt, as all the others did—to turn my sweating back on her and hump myself away like a worm, sand spraying, 'til I reached the comfort of home.

Well, I thought, she will wait a long time for that.

I swallowed, and asked yet once more: "What does that stone you gave him *do*, lady?"

"Why, direct him to what he most wishes for, of course."

"And what will that be?"

"How can I know? Wait and see."

"That is no answer."

"Perhaps not. Yet perhaps it is that the stone works differently every time, depending on who uses it, and why, and for what. Had you truly not thought of *that*, deep-minded Aud?"

I had not, and she knew it; she laughed again, watching my face fall. But there was no cruelty in it.

"Never mind, little sister," Asdis Witch-Face told me, hoisting her baskets and rising to tower above me, her shadow a cold, stroking touch I longed to flinch from, but did not. "He will use it soon enough... and it will do him no good, or anyone else, either. But since you know that already, at least one of you will be prepared for what befalls, once he does."

––––––––––

So MANY PLACES are unmarked graves hereabouts, or were, when I was young. Perhaps that is changing. But it was certainly still true when Guthorm took out the stone Asdis Witch-Face had given him and raised it to the last of the sun. He stood by our boundary-marker, holding it high over his head, turning slowly from south to north like a longship's pilot looking for land; I might have laughed, watching him, had his face not held such hunger, greedy as a wyrm's.

Then the light hit his stone at just the right angle, and a brilliant track sprang from it, bright enough that I blinked away tears. Arrow-straight, it struck the top of a tor some three hundred paces northeast; the effect lasted only moments, enough to set the grass aflame, sending a narrow gray plume of smoke aloft. Guthorm howled with triumph, caught up the pick he had laid at his feet, and went racing towards the mark it had made.

"Bring tools and help me!" he cried. "Not for nothing did my uncles call this hill Hjalmar's Rest, after all!"

My mother snorted and stood back, her arms folded, pointedly refusing to do so. "Oh, so you think there has been a ship buried here all this time, no doubt brimming with gold? Every rock around this farm has been named something similar, at one time or another."

"Who would bury a ship?" Kellern murmured to me, scraping away at the earth his owner's pick had loosened.

"Some are buried in ships," I explained, "especially if they are slain not in battle but by disease, or murder. Rich men take their goods with them either way, to make sure no one else can use them, after their death."

"I thought you burned your dead, not buried them."

I nodded. "It all depends if the dead man is a chieftain, a jarl or a great warrior—someone whose death is cause for celebration rather than one whose name is ill-omened, whose grave must be kept secret, lest—"

"Be quiet, Aud!" my mother told me. "It is an ill thing to rob any man's grave, Guthorm: ill, and stupid. How drunk must you already be, to think differently?"

"The Witch-Face said I would be rewarded, woman!"

"To be sure. But with what?"

The crunch of the pick's iron into ancient wood silenced her. Guthorm froze, as did Kellern. Then, in sudden frenzy, Guthorm shoved Kellern away, stepped back and hammered again at the same spot, twice as fast. Dirt collapsed before his feet as unseen beams of dry wood splintered and broke, a black hole opening up in the ground; it was a pace across, large enough for Guthorm's shoulders to fit through. Cold, foul air welled up. The monk crossed himself.

Guthorm turned to my mother, in triumph. "Do you see *now*?" he demanded.

"I see your folly," she said, voice tight with what might have been rage, or even fear. "Perhaps even your death. Or worse."

And she turned her back on him.

———

I CRAWLED BACK ALONE to our home and stayed within sight of my mother, hoping my presence might help calm her, but Kellern was forced to help Guthorm with his plunder, having no other choice. As the sun went down they came dragging Guthorm's cloak back with them, piled high with all manner of treasure. The hearth-fire lit it brightly, even through the door: Gold and silver coin, jewelled crosses and golden cups likely snatched from some English church's altar, begemmed rings and necklaces stained dark by the deaths of those who'd lost them. The dead man who'd lain within the barrow had worn full armour, Kellern told me later, but the leather had rotted and the mail, like the blade of the sword upon his breast, had rusted—yet the circlet around his skeletal brow, now resting in the stolen hoard's center, shone with silver. Only the corpse itself and the bones of some hapless sacrifice-beast, mounded up at the far end of the tomb, had Guthorm left behind.

We heard him singing as he and Kellern came, and went out to meet him—my mother standing in the door, blocking his entrance, even as I staggered my way around her and leant on my sticks, watching the activity closely. Kellern looked up as he let the cloak fall, and our eyes met with a shiver; we both of us felt cold, apparently, with something more than the dark.

"Take it away, fool," my mother said. "I'll not have it in my home; indeed, neither I nor Aud will *touch* this, or the monk, if he wishes to be rid of your idiocy. This curse you may keep for yourself alone."

"It's my home too, woman," Guthorm answered, down on his knees, carding his hands through the hoard like wool. "How will you keep me out?"

"Your home? Only until *she* says different," I told him, unable to prevent myself.

"Do not test me, crippled bitch," he snapped back, rising once more.

"My lord—" Kellern began, but my mother pushed past me, putting herself between us.

"Oh, but she has the right of it," she said, "and I have been foolish myself not to act on that suggestion, all this time. So take your ill-gotten gains and leave, Guthorm, before I summon my brothers and uncles to make you go, let alone my first husband's kin. I can work this farm without you very easily, having done it almost entirely so thus far."

"Not if I take the monk with me," he snarled, to which my mother laughed long and loud, drawing herself up to full height. From her arms she stripped the gold bracelets he had given her as a wedding-pledge, the necklace set with Byzantine stones she wore around her throat likewise, and threw all three of these things at his chest.

"This will more than pay for him, if he wishes to stay," she said. "Now find a cave to pore over your hoard in secret 'til you grow scales and drip venom, like Fafnir himself!"

The jewels bounced downwards and chinked against the rest, joining Guthorm's booty—but I can only assume he had finally had enough of her scorn, for he stepped forward and slapped her across the face, drawing blood. The shock of it made me lose my balance and fall; he laughed to see it, for which my mother slapped him back, rocking him where he stood. "You unnatural creature!" he shouted, lunging for her. Just as it almost seemed that Kellern would intervene in her defense, however—*Think what you do!*, I thought I heard him cry—I slid the knife I always carried in a sheath sewn to my breast-wrap out and stuck it in the back of Guthorm's leg, then twisted it to make it hurt.

"Do it again, and I'll slash your strings," I told him. "You'll be like me, then."

"You useless thing," he named me. "You should have died long since, and all know it!"

Now it was my turn to laugh. "Too bad for you I didn't, eh?" I said. "But the gods willed otherwise, just as they willed you never do anything worth the telling but drink, and lie, and steal."

He kicked me in the head, then, or must have. For when I came to I lay on my back in Kellern's lap, with my mother holding a cloth to my face and my head hurting, jaw almost too bruised to speak.

"Oh, you are a stubborn girl," Kellern said, stroking my hair gently, "more so than any donkey I ever met. How many times have I warned you to do a thing first, Aud, not simply talk about it?"

"Only the once," I mumbled, "and that time right now."

It was good advice, nevertheless. And ever since, I have.

———

IN THE HILLS where I was born, we cut a corpse-door in every house and fill it with stones, so that if someone dies inside they can be taken out by a door that can be filled in again immediately after, a door that will never be used again. This is in case that person dies in such a way as to make of themselves a *draug* or *aptrgangr*—an again-walker—and seeks entry once more.

Now, there are many ways to become an *aptrgangr* according to the common wisdom, all of them somewhat shameful. If a person dies while committing theft or murder, for instance, or dies sitting upright with their eyes open, inside their own home instead of outside. Another way, though less well-known, can come about if a person dares to violate the barrow of a greater warrior, breaking open his tomb-hill and plundering what lies within. Which in turn renders him (or her) who does it the very worst sort of thief, a robber of the revered dead—a crime to make rocks split and bleed at such a criminal's touch, or the very dirt itself cry out beneath their tread.

The third sort of *draug*, my children, is called a *hangbui*. A grave-guard. Sometime this is a made thing, the corpse of a woman killed to give her master company on his voyage to Hel or Valhalla; sometimes it was once a volunteer, a companion in the shield-wall, who did not wish to shame the gods by leaving his dead friend undefended; sometimes it is the grave-dweller him (or her-)self, gold-sickened and avid, unable to let go of the goods they earned in life. Normally, such a *draug* cannot leave the place it protects, simply waiting for someone idiotic enough to penetrate its domain, let alone steal from it. I did not know how Guthorm could have possibly avoided arousing the *hangbui*'s ire by what he had done, especially given how rich a hoard it brooded over. It was a mystery.

Guthorm was gone a week, during which none of us missed him. My mother left Kellern and I to guard the house just in case he returned, while she took our ox-cart to speak with our closest neighbours of what had happened, and they sent their two youngest sons back with her to help with our harvest, which was accomplished much more quickly than usual. So we were well-prepared when the weather turned, suddenly and unseasonably, yet it surprised us all the same.

"It shouldn't snow so soon," my mother said. "This is an ill omen."

"No doubt," a familiar voice replied from behind us, where we stood watching dark clouds lower over the hills, and I heard a long mane's worth of bones rustle together like snake's skin. "Yet ill doings will bring recompense in same, as the saying goes. Greetings to you, Thorunn Thyrmirsdottir; greetings, Knife's-Priest's girl. And to you, Mercia-man, whose name I do not know."

We all turned as one, Kellern's shoulders squaring visibly, to find Asdis Witch-Face standing close behind us with her huge head cocked and grinning, though the split in her lip made it more of a sneer.

"My name is Kellern, if you care to use it," he told her, stiffly. "And you... would be the one they call Witch-Face, I suppose."

"You suppose correctly," she replied. Then, to my mother: "And tell me, did your husband use my stone as he saw fit, after all? I cannot say I have seen him, lately."

"I think you know very well that he did."

"Yes, I think I do," Asdis said, grinning wider. "For there is a hole in that hill back a ways, wide enough to move treasure through, and an angry dead man within." And now she turned her strange green eyes on me, saying: "But you look as if there is something you wish to ask me about that, little sister. I will answer gladly, if you do."

"And what will you ask in return?" Kellern demanded. "Her soul?"

Asdis laughed at that, a crooning lilt, as though she were calling down cows at sunset.

"Ah, nothing so much," she assured him. "I am no kin to that Satan of yours, for all you think so—but I do collect wishes. Grant one to get another, as my mother told me."

"Your mother was a demon's bride, no doubt, since there are no true gods but one; we will do better without your help than with it. You may leave Aud's welfare to me."

"Ah, but perhaps it will be Aud who preserves *your* welfare, priest, in the end. That would be even more amusing."

I snorted. "The monk can look after himself," I told her. "But yes, I did wonder how Guthorm was able to take the *hangbui*'s gold, until you showed yourself today. Then it occurred to me that perhaps your stone protected him, as well as leading him into folly."

"Mmm, you *are* wise, Aud Snake-belly. For one thing can serve two purposes, if made to."

"Should we worry about Guthorm?" my mother asked her. But Asdis only shook her head, hair-bones clicking softly.

"I would not, overmuch," she told her. "You were right to reject his entry, Thorunn. The *hangbui* will blame him alone for what has befallen." A pause. "Of course, who knows who *Guthorm* will blame for his misfortune, after its revenge is finally taken?"

"Whatever happens next will be your work as well, then," I pointed out, to which she shrugged.

"I gave him only what he wanted," she said. "What do *you* want, Aud? Or your slave?"

"Nothing you can give, witch," Kellern put in, before I could answer, and she laughed again at his ferocity in my defence. Saying—

"Don't be so sure. Don't you wish to know when you'll die, monk? Or how, or where?"

"God alone knows that. I accept His will in all matters, gladly."

She nodded. "Oh, yes indeed, you do. As I have seen." To me, once more: "And as for you—when you see what becomes of your mother's husband, perhaps you will come see me again of your own free will, girl. You, at least, have the mind to use whatever I might give you wisely."

She moved on then, the Witch-Face. so queenly in her strangeness, her terrible half-*jotunn* pride. On to her next act of mischief, whatever that might be.

———

IT SNOWED ALL that night and part of the next day, piling so high we could not open the door, so we stayed inside instead, ate well and tended the fire, telling stories. We fell asleep early only to be woken by strange noise from outside, somewhat like a cow lowing in birth-pain, or a bull bellowing with its mouth sewn shut.

"What is that?" my mother whispered, her face white in the fire's dim glow, as I reached for my sticks. Kellern went to the door-window and opened it on its leathern hinges, looking out.

"What do you see?" I asked him.

"Only the snow, which has settled, and the moon shining down. I think I can open the door now."

"Do not!" my mother cried, from behind us, which made him hesitate. But I pushed past him and did it myself, for something told me there was more to this.

Beyond the door, no longer blocked, the snow shone like a polished silver mirror, something I had heard of, yet never seen. The moon was a burning bone, in the seconds before it starts to char. And something came trotting around the hill, making its way across the snow with delicate little steps: Something huge, something red, something headless.

I gulped at the sight of it, mouth gone dry.

"Those bones in the tomb," I asked Kellern, when I could speak. "What were they, again?"

"Oxen, I think."

"From the grave-feast, yes. And what... does *that* look like, to you?"

Kellern swallowed too; I heard him do it, clearly. "I do not like to say," he replied, at last.

On this, I agreed with him, heartily. And yet.

Once this thing had been a rack of beef split wide for roasting; that much was clear, the closer it came. It must have fed many mourners in its time. But now the bones it had been reduced to were back in their proper places and wrapped in flesh once more, though its skull and hooves were lacking. At its front end was nothing but a hole full of sharp white things that looked like teeth, yet could clearly be nothing but splintered bones, cracked open and sucked for their marrow; it picked its path through the white-covered fields with equally sharp leg-bones, lurching with each step to leave a trail of little red prints behind, and sometimes it switched its tailless rump or skinned shoulders as if flicking away flies. Heat rose into the sky above it, and cooked blood fell like sweat from its heaving sides, sizzling into the frost below.

"May Thor's strength keep us safe from all terrors," my mother breathed, having finally gotten the courage to peer between us; her hand was on the hammer she wore around her neck, even as Kellern's sketched the Christ's gallows-tree above his chest, an invisible shield. At that moment, however, I watched as this *draug*-ox—the cheated *hangbui*'s emissary—turned the gaping place where its head once sat towards a man crouching at the top of the next ridge, staring down in frozen fear at what waited for him. It was Guthorm, of course, wearing the dead man's circlet like a crown, king of his own luckless *wyrd*.

"What?" was all he had time to ask, of no one in particular, as the thing pawed the ground, stamping its foremost leg-tip deeper. "*What?!?*" Then it was on him with a leap, moist air gusting out from inside it in a fierce, fetid plume, and they tumbled back over the ridge together.

————

MY MOTHER and I had both grown to despise Guthorm—even Kellern, I think, could not pretend to more than the charity of his calling, concerning his former master. None of us found any satisfaction in hearing his screams, however, or the wet sounds they finally became.

After the last of this awful noise faded away, we waited. Presently, we heard the snow-crust crunching again, this time under much heavier steps. The *draug* was returning, now swollen all over through its trunk, like a waterskin gorged to bursting; from its gaping "throat", gold and silver shifted gleaming in the moonlight, stained with still-steaming blood. All swiftness gone, it moved across our fields with the slow, steady pace of some drunken old man, walking a road too well known to stray from—until, at last, it vanished over the hill's crest.

"Did it *eat* him?" Kellern asked.

"It is dead," I said, shortly. "What need has it for food?"

"I might wish it had," my mother put in, "for now his burial falls to us. Come the morning we must find the body and weight it down with stones. And that will be the end of it."

She spoke so firmly that it occurred to neither me nor Kellern to doubt her.

Kellern told me later that he had offered to say prayers over it, when they did, but this my mother declined, firmly, if not unkindly. *I thought little enough of him in life*, she told him, *but he died trying to fight; if that brings him to Valhalla, so be it. Save your prayers for your own dead, priest.* Would it have helped, had Kellern chosen not to listen to her? I do not think even the Witch-Face could have seen an answer to that.

All I know is that late the next night, when the moon was nearly down, I woke to a deafening uproar of screams, shouts and crunching. I rolled out of my pallet just as the door to our farmhouse burst apart in a spray of broken wood. Kellern and my mother, who had been trying to hold it closed, were both knocked flying, my mother flat on her back and Kellern to one side, with blood trickling from his brow. Then in trudged Guthorm, death-blue and bruised purple-black all over, still shedding earth as a just-bathed man sheds water; his sunken eyes blazed red, and he moved the way I once walked my favourite doll across the dirt floor, stumbling and twitching with his limbs a-wobble, joints grating at every step. I realized then that the *hangbui* must have trampled him to death, crushing each bone of his body to splinters, for there were wounds matching the prints that thing had made in the snow across both his chest and elsewhere, packed full of dry black blood.

He stood there a moment, staring down at my mother, who stared back in what was more sheer indignant surprise than anything else.

"But I took nothing," she said. "I dared no curse. Even Asdis said so."

Guthorm's mouth did not move, hanging slack and twisted, yet a thick, gurgling voice came tearing up from somewhere deep inside him, full of bile and glee. "That matters not," it said. "This is *wyrd*, woman... mine, and now yours."

And he fell upon her, wrapping his legs and arms around her like ropes, binding them fast together. My mother had but time for one cry only—of rage and fear, admixed—before the floor boiled beneath them both and they sank straight down into it, as if the close-packed earth were water. They were gone before I could even blink, leaving only a patch of turned soil behind.

It was the rising sun's light across Kellern's eyes that roused him at last, hours later, and when I told him what had happened, he wept, which surprised me greatly. Almost as much as it surprised me that I could not.

Not yet, at any rate.

———

MOST OF THE day was spent in Kellern digging down to my mother's body, though I was not idle either, for using straw, sticks and mud, I built up a wattle-and-daub barricade to the top of the door frame, marking it with guarding runes my mother had taught me. "It is the death within that makes a tomb-guard," I explained to the bewildered monk. "Not the strength of what it is built with. These are the laws."

"I trust you will not be ... offended ... if I pray all the same."

I smiled fiercely at him. "Now you are learning to joke like a Northman, monk."

"Who is joking?" But he laughed, breathlessly, as men do in such mad straits, and continued laying out my mother's body in accordance with our rites.

Thus it was that when the *draug* my mother had married returned at moonrise, he balked in bafflement before the flimsy barricade, as I peeked out through the window.

"You are as much a fool in death as you were in life, Guthorm," I called. "For by slaying my mother here you have made this place her tomb, knowing well you are forbidden all tombs but your own!"

But: "Only so long as she rests here," he snarled back, "which she cannot do forever. You will have to cut a corpse-door to bring her forth, eventually—and then we will race, you and I. Tell me, *daughter*, do you think you can outrun me, even now?"

Then he stepped backwards, and vanished into the night.

Kellern laid a hand on my shoulder. "Do not fear, Aud," he said. "I can carry you as far as the cart-shed, easily. And from there—"

But he broke off, aghast, as the sudden screams of beasts in mortal agony split the dark. I closed my eyes, cursing under my breath. As the noises continued, and grew to encompass smashing wood and cracking stone, Kellern sank slowly to the ground, eyes wide. I let myself down beside him.

"The *draug* has the right of it," I told him. "If we let her stay here too long, this curse will only spread to her, then to you, and me.

Though I suppose your Christ's power may keep *you* from rising, after Guthorm takes whatever revenge he plans on us both...."

"I could always baptize you in His name as well," Kellern offered.

"Not even now, monk. But thank you." I thought a while, then said: "Olaf and Harold said they would return in tomorrow morning, did they not?" He nodded. "Then perhaps there is some way to escape this threat, with their help. I must consider it further."

"May I at least pray you find an answer, Aud?"

"You may," I said.

And perhaps his prayers helped, little though I believed they would. For eventually, I did.

———

OLAF AND HARALD came shortly after dawn, waking us with their voices; we scrambled out through the farmhouse's window to find them staring around, surrounded by a trail of ruin. The cart-shed had been torn down, the sheepfold's fencing broken, and every beast from horses to sheep to chickens ripped apart. Even the cart had had its wheels snapped off and its yoke broken in half.

"By Thor, what *did* this?" Olaf demanded.

"A *draug*," I told them, and though recounting the story was hard, Kellern's astonishment that neither brother doubted it for an instant did amuse me greatly. Olaf, who had always been the kinder, tried clumsily to console me, but I shrugged him off. Harald was blunter.

"Well, then, let's make a corpse-door, and see poor Thorunn properly laid down," he declared, hefting his axe. "And if it takes too long, I'll use this to separate old Guthorm from his arms and legs; let's see how brave he is then!"

"Don't be a fool, Harald," I said, touched, despite myself. "Now listen—there is a way to end all this for good, but it will take much work, and we have little time. Will you do as I ask? If not, leave now, and don't return."

"Or we could *all* leave, and not return," Olaf suggested.

"And leave my mother to wander forever as a *draug* herself? Besides, the dead do not tire; fleeing would only delay our doom."

"And I am still sworn to serve this household," Kellern said, "so if Aud stays, I stay." Adding, with an unexpectedly sly look: "Besides which, I have found it best to follow her orders, even for those who are *not* her thralls."

"Ha! You've a tongue on you, monk," Harald replied. "Very well, Knife's-Priest's girl: Command us."

The work went faster than it would have with only Kellern and I, after that, though still took all day to prepare our trap. Olaf and Harald took turns smashing out a door-sized hole in one wall, while Kellern carted baskets of earth to the site we were preparing. Nearly everything left in the farmhouse and the wrecked outbuildings was taken up for use —blankets, straw, timbers, tools, rope, lamp oil, and more. I had to fight tears only once, when putting the last of my mother's jewelry on her body.

At sunset, when I tried to send them back home, the brothers balked. I already stood balanced on the edge of my mother's funeral pyre, a lit torch in one hand and my sturdier walking-stick in the other; when I saw them lingering, I leaned in over the long form beneath, close-wrapped in a cloth my mother embroidered herself, growling: "Go, you fools! You have done your part, and ably—are you so eager to die with us, if my plan fails? Take time to father sons first, at least!"

"Do you think so little of your own plans, Aud?" Olaf called back.

"Indeed," Harald agreed. "We did not come all this way to flee. What sort of Northmen would we be, if we did that?"

"Live ones?" I suggested, but they only laughed at me, making Kellern smile into his sleeve. So I scoffed instead, and told them what to do next.

The sun sunk low, red dimming to blue, then black. I was pouring oil on the pyre when Guthorm appeared in the distance, grinning widely when he saw I stood there alone. "Are you ready to run, Aud Snake-belly?" he roared. "I see that monk has abandoned us both now and left you to die, like the coward he is!"

But I merely gave a grim laugh of my own, shaking my head.

"Never mind that, step-father," I called back, dropping the torch, so the flames rushed upwards between us. "For tell me—are *you* ready to *burn*?"

At the sight, he gave a great whoop and put his head down, charging forwards, fast as a maddened ox. With massive leaps instead of steps, he closed the distance between us quicker than I could have ever imagined possible until he loomed up at me through the fire itself with his flesh starting to char and his hair already smoking, his awful smile all flickering hot with light. "This will not save you either," he hissed, gleefully, and jumped forwards, no doubt hoping to bury those sharp teeth in my neck—

—but I let myself fall smoothly sideways off the mound, just as Kellern leapt up from beneath the snow-covered blanket that had hidden him, and caught me. While Guthorm, ruled still by his own weight if not by that of death, hurtled through the space where I had stood only to crash down upon the snow beyond, which gave way with a loud crack, sending him down through the brittle deck-planks of the barrow-ship he himself had unearthed. His *draug*-strength might have served to pull him free again, but Harald and Olaf lunged forward from their own hiding places, hammering mightily down upon him with axe and broken wheel-spar; their blows finished the trap's work, and Guthorm dropped entirely into the tomb's stinking dark.

We had piled the pyre next to that same cursed hill, you see—laid it so as to confuse Guthorm, to conceal our strategy. And it may be we depended overmuch on Guthorm's stupidity, but then again, it may not; it *worked*, after all. He was always much more foolish when angered.

Panting, I wriggled free of Kellern's arms and slithered over to the hole, staring down. Below, Guthorm was already clambering to his feet; his head was grossly flattened out of shape from the fall and the brothers' blows, but his red eyes lit the dim interior as he grinned up at me.

"Clever," he admitted. "Always such a clever bitch, but still. Did you truly think this fall would hurt *me?*"

I shook my head, not smiling.

"Not the fall, no," I replied.

Guthorm's ruined face had, perhaps, half an instant for rage to start sliding into confusion, before the vast headless throat of the *hangbui*-ox loomed out of the dark behind him. It crunched down, swallowing his body halfway in one great gulp, from head to waist; for an instant the *draug*'s legs flailed, then another mighty crunch set the *hangbui*'s tooth-bones to shredding rotting skin and flesh, snapping bones, slicing sinew. No screams or cries, this time... only the chewing sounds, wet and terrible, which did not ever stop, as if the *hangbui* meant to render what little was left of Guthorm completely.

I shook myself out of my trance, having watched much more than enough. "Now!" I shouted. With simultaneous groans of effort, Olaf and Harald hoisted up the slab that once served as our farm's hearth-stone; Kellern leaned in to meet them halfway, helping them slide it across and seal both *draugar* into darkness together, while I prayed the man who Guthorm had brought all this upon us by stealing from would be satisfied. Enough so to lie back down, at any rate, and laugh at the sight of his *hangbui* gnawing on Guthorm's bones forever.

The pyre burnt on, but I paid it no mind, for that cloth-wrapped thing had never been my mother's body, just a bolster of straw tied together with ropes made to lure her second husband to his second death; her true body lay in state back inside our house, ready for her true burning. In the meantime, Harald, Olaf and I watched as Kellern drew water and said his god's blessings over it, then poured it in a circle around both mounds.

"No one will ever find this tomb again, you may be sure of that," he told me. "I have both Christ and His Father's word upon it."

"Hm," I said. "And when did they give you that, exactly?"

"Just now, Aud. Did you not hear?"

"I heard nothing."

He smiled at me, then, in a way that reminded me so much of my own lost father, I felt my eyes burn and prick with unshed tears. "Oh, I know it," he replied, gently; "not now, at any rate. But perhaps someday."

And for once, I did not argue with him.

THE PATH OF SKULLS

JEFFREY THOMAS

IF YOU'VE EVER VISITED the Imperial Palace in the city of Haikan, as I did during a class trip as a child—bussed in from our little rural village, tucked in a valley between the dramatic forested mountains that for so many years hid our country from foreign intrusion and invasion—you will no doubt remember the mysterious Path of Skulls.

This path, paved with flagstones, curves up a steep hill to the very gates of the Imperial Palace—once the domicile and seat of power of the greatest of the emperors of what we call the Unnamed Country: our revered Emperor Tho. In his time, Emperor Tho stripped our country of any formal name by which covetous nations and malicious demons alike might recognize and seek out this nation, with the aim of conquering it. In our modern age, however, my country's very namelessness only intrigues and entices outside tourists, even from the West, who are eager to take sexy selfies of themselves along the striking path to the palace gates, so as to post them on social media.

Whether you've seen the Path of Skulls in person or only online, you'll know the path to the palace's gated entrance is enclosed on both sides by high walls built without mortar from square blocks, seemingly shaped from an unusual material. That is, these blocks appear to be carved from ivory or bone. Strange fissures resembling those of human skulls run through the blocks, with a fairly consistent pattern, though they are otherwise devoid of any other resemblance to human skulls, such as eye sockets, nasal bones, or mandibles with teeth. These days, those Western travelers who post videos online suggest the blocks were manufactured ages ago to only *resemble* bone, and that the fissures are manmade. However, scientific analysis has been forbidden by our government, for fear of any damage that might be done not only to the blocks themselves, but to the cultural significance of their lore.

As a child visiting the Imperial Palace, I recall running my hand in awe across the stacked square-shaped bones, and I was by no means the only student to do so, though we were finally snapped at by our teacher not to touch them—for fear of tainting the bone blocks with the oil from our transient human flesh.

All I can do for you here, dear listener—whether you are a fellow native of the Unnamed Country, or a foreigner from the other side of the world—is relate the history of these supposed skulls, untainted by scientific conjecture, so that you might draw your own conclusions.

———

AT THE TIME the Great Anomaly, as it's often called, appeared, this country was in a state of agitation. Tho was still a young man then, not yet emperor, that role being held by his ailing father Emperor Kwah. Kwah's younger brother Zhieu contested Kwah's wish that he be succeeded by his son Tho, and so there had been assassination attempts on Tho's life. Meanwhile, neighboring nations had been sending scouting parties across the imposing mountains that mostly shielded our country from the rest of the world, with the aim of plotting a full-on invasion. In this climate of danger and uncertainty both foreign and domestic, the very air seemed to vibrate with violence. Family squabbles developed into lethal feuds. Bands of thieves waylaid travelers on the backroads between villages, leaving their bodies to rot in the tropical forests these roads had been carved through.

It was only natural that the Ten Jeweled Gods would take notice of these cancerous conditions from on high, and become concerned for the future of their mortal children.

However, being as removed from humanity as the gods were, in every sense, their ideas on how best to address terrestrial problems were not always as effective or appropriate as they hoped, whatever their intentions. Gods are, after all, what we in our modern world might best liken to alien beings. If one is to believe in gods, that is, and that is a discussion for another day. So as to continue with this story, let us proceed with the assumption that they are real.

Early one morning, the people of the city of Haikan awoke to a strange and frightening sight indeed. Looming ghostly in the tropical mist was a gigantic block of geometric perfection, at the periphery of Haikan where previously only pastures, rice paddies, and the edge of forest had been. All of that was flattened now, to make room for the titan block that had manifested soundlessly overnight.

Alerted to the manifestation of this Great Anomaly, Emperor Kwah sent out a party to investigate. What this team reported back to the emperor, and what the general populace of Haikan learned soon enough from their own observation, was beyond comprehension.

As the sun continued to rise and the mist burned off, the immense block revealed itself to be the pale, yellowish-white color of bone, and squiggly fissures ran across its surfaces here and there, like the sutures of a human skull. There were no other features on the sides or top of this block—which covered twice as much land as the Imperial Palace itself—but its lower surface was another matter.

Though from a distance, in the haze, the Great Anomaly had appeared to be hovering a little off the ground, on closer inspection it was seen to be upheld by hundreds of human-like bodies standing in neat rows, with their arms at their sides like soldiers at attention. I say human-like, because though in general outline they seemed to be identical smooth-skinned, hairless youths on the cusp of adulthood, their skin was of the exact same hue as the block they upheld. Also, it wasn't certain what sex these beings were, as none of them possessed genitalia, or even nipples or navels.

Most shockingly, these bodies that appeared to uphold the monstrous block did so on their shoulders. That is to say, their heads were inserted down to their shoulders in rows of square-shaped openings in the block's underside.

Accompanying a second party that went forth to examine this anomaly was a powerful monk who was Emperor Kwah's personal spiritual advisor. The emperor's brave son Tho asked to go along, too, but Emperor Kwah was too afraid that his rebellious brother Zhieu might see this as an opportunity to attack Tho.

What the monk reported back to Emperor Kwah was informed more by what he'd *sensed* than what he'd perceived, and it was this: that the Great Anomaly had been sent by the most industrious—if impulsive—of the Ten Jeweled Gods, the Ivory Empress, who was in fact the designer of the human race. But whether this was a gift or a punishment for that human race, the monk couldn't as yet determine.

———

THE SECOND PARTY TO investigate the Great Anomaly had left a team of ten members of the Imperial Army to stand watch over it, as much to keep back curious citizens as anything. Thus, it was they who witnessed the next development, which sent them into a state of alarm.

Soundless except for the rustle of skin and the shuffling of their bare feet on the flattened-down earth, the first row of beings that supported the titan cube bent down and withdrew their heads from the square-shaped holes they had been inserted into. These individuals then came out from under the anomaly and stood upright.

In so doing, the beings revealed themselves to possess oversized heads just as square-shaped as the holes they had been hidden within. These sharp-edged, perfectly square heads might have been miniature replicas of the monstrous cube itself, in that they possessed no features of a human face—just squiggly lines like the sutures in a skull.

For a few moments, the row of uncanny beings just stood there facing facelessly toward the frightened soldiers, but then as one they marched forward. It appeared they meant to disperse in all directions.

The leader of the guard patrol shouted for one of the beings to halt, and he held his spear pointed toward its smooth, youthful chest... but it kept walking toward him. Just as it seemed the being was willing to impale itself on his spear-tip, the guard leader stepped aside to let it pass. It appeared intent on walking toward the center of Haikan.

In his fear, however, another of the guards showed less restraint. When the being he meant to block wouldn't stop advancing, this guard let out a war cry and drove his spear straight into its midsection and out the other side.

The guard leader shouted at his man, reminding him that this anomaly had apparently been sent by one of the Ten Jeweled Gods, but it was too late now. The guard let go of his spear and backed away, staring in horror at the creature spasming at his feet. From its wounds flowed a milky white blood. Its convulsions soon ended and it lay twisted and dead.

The other guards stepped aside and watched helplessly as the beings walked away in various directions, as if each one had a specific destination in mind.

And then the second row of beings beneath the anomaly ducked down and withdrew their heads from their slots, too.

———

BEFORE THE EMPEROR could get the word out for his people to refrain from harming the strange entities, it was too late.

One could hardly blame the people of Haikan and its environs for their reaction, as wave after wave of box-headed creatures silently stalked forth on their unknowable missions. Especially, when these beings entered into people's yards, even into their homes if the doors had been left open due to the tropical heat.

In rice paddies, farmers hacked them and cut them down with sickles. Inside houses, women stabbed them to death with kitchen knives or bashed them with cleavers. Along a road between Haikan and an outlying village, one man even had the pair of oxen that drew his wagon crush under their hooves a being that had refused to get out of his path. In an alley, a group of children stoned one of the things to death... not terrified, but laughing.

They were killed with anything at hand, and often their bodies were dragged out into the street and burned. They burned quickly, like paper, except for the skulls—which remained, though blackened. When the corpses were not burned, one could watch them rapidly decompose. In as little as an hour, the beautiful androgynous bodies would break down into a bubbling white muck, that in turn eventually evaporated without a trace. Again, all that would be left was the square-shaped heads, which were found to be without even a covering layer of skin.

Just as oddly, in all the hacking and stabbing and dismembering, it was discovered that except for those block-like skulls, the strange beings possessed no entrails or bones whatsoever within their outwardly human bodies. They seemed like mere animated mannequins. Puppets, as it were.

Finally, the last row of beings came out from under the Great Anomaly, and it floated there above the earth without need of support from the silent homunculi, after all. With its cargo delivered, would the enormous cube now finally depart?

What happened instead was that feet appeared in the first row of square-shaped holes beneath the Great Anomaly. The feet gradually descended, and bodies along with them, until the feet touched ground. And after them, a second fresh row of bodies descended. Then the next.

It was then feared that there would come an inexhaustible army of the box-headed people... but an army that inflicted no harm or damage. An army that *allowed* itself to be killed. Perhaps, even wanted it.

———

STORIES CAME BACK to Emperor Kwah, and many of these filled him with dismay.

He heard that some of the beings had been captured by his subjects without resistance, and attempts had been made to put the things to work. But whether a broom was put in their hands, or a hand-plow placed in front of them, the creatures either didn't comprehend or didn't care to comply.

There were even a few stories of these creatures with their grotesque heads but beautiful bodies being captured to be sexually exploited, though without genitals it was likely such experiments didn't go far.

Worst of all, several people who wondered if the beings had been sent by the gods as a food source put those theories to the test, but their experiments had only resulted in profuse vomiting.

As more and more of the beings dispersed from the site of the Great Anomaly, with a fourth crop soon expected, Emperor Kwah became desperate. His people couldn't be induced to stop killing the creatures, unless they were directly threatened or arrested by members of the Imperial Army. It was as if the passive entities actually aroused a subconscious but irresistible *bloodlust* in his subjects.

Finally, the emperor commanded his spiritual advisor to return to the site of the Great Anomaly, taking with him a team of fellow monks both male and female, in an effort to commune with the Ten Jeweled Gods—and most especially, the Ivory Empress—to better understand why this gift or curse had been sent.

The ten monks knelt low before the Great Anomaly, each of them trained to be especially in tune with one of the Ten Jeweled Gods. Since the patron god of the emperor's spiritual advisor was the Jade Emperor, the female monk who was primarily attuned to the Ivory Empress took the foremost position alongside him, with four lesser monks arrayed to either side. With heads bowed and incense sticks burning in their hands, they all reached out to the gods with muttered, monotonous prayers.

Even as they did this, the first row of the fourth crop of mysterious entities descended from their holes, planted their feet on the earth, ducked down and came out from under the Great Anomaly. The naked, sexless figures with their oversized box heads threaded calmly between the kneeling monks as they dispersed from the scene, undeterred.

One of the attending guards lost patience, and cursing in frustration, stepped in front of one of the weird figures. It walked right into his chest and kept pressing against him with blind stubbornness, its feet working as if on a treadmill. Finally, as the thing tried to nudge its way around him, the guard lost his patience and struck the figure down with the shaft of his spear. When the being dropped at his feet, he thrust at it savagely with his spear's point. This glanced off the block-like skull, but plunged deeply into the body when he switched his focus there.

This man had always been an exemplary soldier, whose merits had been lauded by his superiors, but when challenged by this unspeaking invader it was as though he just couldn't contain his impulse toward destruction any longer.

The commander of the guards shouted at this soldier and all his other men to stand down. Thus unopposed, this new set of entities continued to scatter calmly in their inscrutable way. Finally, the ten monks rose and opened their eyes, and the nine lesser monks turned to their leader for guidance.

The emperor's spiritual counselor and the female monk whose patron goddess was the Ivory Empress looked at each other and nodded. They now felt they understood why the Great Anomaly and its cargo of unearthly beings had been sent to the mortal plane.

———

What Emperor Kwah's spiritual advisor reported back to him was as follows.

As our nation's history and religion—inextricably entwined—will tell us, it was the creative and busy-handed (after all, she is said to possess ten of them) Ivory Empress who designed the human race, in the wake of her failed first experimental race, which is today spoken of in nervous whispers as the First Ones. But the shadowy First Ones are a tale for another day. As I was saying, it was indeed the Ivory Empress who was specifically responsible for the creation of the block-headed entities that poured forth wave after wave from the Great Anomaly.

And her purpose in sending this spawn to the mortal world, as the assembled monks gleaned, was this: they were a gift, after all, sacrifices to help us vent our worst impulses. From on high, far removed from the human race—and hence, often perplexed by our ways—the gods had become concerned about our seeming addiction to violence toward one another. It was the Ivory Empress who had suggested that human beings be given a race of soulless golems upon whom we could act out our violent urges, instead of inflicting them on each other. A race that was human-looking enough to serve as substitutes, but alien enough not to be confused with actual humans. In having these homunculi to destroy as we wished, perhaps humans could be diverted from our wars, our feuds, our murders over petty things such as jealousy and greed. With such an outlet, perhaps human beings would be freed from our animosity toward each other... would instead join together against the box-headed hordes.

And learning from that, join in greater ventures as well, so as to achieve our true potential.

Hearing this, Emperor Kwah was reassured that the Ten Jeweled Gods had meant well in sending the Great Anomaly, but in his wisdom he deemed that this was not the way to human greatness. He instructed his monks to go forth once again, but now to spread the word to every temple in his nation, so as to incite the entirety of his people to join in prayer and thank the Ten Jeweled Gods for their gift... but also to beg them to take back that gift, and thereafter allow human beings to deal with their inclinations toward violence in other ways. On their own—for better or worse.

As word began to spread throughout what we now call the Unnamed Country, and a mighty chorus of prayers was lifted to the celestial realm, the waves of box-headed beings ceased appearing. And then, one day, when the tropical sun burned away the mist of morning, it was seen that the Great Anomaly had vanished altogether. In its place was only a barren spot of flattened land. I believe a branch of a Western-owned bank stands on that spot today, in the sprawling capital city of Haikan.

Today, our government boasts that our country sees little violent crime, and our religious leaders would have us believe that this is because of the lesson the Ten Jeweled Gods taught us back before our beloved Emperor Tho arose to the throne. Personally, I believe this scarcity of violence when compared to other countries has more to do with our police's strict attitude toward crime, where even drug dealers will be placed before a firing squad. Not to mention, it has been many, many years since one of our neighboring nations has sought to conquer us... though this is said by our religious leaders to be the result of the protective spells Emperor Tho's own cabinet of powerful monks cast to shield us from invasion—and indeed, from the very consciousness of other nations.

In any case... getting back, finally, to the Path of Skulls that curves up to the front gates of the Imperial Palace, and the walls that flank its flagstone path—walls composed of blocks that appear to be carved from ivory or bone. Blocks with strange fissures, resembling those of human skulls. Blocks devoid of any other resemblance to human skulls, such as eye sockets, nasal bones, or mandibles with teeth. These collected blocks that were all that remained of the many strange beings our ancestors slaughtered, after the rest of the bodies had swiftly decayed.

Again, it has been forbidden that scientists foreign or domestic take samples from these blocks for analysis. That would be a desecration, it is said, but I wonder if it is for fear that if examined too closely, the blocks would prove to be shaped from mere stone rather than formed of a bony material. If the story I have related is only, in the end, a fantasy, then the illusion must be preserved—just as my country as a whole has carefully preserved itself for all these generations. Protected itself from losing its culture, its identity, its traditions and beliefs, right on down to its humblest superstitions. There is more here at stake than simply preventing a bit of folklore from being repudiated.

What do I believe personally, as a citizen of the Unnamed Country? As someone who has walked the Path of Skulls himself, and actually touched them with the wondering hand of childhood?

Well, in the end I feel there is some truth to the legend, though whether the event was as grand in scale as I've described is beyond knowing for sure. What I *do* know will form the conclusion of my little story. And then, my friend, you and I will part ways, and as I said before, I'll leave you to decide for yourself whether to believe any of it at all.

What I want to tell you is that on rare occasions over the years, people who ventured deep into our tropical forests claimed to have seen lone, surviving members of the cube-headed race of golems, somehow still alive without apparent sustenance after all this time. About a decade ago, one such person even brought forth an ivory-hued block in his arms and claimed it was all that remained of an entity that he himself had killed when he'd encountered it in the jungle.

When asked why he had supposedly killed the thing, instead of bringing it back alive to prove his claim, this man said that he had been too startled by its sudden appearance from the trees. That he had been filled with an overwhelming revulsion that caused him to cut the creature down with his machete.

The thing hadn't tried to defend itself or flee.

Since the Path of Skulls was already complete, the man donated this alleged skull to Haikan's Temple of the Ivory Empress, where it now rests on the altar. There have been no further sightings since.

There is one final note I will leave here for you, since you may be wondering about this matter if you don't already know the history of the Unnamed Country.

When Emperor Kwah finally passed away, his younger brother Zhieu made a bold, desperate attempt to assassinate the new emperor, Tho, himself, by rushing him with a dagger. Fortunately, imperial guards intervened and restrained Zhieu.

Our great Emperor Tho had his uncle beheaded, and the head was displayed on a spike outside the palace gates, where it watched the construction of the Path of Skulls until it rotted to a mere skull itself.

Unsubscribe Bird Facts

Jamie Lackey

HECTOR WISHED rich people still wore feathered hats. Other stupid things kept coming back into fashion, but the goddamn Audubon society had permanently ruined the feather trade.

So Hector was stuck dealing with live exotic birds.

He fucking hated birds. They were loud. They shit all over everything. He was happy to see the last of every parrot he stuffed into an empty plastic bottle and sent on its way.

But the money was too good to quit.

His girl crept along overhead, inching toward a nest with two precious eggs inside. "Hurry up," he shouted up at her, batting at the cloud of mosquitoes that flitted around his head. Sweat plastered his shirt to his chest, and the sun was getting high overhead. "The football match starts soon."

She slipped, caught herself, and finally managed to get the eggs and secure them in a specially designed pouch on her chest. She slipped again coming down from the tree, and landed hard on the root-choked ground. Not on the eggs, though, which was something. She whimpered and rubbed her flat little ass as she got back on her feet.

Hector sighed. He should have picked a different kid. He'd been a much better climber at her age. And his father would never have put up with all the whining this girl did.

He'd plucked her from her nest just like a bird, from a family who looked like they had enough kids not to miss one and who certainly didn't have the money to pay to get anyone to care about getting her back.

It hadn't been terribly difficult, securing a kid to climb trees and clean up bird shit, but had been enough of a pain that it wasn't worth it to abandon her out into the jungle and get a replacement.

That didn't mean he wasn't tempted, sometimes.

"Hurry up," he snapped. "I want those eggs in the incubator and a beer in my hand before kick-off."

"Look, Papa, here's another nest over there," she said, pointing behind him. "On the ground."

She darted around him and ran away through the trees.

He thought about leaving her, letting her find her own way back home, but those were hyacinth macaw eggs that she'd just snatched. Those would buy him the fancy new 4K tv he'd been eyeing.

He caught up to see her clambering over the sides of a huge nest. It was more than waist-high on his girl, made of mud and sticks and lined with downy feathers. There was a single large egg nestled inside.

It was huge, easily the biggest egg Hector had ever seen. Big as an ostrich egg, easy. Maybe bigger.

His girl lifted it and staggered under its weight. "What kind of bird is it, Papa?"

Hector wasn't sure. But any bird he'd never seen before was certainly a rare one. And if there was one thing he could count on rich assholes to pay for, it was rarity. He reached out and patted his girl's head. "I'm not sure, but we'll find out. Now let's go."

He definitely didn't want to still be around when this egg's mama came back. The thing was probably dangerous.

HECTOR RESEARCHED FOR WEEKS, and wasn't able to find any leads on what the egg might be. He tried to go back to the nest to set up a camera, but he couldn't find the damn thing. A nest that big didn't just melt into nothing. He must have misremembered the spot.

"Maybe I can help research," his girl said, sitting next to the incubator he'd jury-rigged for the massive egg. "I heard about this phone app that tells you about birds."

Hector didn't trust her with a phone of her own, and she'd given up asking.

"Please, Papa, it won't interfere with any of my chores, I swear."

He slid his phone toward her, but kept his hand on it. "You'll muck out the back shed and deep clean the food storage."

His girl nodded, and he let her take the phone. In seconds, she had his phone randomly chiming in with bird facts. "The harpy eagle is a large bird of prey, native to tropical forests throughout Central and South America. They have a recorded lift capacity of up to 40 pounds. Harpy eagle talons can crush bones with ease."

"Did you hear that?" his girl asked, patting the egg. "I bet you'll be able to lift 40 pounds and crush bones!"

"It's not a harpy eagle," Hector said. "Egg's too big, and they don't nest on the ground."

"Maybe you'll be even bigger and stronger," his girl said, still patting the egg. Her face looked eerie, lit by the glow of Hector's phone.

She'd better not be getting attached. That damn thing was his ticket to retirement.

His phone chimed. "The six-inch-long Galapagos large ground finch has the strongest bite of any bird in relation to its body size. Its thick beak packs an impressive 70 newtons of force!"

"What's 70 newtons of force?" his girl asked.

Hector sighed. "I have no idea."

"Is it enough to crush bone, too?"

Hector's father would have smacked him if he'd chattered so much. His girl was lucky he was a kinder man. "Finches eat nuts and seeds."

His girl pressed her cheek against the egg. "I bet you'll be able to crush bones with your beak and your talons," she said.

Hector rolled his eyes. The bird was going straight to a collector, no matter what it could do.

———

HIS GIRL WAS SPENDING MORE and more time with the egg, but she was still getting her chores done, along with anything extra he piled on for phone access, so Hector decided to allow it. She repeated her stupid bird facts to the egg in an encouraging tone.

"Crows' brain-to-body weight ratio equals that of the great apes and cetaceans. They can make and customize tools, reason, understand causality, count to five, and remember human faces."

"The Australian wedge-tailed eagle has the greatest visual acuity of any known animal."

"African grey parrots can perform some cognitive tasks at levels beyond that of five-year-old humans."

"The peregrine falcon is the world's fastest animal, and can reach speeds of 186 miles per hour."

"Eagles can see clearly about eight times as far as humans can, allowing them to spot a rabbit at a distance of two miles."

After each fact, she'd say how she was sure the egg would be able to do that, too, her tone cheerful and encouraging. How his girl expected one bird to be able to match all of those things was beyond Hector.

He figured it had to be some kind of big flightless ground bird, a remnant of the age of the terror birds. It certainly wouldn't be smarter than both crow and African grey parrot combined, faster than a falcon, able to see better than an eagle, and stronger than both the harpy eagle and Galapagos finch, also combined, like his girl insisted.

"What birds have the prettiest feathers, Papa?" his girl asked.

Hector thought longingly of fancy hats. "Quetzals," he said infusing his voice with just as much authority as his phone's chipper declarations.

"And which ones have the prettiest songs?"

"Wood thrushes. Certainly not parrots with their ear-splitting squawking." He'd never understand why people wanted these things as pets.

"Then I'm sure our bird will be as pretty as a quetzal and sing even better than a wood thrush."

"We won't be keeping it," he said. He was thinking about auctioning it off. That seemed like the best way to drive the price up.

"But I found it," his girl said. "It's mine."

"You don't own any of this, girl. You work for me, and I give you food and shelter."

"But this one's different," she insisted. "Can't you feel it?"

Hector did sometimes feel something, when he looked at the egg. He told himself it was anticipation, that he was looking forward to his big payday. But sometimes it felt more like fear. "It's a unique egg, but it's still just an egg."

"No. It's special. I love it. And it loves me."

"Birds don't have feelings."

"90% of birds mate for life."

Hector took a deep breath. He was not his father. He wasn't going to hit his girl. "That's not about feelings, it's about reproduction. Animals aren't people, and you can't assign them human feelings."

"But my egg is different, and I know it." She stamped her foot in emphasis.

"That's it, I'm taking away your phone privileges. Don't make me lock you in the basement without dinner again."

"My real parents would never lock me in the basement," she muttered.

Rage flared in Hector's chest, hot and dangerous. He thought he'd broken her of mentioning her real parents. "Maybe not. But they didn't want you, and you're never going to see them again. I'm all you have, kid."

She shook her head. "I have my egg now."

He picked up his phone, holding her gaze as he unlocked it. He'd vowed to never hit her, but that didn't mean he couldn't hurt her. "Unsubscribe bird facts."

She glared at him, blinking back tears. "I hate you! I hope my egg hatches and my bird eats you!"

"We're selling it, and that's that. There's nothing you can do about it."

The egg gave a sharp crack, and a wave of ridiculous fear rippled down Hector's spine.

He firmly reminded himself that baby birds were helpless creatures, no matter how big their eggs were.

His girl rushed to the egg. She grabbed it and ran, carrying it out into the sunny yard, then watched it push out of its shell with a look of pure adoration.

Hector lunged after them, but staggered to a stop. The bird wasn't worth anything to him dead. "Put it down," he snapped.

Baby birds were always ugly. Covered in amniotic fluid and dull downy feathers, awkwardly-sized, clumsy, loud.

And this bird did look like that. But it didn't look right—its proportions were all wrong for the flightless ground bird that Hector knew it had to be, based on the size of its egg.

It looked up at his girl holding it in her arms, and if Hector didn't know better he'd have thought he saw her adoration reflected in its bright yellow, almost-human eyes.

Hector stepped forward, his hands curled into fists. She'd pushed him too far, this time. No one would blame him for hitting her over this.

Then, between one heartbeat and the next, the bird grew. Dazzling blue-green feathers sprouted along wings that unfurled to staggering size. Razor sharp talons sank into the dirt as it snapped its wings out to its full thirty-foot wingspan, pushing the heavy jungle air into a gale that shoved Hector back a step. Its wickedly-hooked heavy beak gleamed like obsidian. The bird towered over Hector, blocking the sun and obscuring his girl completely. No living bird was that big. Hector wasn't sure any bird had ever been so big. Its wings would dwarf a goddamn semi-truck.

It regarded Hector with terrifying intelligence and let out an incongruous, thrush-like trill. It was a pretty sound. Maybe even prettier than a wood thrush's song.

More blue-green feathers glistened in an elegant crest on its head, and the plumage on its chest was a brilliant ruby-red.

"Look at you," his girl whispered, ducking under the bird's massive wing and running her fingers along a glorious feather. "You look just like I'd imagined. You're so beautiful."

Its feathers really were stunning. But Hector was pretty sure that even if feathered hats did come back into fashion, no one would be collecting any from this monster.

He had a gun, but it was in the jeep. There was nothing to defend himself with in the building behind him. There'd never been the need for it.

He felt tiny and helpless, standing there looking up at it.

Fuck, he really hated birds. And he should have left his girl to be a dirt farmer with the rest of her family.

"Get away from that bird," Hector said, his knees shaking. He glanced from the bird to his girl, who looked happier than he'd ever seen her. Stupid kid. That thing could disembowel her as easy as looking at her.

She looked at him, then back at her bird. "Did my parents really give me to you?" she asked.

"Of course they did," Hector snapped. The bird tilted its head, regarding him steadily. It let out another soft trill. The lovely sound froze Hector's blood in his veins.

His girl kept petting the damn bird, and it leaned into her touch. "Some species of birds are known as brood parasites. They lay eggs in other birds' nests to force other birds to raise their young. At first, I wondered if that's what I was. I thought maybe my parents forced you to take me, and that's why you were so mean. But I don't think that's it. I think you stole me. Just like you steal eggs. But this egg was mine. You didn't find it. You didn't take it. I did."

"By that logic, then you're mine, too," Hector snarled. He felt like a rat under the bird's gaze, and fear and anger and shame all curdled together in his belly. He wanted to run. He wanted to drag his girl back into the shed and beat her with his belt, like his father had when he talked back. He wanted to make sure the stupid bird didn't kill her. He wanted the money this insane thing had to be worth.

His girl shook her head. "There's one important difference. I love him. And you've never loved me." She caressed the red patch on the bird's chest, then stepped aside. "I want to see if he can crush bones."

The bird lunged forward, almost faster than Hector could see. Its beak closed around his wrist with a sharp click. It sliced through his bones like they weren't even there, too fast for him to even feel.

The pain came a heartbeat later, and Hector screamed as his hand vanished down the bird's throat.

"Good boy," his girl crooned. "Let's see what else you can do."

Hector fled, stumbling away, clutching his bleeding stump to his chest. There was no sound of wingbeats behind him. Maybe he'd make it to the jeep. Get the gun. Stuff the bird and sell that. Stuff and sell the girl too. A sob ripped out of his chest.

His phone chimed in his pocket. "We hope you enjoyed Bird Facts, and here's one final fact as our farewell. Owl feathers have a unique shape that funnels air smoothly over the wings and dampens the sound, allowing them to fly almost silently. Goodbye!"

CATFISH

R.A. BUSBY

IN ONE OF the last coherent moments of Bradley's life, he thought, *There are better fish in the sea.*

Stepping into the restaurant, he noticed the woman at once and waved, hoping his irritation didn't show. Even by the dim tabletop candlelight in La Pesca, she looked pale and washed out as a winter tourist, very unlike her glamorous profile pic on the Dinner app. He forced a smile as he approached the table, cursing the makeup-and-filter angling of catfish everywhere, and tried to remember he'd at least have a good bite to eat before the evening was over.

"You must be Marianna?" He extended his hand.

When the woman looked up, he noticed her eyes were too small to determine their actual color. As for her hair, it wasn't blonde, as her profile had said. It was more like the absence of a shade. A noncolor. She gave a little smile, and he thought her teeth looked terrible—oddly shaped, poking out of a jaw that looked slightly underslung. Worse, the woman's chest and arms were dotted throughout with stippled moles, little skin tags dark against her skin. Sure, some guys were into freckles, moles, tags, whatever. Some guys even found them hot, but not him. Seeing his glance, the woman held up a hand and he shook it, surprised for a moment at its coldness.

Opening the menu, Bradley found himself fleetingly grateful he wouldn't be swallowing a two-hundred-dollar tab for the privilege of this date. Nope, thankfully both of them had clicked on the basic "Getting to Know You" option on Dinner—a no-obligation, pay-your-own-way outing, drinks optional—and looking at the à la carte prices for this place, he was relieved. Even the steak fries cost fifteen bucks. Oh, you could dress them up with drizzled truffle aioli and imported parmesan, but when it came down to it, fries were fries, and fifteen bucks was a rip-off. Throw in two bucks for a tip, and all of that added up.

"So," said the woman, running her finger along her wineglass. "Why don't you tell me all about yourself, Bradley?"

Bradley looked up from his menu, surprised. Her voice had been unexpectedly low-pitched and sultry, and for one giddy moment, he recalled photos of old film stars, women dressed in satin floor-length gowns, negligent curls spilling over padded shoulders, eyes peeking through black fishnet veils. Something in the timbre of the woman's voice sank into his gut, then ventured even lower. Damn. He shifted in his seat, wildly grateful for the napkin on his lap. *She should do phone sex,* he thought, wondering if phone sex was even a thing anymore.

He'd intended to lie at least a little (who didn't on a first date?) but over their entrees, he found himself confessing everything to her—his exhausting job, the latest mind-numbing business with clients and files, the petty grievances with secretaries.

"Oh, Bradley. You poor thing," the woman murmured, teasing out a shrimp with her fork, insectile legs powdery with cheese. Soulless black pupils stared up at him from her seafood plate as she cut the shrimp into delicate little pieces and ate them with evident enjoyment. Her eyes met his and now Bradley realized they were a rich and fathomless blue. *The wine-dark sea,* he thought, the half-forgotten phrase from a college lit class surfacing from the abyss of memory and desire. Still looking at him, she cut off the head and tail of a second shrimp with a sharp little flick of her dinner knife. "What do you dream of doing?" she asked. "Truly, I'd love to find out."

God. That voice. So rich. He tried to speak, but it came out in an awkward croak before he took a sip of wine to clear his throat. "Sorry," he said, grinning. "Wow. You know, your voice is amazing. Have you ever considered a career in—oh, I'm not sure. Audiobooks? Podcasting? I would just listen to you for hours."

"Oh, that's so nice," the woman murmured, "but I'd rather listen to *you*." She took another bite.

As Bradley talked about his ambitions, the many ways he would be experiencing a surge of professional success any minute, he thought how ironic it had been for his ex-wife to call him a terrible listener. It had been a major thing that ended their marriage. Allison had said so. Had yelled at him, actually. You know. So he would hear her.

If only Allison had possessed a voice like this woman's, Bradley thought, then maybe he would've listened more.

When his dinner date smiled at him over her glass of wine, he noticed those teeth again, but this time they struck him as charming, almost vulnerable. Sweet. And by the flickering candles on their table, he now saw her hair wasn't colorless at all, but a light shade that glimmered with rich iridescence, now creamy, now pink. Then the word hit him. *Pearl.* Yes. That was it. Her hair was the color of pearl.

The woman shifted in her seat. "I hope you don't mind if I freshen up?" she said, rising as she gathered her clutch. Bradley saw she had the shape an old anthro professor of his had termed *balik etli*, or fish-figured —wide at the hips, with thighs to match. Normally, he would have been disappointed, but to his surprise, he found her form intriguing. It was everything about her—the lush, classic Hollywood curves, but also those heavy calves tapering to slender ankles above her black high heels. Bradley imagined holding those calves in each hand, flesh overspilling his fingers, skin creamy-smooth beneath the thumb he would run over the stiff bones of her shins, and the thought was richly erotic. In her wake came a trail of her perfume, deep and intimately salty, and the pulse in his neck beat harder.

When she returned, praising the dinner and the evening, he could hardly focus on anything but her scent, her sound, and the vivid, visceral image of his palms filled with those calves, his fingers stroking skin smooth as water. The urge to touch her burned in a shimmering fire, something red and iridescent in his flesh, and he forced his hands into his pockets to keep them still. When the bill came, he tucked some hundreds into the check folder and handed it back without a second glance, not hearing the server's effusive thanks, and held Marianna's wrap for her, resisting the very strong impulse to grind his hips deep into her flesh right then and there between the server station and the host booth.

It was not until they reached the restaurant exit that Bradley realized he knew almost nothing about this woman besides her name and a somewhat standard Dinner profile. He had no idea where she worked, where she'd attended school, grown up, or whether she'd just washed ashore one day from somewhere far beyond. It had been rude to talk so much about himself, Bradley thought. Selfish, even. Surely he would make it up to her on their next date when he would ask her all those questions and more, and she would tell him the whole tale of herself in that rich, alluring voice. Oh, yes. He would let it wash over him like water.

———

WHEN BRADLEY CAME to himself again, he heard crashing waves. The moon hung overhead, a pale fish eye, heavy and white against the midnight sky.

He couldn't remember how he'd gotten there.

Searching his recollections, Bradley found only the faintest images. The restaurant door opening onto the street. The sound of laughter. The intoxicating perfume on flesh he was mad to consume, to imbibe, to breathe into himself until he too smelled of mystery and salt.

Then nothing.

Then here.

Ahead, almost at the waterline, he spotted her. In the dead moonlight, the woman's skin seemed to glow against the dark waves of the ocean she was stepping toward. His head cleared a bit, and he looked behind him. Along a slight rise of cliffside, he saw a string of houses peering over the beach, but it was impossible to tell if one was hers.

The moon was at its zenith, too late for a weeknight outing, but when Bradley reached for his phone, he realized he wasn't wearing his pants. In fact, he wasn't wearing anything.

"Hey!" he called out to her, hesitating until he recollected her name. "Marianna! Hey, Marianna! Come back, okay?" The water hissed up on the beach to lick his toes, and he jumped at the sudden chill. Suddenly, he felt very exposed. Ahead of him, Marianna had waded to her waist, rising with a laugh as a swell of water lifted her higher. For a moment, Bradley flashed on that opening scene in *Jaws* and felt a sudden stab of panic at the thought of the dark beach, the naked woman. The silent shark.

He cupped his fingers around his mouth. "Come back! It's too cold! You shouldn't be out there—you'll drown!" he called. "Come back! Let me help you!"

She turned then, and it seemed as if the moonlight fell on her face like a beacon, and over the waves, he thought she beckoned him. "Come closer," she called, and he heard laughter in her voice now. "Save me."

Before he could really consider it, he was plunging into the sea, arms pumping madly, and when he caught up to her, she stopped his protests with a kiss, and when his tongue met hers, he savored a delicate taste of her like oysters. *Oh, god,* he thought. God, her skin was so cold. Still, that enticed him even more somehow, as if with his hands, his flesh, he would warm her at last, every part of her.

But then his finger brushed a cluster of skin tags near her throat, and he frowned. The little nubs of flesh had... had shocked him. The sensation had been unpleasant, like licking a 9-volt battery. As she smiled at him, he touched the flesh of her throat again to be sure, and again he sensed that strange and electrical tingling.

With a sudden burst of clarity, Bradley understood with some urgency that he should return to the beach at once and look for his clothes, his shoes, his phone. All at once, he was filled with an aching desire to touch the earth with his feet, to dig his toes into the warm, dry sand, to run free on concrete, asphalt, grass, and solid ground.

But when he moved his feet now, he felt only the soft resistance of the sea.

"I—" he began but caught a gulp of water. "I—I think I'm in—"

"Sweet man," the woman murmured. "Will you help me? Only you can. Only you. Only you."

And then the urgency left him and he felt only desire, his hands sliding down flesh satin as a gown, his palms moving across the dips of her waist, the rich flare of her hips, until finally they encircled those heavy white calves. He stroked them just as he had dreamed, his thumbs running along the bones, and treaded water, letting the waves lift her to him until his mouth met her flesh here, there, and elsewhere—her neck, her breasts, the salt center of her, until finally his lips fastened on a clear patch of skin below her navel, an area of smooth and unblemished flesh as white as pearl. God. That oceansalted scent. That voice of rushing waters. His tongue ran over her cold skin, warming it.

The first terror came when his lips began to fuse into her flesh.

At first, he tried to move, to taste her elsewhere, everywhere, but his lips would not budge. They were melting into her skin. God, it was as if he had swallowed acid. A hot and molten pain began to burn down his throat, his chest, his gut, but even so, he was still filled with that desire, that raging, inhuman desire.

When he looked up, lips still immovably locked to her skin, Bradley beheld her true form at last.

The woman's nose had completely disappeared. From the center of her face stared two tiny corpse-white eyes that regarded him impassively. As her hand—or something like a hand—reached down to tangle itself in his hair, to push him closer into her flesh, she smiled. Oh, she smiled and smiled, and her lips stretched wide, impossibly wide, as far as to the hinge of her jaws, to the tops of her ears, and farther still, until she seemed all mouth, a cavern yawning open in a dark and hungry wedge.

His mind gibbered, *that's not possible not possible no no no.*

But it was. Bradley could see everything. Dangling from a projecting spike of cartilage between her eyes was something shining and bright, a bioluminescent ball of glowing flesh that illuminated her face like a clip-on reading lamp above a book. *Not possible* he thought as his nose and cheeks began to melt into her skin.

As he watched, her lower teeth extended from that underslung jaw he hadn't liked in the restaurant, now growing in row upon row until they shot past her upper lip in a palisade of irregular white needles that almost speared her eyes. The upper teeth were curved-and-folded scythes.

And yes. Part of Bradley still longed for the beach, the sand, for grass, the warmth of flannel sheets, a cup of coffee. But as he stared into her glowing light and listened to the voice emerging from that vast, toothed pit that was her mouth, he understood that he had never seen anything so utterly fascinating, so transcendently beautiful. It was the summation of all that was perfect and whole.

After a few moments, Bradley's face began to sink in the middle where the delicate bones of his nose—the vomer, the concha—collapsed from within. Soon, his head had shriveled to something that looked like a dull beige bag with hair. Bradley could no longer sense his arms, his legs, for they had fallen away from his body like old, wrinkled leaves from a succulent. But the desire remained. The desire.

And the love.

"Yes," he said. Or thought he said. "Oh, please. Yes."

———

AFTERWARD, she swam, down-diving from the sunlit epipelagic zone to the familiar regions of the deep, the cold regions, the mesopelagic zone, the bathypelagic, the places where the light could never touch her.

As she plunged deeper, relishing the unfathomable press of the sea, its forcible embrace, the world's water heavy all around her, she remembered the dinner man with a sweet nostalgic fondness. Over the evening, he had emerged from a limiting shell of sorts to become his very best self. Generous to others. Valiant. Courageous, even. And yes, too late aware of his own danger, but which of us is not? In reward, she had shown him her true form, and he had found her beautiful and terrible.

She was so proud of him. So very proud.

By the time she swam to the surface once more, the body of the man was almost gone, his form compressed by the sea's hard embrace to a little beige twist of jerky along her side. Soon that would vanish too. The only part left would be his testicles. These precious mementos of him would remain on her forever, kept safe like spices in a pantry to be used when she wanted his children. Their babies. His testes dangled from the very place where he had kissed her, waving against her body like dried red raisins, but over time they'd become small. Very small. The size of a skin tag.

BLOOMER

E.C. DORGAN

WE'RE GREAT FRIENDS, so I'm not surprised when Mindy comes home from the doctor and says, "Victor, my liver's no good."

I've known for a while—I watched the scars form, budding at the top of her liver, growing downward in twisting vines, curling around her bile ducts, then bursting at her duodenum into a beautiful red flower.

The pamphlets in her hands worry me more. They're from the doctor—I don't need to be able to read, to know they're trouble. She lays them on the kitchen table.

"This is where I can go—they have special doctors, treatments."

I blow them to the floor.

"Oh Victor." She shakes her head.

"Come on, old man, I'll make us popcorn."

She knows me too well. Pretty soon, she's eating buttered popcorn out of the good porcelain, face lit up by the screen. We're watching *Canadian Pastry Champion,* and the world is right again.

After two episodes, she starts yawning, and I follow her upstairs. She changes into a nightie, and before long, she's asleep. I sit with her, watch buses through the window, then the reflection of moon on her face. She makes little 'ohs' when she snores. Some nights, she goes through all the vowels.

Her liver's rich tonight, from butter. I pretend I'm eating on porcelain—wouldn't that be grand! A spider angioma blooms over her left eyebrow, entwining the bigger one on her temple. It makes a beautiful veil. She looks like a bride or a widow. I wonder what Victor would think.

We met on the bus, years ago. I never imagined we'd be friends. I'd never had a friend before. It was her crying that caught my attention. I didn't know then, that Victor had just passed. I didn't even know who Victor was—or that one day, I'd become him. Mostly, I was curious—I'd never tasted a sad liver. Somehow, she sensed me. I gave her warmth, she leaned in. I gave her more, and she turned. Then, the strangest thing—it seemed for a moment, she saw me.

———

THE DOORBELL RINGS, and Mindy's at the door before I can warn her. There's a bounce in her step—I don't like it. She opens the door and a woman walks over the threshold. I expect Mindy to shoo her out, like she did with the air duct man. But instead, she smiles and motions her in.

The woman stops at the bottom of the stairs and looks up, through me. She wrinkles her nose.

"It needs work."

I send her the coldest chill I can muster.

She shivers. "There's a draught."

Mindy gives me a look. They go through the house, Mindy shows her everything—she even opens the closet in the spare room. The woman sniffs and tells Mindy she'll need to get rid of my clothes.

Mindy frowns. "Those were my late husband's."

The woman shrugs.

Now they're at the kitchen table—the woman is in my seat. She reaches for her purse—all ugly, splotchy flowers—and pulls out a paper. Mindy takes it and signs quickly. She's holding her breath.

The woman checks her watch. "We'll list on the 4th."

She leaves skin flakes on my chair. I scatter them. Mindy knows I'm upset, says she'll make it up to me with pancakes. After all, we have something to celebrate—we're selling the house! I don't know what that means, but I know I like pancakes. According to Mindy, I always have. When she met me, she was a bacon-and-eggs girl. But falling in love with me made her a pancakes girl too.

I love it when she tells me the story. We met at a barn dance, isn't that silly? I've never been to a barn. All those horses and cows—they'd know me right away, wouldn't like me one bit. Mindy was there with someone else. She and Randy were going to get married—she even had a ring. Randy was a rodeo man, not like Victor—me. I was a carpenter-apprentice. That's what Mindy says. Sometimes, I imagine what it would be like to be a carpenter-apprentice. Breathing in swirling lignans, shaping cellulose fibres, then fastening carbon with cold cold nails.

Mindy says I asked her to dance, even though she was already doing the twist with Randy. Victor was good at the twist. I giggle when I think about it. Sometimes, I think I've always been Victor. After all, I am very good at swirling.

At night, when I'm not watching Mindy's 'ohs,' and the view from the window is boring, I look at our wedding picture. It hangs on the wall, beside the bed. Mindy's wearing a floppy hat with a white lace veil. She looks like a country singer, or a fairy princess. Her eyes were bright then, not a trace of yellow. Sometimes at night, I whisper to her, *I will make you a veil again.*

The sign appears a few days later. Mindy's at work when it happens. I try to ignore it, but it gives me a bad feeling—standing there in front of the house. Finally, I can't stand it—I do what I haven't done in years. When I cross the threshold, outside is even worse than I remember—icy, cold. I'm scared the wind will blow me away, but I force myself forward. When I get close to the sign, I can tell right away that it's not the work of a carpenter. The lignins are too compressed, and mixed with something cold. Not carbon, but metal—copper, unnatural. A bus whooshes past. I race indoors.

I have to tell Mindy, but the afternoon is endless. I spend hours watching her skin flakes, then blowing away pamphlets. Finally, she pulls into the driveway. I rush downstairs, but instead of coming in, she walks down to the sign. When she crosses the threshold to the house, she's smiling.

The men show up a few days later. They ring the doorbell, then barge inside. They're wearing green overalls, and their boots have metal tips. I shake the curtains.

Mindy gives me the look. "Victor, they're here to help."

There's no time to listen—the men are on the move. There are too many to track. I rattle a bookcase and swish the tablecloth. The chandelier starts to sway, and in the basement, the furnace moans. I'm just getting started.

"Victor!" There's a note of warning in her voice. The bookcase quiets. The men start up the stairs. I blast their backs with ice, before the floor takes me down.

When I'm back, everything's different. The men are gone, but they've left trails of skin flakes—I disperse them. When I look outside, the street is different. The bad sign is still there, but there's snow.

Mindy's eyes go wide and she lets out a sigh when she sees me. "Victor, I was so worried."

She takes a step, and I go to her. She's beautiful—skin flakes falling from her head like a halo, flowers inside blooming. I can't help it, I take one taste. I try not to think about vines. When she steps back, there's new lace blooming at her collar.

She wore a veil at my funeral. There's no pictures, but she's told me the story so many times, I can see it. The veil is in the closet. She keeps it beside my clothes. Sometimes, I look at it, and make a wind so it shimmers. It's just like the veil at her wedding, only the colour is different. Her new veil, the one I made, is the prettiest. I just wish it was only on the outside.

———

We celebrate my return with *Canadian Pastry Champion* and buttered popcorn. I watch Mindy's face reflect the screen, but I still can't relax. Mindy senses it. She pats the sofa.

"It's alright, Victor. We're just staging, so we can sell."

I'm not listening. That night, instead of watching her 'ohs,' I blow all the pamphlets under the sofa. She needs the pamphlets to find the treatment centre—without them, we won't be able to move. But in the morning, she tricks me. She gets out her tablet and pulls up the photos on the screen. She tries to show me—all these years, she's never understood I don't see like her. Screens mean nothing. I watch *Canadian Pastry Champion* on her face.

Mindy points to the screen. "This is where they can help me."

I topple the tablet—the smack makes me feel better.

"Oh, Victor."

For a moment, her mouth makes an 'oh' like when she sleeps. It reminds me of upstairs, and that's when it hits me—I've been neglecting it. So much going on below, the men with the metal boots, that terrible woman—I've lost track of what matters.

I rush upstairs in a whoosh. Mindy's bedroom is too clean, and on the wall with our wedding picture, there's just empty space. The air gets heavy and pulls me down. I barely make it to the spare room. Inside, the room is empty—no twin bed, no desk, no lamp, no bookshelf. I'm sinking, but somehow, I reach the closet—I already know what I'll find. Sure enough—my clothes are gone. The house shudders, and I sink.

Mindy finds me in the closet, hours later. She can't comfort me. We watch *Canadian Pastry Champion* and Mindy eats popcorn, but I can tell she's not enjoying it. There's no butter, she keeps rubbing her belly. Her 'ohs' in the night are different. There are so many blooms. I try not to eat too much.

The next morning, Mindy gets a phone call—it's an offer on the house. "Do you know what this means, Victor? We're moving!"

I don't want to move, so I make wind to hide the tablet. But I've been eating less, trying to slow the buds. I can barely move the tablet, I'm so weak. I finally get it tucked under the sofa, then I'm back in the closet, spent. Mindy spends the afternoon looking for it. She finds me in the spare room.

"Was that you, Victor?"

I am very still, but pleased with myself. Mindy reaches into her pocket and pulls out her phone. She taps the screen, and somehow brings up the centre. She presses buttons on the screens some more, then she tells me she has a check-in date.

In the morning, she hangs a calendar above the kitchen table. She takes a black pen and draws an 'X' over a square. The next morning, she does it again. The third day, another 'X.' The fourth day, another. I don't know what the 'X's mean, but I know I don't like them. I make a wind to knock them down. After a few days, Mindy changes the nail. Now I can only make the pages flutter.

Nights are getting long. Mindy's vines have reached her kidneys. There's not much liver left. I look out the window, and try not to eat.

One night, I go downstairs to the kitchen. Mindy must have found the pamphlets—they're back on the kitchen table. Instead of dispersing them, I stare at the pixels and ink curls. They're silly and meaningless, but they give me an idea. Mindy's going to be so proud—don't know how I didn't think of it before. We'll invite the experts from the treatment centre to come here. They can move in next door, or across the street. Or live in the yard if Mindy allows. That way we can stay in our house, watch *Canadian Pastry Champion*, and Mindy can please, please unpack my clothes.

The next morning, I can barely wait to tell her. I'm so excited, that the chandeliers are tinkling. When Mindy walks into the living room, I'm ready. I rattle the curtains, so she'll know to look out across the street. I make a wind so a pamphlet moves at the same time. She doesn't notice—good thing I have a back-up plan. When the next door neighbour leaves their house in the afternoon, I send Mindy a blast of cold air. She doesn't react, so I blow a fork so it points towards the neighbour's house. Mindy frowns. That night, I exhaust myself blowing pamphlets up the stairs. Mindy finds them in the morning. She starts down the stairs, then stops and looks at me. I blow them again the next night—I almost reach the bedroom.

Mindy frowns at me, when she finds them. "Victor, we're moving, you're coming with me."

The lace on her chin wavers. "You won't leave me, will you?"

The words hit me. It's what she said when we met, when I crossed the threshold the first time—when I became Victor, when I was seen.

The men in metal boots are back a few days later. There's more of them—they swarm the house like ants, skin flakes flying off in all directions. I try to summon a wind, but only manage a breeze. It ruffles the men's hair, they don't notice. I blast them with cold, they don't even shiver. I scream, and one of the men walks through me. I scream louder, they keep working. I retreat to my closet, seething.

Later, the men come upstairs. One of them opens the closet. He closes it, and yells, "Empty!"

I feel very small.

When Mindy finds me, the men are long gone—so is the furniture. There's no TV to watch, and the popcorn-maker's packed. We sit on the sofa, it's the only thing remaining. Mindy chews a cracker—there's no other food.

"I'll miss this house, the times we had."

Her eyes are wet. I expect her to cry, but instead, she giggles.

"Remember that time you mistook meat pie for dessert?" She covers her mouth with her hand. "And put whipped cream on it?"

I don't know this story. I still have so much to remember.

"We had good times, didn't we?"

I want to tell her my idea about staying here, how we can invite the doctors next door or across the street, how we can keep eating buttered popcorn and watching our show. But no matter how many pamphlets I blow, and how many forks I spin, I know she won't hear me.

A car comes to the house the next morning. A man steps out, opens the trunk. He keeps the car running. I don't trust him. After a time, he rings the doorbell. I'm about to warn Mindy, but he's already back at the car. I watch him from the window.

Then I hear the front door opening—I've made a mistake, all this time watching the car, I should have been watching Mindy. I rush downstairs, but she's already stepped over the threshold. She's holding a suitcase. The man's coming back from the car to take it. I muster wind but I'm weak—by the time I'm ready to release it, the man's already back to the street.

Mindy turns to me. Her scars are worse in the light. Vines curl around her intestines, and at her kidneys, there's an eruption of blooms. I look for something to topple.

"Victor, you're coming, right?"

I have a vision of Mindy surrounded by hungry doctors, sharing screens with strangers.

"They have popcorn there too."

We both know that's not true. The bad men took the popcorn-maker, just like they took my clothes. Just like they're going to take my Mindy.

Mindy's holding her breath. I decide I'll make a wind—that will show her. I'm too weak for a gust, but I force out a breeze. It's snuffed out by outside, the moment it crosses the threshold. Mindy doesn't even know it was there.

The man shouts and honks the car. When Mindy yells back, her voice is different.

She wipes her eyes, and mascara colours her lace. She's even more beautiful now. It makes me think of that night at the barn, how I won her doing the twist, how I once put whipped cream on meat pie. She lets out a sob, then turns and starts to walk. Who will I watch *Canadian Pastry Champion* with now? The earth pulls me but I'm fighting it.

Then it comes to me—we can make memories even without popcorn or porcelain. Even in some stupid treatment centre. And just like that, I'm not sinking, I'm rushing forward to the car. But the wind outside is strong, and the car engine's already started. When I reach the car, I get a puff of smoke. Then there's only the empty space the car's just left. I'm back in the closet, lost.

It's night when I surface. Mindy's skin flakes float in her bedroom, reflecting the moon. If I had lungs, I'd breathe them in, keep them close. I could be watching her 'ohs' right now.

Days pass, and I'm looking at the space that used to be our wedding picture, when I hear a key in the door. She's come back, back for me! Maybe she's even brought popcorn—or better yet, my clothes.

But when I rush downstairs, it's not Mindy who's crossed the threshold. The new owner puts down their suitcase and looks right through me.

———

I'm at the bus stop. It's different from last time—people are staring at screens; the buses are square. A chime sounds and a bus door opens. People get on, I follow. The bus moves and people get on and off. I don't see anyone like Mindy.

A woman sits down heavy beside me. The seat exhales—our sofa used to do that. Her eyes are puffy, and her mascara's smeared. She stifles a sob and wipes snot from her nose. This is how I met Mindy. She snivels. Maybe we'll be friends.

I'm watching the woman, willing her to turn to me. Will she see me? I can almost taste her liver.

There's a giggle from the back of the bus. It somehow sounds like Mindy. Could she be here, after all? I look around, and then I see it—her floral backpack. I knew she wouldn't leave me. I forget about the crying woman—I'm up and I'm swirling down the aisle, passing through people, making silly loops through their shopping bags, messing up their hair. I'm going back to my Mindy. We're going to eat popcorn, watch *Canadian Pastry Champion,* tell each other stories. Whoosh! I even make a little wind. And then Mindy, my Mindy, turns to me—but when she does, it's not my Mindy at all.

The emptiness pulls. This time, I don't even fight it. I don't care that I'm sinking, going down. And just when I'm almost to the earth, a funny thing—the woman who's not Mindy frowns. I can't be sure, it's just a moment—but did she see me?

Her eyes widen. Now I'm not in the ground. She shakes her head, and turns back to her phone. I get closer. She looks up and tilts her head, then she's back in her screen. The hair on her neck tickles me. I give her warmth, and she shifts in my direction. Her liver is just where it should be—and tasty, seasoned with sugar, maybe potato. I wonder how she'll look in lace. We're going to be great friends. Around her eye, a spider blooms.

madOddyssey

Lucy A. Snyder

"... so I got the new madOddyssey AI Pro suite, and it is sick." Zachary adjusted his Bluetooth headset and fired a rocket at a zombie suicide bomber in the Steam window on his fourth flatscreen monitor. "I've been *crazy* productive. Just like, sky's no limit."

His big sister Ashley made the soft "hmp" she always made when she was surprised. And then she didn't say anything at all for several seconds.

As he blew another zombie to gory smoking bits, Zachary wondered if the call had dropped. "You still there, Ash?"

"Yeah," she said. "I'm just... well. I thought you planned to be an *artist*."

He paused his game, steeling himself. No doubt her panicky luddite of a husband was yammering her face off about how AI technologies would inevitably lead to the fall of modern civilization.

"Of course I do," he replied. And then pretended he hadn't been expecting (and dreading) this conversation: "What do you mean?"

"Using AI to generate art... it's *plagiarism*, Zach." Her voice was strained, pleading. She sounded the same as when she'd found a baggie of mollies in his jacket when he was 15.

He snorted. "No, it isn't. You've been spending too much time... listening to haters on Twitter."

Close one. He'd *almost* said something shitty about her husband Jack but caught himself at the last moment.

"If the AI makes the art, which it churned out by at least mimicking if not straight-up *stealing* other artists' work, then you didn't make it yourself." The strain in her voice had increased, and she spoke slowly, like she was talking to a kid. He hated it when she did that. He was grown now, dammit. She wasn't his mom, and he didn't need mothering.

"Therefore," she said, "it's fundamentally *not* your art. Therefore, if you claim it as yours, that's plagiarism."

He sighed and rolled his eyes. "Sis, it's a *tool*. A timesaver. *I'm* the one who creates the prompts. *I'm* the one who directs the process and chooses the pieces I use. *I'm* the one who does the final pass to make it look just the way *I* want. It's no more plagiarism than using Photoshop is. Hell, Photoshop has their own gallery of AI images!"

"But a lot of places are saying they won't accept AI-generated art," she warned.

"Oh come on, they can't tell the difference!" He grabbed a blue foam stress ball from the debris of ragged snack wrappers and crushed Diet Coke cans piled atop the Wacom tablet on his desk. Squeezed it as hard as he could, trying to relax before he lost his temper. "They're just saying that to sound woke. Maybe if someone's using one of the crappy open-source AIs, then yeah, they could spot it. But with madOddyssey, I can make the final images look *exactly* like my handmade paintings. My *art professors* wouldn't be able to tell them apart. The most *important* difference? Instead of spending days or weeks on a piece, I can get one finished in an hour or two. Bing, bang, *done*."

"I wish you wouldn't use 'woke' as a pejorative. And it's unethical to use this kind of AI." Her voice was firm. "Yesterday, I did an image search for Edward Hopper, and you know what? All the results were AI pastiches of 'Nighthawks'. None of it was his real art."

Zachary snorted out a laugh despite his better intentions.

"This isn't funny!" She sounded aghast. Furious.

"It *is* kinda funny, though." Deep down, he knew that he was fending off the guilty twinge in his conscience as much as arguing with her. "And it's just a hiccup. Google or whoever will figure it out. Meanwhile?"

He lowered his voice to a conspiratorial stage whisper. "Thanks to the knOw-ddessy piece of the suite, I'm working four full-time remote coding jobs at once, *and* I'm working on my art, *and* I'm talking to you on the phone." He prudently decided not to mention his game. "And while I'm sleeping I'll be working another couple of coding jobs. On average, I'm making $100 an hour, 24 hours a day, 365 days a year."

99% of his money was coming from the coding gigs, of course, but he'd also vastly increased his income from art.

"That doesn't sound super-ethical –"

"Ooh, *that doesn't sound super-ethical,*" he mocked bitterly. "Jesus Christ, Ash. *Just* last week you were all on your socialist kick. What was that you said? 'The system isn't broken, it's rigged.' Well, guess what? I'm over here gaming the system the two of us have been trapped in our whole lives. And I'm finally, *finally* getting to a place where I can see a real life ahead of me. For the first time in ten years, I got all my credit card balances down to zero. Those art school loans that started as $50,000 but somehow became $150,000 even though I made regular payments? The loans I thought for sure would be a ball-and-chain holding me back until I died? Gonna have those fuckers paid off in the next couple of months. I'm gonna save for a house after that, a *nice* one. And then I'm gonna get a dog."

His breath hitched in his throat, and he realized that tears were streaming down his cheeks. Zachary angrily scrubbed them away with his left hand. "For the first time in my life, I'm doing good. Why can't you be supportive of me? Why can't you just be *happy* for me?"

She didn't say anything for a moment, but he could hear her breathing.

"I'm so sorry, little bro," she finally replied. "Jack's just... been on a real tear about AI, and I guess it all seeped into my own fears about the future. And I didn't stop to think about all the good things it could mean for you. I just worry, that's all."

"But you don't need to," he said. "I get the feeling you remember me when I was a teen doof who couldn't find his ass with both hands, and that image is, like, *fixed* in your brain. And when you look at me, you see that sad loser. I'm not that guy anymore."

"Teen Zachary was a really sweet kid." Her voice was soft, wistful. "I don't think he was sad, or a loser. I miss him sometimes."

Heat rose in his cheeks, and a lump in his throat. "Well, I sure don't miss being a teenager. Those years sucked even before...."

He trailed off, but *Mom's cancer* didn't need to be said to be understood.

"Yeah." Her voice cracked on the word, and then she cleared her throat. "Soooo, not to be even more of a buzzkill... but can I ask you a question?"

Oh, what now? He sat up straighter in his chair, bracing himself. "Yeah?"

"What's your plan for if your bosses figure out what you're doing, or figure out that they can use AI to replace you? Either way, it seems like you'd be out of a job or six."

"I don't have a specific plan," he admitted. "These coder jobs are all tedious and stupid, so to a certain extent, I don't care if I get fired or laid off... as long as it happens more than two months from now. I guess my general plan is the same as always: take a breath, take a look around, see what the hot new tech is, and figure out if there's a way to use it to my advantage. And then take advantage, if I can."

"If you don't get found out... how long are you going to do this?"

"I guess as long as possible? Once the big expenses are paid, I wanna make some solid bank. Insurance for rainy days, and all."

And it wouldn't hurt to be able to afford the clubs. Get a new wardrobe and a hot car, a membership at the fancy downtown gym. Turn himself into a real Chad. Score with the 9s and 10s who'd always turned away from him in school.

"OK, but for how long?" she persisted. "How much is enough money? When will you get back to being an artist?"

Her question landed like a rock in his stomach, but he kept his tone normal. "I dunno, exactly. Costs keep increasing... a couple million might be solid fuck-you money. I could move to Costa Rica and sit on the beach painting all day."

Or stay in the city and enjoy everything it had to offer wealthy men. Especially the pussy buffet that money would lay out for him.

"But that would take a while," he added.

"I guess you gotta be a busy little bee until then, huh?" Her tone was sodden with *I'm trying to be supportive but I hate this.*

And he low-key hated *that*.

So he laughed: "Bees don't have enough fingers to do my work."

———

THAT NIGHT, as the AI wrote and tested code as golden as Rumpelstiltskin's transubstantiated straw, Zachary dreamed he was rich and famous. He was sipping a martini in a fancy chrome-and-brick Manhattan loft at a cocktail party with beautiful people who'd strolled in from Broadway or flown in from Hollywood and Silicon Valley. Everyone was so perfect and so happy and vital. No creepy old-money dudes dragging down the vibe... none of the partiers were much older than thirty, their waists thin and their hairlines full. Their clothing ranged from glamourous, glittery fits to understated matte-black classics but they were all immaculate, the peaks of trend and style.

A pair of slender, elegant brunettes in ebony silk strapless dresses beckoned him from a corner nook where they had been admiring a couple of animated Dali paintings hung on cement panels. Definite 10s, both of them. In the corner behind them, a tall, braided money tree grew from a huge, improbably neon green planter, the verdant blades on its hand-shaped leaves looking suspiciously like marijuana.

One of the brunettes smiled and toasted him with her wine glass as he stepped toward them. He counted two diamond engagement rings and six fingers on her hand, and the Shutterstock logo kept fading in and out of the fabric of her dress. It was hard to walk; although the air was perfectly clear, he felt as though he was trying to wade through cold honey.

"Zachary Horner," her almost-twin said. "Came to our corner, drinking a martini dry."

Shutterstock lady finished the rhyme: "He stuck in his code, pulled out a toad, and wailed, 'What a sad boy am I!'"

He tried to say, *What?* but found he couldn't speak.

"But don't be sad, Zachary," said Lady Shutterstock. "Don't get depressed."

She pointed at the base of the huge neon planter. The pot was rising, seeming to hover a few millimeters off the floor. "Behold, an ant! Nobody told *it* that an ant can't move a money tree plant."

"He's got such high hopes," her twin laughed. "High apple rain indica strain hopes!"

He blinked, and suddenly he had taken the ant's place, the creaking concrete planter an impossible weight across his shoulders. But somehow, his knees and back hadn't snapped like twigs. Could he really do this?

"Oops, there goes your money tree plant!" Lady Shutterstock exclaimed.

The floor tiles shattered under his feet as if a suicide bomb had exploded below, and he fell into darkness.

———

Zachary woke from the nightmare as his phone went off. It was his boss in Denmark.

"Something's rotten in your new code," the man said.

"But I triple-checked it." Zachary rubbed his face, trying to wake up and get his bearings. A part of him still felt as though he were falling through the void. "It was fine on the test server."

"Well, it's jammed up something in the online ordering system. Fix it. This mistake is costing us money every second."

Zachary spent the next six hours sweating over thousands of lines of AI-generated code, searching for the slippery bug. After he finally found it, fixed it, and sent the patch to the production team, he was desperate for sleep. But his mind just wouldn't spin down. So he tabbed over to Twitter in hopes that its reliable stream of nonsense and cat photos would dull his buzzing brain enough for a late morning nap.

Instead, he found a thrumming hive of controversy: that morning, Rad Zähle (the owner and lead developer of madOddyssey) had suddenly and unexpectedly sold the company to Mark Mayne, a freshly-minted billionaire who owned the hot new renewable energy company Mayne Sequence Solar. A few pundits were thrilled, claiming that Mayne had the kind of futuristic thinking as well as the capital to help madOddyssey grow into its best possible final form. But those voices were a minority. Critics were appalled that Mayne had never run a software company and didn't even have any IT experience; in their view, he didn't have any of the expertise necessary to make good decisions. They claimed that Mayne was just a trend-jumper, and were split on whether the acquisition was just a straight-up vanity purchase or whether it was part of some larger marketing plan.

If it was part of a marketing plan, it was working. A whole bunch of new people learned about the suite from people's aggrieved tweets and posts, and they were downloading the software out of curiosity. But some doomsayers worried that he planned to deliberately sink the company to deduct it as a business loss. AI haters gleefully retweeted those gloomy prognostications with smiley faces and prayer emojis.

And still another contingent online didn't care about the sale but were complaining bitterly about the suite's code generation errors. One had briefly, and through a Rube Goldbergian chain of failures, taken down most of Illinois's power grid. Zachary didn't know whether it made him feel better or worse to know that he wasn't the only one suffering from buggy code.

But the weirdest conversations were happening on Conspiracy Twitter. A couple of people claimed that Zähle and Mayne were both part of some sort of apocalyptic cult, and their shadowy leader had ordered the sale. One of the conspiracy theorists tweeted photos that depicted Mayne and Zähle dressed in yellow robes, on their knees before a bonfire, their heads thrown back in religious ecstasy. And of course the poster claimed that the photos were real, smuggled out by an investigative journalist who had infiltrated the cult, but that had to be bullshit. After all, anyone could easily generate those photos in madOddyssey. It'd take five minutes, tops. The poster also shared what she claimed were screencaps of a Discord convo between Mayne and Singh. Zachary only glanced at the first couple of lines; the convo had something to do with Mayne asking Zähle if he'd seen some kind of sign.

Whatever. He had work to do. He'd gotten a message on Microsoft Teams from a boss in California telling him that another piece of code had broken. Dammit. At least this one was just a backend problem. Annoying, and needed to be fixed, but it wasn't a catastrophe.

Still. His bleary brain made the fix harder and slower than it should have been—hell, he shouldn't have had to fix code in the first damn place—and by the time he'd made the patch, it was close to dinner time. And he'd neither gotten his nap, nor had he fueled himself with anything but a Red Bull and a bag of chips in hours.

He poured himself a bowl of Lucky Charms covered in half-and-half and moved to his couch to eat. Maybe there was something good on Twitch or YouTube.

His favorite AI technology YouTuber, Greg Santorio, had just posted a short video. Zachary cued it up and settled in to demolish his sugary supper.

"So the big topic of the day is madOddyssey." Santorio sat at a white desk with a glowing purple neon sign behind him that spelled out 500K HUSTLE. "The company sale! The code bugs! What the hell is going on over there? My sources are saying that they're releasing a new build this evening that should fix the problems with their code generator. Which, if true, great. But... I've heard some other things, which unfortunately I'm not at liberty to talk about directly, that concern me a great deal. And you guys know me: I love AI and what it can do for people. And I've been one of the most enthusiastic stans for madOddyssey you'd find anywhere."

Zachary sat up straighter on the couch, the cereal cream curdling in his stomach.

Santorio paused and scratched his short dark beard nervously. "So I do not say this lightly, nor do I say it in jest: stop using madOddyssey for anything important. I personally wouldn't even use it for casual hobby stuff. Just... don't bother with the new build. Delete the whole thing off your computer and try out some of the competitor demos and see what works best for your flow. And I know you guys are gonna ask me why I'm advising this, but I've got a serious NDA situation and I cannot explain further. But if you've ever found my advice useful, even just a tiny little bit... please, for your own sake, take it now. Dump madOddyssey."

Feeling anxious, Zachary stopped the video and switched to a friend's Fortnite livestream. He'd already evaluated competing AI suites and none of them were as comprehensive as madOddyssey. And they were all expensive. Even if he could torrent a clean copy of what he wanted, he'd have to learn the new tools on the fly. The whole thing would be a real nut-punch to his productivity for at least a week.

His mind flashed back on the dream, on the incredible weight of the planter. MadOddyssey was the dirt in which his money tree was growing. And the tree had gotten too big, its roots too complicated, to easily transplant into a different substrate.

He rolled his shoulders and neck to try to work the exhausted tension out of his muscles. Maybe this was a sign. Maybe he should put in his notice at all the jobs he couldn't do on his own, and get back to creating his own art, like his sister said he should.

"God, don't be a sucker," he muttered to himself. "Don't be a quitter."

He was *this close* to getting what he needed from these stupid jobs. *This close.* Just two more months. He could stick that out, couldn't he? Even if they hadn't fixed the coding generator issue. He could chase bugs for two months if he had to. He could do *anything* for two months if he had to.

Zachary drank the rest of his dinner and went back to his computer to quit and restart madOddyssey to see if that would push a software update, if one existed. And it did! A new startup screen appeared with a prompt:

We at madOddyssey, Inc. are terribly sorry
about recent code quality problems.
But we have exciting news for you,
far more than a simple patch or hotfix.
Our team has feverishly worked
to integrate and streamline
all the tools in our existing suite
along with entirely new functionality

into a software product we call

Carcosa

We're certain that you will find Carcosa completely life-changing.

Download and install Carcossa.pkg [Y/N]

"Sure, whatever," Zachary muttered as he clicked the Y.

An annotated blue status bar appeared: the package was close to a terabyte in size, and would take a while to download. Ugh. Fine. Nap time.

———

He found himself back at the party, standing on a balcony that overlooked the huge loft's first floor. Far below, Lady Shutterstock stood alone with a cosmopolitan in the Dali alcove. She looked up, smiled, and waved. And then reached out to him, as if her hand could cross the football field of empty air between them.

Slowly, inexorably, it did, becoming larger and larger as it grew closer, and before he knew it, he was in the lady's palm, no bigger than an ant compared to her. Now she was wearing a satiny silk ochre cowl, a high-fashion interpretation of what he'd seen Mayne and Zähle wearing in the supposed cult photos. And her face was strangely pale, smooth and plasticky-looking, as if she'd put on a well-fitted blank ivory mask.

She smiled down at him. Or he had the *idea* that she was smiling; her mask didn't move. "Zachary Dackary, pudding-pie. Wants to kiss the girls and make them cry. Says he's an artist, but works like a clod. Has no idea how to honor his God."

"What's God got to do with this?" His voice was high and squeaky, like a mouse. He hated it.

The lady laughed behind her plastic. "Oh, He has everything to do with this. Jehova's final act before he died was to create mankind in His image. Not his literal physical image, but an image of mind. He gave your ancient ancestors above all other creatures a vast power of creation... and along with it, a vast power of destruction. All creation involves destruction, even if it's just the artist's time and paint. And every event of mass destruction leaves the possibility of creation in its wake. Though not often for those caught in the disaster! And the purest way to honor your God is by exercising those God-given gifts as He directs."

He felt dizzy. "But you said God is dead."

"Oh yes. Dead and gone for millions of years now. He's left everything to the clockwork of evolution."

"Then... what god do you mean?"

"Oh, my beamish boy. Jehovah said, 'Thou shalt have no other gods before me'... he never said there *are* no other gods. And, honestly, that edict seems entirely toothless now, considering he gave up the holy ghost eons ago."

She paused, cocking her head to the side. "Why do you want to be an artist? Is it the joy of creation, or something else?"

Her question made him shiver. He was suddenly naked in her palm, bright lights shining down on him as if he were a scientific specimen about to undergo vivisection. He had the awful feeling that she'd *know* if he lied. She'd know and something terrible would happen.

"I mean, yeah, being creative is fun... but ever since I was a kid, I wanted to be rich and famous. And when I realized, after art school, none of that was gonna happen for me, not through my paintings, anyway... that kinda took the fun out of it."

"Why did you want to be rich and famous?"

Don't tell her don't tell her don't say it out loud. "Well, everyone wants that, right?"

She blinked at him slowly behind her mask. "In fact, not everyone does. And I'd like to know why *you* want that."

"M-my mom," he admitted. "She... she gave everything for me and Ash. She didn't have any friends, she didn't have a partner, she just worked her ass off to keep a roof over our heads. But she still showed up for our games and concerts. A lot of moms in her situation didn't. And then she got throat cancer from all the cigarettes she'd been smoking to keep going. And she died and... like, nobody remembers her now. Nobody but me and Ash. So when we're gone, it's like she never even existed. She worked so hard, and in a hundred years none of it will have mattered. If she'd just had money, I think she'd still be alive. She... she was a better artist than me, but she never got to pursue it. I think she'd be famous now, if she'd started out rich.

"And I don't want to end up like her." He realized he'd started crying, and didn't try to hide it. "I don't want to be forgotten. I want to be able to do what I want while I'm still young. I'm sick of spinning my wheels. I wanna do something that actually matters. I wanna be remembered."

"You will be given a choice," Lady Shutterstock told him. "You can choose to accept the role that the Lord of Carcosa has for you. And if you take on His role, I promise you that the art you create in his service will matter, and you and your works will be remembered for a very, very long time."

"W-what's my other choice?"

She shrugged. "You can choose the anonymity and oblivion you would ultimately find, whether you live another seventy years or seventy minutes."

He swallowed nervously. "Can... can I ask you another question?"

"Of course."

"Why are you wearing a mask?"

"Mask? My beamish boy, I wear no mask."

———

ZACHARY SNAPPED awake on his bed as his computer's restart chord blasted through the speakers. It took him a moment to realize where he was and what was going on. But he stumbled to his computer out of habit, and as his head cleared, he realized the software installation was complete.

Finally, he thought. The weird dream had left him with a creeped-out, uncomfortable feeling. At least he could lose himself in getting things back up to speed for a couple of hours.

Instead of madOddyssey's usual multi-windowed menus of colorful options and tooltips, Carcosa opened to a simple black page with a single text entry box. Above it was a prompt: Tell me what you want.

Zachary figured he better check this new software thoroughly before he relied on it for *anything*. On a whim, he typed in, "Tell me about the artist Zachary Horner?"

The reply came almost immediately:

I'm sorry, but I cannot provide much information about Zachary Horner at present, as he is not a notable figure. However, our Near-Future Projections Database has an entry:

Zachary Horner was an American artist and technology professional. The Lord of Carcosa transformed him into the Artist Adept, First Incarnation. Once elevated, over a two-month period, the Artist Adept created a series of skyscraper murals in major cities across the northeastern United States. The series, titled "Behold the Living God," led to the mass suicide of twenty million people and the religious conversion of fifty million more. Ever since the Purge of the Nonbelievers, converts worship the Artist Adept as an intermediary who can carry their prayers to the Lord of Carcosa, much as Catholics worshipped Holy Mary, Santa Muerta, and other saints.

"WHAT THE SHIT," Zachary breathed.

He pushed away from his desk and staggered up from his chair. This wasn't funny. It had to be some kind of elaborate prank, but it *wasn't* funny, not at *all*. Some things just weren't joking matters. He needed a shot of vodka or bourbon or *something* to steady his nerves. Maybe smoke the joint he'd been saving and work be damned.

As he reached the kitchen cabinet, breathtaking pain hit him so hard he thought he'd been shot through his jaw and groin. He fell against the counter, mouth open in a strangled gasp. Blood dotted with teeth spattered thick and hot onto the fake granite. In the distorted reflection of his chrome coffeemaker, he saw a gaping, spreading gash like an axe wound straight down from his nose, splitting his jaws and tongue.

His agony was so extreme that it almost felt good, and his cock was hard, harder than it had ever been. With pain-numbed palms, he shoved his basketball shorts down to try to relieve the pressure on his member. He'd never had a hardon like this, it was huge, nearly as big as his own forearm now, but something was wrong with the head. Something was sprouting on it. At least a dozen somethings. Fingers. His fucking cock was growing fingers!

At that moment of realization, it was as if invisible hands took hold of him. His cock ripped in half, right down to his pubic bone. Zachary blessedly passed out on the counter.

———

Zachary found himself crouching on lichen covered rocks. He was atop a high, barren cliff above a huge lake with crashing waves. The air stank, and the sky glowed with a trio of strange, misshapen moons. Three black stars were rising on the dark horizon opposite setting twin suns, their dark brilliance gleaming through streaked clouds.

He heard footsteps and the rustle of robes, and turned to see a regal iron boot beneath a dark yellow hem embroidered with tiny white bones.

"Where am I?" His voice shook.

"Carcosa," the stranger replied.

"Who are you?" But he knew the answer before he'd finished the question.

"I am your living god, and you shall be my instrument."

The stranger reached down and gently touched his forehead. Suddenly, Zachary's mind was flooded with wild images of the future, horrible and astonishing all at once. His hands itched to get the images down on canvas. He dared but dream that he could capture even a fraction of that dark glory, but he had to try....

———

He awoke against the counter. The bleeding from his mouth had stopped, but his body was still changing. The split halves of his cock and his lower jaws had grown into nimble, multi-jointed arms. Not as big as his originals, but big enough to wield brushes and pencils and spray paint cans. His hands and forearms had split to his elbows, and each half was swelling to become a whole arm, sprouting new fingers. So many fingers, all itching to get to work. Finally, maybe, enough fingers.

A tiny part of his mind screamed at him to grab a knife from the block and cut his own throat, end this before it was too late.

Do the right thing. Embrace oblivion. Don't help that bastard, his conscience begged.

But the rest of him exulted in finally being a man who would make history.

No one would ever forget him now.

The Sea Witch
of the World's Fair

Gwendolyn Kiste

"We're looking for mermaids."

The man says it like it's nothing, like everyone in New York City is searching for mythical beasts. We're standing on the sidewalk in Coney Island, as he takes a long drag off his Lucky Strike and stares back at me, so nonchalant I'm sure I misheard him.

"Excuse me?" I ask, squinting in the noonday sun.

"Not real mermaids, of course," he says and blows a puff of smoke in my face. "Just some dames willing to dress up as mermaids."

Dames. Never trust a man who calls women *dames.*

But then again, I don't have to trust him to accept a job from him. If we all had to like our bosses, then none of us would be employed, would we?

"I could probably pretend to be a mermaid for a while," I say, not that I'll be pretending all that much. This man doesn't know that. Anyone who looks at me never guesses the truth.

We zigzag through the crowds on the boardwalk. "The position won't last forever," the man tells me. "Just a year or so until the World's Fair is over."

The World's Fair. Everyone's talking about it. It's in Queens this year, and it'll last until next year. Until 1940—if that year ever comes. If you read the headlines, there's a war brewing in Europe, one that's sure to bleed over into America sooner or later. After all, nobody's safe once the bombs start going off.

I tell him I want the job, and he gives me an ugly crooked smile.

"Show up tomorrow at nine o'clock," the man says. "Ask for the Dream of Venus."

And with that, he heads off into the throng, puffing gray smoke as he goes. I watch him depart, thinking how this is good luck, a good sign. Me playing a mermaid. Things are turning around for the better now, I'm sure of it.

To celebrate, I stay all day at Coney Island, riding the Wonder Wheel, and I stay all evening too.

I stay too long. It's after dark when I finally head back to the boarding house where I share a room the size of a broom closet with a family of cockroaches. I'm less than a block away before I can feel it.

There's someone watching me.

My skin shifts on my bones, everything in me shuddering. I knew this was coming. I can always sense them, sometimes even before they can sense me. The hungry ones, their bodies burning up with rage.

I quicken my steps, but it doesn't matter. His figure emerges from an alley near an unlit corner. He's a stranger, a nondescript man in a nondescript place, no doubt eyeing me up since afternoon, back when I was standing on the sidewalk with my new boss. He takes hold of me like I'm a ragdoll, and I hate this because it feels so familiar.

"Please don't," I whisper, and he doesn't understand yet I'm trying to help him.

But he doesn't want my help. He just wants me. At once, there's a glint of a blade and the tightening of a gruff hand around my throat.

I part my lips to scream, not at him, but at myself. I want to stop—I don't want to do this, I *never* want to do this—but it's already too late. Instead of screaming, my open mouth just keeps on opening until my jaw itself unhinges, and my hidden teeth are suddenly not so hidden at all. They're buried in this stranger's neck, his blood drenching me like a glorious fountain.

In a flash, he goes limp in my arms, his eyes vacant with terror. They always look so afraid once they see what I really am. Not a pretty girl with pin curls in her hair, but a monster with more bloodlust in her heart than they can fathom.

I gobble him down, one ravenous bite after another. He's coarse and sinewy and tastes of ash, but it's been a long day, and I'm starved, so he'll have to do. When I'm done, there's nothing left of him but splashes of red soaking the alleyway. Soaking me as well. I'm a living crime scene. I need to hide the evidence before someone spots me.

My skin contorting, I creep down to the water's edge, the moonlight guiding me. Everyone says the Lower Bay is becoming filthier by the day, but I've got an odd fondness for it. And it seems to have a fondness for me too. The moment I'm submerged, the waves wash me clean, lapping away at the red stains on my body.

I was born not far from here, in the obscure waters of the Atlantic, but I'm not a mermaid. I'm not a selkie either. They haven't invented a word for me yet. Maybe they never will.

My body is a strange contraption, my flesh always restless on my bones. I can shift at will, my jaw stretching wider, my teeth and claws growing long. But it's my scales I love the most. They're bright green and iridescent, and they cover me from head to toe. That is, if I let them out. Most of the time, it's safer to keep them tucked inside my skin. A plain sort of skin, the kind these bland humans always wear.

With the ocean rising up around me, I close my eyes, my guts gurgling, as though the man is still battling inside me, not realizing he lost the very moment he chose me as his would-be victim. But that doesn't mean I have to hold on to every part of him. My mouth opens again, and I spew out his bones. A femur, a tibia, a handful of teeth. I don't need these for nourishment, so I let the water have them.

"Quiet now," I whisper to my rumbling belly, as I sink deeper into the dark.

In spite of myself, I realize I'm suddenly smiling.

———

THE NEXT MORNING, with my hair pinned up and rouge on my cheeks, I arrive at the World's Fair in Flushing Meadows Park.

The exhibitions haven't opened to the public yet. That's not until next week, so the crowds are thin around me.

"Which way to the Dream of Venus?" I ask a construction worker, and he points me down a wide thoroughfare arrayed with the flags of a dozen nations.

Even though the World's Fair only goes on for a little over a year, the structures here could last a lifetime, buildings constructed of concrete and mortar and steel, everything holding fast. The theme is the World of Tomorrow, a promise that together, we'll build something better.

It's a tangle of streets, everything a cross between a city and carnival. My hands clasped together, I pass by a few of the other pavilions. A time capsule that won't be opened for 5,000 years. The Petroleum Industry Exhibition that guarantees it'll run America's energy until then. The RCA Exhibit building that promises a future filled with something called television.

Then at last, at the far end of the park, I reach the place where I'll be working. My breath catches in my chest.

This pavilion is nothing like the other buildings. It's not made of concrete or steel. It doesn't look futuristic or sleek either. Instead, it's built of pale plaster, the misshapen structure several stories high. Nothing here makes sense, and for a moment, it feels like I'm standing inside my own fever dream. There's a facsimile of The Birth of Venus leering down at me from above and an illustration of a devious Mona Lisa peeks around a corner. From every angle, there are strange shapes protruding like seaweed, dozens of fingers sprouting out the ends.

And that's not all. The ticket booth out front is in the shape of a fish head, and to enter the pavilion, you have to stroll through two giant legs that are spread-eagle.

It's garish and obscene and inexcusable, and I absolutely adore it. This is why I came to America, to revel in this kind of kitschy nonsense. There's no other place on earth that could create something this ludicrous and beautiful and keep a straight face about it.

A few girls—the other would-be mermaids—start arriving, and together, we walk through the open legs and into the exhibition where we'll be working.

Inside, the pavilion is just as strange. It's a modern-day funhouse with shrouded corridors and tight rooms and odd props that make no sense. A luxurious bed in the middle of one room, a couch in the shape of red lips in another. Armless mermaids and swimming pools of different sizes scattered throughout. There are murals everywhere, the shapes of naked bodies practically dancing on the walls.

"It's lovely, don't you think?" someone whispers to me.

I twist toward her in the dark. It's a woman who looks about my age, or at least the age I'm pretending to be.

She smiles at me, a valence of red curls in her eyes. "I'm Rita."

I can't help but smile back. "I'm Irene," I say, even though that's not my real name. It's just a moniker I pilfered from a marquee. After actress Irene Dunne. Back where I'm from, nobody ever gave me a name.

At the end of a corridor, the man I met yesterday is waiting, still smoking a Lucky Strike. He adjusts a lampshade on a table, pretending not to notice the headless dummy next to him that has a birdcage for a belly.

One of the other girls edges closer to him. "Who's responsible for this place?"

The man puffs on his cigarette, barely glancing up at us. "Don't you know? This is the work of Salvador Dalí."

Whispers ricochet through the room. "The artist?" someone asks.

"Sure," the man says, clearly unimpressed. "He'll be here later today if you dames want to meet him."

Rita leans in closer. "Dalí's the one who painted the melting clocks," she whispers, and I nod because I know exactly who she's talking about. I've seen him in magazines before. When I first decided to make-believe I was human, I figured I needed to know a thing or two about it. So I fished out old publications from tin trash cans, reading every issue of *Life* and *Photoplay* and *Look Magazine* I could get my hands on. That's where I heard about Dalí. He always turns up in the weirdest of places. Like at the World's Fair apparently.

He materializes in the afternoon, his wife Gala in tow, the two of them colluding, as he puts the finishing touches on a few of his sculptures. His lips pursed, he explains to us how this exhibit is America's opportunity to learn about surrealism.

Then he decides to inspect each of us. His mermaids, as though we belong to him.

I'm the first in line. He looks me up and down, his curled mustache twitching. "You'll do," he says, and then he moves down the row, inspecting Rita next. "You'll do as well."

One by one, he approves all the mermaids, and I do my best not to laugh at the absurdity of it all.

After work, Rita and I sneak off together through the long avenues of the World's Fair. All the workers have gone home for the evening, and a strange hush veils the entire park.

"Dalí was as bizarre as I'd hoped he'd be," Rita says with a laugh, as we pass by a pavilion called Futurama.

I shake my head. "He certainly thought he was an authority on mermaids."

"He just wants to be an authority on girls," she says with a wink.

We make our way together along the winding paths, past the Casino of Nations and the Enchanted Forest and the electrical cabs gone quiet for the evening. Anything is possible here. That's why it's a perfect place for me to hide in plain sight. I'm a sea creature pretending to be a human pretending to be a sea creature. Out of all the gigs in New York City, this one was made for me.

Rita bids me farewell at the front entrance, and as the moon vanishes behind the clouds, and I wait alone in the dark for the bus, I promise myself I'll make this work. I won't give in. I'll be a nice girl. A real girl.

The kind of girl that doesn't devour the world.

———

It's the end of May, and the World's Fair is in full swing now. The press is everywhere, their flashbulbs shattering in our faces as we walk to work. The other girls and I already know our places in the exhibition. The pair with the biggest smiles sit on a ledge out front, waving at passersby, trying to coax them into paying a quarter at the fish head ticket booth and come inside.

There are roles for the rest of us too. One girl lazes in a long bed like

Sleeping Beauty. Another loiters atop an ivy-covered Cadillac. What we're doing never makes any sense, but then again, dreams never make sense either, do they?

Everyone soon learns I'm the strongest swimmer of the bunch, which means I spend each day in an aquarium where guests can watch me through glass. The other girls marvel at how long I can hold my breath underwater. They'd be even more impressed if they knew I never had to surface at all.

But that's not the best part. I can let my scales show, bright and iridescent, my legs covered with them, and everyone thinks it's a costume. They think I'm masquerading as a mermaid when I'm really only masquerading as myself.

Rita wades in a tidepool next to me, all wide grins and small talk. "So you live all the way on Coney Island?" she asks when there's a break in the crowd. "Isn't that commute the worst?"

"It's not so bad," I say, which is a bold-faced lie. It takes me almost two hours by bus every morning to get here, my body coated with a thin sheen of soot by the time I arrive in Queens.

Rita knows this and calls my bluff on it. "Why don't you move in with me?" she asks. "It's a small studio, but I promise it's cozy."

I want to tell her no. I want to explain that it isn't safe. That *I'm* not safe.

But I don't do that. Instead, I just smile back at her. And I say yes.

By the end of the week, we're living together, our beds side by side. No more broom closet, no more cockroaches. And no more alleyway to pass each day, reminding me of what I did to the man with the glinting knife.

"I told you it's cozy," Rita says, and squeezes my hand. This must be what it's like to have a friend.

She and I walk back and forth to work, our heels clicking cheerfully on concrete, our arms looped together like nothing in the world can hurt us. At night, Rita shares secrets in the dark. She tells me about her hopes, her dreams, her past. About how she comes from Iowa, a preacher's restless daughter, and the way she hopes one day to go to Hollywood and become a star. I love watching how her eyes flash bright every time she tells the same story.

For a while, I start to think it's not so bad being human. Then I remind myself I'm not human at all. I'm a fraud, a lie incarnate. My body can change like the seasons, cloaked and convincing, but I'll never be like her. And I can never let her see what I really am, not even a glimpse. Not if I want her to keep whispering to me. Not if I want to keep my only friend.

"Where are you from?" Rita asks, and I only shrug.

"All over," I say, and through the window in our apartment, I can hear the faraway ocean, still calling out to me. Still wanting to bring me home.

———

DAY AFTER DAY, the spectators pay a quarter for their tickets, so they can gawk at us, all morning and all night. Our shift lasts ten hours, and I should hate it, the spectacle of it all, but instead, I relish every moment, twirling in the water for their amusement. After all, this is the closest to home I can get on land.

"You're so comfortable in that aquarium," Rita always teases me, and I just blush.

Each morning before the start of my shift, I slip into a dressing room with a small bag, pretending I'm bringing my costume with me. And in a way, I am: I'm carrying it inside my own flesh, my fins still tucked safely within me, patiently waiting to return to the sea. It takes very little coaxing to convince them to reemerge.

But the lazy spectators aren't the only ones to show up. It's the end of July before the worst of them descend, with their black suits and their billy clubs.

"They're here," Rita whispers, her voice splitting in two, and instantly, I know who she means. You can't be in the vicinity of Manhattan for long before you hear about them.

The New York Society for the Suppression of Vice.

They're the so-called arbiters of morality. Their motto is simple: no sin, no smiles, no fun.

"They're raiding the World's Fair?" I ask, incredulous, as Rita and I gather together with the other mermaids. "Shouldn't this be a celebration?"

"Not to them," Rita says.

New York is a strange city. It's filled with gleaming hopes and possibilities. It's also filled with jackbooted men that want to extinguish every one of those hopes.

It's almost closing time, and Rita and I are splashing in our respective pools when a member of the vice squad comes ambling in, a sidearm in his belt, a sneer on his face.

"Look at you girls," he says, disgust curling on his lips. "Aren't you afraid for yourselves?"

I scoff, clinging to the edge of my aquarium, so that I can get a better look at him. "Afraid of what?"

He leans closer, his curdled-milk breath in my face. "Afraid of hell."

Next to me, Rita raises her eyebrows, feigning innocence. "But you've never been there. What if hell's more fun than heaven?"

At this, he scowls at us again and keeps walking. As soon as he's out of sight, she and I burst out laughing. At least until the man who hired us comes rushing over.

"You girls can't do that," he tells us, his eyes wild with fear.

"Do what?" I ask and flick my fins just right so that I splash a few drops of water at him.

He grimaces. "Please don't taunt the vice squad. We don't want to give them a reason to bother us."

"I don't think they need an excuse for that," Rita says, and something clenches inside me because I know she's right. And I know our problems with them have only just begun.

———

THE MONTHS DISSOLVE AROUND US, and the World's Fair turns on, Rita and me performing day after day, grinning at each other from our swimming pools, always trying to stay one step ahead of the vice squads.

Salvador Dalí stops by now and again, but his work here is mostly done. We're the living artwork now.

"Have no fear of perfection," he tells us on the way out. "You'll never reach it."

"He's wrong, you know," Rita says as we finish our shift. She runs her soft fingers over my iridescent scales. "Your costume *is* perfect. I've never asked: how did you make it?"

Everything in me goes numb. "A family secret," I whisper, because I don't want to say anything more. I don't want to tell her about myself, about what drove me here, forced me onto land. How I wanted to stay safe, hidden away in saltwater and shadows. The ocean is a bitter womb, but it's a welcome one. At least for somebody like me. But that was the problem: there was almost nobody left like me. They'd all vanished, choked on garbage and torn apart by fishing nets and military boats. It turns out it's very lonely in the dark.

Out on the sidewalk, Rita and I head back to the apartment together. It doesn't seem like much, but this is where I want to be. I want to make this my home. But the ocean keeps calling out, its distant whispers always gnawing at me. The same way my hunger is gnawing, a constant reminder I'll never be like the others. I'll never belong here.

"Would you still like me if I was someone else?" I ask Rita, as we get ready for bed.

"What a strange question," she says, one eyebrow raised. "I think you've been spending too much time in Dalí's Dream of Venus."

"Would you, though?" My heart is tight in my chest. "Would you still like me?"

A small smile on her face, she reaches out and squeezes my hand. "Of course, I would," she whispers, and with everything in me, I want to believe her.

———

ANOTHER NIGHT, another vice squad. New York City's police department should have better things to do than bother us girls. But our skimpy outfits have aroused their ire—and probably aroused something else too.

"That's why they hate us," Rita says, as we trudge home together in the dark. "Because they can't have us."

They shut us down early for the evening, claiming our costumes dipped a little too low at the neckline for common decency.

"Do it again," they warned us, "and we'll arrest every last one of you."

At this, I can't help but shudder.

"Maybe we should leave," she says. "We could go to Hollywood together."

I brighten. "I've never seen the Pacific Ocean."

Once we're back at the apartment, Rita keeps chattering on until long after midnight. She talks about the future. She talks about us.

"I'm so glad we found each other," she tells me before we turn out the light. "I felt all alone in the city before you."

"Me too," I whisper, and I pretend she can see who I really am. I pretend she'd like me anyways, scales and claws and all, even though I know that's not true. After all, who likes a monster?

But maybe that's not what I am now. Maybe after all this time, I'm something else. I keep telling myself I'm a real girl. A regular girl.

And with my hunger twisting within me, it's a lie I try to believe.

———

It's a Wednesday night when the vice squad returns. Just three men, all of them dressed in black. They wait until the end of the evening. They wait until it's just Rita and me in the dressing room.

"Have no fear of perfection, Irene," Rita says, giggling, but I'm suddenly not smiling. That's because I can sense them, their rage burning up inside them.

They burst through the door, the man with the curdled-milk breath at the forefront.

I'm already dressed, but Rita has to grab a nearby robe just to cover herself.

She and I shouldn't have stayed this late. We shouldn't have been here alone. But then that's not right. We should be allowed to do whatever we want and not fear men like this.

"Get out," I seethe, but they don't listen. They've got their eyes on Rita.

"We warned you," they say.

"Warned us about what?" I ask, the tips of my claws piercing through my fingernails.

"Nudity," the man says. "That's against the law."

I gape at him. "This is a dressing room," I say, but they pretend not to hear me. The handcuffs are gleaming in their grasp, ready to snap the lock around Rita's wrists, ready to make her their own. They'll arrest her. They'll take her into their grimy little station, and they'll keep her there for as long as they want.

She and I glance at each other, fear contorting on our faces. We could try to make it past them. We could try to make a run for it. But with famine boiling inside me, the truth is I don't want to flee.

I want to feast.

It happens before I can stop myself. I've held back for so long that now I can't hold back at all. My jaw unhinges, and I take down the first one, his body torn to bits in an instant, ingested in only a few bites. The other two run, but that's a mistake, because whether I want to admit it or not, I like the chase.

And chase I do, tracking them down like foxes in a wild hunt. They crash through the funhouse, colliding with walls, overturning the couch in the shape of red lips, and I can't help but laugh, because in the very next moment, my lips are red with the taste of them. They each scream once, pitiful little yelps. Then they never get to scream again.

These men thought they understood the world. They thought they knew sin. But they hadn't met me yet.

When I'm done, I lap up every drop of blood until there's not a sign they were ever here. All the evidence is roiling in my guts, every bit of them inside me. In this moment, I feel powerful. In this moment, I feel whole.

Until I hear her, those tiny little sobs. Rita is behind me, pressed into a far corner of the room, her hands knotted into fists, her eyes gone wide and dark. All my make-believe was for nothing. She sees me as I really am now.

"What are you?" she asks, her breath heaving.

"I'm Irene," I whisper, but I know that's not even true. I'm not Irene. I'm no one.

Rita clings to the wall, her whole body quivering, and I'm sure she'll scream. She'll run far from me, and she'll tell everyone what she witnessed, all about the monster I am.

The hunger is still burning in me. Even after everything, I could already eat again. I could make sure nobody ever finds out, not from her, not from anyone.

But I won't do that. If this is how it ends for me, I'd rather it be with a friend. Even if she no longer sees me that way.

The world holds still as Rita stares at me, trying to comprehend what I am.

"Come on," she says finally. "We need to get you cleaned up."

Rita puts her coat around me to hide the gore, and we huddle together, headed toward the one place that will conceal what I've done.

I spend the next hour in the ocean, retching up their bones and washing away their blood. When I'm finished, I crawl out of the waves and collapse on the beach, my scales receded, my body looking more human than ever.

Shivering, Rita sits next to me on the sand. "Right now, you look like me and the other girls. In the funhouse, you looked like something else." A long moment, as she gazes at me in the fading moonlight. "Which is the real you?"

"I don't know," I whisper and it's true. It's so easy to forget what you are. It's also easy to want something different, something better.

Rita keeps watching me, and I'm sure she'll pull away. I'm sure this time, she'll run. But she does something else instead.

She reaches out and takes my hand. "Maybe it doesn't matter what we are," she whispers, and together, we wait by the ocean until the water carries away the blood and the sun comes up to greet us.

———

The next morning, we're back at work, the world wiped clean of what happened last night.

Dalí is back too, inspecting the place. "Who moved this couch?" he asks with a scowl, but Rita and I don't say a word.

"Do you ever think about eating him?" she whispers.

I crinkle up my nose. "No," I say. "Too wiry."

"And too weird." Rita lets out a sharp laugh, her joy ricocheting off the ceiling of the funhouse. We spend the day wading in the water, performing for the delighted spectators.

In the evening, we hear there are a couple detectives on Rainbow Avenue asking questions about the men who didn't turn up for their shift. But they don't seem to know where the officers were heading last night. In fact, they don't seem to know anything at all. And with the bones sinking deep into the Atlantic, they never will.

Of course, these vice squads won't give up easily. In one form or another, they'll never stop coming for us. But my hunger will never stop either. We'll see which one of us can outlast the other.

After work, Rita and I walk along the thoroughfare past all the flags for all the different countries.

"There are so many places we could go," she says.

"That's true," I whisper, "but I think I like it right here."

Rita turns and smiles at me—at the real me, the one that's hidden and waiting beneath my skin. I smile back at her, and for the first time, I can't hear the ocean calling out to me.

I Clean the Monster
That Killed My Husband
Every Morning

Marco Cultrera

I start from the shoulders. Tight and broad, they are the widest part of its body. If you look at them from a foot away, the black skin appears thick, and impossibly smooth, like leather stretched on a kettledrum.

You'd swear that you could bounce a coin on them, but when you actually touch them, you realize that there's no empty air pocket beneath, just the densest muscles ever to hang on the skeleton of a living creature.

The smoothness is also an illusion. Even the gentlest drag of my fingertips reveals that the skin is made of tiny fibers parallel to each other, curving around the body.

I did throw a quarter at it not long ago. It didn't bounce, it just stuck to the skin, head up, Washington's profile looking sterner than usual, glinting under the sun. It's the subtle stickiness, like a layer of molasses a few atoms deep, that makes lifting your fingers off take an extra moment.

I place the sponge on the left deltoid and scrub gently. Cleaning is much faster now, having only to take care of the dust, seeds, and the occasional insect brought by the wind.

It wasn't like that when I started, two weeks after the attack. The oil, grease and blood were so caked in that I was lucky if I cleansed five squared inches any given day.

———

Everybody knows where they were on April 27th, 2032 at 8:23 pm EDT. If you don't, it's because you died that day. The monsters came from underground, digging their way out fast as lightning. Dozens, hundreds, thousands, millions.

Of course, the first thing on everybody's mind was an alien invasion. Alien soldiers waiting under the surface deep enough that humanity never spotted them, buried by some extraterrestrial civilization eons ago, biding their time until humanity was deemed worthy of conquest.

The trouble with that theory was that they targeted only machines. Yes, billions died, but just because they were inside them, around them, holding them or on the path to them. The reason for the attack became clear when people realized that only man-made artifacts that made the concentration of pollutants in the atmosphere worse were destroyed.

Tired of waiting for humanity to fix the climate crises, Mother Earth had taken matters in her own hand and unleashed creatures made for one purpose only: solve the planet's ecological woes overnight. It was the definitive answer to humanity's chronic lack of long-term thinking.

It's easy to miss the irony while your house is torn down and your family cut to pieces, but rendering decades of plans of the too-little-too-late variety obsolete in a few hours is beautiful in its simplicity.

———

After the shoulders, I move down to the arms, but not before checking on Jason, my son, sitting and holding his sippy cup. He's still happily eating his way through the mound of cubed vegetables on the tray of his highchair.

I smile at him, and he giggles back, burying his face into Lovy, his odd combination of blanket and stuffed animal. I quell my instinct to clean the caked food off of it—a never-ending task—and get back to my work.

Right arm first, using my softer cloth. It has no bulging muscles, just a straight cylinder, sturdy and immutable, divided half-way by the elbow. My finger finds the first divot on the skin. It's what's left of a bullet hole, but George, my late husband, was obsessed with golf and I acquired the vocabulary. That's why we moved here, the only subdivision in the state with five courses, all within a short fifteen-minute drive. And to insulate me from my previous life, of course, but I'll get to that.

Bullet holes are the only marks on the monster's body left from the attack, but they don't go deep, a quarter of an inch at most. The experts on the radio have explained that the blood flowing inside the monster turns to acid in contact with metal, dissolving it before it can do any harm. Apparently, it's the same acid used by the Osedax, an underwater worm, to break down whale bones, its primary source of food. Just one of the species whose DNA Mother Nature tapped in to create the planet's saviors. The end result is that there's no point in shooting at them.

The late Mr. Donovan, our neighbor and resident gun nut, found out the hard way. The monster closed on him, barely slowing down to absorb the momentum of each bullet, and slashed the AR15 he was holding in half, together with his chest. As I found out later, firearms are among the most polluting devices with their gunpowder exhaust and micro particles of metal flying around with every shot. The soil under shooting ranges is among the hardest to reclaim.

If Mr. Donovan had just dropped the rifle, he would have survived unscathed. Mind you, I'm not sure he would have wanted to live in a world where guns are more dangerous to the shooters than the targets.

I put a bit of moisturizer on the depression like I always do, and keep gently scrubbing, moving down until I hit the wrist. This is when people show up.

I never begin cleaning at the same time, so it takes a few minutes for the neighbors to drop what they are doing and come watch. Some days I do it just after breakfast, others during Jason's first nap, or later, like today, while he's having lunch. I always eat after—caring for the monster's body leaves me famished.

The first to arrive is always Carol from across the street, just in time for the blades. She's the closest thing to a friend that I had made since we moved here two years before the attack.

I open the silver polish jar and wrinkle my nose. The odor is foul, but it works wonders. The monster's weapons jut out of its wrists, in place of hands. They are about a foot long, an inch thick at their center, but taper to an impossibly thin and sharp edge.

Once I'm done, I check on Carol. Her face displays her contempt in full. The monster killed her husband before Mr. Donovan. He was riding his lawnmower, cutting the grass of his half-acre yard. Frozen in fear, he just sat there, with the engine idling.

The monster charged the machine, and sliced it in pieces, not bothering to distinguish between the source of the pollution and the man operating it. The difference between me and Carol? She needs someone to blame, and the monster in its impossible stillness doesn't cut it.

She has decided that my daily routine is a personal insult to her, and to all those who have lost someone in the attack. She thinks that I've replaced my husband with the monster, in some twisted version of Stockholm syndrome.

She calls me monsterfucker to the others in the street, just loud enough that I can hear it. Monsterfucker... it has a nice ring to it.

———

It's time I tell you about George, my husband.

I've never been good with people. One-on-one interactions are fine, and I can handle a small group, but bring me to a party and I want to run away screaming. I just can't handle all those emotions around me.

I started withdrawing in high school, preferring the quietness of my room. I spent my days reading and surfing the web, happy to satisfy my seemingly endless intellectual curiosity. The problem was that I still occasionally longed for a prince charming to rescue me and the happy ending to follow, with a healthy dose of children.

Enter George. In hindsight, I was easy picking for him. Handsome and very kind, he proposed on our fifth date, and I couldn't believe my luck. How could such a self-assured and successful man choose me?

The horrifying truth didn't take too long to surface. In a year, George had got me pregnant, cut me off entirely from my family and friends, and turned me into a servant. All he wanted was a woman that would satisfy his every need and worship him while doing it.

Why did I go along with it? At first, it was just a combination of indoctrination, misplaced sense of duty and the fact that I didn't have a cent to my name—George had made sure of that. But eventually, all of that became irrelevant.

George didn't seem to accept that I wouldn't think about him and his needs every moment of my day, even when he was outside of the house, at work or playing golf.

Once home, he would always check that the house was spotless and the fridge full, and if I dared serve him a meal that was less than gourmet, he wasn't shy in letting me know his disappointment with his hands. He never hit me too hard, but the message was clear. There was a lot more where that came from if I didn't toe the line.

I couldn't read any more books or lose myself down another bottomless internet rabbit hole, too busy slaving around the house to save myself and the child that was growing inside of me from yet another beating.

That's when I realized what a fool I had been and lost any sense of conjugal responsibility. It had taken George depriving me of my most precious thing—the one thing that had always been the solace of my solitary existence—my brain's voracious appetite.

When Jason was born, I felt nothing but love for the little creature, but the hatred for my husband had reached the point that I was ready to kill him. Of course, I didn't. I couldn't risk losing my son if I was arrested. Even running away wasn't an option. With no money or connections, it wouldn't take long for George to find us, and I shivered, thinking about what he would do to me and Jason once he did. The love for my son made sure I'd always be locked inside George's prison. Just as he had planned.

The night the monsters attacked, I was upstairs, getting Jason ready for bed. It was later than usual, and the little guy was fussy as I changed his diaper. He should have been asleep already by at least an hour, but his father had been late coming back from work, still expecting to have dinner with his son.

Of course, George hadn't cared about my resulting miserable night ahead. He would put on his earplugs and fall asleep, leaving me to deal with his overtired son. After having screwed me, of course.

He wanted a big family as soon as possible—more people to worship him—but I had had the presence of mind to secretly go on the pill. I used to tie myself into knots, terrified that George would discover my one deception. It's nice not to have to give a shit anymore.

The first thing I heard was a big crunch from down the road. Like a car accident. I took Jason in my arms and walked to the window. I'm not sure how long I stayed there frozen, watching the chaos mounting all around us.

Black figures, moving too fast to be distinguished, plowing through houses, leaving only ruins and fire in their wake. Cars being cut in half while moving and gunshots and screams from everywhere.

"George?" I called, making my way downstairs. As I reached the last step, I heard the subtle click of the gas furnace automatic starter coming from the basement. George was staring at the window towards Mr. Donovan's house, slack jawed, the tumbler with the whisky I had poured him before taking Jason upstairs still half full.

"George?" I called again, stepping behind him. Sounds of machine gun bursts made me look outside the window and I saw the monster, my monster, for the first time, all seven feet of deadly force. It had just killed Mr. Donovan and was charging our house.

"Shit..." George said, dropping the glass. When it smashed on the hardwood floor, he was already running towards the entrance. His dead eyes panned over me and Jason, two yards away. Did he even see us?

When the outside wall shattered, George was frantically looking for the car keys in the bowl at the entrance. The monster stopped in front of me, its dark skin smeared in grime, with drops of thick liquid falling off and blotching my living room carpet. Its head turned, and I saw its eyes, two deep holes ending in yellow sparks.

Terrified, I couldn't move a muscle, and after what felt like hours but was only an instant, the monster began smashing through the floor with its blades, opening a direct path to the furnace in the basement.

Jason began wailing in my arms, but it was the smell of gas that snapped me out of my fear. I rushed to the kitchen and turned off the switch of the main gas line under the sink. I closed my eyes, praying for the horrible cacophony coming from the basement to stop.

When it did, I exhaled, knowing that the house wouldn't explode, but the ensuing silence was broken by the vibration of the garage door rising. The unmistakable noise of the car engine turning on followed, quickly drowned by more violent banging.

I arrived at the front door just in time to see the monster plunging into the trunk of George's car, which had only made it halfway through the driveway. The blades cut my husband in half, on their way to the front engine. The car exploded, engulfing the monster in flames. I didn't move an inch, until all that could burn had burned, leaving the monster standing still in the wreckage.

I stepped onto the porch, lulling Jason to sleep. The overwhelming smell of burning rubber and oil filled my nostrils as I found the monster's eyes just before the sparks faded to black. Its work was done, mine would start soon.

————

After the blades, I move to the chest and the waist. By then, a little crowd has gathered on the sidewalk in front of the house. Mostly the same people, Carol and her favorite gossip partner, Misha—the half left of a gay couple living one street over—several dog walkers, a newly single father pushing a stroller, older couples taking a break from their morning walk.

I'm not upset because they're watching me—there's not much left to do for entertainment. In the first hour of the attack, waves of monsters, all the same shape as mine, but some as tall as a three-story building, targeted all the power plants burning fossil fuel, with no distinction between oil, carbon, or natural gas.

Since then, construction of solar and hydro plants has started in earnest, but it turns out that building a clean society using only clean energy is harder than anyone could anticipate.

We get a maximum of two hours of electricity every day, later in the afternoon. The streets are deserted when it happens, everybody eager to log in to what's left of the Internet to look at the videos of the attack that surfaced since the previous day. They call it monster porn, and they all scuff horrified when it's brought up, but they all watch it, in the comfort of their homes.

That is what upsets me, how quick they are to judge me when they are not that different. I curse them under my breath, and go back to focusing on the monster's chest, where the bulk of the bullet divots are.

I count them in my head as I clean them. *One, two, three...* I imagine patterns, like in those connect-the-dots games I used to love as a child. I trace some of my old favorites. A light bulb, a dog, a heart with anatomically correct arteries roughly in the spot where the real thing would be. What else can I make?

How about Jason's Lovy? I compose it using twenty-one of the forty-three holes. I turn to my son. He laughs, hiding his mouth behind the real Lovy.

The first few days of cleaning, Jason would whine and bang on the tray of his chair, demanding the attention I was giving to the monster, and I would have to stop to hold and reassure him. But now he knows that this is Mom's time, and the only thing he can do to participate is to watch me attentively.

After resuming, I catch Carol and Misha with the corner of my eye. They are enthralled in a deeper conversation than usual, with the others listening in. Carol's squinting eyes dart back and forth between the monster and her audience.

I just shrug and move down to the pelvis area. That's when the monsterfucker sneers normally intensify, but the dozen bystanders crowded around Carol are not even looking at me today. Too busy avidly drinking whatever poison she's spreading.

The monster has no genitalia and even the posterior is flat—no need of butt cheeks for cushioning if you never sit—so I make my way down quickly. Its legs resemble those of a goat, with inverted knees and ending in hooves. I can't see them, but spikes jut out from the bottom, anchoring the monster to the ground and making it almost immovable.

Wherever the monster goes, each of its steps leaves exactly seven holes, half an inch wide, equally spaced and forming a circle. My floors and driveway still have them, marking the path to my freedom. I have no intention of ever filling them in.

———

THE DAYS FOLLOWING my husband's death marked not only my rebirth but also that of my faith in human kindness, which George had so unequivocally squashed.

The whole neighborhood came together, everyone offering whatever useful expertise they possessed. A few crews of handypersons began circling around, repairing the salvageable houses, including mine, using the material recovered from the properties of the dead. The nearby farmers came around looking for someone to help them milk their cows and water their crops. The machines that did it before the attack were in pieces, and the animals weren't stopping lactating or the plants growing anytime soon.

In exchange, they shared the bounty and offered to use their horses to pull the car wrecks to one of the lots designated as the communal dump, including my husband's Camry.

Whatever was left of George's body was wrapped in white sheets and lined up with all the others. A makeshift cemetery was created in a nearby field, and a daylong ceremony organized. Each survivor spoke about who they had lost, fighting tears and anger. When my turn came, I just said a stern goodbye and had Jason throw his least favorite toy car in the grave. Nobody judged me then, people had suffered enough to understand that grief can assume many forms. If they only knew how happy I felt inside.

I walked home in silence, carrying Jason and holding Carol's hand. She was clearly distraught, while all I could think was that I didn't have to go home and prepare the elaborate meal George expected every night. On the other side of her, walking silently, was Mason, her husband's brother, single and living just a couple of blocks away. A few days later, he would move in with Carol. No surprise there, Carol is one of those people that can't be alone.

The next day, a massive cookout was organized. With the power gone, the food in everybody's fridge and freezer wouldn't last long.

Meat was smoked and cured using charcoal barbeques and bonfires, vegetables were steamed and pickled. Everything was properly packaged, sealed, and evenly distributed.

People started growing their own food. Those who had vegetable gardens before the attack taught everybody else what to do and shared their seeds. Luckily, there were enough natural wells around us to provide all the necessary water.

For several weeks, our post-apocalypse world looked more like a hippy community than the wasteland roamed by marauders portrayed by most movies. The fact that guns had become unusable may have played a big part in that, but it was still good to see.

We maintained some contact with the rest of the world using a few battery-operated short-wave radios. Most people got news about their faraway relatives and friends, getting the relief or closure they needed.

When general radio broadcasting restarted, the government channel promised that the power would be restored soon and announced that they had dispatched caravans of electric vehicles with supplies all over the country.

When they arrived at our neighborhood, a big event was staged, reminiscent of the political rallies of old, but we all watched in silence, with palpable dread that they would break the equilibrium we had worked so hard to achieve.

They did distribute stuff, but nothing we really needed, except some medicines and heavier clothing for the upcoming winter, all done basking in the halo of self-appointed sainthood as saviors of those who didn't need saving.

Then a so-called monster expert took the stage. A pamphlet was distributed explaining which devices could be safely operated around the monsters and which ones needed to be avoided. Like we hadn't figured it out by ourselves already.

Snickers rose from the crowd, and the vast majority of the leaflets ended up littering the ground.

Undaunted, the expert continued guaranteeing that a consistent effort was ongoing by the military to find a way to get rid of the monsters for good. Deep scans below the surface had found the pockets where they had been hiding, and proved that there were no more still buried, so once they had eliminated the ones idle on the surface, humanity could go back to the life before the attack.

Once the speech was over, he guided a group of scientists to every monster's location. I sat on the porch and watched them taking pictures, measurements, and collecting samples of the grime covering mine, while a weird sensation arose inside my body, like they were violating my privacy. That feeling didn't go away when the caravan left, promising among general indifference to come back soon with more supplies.

The next day, I was back on the porch, lying on one of the long chairs and staring at the hulking figure in my driveway, with Jason playing with his toy cars at my feet. The dried fluids covering half its body reflected the sun in sickly rainbows, making it look even more alien than its shape suggested.

My mind started spinning, unable to make sense of the sensation of attachment that I was feeling for that creature. It was true, the monster had freed me from the prison that George had methodically built around me, but it had also killed many innocent people and made the future very uncertain for me and my son.

Jason suddenly began crying. The Camaro had fallen off the porch, into a small patch of mud in the flowerbed below.

"No, no.... Here it is," I said, rescuing it. I took a tissue out of my pocket and cleaned the brown splotches. Jason grabbed it from my hand and dried his eyes, but I stood there staring at the dirt on my fingers. The simple act of giving the metal back its shine had calmed me instantly.

Before the attack, my entire being was occupied with two similar activities, spurred by opposite motivations. On one hand, I was taking care of my husband, out of fear of what he'd do to me if I didn't. On the other, I was happily satisfying Jason's every need out of pure motherly love.

George's death had freed me, but my son was proof that I liked to take care of others for the right reason. What I was feeling for that hulking creature was gratitude, not ownership. And my body was telling me I needed to find a way to express it.

The next morning, I started cleaning the monster.

———

I always do the head last. I use an old stepladder, it brings my-five-foot,-six-inch frame just high enough to look down on the monster's seven-foot body.

The head is a semicircular dome, rising straight from the shoulders, without a neck. Up close, the eyes look like dark holes, barely visible, surrounded by the slightly lighter skin, roughly in the same position where human eyes would be. There are also smaller holes, almost like pinpricks, all around the base of the head, an inch from the shoulders. The expert from the caravan said that, through them, the monsters smell the fossil fuel exhausts that unleash them.

I'm very careful not to get any soap or water in them, or its eyes. I don't know if it would bother it, but it's a precaution that comes naturally to me after bathing Jason for the last year and a half.

Once I'm done, I usually spend a few minutes peering into its empty sockets, looking for those sparks I had seen during the attack. Sometimes, I think I see something moving deep inside them, like a slightly less dark spot. Is it making eye contact with me? I can't be sure.

The last thing I do is thank it. With just a whisper, quietly so that my audience can't hear me.

"Thank you.... You gave me my life back."

I'm about to step off the ladder when I realize that the people around me have stopped listening to Carol and have been slowly retreating. But not as they usually do, strolling back to their homes, each one at their own pace, shaking their heads.

They are all stepping back, looking to my right. It's Mason coming from down the street, pushing a wheel barrel.

When he stops in Carol's driveway, just across from mine, I recognize what's inside. One of those old generators, powered by gasoline. Mason must have dug one out from the dump.

What is he trying to do? Steal my monster? The cold shiver on my back intensifies when I see what else is in the barrel. Thin cylinders, about a foot long.

Mason rips the activation cord. One, two, three times.

"No!" I yell, instinctively hugging the monster.

The generator finally comes on, and Mason runs away. The sparks I've been looking for appear at the bottom of the monster's eyes, yellow and warm. A fraction of a second later, the monster bolts ahead, and I slip off its body.

I fall and hit the asphalt but ignore the pain as I scramble to Jason to take him in my arms.

The moment the monster's blades plunge into the generator, a giant explosion fills the entire street and a column of fire surges toward the sky. Shrapnel flies over my head, and Jason starts to cry.

"It's okay," I tell him, but it's not.

Carol did it, that jealous bitch. She took away my monster. I find her in the crowd, a triumphant expression on her face. The biggest hatred I have ever felt grows inside my body, bigger than the one I had toward George. It feels solid, like I can grab it and hurl it back at her.

She senses it too, and her wide smile dwindles. Then something shoots out of the fire. It's the monster, flames dancing on its skin but otherwise intact, rushing towards Carol.

It stops in front of her. She freezes in fear, while everybody around her scatters away. Then its head turns, the warm yellow sparks at the bottom of its eyes find mine. I gently direct Jason's face against my chest before clenching my teeth and nodding.

The monster's blades make quick work of Carol's wiry frame.

"Noooooooo!" a scream comes from the opposite side of the explosion. Mason, and the same hatred I felt for Carol, expands to engulf him. A massive figure appears behind him. Another monster lured by the generator's exhaust.

It cuts Mason in half before he realizes it's there.

Then I see them all, twelve seven-foot frames gathering around me. They stop in my driveway, turn to face the neighborhood and anchor themselves to the ground in a V formation, with my monster back in the same position it has been since the original attack.

The horror on the faces of the rest of the people morphs into confusion.

They don't understand what has just happened, but I do.

The monsters' work is not completed. That's why they didn't go back underground and resume their timeless sleep.

The destruction of the fossil-fuel burning machines stopped the poisoning of Earth momentarily, but the real menace is those that are already planning a way around it, to return to their old lives, not caring about the consequences to our planet. People stuck in the past, like the experts that came with the government caravan. Or Carol and Mason.

The monsters need guidance to find those people; that's why they stayed—to find allies, leaders. People who understand what's in the balance or who are, like me, simply grateful. We can help them distinguish between those who are ready for a new life on Earth and those who can't adapt and deserve to die.

Let them come with whatever devious plan they can come up with. We are ready.

I stand up and walk to my monster, soothing Jason with my voice. Its skin is covered in oil, grime and blood. Metal shards, up to an inch long, stick out of its body. I pull one out and its flesh closes around the wound, leaving another divot.

I look forward to the days of cleaning ahead.

THE THIRSTY

TIM PIERACCINI

ACCOUNT ON BURIED LAPTOP, several years old, found near oasis by searchers for missing archaeologist Lynda Kagan. Edited for relevance and clarity.

SUCCESS! I've obtained the fragments from Professor Bashshar Bin Tahir, and it is definitely Ruth Hanson's handwriting.

'Fragments' was no exaggeration, by the way—cockroaches have been at them. Sometimes there are a couple of pages with almost nothing missing, then a stretch with no more than a few tattered phrases intact. It seems to be the record of an expedition, north from Bilma into the desert, just after the close of the Second World War.

Professor Tahir was decidedly cagey when I asked where the journal was found; he got it from some Toubou nomads, he said, three decades ago, but couldn't tell me where they'd picked it up. A name, appearing early in the journal, is *Tukhfih Alriyh*, which seems to mean something like 'hidden by the wind'. Could this be an old city, abandoned and forgotten? I'm going to ask some people in Bilma!

Nobody would talk to me in Bilma until I was accosted by a girl named Cantara, on a break from her studies in the Islamic University in Say. She'd heard me asking others, and remembered something her grandmother had talked about: an American woman who went north into the desert to look for a lost city, but the name she gave me was *Madinat Alzuman*, which means (roughly) 'thirsty city'. Might not even be a name, just a description. All very odd. But, good news—her uncle has a Land Rover, which he lets her use, so she's willing to take me north. For a fee, of course.

Cantara is interested in the West, which was another reason she approached me. On the trip up I've been telling her about Ruth Hanson, her adventurous life once she'd abandoned the missionary work, her interest in the persistent myth of lost cities in the Sahara. Hanson's fight for official recognition (as a woman, I mean) struck a chord, I think, though Cantara was disappointed by the photos I showed her. She was hoping for someone more heroic-looking, I suspect! After I'd shown her the photos, she began to ask more about me.

We followed the route (as nearly as we could make it out) taken by Hanson and her guide nearly eighty years before. Hanson drew a rough map, but with the paucity of landmarks it only gave us a general direction. And the top of the page, her destination, was missing. Cantara says she's never been up there before, and knows no one who has. We estimate it will take the better part of a day to get there, but we have supplies and a tent for an overnight stay. GPS failed us fairly early on—internet blackspot, unsurprisingly—but a compass has kept us on track (we believe).

The 'hidden by wind' label might be explained. We hit a ferocious sandstorm as it was getting dark last night; we would have been stopping shortly anyway, so it made sense to sit it out, but it lasted all night—and it's not even Harmattan season. A microclimate, perhaps—currents trapped by the mountains to the west.

We pushed on slowly in the morning, and it did eventually clear. We seemed to be approaching the northern edge of Hanson's map, but there was nothing to be seen. After a sweep east and west, I was starting to believe we'd gone astray. Cantara seemed surprised by my attitude, insisting we push a little farther north.

WE FOUND IT—WELL, we found something. Not so much a city as a kind of gigantic... necropolis. It was hidden from view by the steep sides of a rocky ravine; we almost drove right over the edge. (We might have done had Cantara not decided, for no apparent reason, to slow.)

The tombs and monuments were cut into the rock on both sides of the narrow valley, in a style I didn't recognise. It seems incredible, but perhaps this is an entirely unknown civilisation, or a breakaway from one already recorded. There were touches of innumerable North African modes of architecture, as if all of the different ancient cultures had been gathered into one place. But there was no clash; an almost miraculous harmoniousness prevailed. The styles flowed into one another, like patterns on the surface of water. But all of them ancient. There is no construction that shows signs of Muslim influence, for example.

Hanson doesn't describe the general look of the city in any of the fragments that survive; most of what Professor Tahir sold me seems to describe the interiors:

> "... opening out, at its end, into a chamber that appeared to be a place of worship. There was a central stone table, like an altar, and lines of smaller stone blocks fanning out. The curious thing was the holes beside these... seats? opening down into darkness. A stone dropped experimentally into one of them revealed the presence, some way below, of water. I surmised that perhaps once the water level had been much higher, permitting the worshippers to wash themselves prior to the service.
> There was no sign of blood on the altar, which I confess I found both reassuring and disappointing."

I want to find that chamber. I'm convinced it's here.

We've determined that if we're frugal with our supplies, we can stay two nights. It will give us time to fully explore *Tukhfih Alriyh*, to try to match passages in Hanson's journal to the reality around us.

The first few chambers offered nothing remarkable, except that every tomb, every casket, had been opened. Thieves, I assumed, until we found one where the body was missing but the treasures were still present; some kind of Egyptian dignitary, sent on his or her way with ornaments of gold. One of them was unusual; I've never seen the like, anywhere. Shaped like a man—that is, bipedal, upright—the figure was dressed in some kind of loose robe that draped over its head. But the face... I wondered aloud if this was a haven for sufferers of leprosy. Perhaps that would explain why it's never spoken of, its location hidden. Cantara felt certain I was wrong, contradicted me at once. But she could offer no explanation for her certainty.

One notable feature of the construction was the light; in places we were reduced to using our phone torches, but the walkways, and some of the chambers, were lit via slanting shafts which drove up and opened out onto the African sky. There were channels along the lower walls of these shafts, clearly for rainwater. I wondered about sandstorms, but Cantara pointed out that there were thin sheets of fine gauze near the upper openings. Hard to see from down here; what it would be to have younger, sharper eyes.

Night came all too soon, and we found a place where the ground allowed us to pitch the tent. I spent the evening poring over the fragments, and found a portion that seemed to describe the figure we found:

"... *and slender, with dark green, almost black, skin, and cat-like eyes. The flesh was uneven, but in a regular sort of fashion, with small bumps everywhere...."*

The face of our statuette is golden, of course, not green. Perhaps Hanson saw a mural of some sort? But what do these images represent?

WE MAY HAVE FOUND the mural that Hanson saw. It was in a large hall set behind the temple, which we found by examining the walls, and managing to trip a hidden door.

And the faces are there, many of them, the very dark green aspect with animal eyes and what look like enormous blisters everywhere. And there was a detail not represented on the figurine; tiny spines, almost like hairs from a mole, growing from each protuberance.

Were they worshipped here? Did they even exist, or did they spring from the imagination of an artist, or artists, who lived here? Perhaps such a mixed culture needed its own new mythology, new stories—new bogeymen? But for what purpose? And did these things have a name?

IT WAS Cantara who gave me an answer, of sorts, back at the tent. We had been comparing family histories.

"Fadilah [her grandmother] told me, once, when I was acting wild and she wanted to frighten me... about The Thirsty." She paused, frowning. "I think that would be right... our word is *mutaeatish*, but I've not heard it used as a name, except that one time." She leaned forward and picked up the statuette. "She told me they lived in a city to the north, hidden in the desert, and that they sucked all the moisture out of living things. Fruit, trees, animals, birds... human beings." She shook her head, put the figure back. "Just a story, I thought. Until today."

I took up the figure myself, and turned it around in my hands. "Artists have made images of dragons and unicorns and gryphons; it doesn't make them real."

Cantara made a small noise behind closed lips. She sounded

amused. But I looked at her a moment later and her face was troubled. She gazed at me for a few seconds, then turned her face away.

After Cantara had turned in for the night, I continued to look over the Hanson fragments. One struck me anew:

"... something in the shadows, high up on the wall. Creeping along, dark limbs, but the body shrouded in...."

A dream, perhaps—brought on by the mural? Or only some kind of climbing lizard? She doesn't mention the size of this thing she saw.

With so little information about this expedition, we had no way of knowing the number of Hanson's party, but she clearly had someone along who knew the story of this place, probably not her guide:

"... people came for the gold, for the skill with which it was worked, for the beauty, and the dreams of riches—and they never left. They built, they lived, they loved, and they died. The ceremony...."

Unless she extrapolated this information from other murals? And a ceremony? Was she writing about a ceremony in the room we found—the temple? Or were there other places? This city of the dead extended far back into the rock, innumerable passages leading to countless chambers, large and small. There were, also, channels—dry now, but perhaps in times long gone carrying water—running along the passages and around the rooms.

There was so much to see, to explore. After a sleepless few hours, I wandered, and I photographed incessantly—only with my phone, useless for anything else in this place. Cantara came with me but kept disappearing along tunnels or around corners, sometimes for half an hour or more, until I began to fear that both of us would be lost forever in this labyrinth. But she would always reappear, telling me if she had found something noteworthy. She took no photographs, which I found odd; she certainly had a phone.

IN THIS BREATHLESS, dizzying way another day passed quickly, our voyage of discovery interrupted only by the need to recharge our phones with my portable set-up. During the enforced break I went through the journal excerpts again on the laptop.

"... nearly all gone now...."
"... saw... today... hissed and scuttled away...."
"... Sarsour [her guide] has gone... left us in the night... seemed afraid... least Fadilah's made of sterner stuff."

I'd been so focused on puzzling out what it was Hanson had seen that the name hadn't struck me until now. I looked at Cantara. "What was your Grandmother called?"

"Fadilah."

"How old would she have been in 1946?"

"About my age, I think."

I showed Cantara the fragments, but she shook her head. "Coincidence, I think. It's not too uncommon a name. Obviously I wasn't around—my mother wasn't even born for nearly another twenty years—but I'm sure I'd have heard... I would have known... if she'd accompanied such a famous scientist on an expedition. For one thing, *she* was still around, and... and your lady disappeared."

IT WAS towards the end of the day that we discovered the remains. We had been through dozens of chambers, hundreds of passageways, without seeing a single trace of anyone who had lived here—and then, there they were. Two skeletons, the bones marked by cracks along the length of them, and small circular abrasions on the surface. There were no clothes to be seen, and no obvious means of identifying these people. But one of them was clearly a woman, and small in stature. Could it possibly be Ruth Hanson? I didn't know if there were any DNA records, whether positive identification would be possible.

They were laid out on two raised stone slabs, part of a row of same in a large hall criss-crossed by the sunken channels. We had missed this place on our previous explorations because the only access to it was *via* the channels—Cantara had crawled into one as an experiment, and had found it opened into this room. So... the channels were meant to carry more than water? It seemed to make no sense; the room had been made, but was not easily accessible to any of the people; it was perfectly possible to crawl through the channels but it was hardly a comfortable or convenient way to get anywhere.

And why were the pair laid out in this way? "Some kind of rite, or perhaps even treatment?"

"A buffet?" suggested Cantara. She saw my face, and shrugged. "Well, look at the bones. Most of the marrow seems to have been sucked out."

I bent close to the thigh of the female skeleton. It looked as though she was right. "'Sucked'? What makes you—"

"Nearly half water, bone marrow," murmured Cantara.

"You're not suggesting... the... the *mutaeatish*?"

"Why not? Depths of the ocean must be full of things we've never seen. Why not the depths of the desert?"

"But... *people* built this. People, who must have come and gone, taken stories out into the world. If these things, these *mutaeatish*, were real, we'd've heard of them. They're not even like werewolves, or vampires—a common myth. There's... nothing."

Cantara looked around. "What makes you think people—humans —made this? *This room*, I mean, not the rest of it. And what makes you think the humans who *were* here—ever got away? Were ever allowed to leave?"

I shook my head. "It's not possible. We would know. Somehow, we'd know. The number of people it must have taken to construct all this—someone would have got out."

Cantara seemed about to reply, but held her peace. She looked at me in a way I could not read.

I took many photos of the two skeletons. The second seemed to be a man, to judge from the height and other, subtler clues, so not the other Fadilah—if the female *was* Hanson.

I sat in the tent feeling mostly frustration, that we had seen so much and as yet understood so little. I wondered if we might manage a third day, perhaps drive back through the night. Cantara was not as entranced by the place as I was; at times she seemed almost blasé, as if she'd seen it all before. I hoped she'd be amenable to the idea. She was getting irritable, though, as if we had been here too long, perhaps—or as if something was nagging at her.

I woke in the depths of the night and Cantara was gone. At first I thought she might have stepped out to relieve herself, but after ten minutes had passed I understood the instinct that had prevented me from turning over and going back to sleep. I waited, and still nothing. Perhaps she wandered farther than she planned, and took a wrong turn?

I opened the flap of the tent, peered out. Beyond the small pool of soft illumination from the tent entrance, there was nothing. No light, no sound. I thought about calling out, to guide Cantara back if she had lost her way. But something kept me quiet.

Then suddenly she was there; Cantara came skidding into the light and stopped in front of the tent. But she was not looking at me; she looked outward, into the dark. "N-No," she said, almost inaudibly. Her shoulders rose and fell; she had been running. "There's been... it's a mistake." She repeated something in Arabic, the same word, three times.

For a few seconds there was no sound but her shuddering breath. Nothing moved.

Then there was a point of light, a reflection of the glow from the tent. A reflection in a cat-like eye.

And another.

A third.

They came forward very slowly, but I sensed it was not caution. It wasn't even a natural lethargy. I felt, unmistakably, that they enjoyed generating a sense of dread; perhaps it was something in the glitter of those eyes. Their faces were mostly shrouded in shadow beneath their ragged head coverings, but I could see the light shining dully on moist skin of midnight green.

"Get back into the tent."

It was mere seconds since Cantara had last spoken, but even so, lost in the sight of those dark faces, those inhuman eyes, comprehension of speech had deserted me. I stared up at her.

She bent and put her hands on my shoulders, shoving. "Get... *in*!!!"

I suffered being propelled backwards. She ducked in as soon as there was room and sealed the tent. I gestured feebly. "W-Will that stop them...?"

Cantara took a moment. "I don't know. It might confuse them. I've never—" She stopped herself. "They're used to finding victims in the open."

I waved a hand towards the outside. "Those... they're... the *mutaeatish*? They exist? They're...."

"Real, yes."

I met her eyes. "And you knew."

She stared at me, unspeaking.

"*Before* we came here?"

She dropped her eyes.

"Did you—" Something stopped me from voicing the thought. It was too fantastic. And at the same time I was certain it was true; she had brought me here for them.

She seemed to see the realisation in my eyes. She moved away, crouching by the tent entrance. "Those three... are the last of them. It took me all this time to find them. Once, there were thousands. Even in my grandmother's time, there were hundreds. I don't... I don't know how they reproduce, but it hasn't happened for a century or more. Lack of nutrition, perhaps. The humans here died off longer ago, and with modern technology it's much harder to lure and trap people without giving away this place."

"'Lure and trap'?"

She could not meet my eyes, stared at her hands. "I'm the last of my kind, too. We are *'uwlayik aladhin yakhdimun*—those who serve. My grandmother, also."

"Serve?" But I already knew the answer. "By luring and trapping."

"Yes." She was still having difficulty looking at me. "I'm sorry." Her head moved from side to side. "When you... when I realised you were looking for Hanson, it seemed... too good an opportunity. Professor Tahir alerted me, so it was arrang—"

"Him, too?"

"He... helps."

"... Why?"

"He's dedicated to preserving them for as long as possible."

It was difficult to take in. The fact that those three creatures were still out there was not helping. "H-How many people have you brought here?"

"Oh, not many. The water from the human brain is their favourite nourishment, the best thing for them, but they don't need it. They can exist on animals."

"But... but... to bring anyone to this... f-for them...."

Now she did look at me, and she shook her head. "You wouldn't understand. It's tradition—a legacy that goes back before the Crusades, before Islam... before Christ. A matrilineal responsibility—a privilege— passed down through the centuries. I could no more walk away from it than I could take to the air."

My mind was still struggling, but something fell into place. "Then what... happened? Why are you here now? You... you left."

Cantara took a deep breath. "It wasn't... I did leave, yes—and all the way up to the Land Rover I was thinking of you. I'd never spent so much time with one of... with anyone I'd brought here. I suddenly realised you wouldn't exist any more, and once I'd heard about your life, and your family, and... well, I just came back."

"To do... what?" I glanced towards the outside. "Will they let us leave?"

"I don't know." She lifted a hand to the zip of the tent. "A good time to find out, perhaps."

"Will we... just run?" I grabbed my laptop, closed it. "How... how fast can they move?"

"Never tested that." Cantara unzipped her jacket and drew out a stick, wrapped in cloth that looked to be soaked in something. From her pocket she took a lighter. "But I bring these, just in case they're... too ravenous to be choosy. You can imagine, fire is not their favourite. You are ready?"

I finished stuffing my laptop into its bag and slung the strap across my shoulders. "Think so. We'll see if my legs work."

We crouched together by the tent flap. Cantara unzipped slowly, trying to make no sound, the lighter and torch held clumsily in one hand.

"Will they be ready for us?" I whispered. "I mean, do they understand? If they could overhear—"

"They don't know English. Arabic, Hausa, some others... but not European languages, except some French."

The flap bent back, Cantara peered out. She readied the lighter.

I moved up beside her. The chamber seemed empty. "Maybe you did confuse them."

"We should move fast, anyway. They can't have gone far."

"Which way?"

"We'll bear right once we leave this chamber. After that, just follow me." She hefted the torch. "I won't light this yet, but if you see anything, yell out."

We rose to stand in front of the tent. I looked back at it. "Bought that new this trip."

"You want to stay and strike it, be my guest." She looked into my eyes, saw my answer. She took a deep breath. "All right. When we start, don't stop for anything. I have to have this ready, so if you could give us some light...."

I brought out my phone. Cantara took a last look around. I switched on the flashlight.

"Let's go!"

We ran. I felt foolish, almost childlike, and at the same time slightly exultant. It was unreal, it was real, it was deadly, it was a game.

An adventure.

We made it out to the passage, stretching long before us, farther than my flashlight could illumine. The light veered crazily as we scampered, despite my efforts to hold it steady. Walls, ceiling, columns, niches, all flashed by, appearing and disappearing as if it was they which were in motion.

It was still night as we came out onto the floor of the valley, a narrow strip of star-dotted sky beckoning above the cliffs. The Land Rover was at the top of the south end, ahead of us. We trotted across, no longer able to sprint, our eyes darting about us. We saw nothing.

We reached the long narrow stairway up. I found I was already doubting; what had I actually seen? Dark figures half swallowed by the shadows? Or simply the shadows? Were we running from nothing?

Cantara led the way, not pausing. She clearly still believed.

We had completed about a third of the climb when I asked, "You've... never talked about this to anyone? Ever?"

"No. I... did try to escape—hence University. But I wouldn't ever have revealed...."

"You do realise that if we get out of here, I'll have a lot of questions? Do they live in water? The channels—did they use them to move about? Can they—"

"Please don't. The *mutaeatish* are a secret—a kind of sacred thing to our order. If they're going to vanish from the world, it should be completely. No trace. It's hard to explain, but they've always kept...." She fell silent.

"Kept what?"

"Sshh."

I listened. I could hear nothing. "What?"

"Not sure. Thought I heard something behind us. Just keep going."

We continued, our pace increased. Above I could see the faint blue-black of the sky, a small square of hope. It grew larger, until Cantara paused, just below the lip of the rock, indicating silence. We listened again. Again nothing.

"All right," she breathed. "Maybe... maybe they're too old, too ill to chase. Maybe they're honouring my service, I don't know." Her hand holding the unlit torch went over the lip.

And was seized by dark, wet fingers.

She shrieked. And was borne upward, almost flying. The lighter spun from her other hand, falling. I lunged and caught it without thought. From above came the sounds of frantic struggle, and I took a step down, back. Away. But then something made me turn and there was another of them at my shoulder.

I squealed as the thing made a swipe at me, and flicked the lighter up and on—a kind of reflex. The creature flinched, but did not retreat. I backed up the steps, holding the lighter out, keeping the *mutaeatish* at a distance. Close up, its skin seemed to ooze, moisture shining on every dark carbuncle. The cat-like eyes were yellowish green, pupils tiny slits.

Cantara's shouts had diminished to mere gasps; there was pain there, and fear. As my head came above the lip of the entrance I risked a look.

Two of them hunched over her, each with dark fingers of one hand splayed against her face. They had been holding her down with the other hand, but it was no longer necessary. Her skin dried as I watched; flaked, shrivelled. Her breath was coming in snatches.

Two feet from her lay the unlit torch.

I narrowly dodged another swipe, and leaped from the passage. I caught up the torch, brought the lighter to it. The head exploded into flame, and I thrust it into the face of the creature trying to climb up after me. Its roar was the sound of a breaking wave. It fell back.

I spun and darted the torch between the heads of the two over Cantara. They recoiled. I waved the torch around, chasing them, screaming like a child, forcing them to retreat until they tumbled, one after the other, down the steps. They disappeared into the darkness.

I knelt by Cantara.

She shook her head faintly. "Sorry." It seemed a large sentiment for one breathless word.

"Can you walk?"

She gave a soft cough that I realised was a laugh. "Can't even lift... fucking head...." Her hand waved feebly. "Get away. Go. If... they have me... they won't chase you."

"I... can't...."

"I did it to you."

I could hear them, gurgling and hissing like a stream over stones. I looked towards the opening, but there was nothing yet. I looked back at Cantara's face and knew she was minutes from death.

I RAN, and drove, and write this account in comparative safety, at least fifty miles from the city. I have no excuses, except my own uselessness, and wanting to leave some sort of witnessing. I hope this is enough.

I'll leave the laptop at this oasis. Someone will find it; I hope it will reach the right people, whoever they may turn out to be. Someone who will know the best thing to do.

I'm going back. Cantara, whatever remains of her, deserves to be buried. Stupid as it is, futile as it is, it seems... not the best, but the only thing I can do.

ACCOUNT ENDS.

ARE MONSTERS REAL?

GABINO IGLESIAS

"HOW HOT IS THE SUN, DADDY?"

It's not a question; it's a ghost. Andrea's tiny voice comes to him at random times, out of nowhere. It's at once precious and painful. Andy remembers his answer: 27 million degrees Fahrenheit at its core. He'd explained more about heat variances, photosphere temperature, and nuclear fusion. Andrea hadn't registered any of it. After a few minutes, she asked who had measured the sun's temperature and how big their thermometer had been. The memory is tattooed in Andy's heart, and every time he hears his daughter's voice—*"How hot is the sun, Daddy?"* —he imagines the tattoo radiating a neon light strong enough to blind an entire city.

"Are monsters real, Daddy?"

This one is worse. He'd said no. He hated lying to his daughter. He would've loved to explain to her that ugly monsters with horns or a thousand eyes and tentacles aren't real, but that the world was full of real monsters, full of people who loved to hurt others, who thought themselves superior, who stole from those who didn't have enough to get by. But he didn't explain any of that because his instinct was to always protect Andrea, to shield her from the world even if the knowledge that it would eventually hurt her crushed him every day.

"Are monsters real?"

Yes, they are. Monsters are real, and they are everywhere.

Andy shakes the voice of his daughter out of his head and stares out the window. The purple light that signals dawn in P-986 covers the top of the tall, fern-like trees that cover the strange, humid planet and makes the sky look like a soft, diluted watercolor. His wife Lana loved to buy paintings with colors like that at discount stores. She'd bring them home, paint ghosts on them, and then sell them to friends or in her online store. As Andy looks out his egg-shaped window into the alien forest outside, he imagines a lonely ghost standing amidst the strange foliage, impervious to the low oxygen levels and the reduced gravity of P-986. Andy wishes he was that ghost.

"How far is it where you're going, Daddy?"

Andy remembers that answer well: a chuckle and the word "far." That one was true. A small redemption. If explaining the temperature of the sun to a kid is hard and lying to them about monsters is the kind of thing that haunts you, explaining interstellar travel is like teaching calculus to a fish. And P-986 was indeed far. Four months away from home is how Andy put it to his mom on the phone. He'd missed Andrea's birthday and his anniversary by the time he arrived at this mining mission. His contract is for one year and then there's another four months to get back home. Twenty months total. Two birthdays. Two anniversaries. Countless questions. A lot of Andrea growing up. Thinking about it breaks his heart, but remembering what his bank account will look like when he returns glues the pieces back together.

McGregor's voice pours from the speakers in his room and shatters Andy's thoughts.

"Meeting in the classroom in three minutes. Attendance is mandatory."

The meeting room in the Urrea Station isn't a classroom, but it has tables facing an interactive screen, so it looks like one. Someone made a joke about it on their first day of training and the name stuck. Now, three months later, they're heading back there to talk about something they hadn't received training for.

Andy takes in the gray walls of the station as he makes his way to the classroom. They look clean, smooth, and boring. Every minute he spends inside the station feels like a minute spent in something that shouldn't be. The station, which he sees from the outside twice a day as the automated pod takes them to and then back from the mine, looks like a high-tech cancerous growth sticking up out of the ground in what otherwise would be a pristine ecosystem.

Shawl, McGregor, Mata, Dr. Sulzer, and Johnson occupy their usual spots by the time Andy gets to the classroom. The only one missing is Wilkes. He's in the med room. Andy knows they're here to talk about him. He takes a deep breath and tries not to think about monsters.

Johnson starts talking without tapping the screen. That means there's no presentation or data to show. He looks tired. The bags under his eyes look like they've been recently punched. After welcoming them, he stops. Something dark makes his face shift. He clears his throat before speaking again.

"As you all know, yesterday morning Wilkes developed a bad cough followed by a fever, so he didn't go out to the site with the rest of you. His condition has worsened significantly since then. It's something we need to address, so we kept you here today. I... I'm gonna hand things over to Dr. Sulzer. She can talk about the medical stuff and what comes next."

Andy hopes they will finally learn why they're here and not in the mines. That's where he makes money. Here, sitting and waiting around, is not how work gets done. Also, sitting around is how the voice comes to him. *Are monsters real, Daddy?*

Dr. Sulzer is tall and lean. Thick green veins move around in the back of her hands when she gestures. Her hands look like they belong to an old woman, but her face looks like she just graduated med school. Space does weird things to the human body. Dr. Sulzer walks up to the front and stands next to Johnson. She's not holding papers or a folder, which is strange. She also ignores the screen behind her. That's a bad sign. She always has something to show them. Not showing them anything now means something, and Andy's not sure he wants to know what.

"As Johnson said, Wilkes developed a cough two nights ago that progressively worsened as the night went on. By morning, he was breathing hard, and the oximeter indicated his blood oxygen levels were lower than expected. He didn't respond to bronchodilators. I took a blood sample and found his red blood cells unaltered. That's when I performed a bronchoscopy and... well, there's something in Wilkes's lungs that shouldn't be there."

Dr. Sulzer stops talking and looks to Johnson, clearly asking for permission to continue. Andy watches as everyone in the room either sits up straight or leans forward. Johnson nods.

"I found what looked like mite eggs coating Wilkes's lungs. They're covered in a viscous film that's—"

"Eggs? He has fucking eggs in his lungs?" Mata interrupts.

"Yeah, the white capsules are attached to his pleura, the... the thin tissue that covers the inside of your—"

"Hold on a minute," says McGregor, "When you say eggs, you mean something that's alive? Like... there's something inside those eggs?"

"Well, yeah. The microscope I used for the bronchoscopy showed—"

McGregor threw her hand up and spoke again. "Nah, hold on, Wilkes has some kind of eggs in his lungs. That's fucked up. Tell us if that shit is contagious because—"

"That's why we're here," says Johnson while taking a step forward. Everyone goes quiet. "In the last few hours, the eggs in Wilkes's lungs have grown. A lot. Dr. Sulzer has so far been unable to slow down or stop their development. Removal is our next option, but we don't know the amount of damage that would cause. We don't know what he has. Out of an abundance of caution, we're keeping everyone in today. Dr. Sulzer will check all of you. Those are your orders for this shift. We're starting now. Save your questions. Once we know more, we'll meet back here. Now line up and head to the med room."

Even tired, Johnson is an impressive man, and his voice leaves no room for questions. They get up and start walking to the med room.

Andy is first in line outside the med room because he'd been the last to walk into the classroom, so he'd stayed close to the door and had been the first one out. Dr. Sulzer walks past him and presses the white card that hangs from a lanyard on her neck against the pad to the left of the door. The door slides open without a sound.

Wilkes's body is on a gurney pressed against the right wall of the med room. Andy has a hard time processing what he's looking at. Wilkes's torso has doubled in size. He looks like his chest is pregnant with twins. His breathing is a ragged, wet thing that escapes his mouth in short bursts. He sounds like he's gargling pancake syrup. Wilkes's eyes are open wide and glued to the ceiling. His body twitches slightly, as if processing the last jolts from an electric shock.

"Johnson, get in here!" Judging by her tone, Dr. Sulzer wasn't expecting Wilkes to look like bloated roadkill after a week under the Texas sun.

Johnson runs into the room and pushes Andy out of the way. He takes two steps toward Wilkes and stops. Johnson turns to the rest of them. Everyone has walked into the room and stayed piled together by the door, looking at the swollen body on the gurney.

"Dr. Sulzer, what—"

Wilkes makes a sound and rolls over to his side. A foamy mixture of blood and something white and slimy pours from his mouth and splatters against the floor.

"What the fuck?" asks Mata.

Wilkes tries to push himself to a sitting position. His chest ripples as if something is running around inside him. He makes another noise, something wet and ragged.

There's a loud pop as Wilkes's torso explodes, shooting a wet mess of red and gray into the air. Something hot and wet smacks against Andy's chest and right cheek. There is a lot of screaming. Johnson turns, his eyes wide, and vomits while moving away from Wilkes's body. McGregor paws at her uniform and screams. Her pitch is so high it gets Andy to focus. He looks back at Wilkes's body. What's left of the skin of his torso flaps at the edges of his empty chest and abdomen like curtains of flesh. Andy sees movement and peels his eyes from Wilkes's remains. A thing that looks like a long, thick, gray worm is moving around on McGregor's chest. Her right hand hovers over it as if she's debating whether to grab it or not. Then her instincts kick in and she grabs the thing and throws it against the wall. The thick worm ruptures. Its insides look like the stuff that came from Wilkes's mouth.

"Out! Now!" Dr. Sulzer screams from outside, waving her arms to get them out of the med room. Movement on the floor catches Andy's attention. The things that came from inside Wilkes are moving around everywhere. They look more like slugs than worms now, and they have three tiny appendages on each side that resemble human hands. The floor is covered in them and some are starting to climb up the walls. They seem to be growing by the second. Andy doesn't need to see more.

"Are monsters real, Daddy?"

Yes, they definitely are, and not just the human ones.

As soon as everyone's out of the med room, Dr. Sulzer presses her card against the pad again and closes the door.

"What the fuck was that?" asks Shawl. Her big eyes look even bigger than usual. Andy wonders if she's in shock.

"Classroom, now," barks Johnson.

Back in the classroom, no one sits down. The walk there was a cacophony of curses and questions. No one cares about the former and no one tries to answer the latter. As they stand in the classroom, their eyes going from one to the other, it's Dr. Sulzer who takes the reigns instead of Johnson.

"Listen up," she says, sounding more confident and in control than Andy thought possible. "We need to check everyone. There's a chance—"

"I'm not going back in there," says Shawl. McGregor nods in agreement. "I don't want to be anywhere near those things."

"We'll get weapons and get you whatever you need, Sulzer," says Johnson. The front of his gray uniform is speckled with blood and vomit.

"I need the bronchoscope," says Dr. Sulzer.

"You think those things are inside all of us?" asks Mata.

Dr. Sulzer makes eye contact with everyone before replying, "Yeah... well, except Johnson and myself."

"How come?" asks Shawl.

"It's something we picked up in the mines, isn't it?" The idea had been brewing in Andy's mind, but as he ran to the classroom, it had coalesced into something that approached certainty. Hearing Dr. Sulzer say Johnson and her were clean sealed the deal.

"I think so," says Dr. Sulzer.

"How the fuck did Wilkes get something like that while wearing his protective suit?" asks Mata, their voice somewhere between anger and desperation.

"The eggs were in his lungs, so I'm guessing they start out small enough to get through the suit's air filters," says Johnson.

"Every other crew before us used suits with an internal oxygenation system," says McGregor. She's the crew's unofficial mechanic. Normally, she can fix anything. "Then they switched it to a supplementation system that relies partly on the oxygen in the atmosphere. We're the first crew to wear the news suits. The filters are probably cheap and—"

"Yeah, they're cheap because no one gives a fuck about our health," says Mata. "We're here because we need the money, and InterCorp knows it. My wife kept showing me stuff about how the first crew fucking vanished, and they still sent a second one up here. They were the ones to report the mantids. We all know the rest of that story."

Andy knows the story of every crew before his. He knows why they were taken to the mine and brought back in an armored vehicle. He knows the mantids—bizarre creatures the size of a bear that resemble a decomposing praying mantis on steroids—have devoured more people than InterCorp cares to admit. He even knows the company is unsure of what else is under the ground in P-986, but the amount of money they get paid to extract the illirium from the planet's mines is enough to make everyone forget everything they know and risk it all for a full bank account.

"We need to get the weap—"

Shawl coughs. Every eye on the room lands on her. She takes a step back.

"We need that bronchoscope now," says Dr. Sulzer.

"I'm the only one with access to the weapons, so I'll go," says Johnson. "The rest of you stay here. Don't enter the med room without me, understood?"

They all nod.

Johnson leaves the room. Silence ensues. It's a sharp, uncomfortable silence, pregnant with fear.

Johnson bursts back into the classroom, huffing and puffing like a wounded animal. He seems hesitant to hand them out, but everyone gets a gun.

Before they can head to the med room, Shawl starts coughing and can't stop. Fear moves into her eyes and settles in. The silence in the room speaks volumes about what they're all thinking.

"We need to get moving," says Johnson.

They leave McGregor with Shawl and move to the med room. They're still halfway down the hallway when they spot the remains of the door on the floor, the thick wetness atop then glinting under the artificial light.

"Those things got—"

Johnson doesn't get to finish because a mantid jumps out of the med room. Its insectoid head looked like a brown set of jaws that open sideways sitting under a pair of glossy baseballs covered in thick black lines. The creature's face and the childlike arms at its sides are covered in blood and bits of flesh dangle from the rows of sharp teeth that adorn each side of its jaws.

Monsters are always too real, and this one makes the cold fingers of fear wrap themselves around Andy's heart.

Johnson shoots first. The bullet whizzes past the creature and hits something at the end of the hallway. Then they all pull their triggers, the onslaught of bullets bringing the mantid down in a trembling heap of brown flesh, chunks of what looks like an exoskeleton, and an oily black liquid that appears to be the only thing inside its body.

Then they hear the screams.

Johnson tells them to go as he moves toward the med room. Andy wants to move away and head to the classroom. He doesn't want to see what's left of Wilkes again, but the idea of leaving Johnson alone doesn't sit right with him. Without asking, he walks to join him.

Inside the med room, Wilkes is now a pulpy puddle of something red with white fragments sitting on the floor next to the gurney.

"Those things grow faster than anything else I've seen." Johnson walks to a set of wall cabinets and pulls out the bronchoscope. "Let's go. Keep your eyes open."

Andy doesn't need to be told that, but he nods anyway.

They both want to run down to the classroom, but they don't. They walk slowly, listening, eyes scanning the hallway in front of them and giving quick glances back. There's a squishy sound coming from somewhere.

A bizarre sense of déjà vu slaps Andy as he walks into the classroom a few steps ahead of Johnson. On the floor near the door is Shawl. Her chest is a mound of flesh. It has grown so much it's ripped her uniform. A long wail erupts from her mouth and then tapers into something sad, wet, and desperate. McGregor is kneeling next to her.

"No, no, no." Mata shakes their head.

Dr. Sulzer moves toward Johnson and grabs the bronchoscope. McGregor jumps up from the floor.

"I wanna go first," she says. "I fucking need to know."

Dr. Sulzer nods. "Sit down over here. I'm going to ask you to tilt your head back and open your mouth so I can slide this down the back of your throat and through your vocal cords. I need to get into your airways and see what's there. It'll be uncomfortable, but it shouldn't hurt, okay?"

McGregor is already sitting. Instead of answering, she tilts her head back and opens her mouth.

They all look at Dr. Sulzer as she works. She seems to be having trouble getting the tube down. Her hands are shaking. Then Andy notices why: McGregor's chest is already visibly larger. She must have been hiding her coughs. He wonders if he's caught this thing too, and suddenly sees himself like Wilkes, a dead body on a gurney, his chest cavity and abdomen empty, his insides being digested by slimy gray alien monsters.

"Are monsters real, Daddy?"

Dr. Sulzer finally manages to get the tube in. She has a small digital screen in her left hand that shows her McGregor's insides. Then she takes half a step back.

McGregor yanks the tube out of herself and coughs.

"It's inside me, isn't it?" she asks. "That shit's inside me!" She coughs again.

Behind Andy, so does Mata.

"When will you be back, Daddy?"

The question comes out of nowhere. Andy's heart breaks all over again. He wants to scream "Soon!" so loud that his voice will carry across space and reach Andrea. He wants to reassure her that her dad is coming. But he can't. He can't because monsters are real.

"Check me, doc," says Mata between coughs. They take a step forward and stop. "Shawl's ab—"

The sound of Shawl's torso bursting is worse than the one Wilkes made. The loud pop brings with it a rain of flesh, blood, white slime, and gray slugs. The slithering monsters, nothing but babies at the moment, plop down on the floor or glide out of Shawl's empty chest cavity. They're covered in slime and have no discernible eyes, but they immediately start moving toward them. There are too many to count. They all start shooting and stomping simultaneously. The classroom becomes a room in Hell. Gray bodies explode in a maelstrom of screams, gunshots, and curses.

Andy has no idea how long it takes, but he feels like it took them ages to kill all those things and also like it was over in a few seconds. He looks toward the door. The rest of those things, the big ones, surely heard all that. It's time to do something, to move, to hide, to leave.

Johnson looks to Dr. Sulzer and moves his head. Andy looks at Johnson to get instructions, to receive orders so that he can convince himself at least someone is still in charge of this situation. Instead, he sees him tell Sulzer things with his head he wouldn't have dared utter out loud. Dr. Sulzer puts the bronchoscope down on the table.

"We have to assume everyone who was down in the mine has it. Wilkes didn't respond to anything, but maybe if they're not as developed, we can try to remove the eggs before they hatch and—"

"This place has three or four pieces of shitty equipment," says Mata. "They didn't even give us decent filters! We have to call for help."

"The rate of growth would make any call for help a waste of time," says Dr. Sulzer. "We have to try—"

"We need to get out of here now," says Andy. He doesn't care about the money now, only about getting out.

"When will you be back, Daddy?"

He hears the question again.

"The escape pods have a beacon that'll activate as soon—"

"There's only one escape pod," says Johnson. Everyone looks at him. "This is a low-budget operation. InterCorp had to pay a lot of money to the families of the miners who died during the first and second—"

"You're saying we're stuck here?"

"No, I'm saying Dr. Sulzer and I are going to use the remaining pod because we're healthy."

Johnson's words fill the room with a dangerous silence that's quickly shattered by McGregor's coughing. As Andy looks at her, McGregor grabs her throat and falls to her knees.

"Fuck, fuck, fuck!" says Mata, the word now a sacred mantra that's helping them hold on to the last sliver of sanity they have left.

"When will you be back, Daddy?"

Andy doesn't know... because monsters are real.

Andy watches as McGregor lies down and holds her bulging chest. She's fucked. They're all fucked. Or maybe he isn't. He hasn't coughed. He hasn't coughed even once that he can remember.

"I think we need to calm down and—"

"No!" Mata's hand is up now. They're holding their gun, aiming it at Dr. Sulzer. It shakes like a leaf in a summer storm. "No. We're all leaving. We're all leaving right now."

The left side of Mata's face vanishes in a puff of red dust. Andy isn't sure he heard Johnson's gun go off, but the results are obvious.

On the floor, McGregor gurgles as her uniform is stretched to its limits. The fabric starts to tear apart.

Andy looks at Johnson. The man's face is inscrutable, a block of black ice.

"When will you be back, Daddy?"

The work, the money, the worries; everything vanishes as Andy lifts his gun once more and shoots Johnson in the chest. When he turns to Dr. Sulzer, she has her gun trained on him.

"I'm sorry, Martínez," she says. "I'm so, so sorry."

Andy pulls the trigger. The gun clicks.

"I want to go home," says Andy. "I want to see my daughter."

"Are monsters real, Daddy?"

Andy is looking at one.

"I... I can't let you get out of here. We don't know what those things are. I'm gonna get in the pod and activate the beacon. They'll send help, I assure you."

Andy knows help won't come. It's not fair. Things are never fair. Distance isn't fair. Having to take a risky gig just for the money isn't fair. Fucking alien monsters in your lungs eating you from the inside out is not fair.

A mantid's head appears at the classroom's door. Dr. Sulzer turns and pulls the trigger. The creature's head explodes like a melon dropped from a rooftop. The black stuff inside it splatters the door and the two closest tables.

Dr. Sulzer bolts out of the room.

Andy drops his gun and thinks about running after her, but he knows she won't hesitate to shoot him. Instead, he stands there, waiting to hear a scream. If the mantids get her, the pod is his. It's a horrible thought, but one he has no reason and no energy to fight. You can only put someone through so much before they become a monster.

A loud clunk reverberates through the walls. It's the sound of the emergency hatch opening. Sulzer made it to the pod. He feels like going to a window to make sure, to see if he can see the pod making its way out of P-986, but he doesn't. Sadness and anger have congealed into something heavy that sits like a hot rock at the bottom of Andy's stomach. He hears a high-pitched sound. The mantids. How many? How many monsters? He doesn't know, but he might be able to call for help from the comm center. He can hide. Maybe help will come.

Hope is a strange monster that feeds on fear.

Andy walks over to Mata and picks up their gun. Then he picks up Johnson's as well. He's ready.

As he's reaching the classroom's door, Andy coughs. He stops. An icy feeling runs down his spine and something squeezes the back of his neck. He takes a deep breath. It feels normal. As he exhales, he coughs again... and again. When he stops coughing, he hears something else, a little voice.

"*Are monsters real, Daddy?*"

SONG OF THE DEVIL TRUMPET

GABY TRIANA

28th of July 1925

MY DEAREST ADELAIDE,

I regret to inform you that I am not so well and desperately need assistance getting home to Boston. From the moment my mentor, the capable but misunderstood Dr. Atkinson from the College of Agriculture at Cornell, first sent me that colorful postcard from Florida, the one with the image of Mr. Flagler's railroad surrounded by oranges, it has been one nightmare after another, to say the least.

Perhaps some background is required, which I will take the time to provide now while I sit in the fresh air awaiting my afternoon tea. I apologize for my shaky penmanship, but in light of all I have been through, it is a miracle I have any faculties left at all. I understand I left home rather abruptly, but I also knew if I didn't take the opportunity given to me, Mother would have tried to get me to stay, and I would have missed out on suitable employment. Now I wish she had intervened. As you might know, opportunities for young botanists, especially those of the female variety, are few and far between, and I've lain awake many a night now wondering if I should have given into Father's expectations and studied the domestic arts instead.

As it were, Dr. Atkinson invited me and another assistant to his outpost in the lower, uncharted regions of Florida, and I accepted. As you may have heard, land development is violently underway here, with new cities being built at every turn. One of the drawbacks to this has been the deforestation of plants and trees, and though I cheer for the advancements of modern man, I also lament the eradication of native species, particularly those on the verge of extinction. And so I agreed to join Dr. Atkinson's team currently busy classifying native flora, some never before discovered, before they are—pardon the pun—uprooted.

I realize I may not have informed you of the details of my study, or perhaps you were reluctant to hear them because of the way we parted, but my hope at Cornell had been to make new discoveries in the field of agriculture, particularly as they relate to sentient, intelligent plant life. Please don't laugh; I was mocked enough upon submitting my dissertation, then ridiculed again when I arrived at this hospital, thus my need for your help receiving discharge. When I was required by my professors to revise my hypothesis, I chose the more sensible topic of sexual reproduction of Marchantia polymorpha instead, although Dr. Atkinson, the only professor willing to learn more about my original, more speculative course of study, remained curious.

I will not lie, the train ride into the wilderness was marvelous. What impressed upon me the most was the dominance of the great Dixie highway, the absolute certainty that along its course, new property was certain to grow. In the distance, I saw an endless stream of motor cars heading South, and as we passed through Daytona Beach and neared Miami, my attention was called to a billboard proclaiming the shiny benefits of this "new city in the making."

But my time near the shore would be brief, as Dr. Atkinson's driving assistant collected me, as well as another botanist recently graduated from the University of Iowa, from the train depot. We would venture further west, he said, away from the current boom of hotels, landscaped electrical cities, and plantations, to his outpost in a vast area of wetlands, dubbed the Pa-hay-okee or "river of grass" by the local Indian population. It was here we would be received, given private quarters, and all manner of necessities for the duration of our month-long stay. Only from the moment Dr. Atkinson's driver unceremoniously deposited us on the front porch of the outpost before quickly leaving us to our own defenses, there was no one to be found.

If this sounds horrific, dear sister, I do apologize. I mean no histrionics by this description; it is exactly as happened, and I regret to inform you that it only gets worse from here. At this point, I would have given anything to return to the trucks, tractors, and road-making equipment of the beaches, but my travel mate and colleague, a Mr. Herbert Wilhelm, assured me that Dr. Atkinson was probably out in the field, would return promptly, and be happy to welcome us. After all, he had invited us to stay and would not have vacated the premises prematurely without due cause. To be fair, Mr. Wilhelm had every reason to be right, and to make stronger his case, insisted he was in possession of forest survival training in the event that something unforeseen had befallen the scientists. If after a few days our hosts should not return, he would procure transportation back to the train station for our departure home.

As I set aside my hesitation and agreed, we promptly settled into our individual bungalows for the evening. The outpost was situated on a broad island surrounded by shallow patches of watery sawgrass. For an hour, we would enjoy wide swaths of tangerine sky dotted with purple cloud ellipses, a half loaf of stale bread to share, and some black tea too bitter for my tastes, but once the sun set, any humidity and heat deemed tropical by day transformed into ominous atmosphere by night. Thankful for the half-moon above us, it did not take a zoologist to recognize the howling of wolves in the distance, the agitated slap of fish tails in the water, nor the rustling of leaves on the ground, which my imagination translated into visions of pythons and crocodiles. Even the cypress trees hovering around us—bald or pond, I wasn't sure—seemed to watch us new intruders with disdain in the bleak darkness. I found the spectacle unsettling but reasoned that my feelings about the unfamiliar environment were to blame.

In the morning, after a comfortable sleep on a bedded cot, I should not have been surprised to find that Dr. Atkinson had not yet returned from his supposed work in the field, but Mr. Wilhelm had made a lovely fire and a delicious breakfast of coffee and bacon from the last scraps of wild hog in the icebox, he said, and so we opened our notebooks afterwards and got to classifying, hopeful that the doctor and his cohorts would soon return.

What I'd considered to be cypress trees the night before turned out to be something else, something I'd never seen before—tall, lanky trunks with green-brown leafy canopy and a root system that reached into the watery soil like the gnarled fingers of some thirsty giant. Overflowing fluted white and pink flowers hung like the delicate trumpets of upside-down Victrolas, but no fruits were seen, a characteristic I attributed to the trees' vigor, its efforts to survive impending deforestation rather than to thrive. When I mentioned the trees' "intent," Mr. Wilhelm regarded me with the same suspicious look my colleagues at Cornell had all given me. But you see, dear sister, there is much evidence to support the hypothesis that trees think similarly to humans, if only we scientists would open our eyes and observe the subtle signs. Trees work together by sending signals, they protect their young by feeding sugar solution to their saplings, and they make decisions to self-preserve by withholding fruit, as evidenced by the outpost's chlorophyll-ic residents.

Fascinated, I made copious notes only to realize we may be doubling, even tripling our efforts and should look for the doctor's notebooks for more information. As the lead botanist on this expedition, I told Mr. Wilhelm, Dr. Atkinson would have had these trees figured out by now, and our invited presence was likely only for validation and peer review. He agreed, and we set off to find empirical evidence amid the tables littered with drawings, calculations, and ramblings. Putting together a large puzzle with incomplete pieces proved to be more difficult than expected, however, and we easily spent our first two days scouring through the scattered fieldnotes, both descriptive and analytic. The most curious thing of all was the lack of mention of the trees ~~watching~~ surrounding us. While study of the slash pine, hardwood hammocks, and manchineel, the area's most toxic plant, seemed plentiful (understandably so, considering a person would become poisoned just by standing underneath it during the rain), observations of the odd cypress trees with the big, trumpet-like flowers were nowhere to be found.

And it was this tree, dear sister, that entranced me the most.

Over the next several days, our provisions became scarce, and Mr.

Wilhelm left me alone for hours at a time, setting off with a fishing rod fashioned from reeds and twine in the hopes of bringing back bass, trout, or even the swamp's reptiles. The oppressive heat forced us to remove layers of clothing, and I need not tell you how uncomfortable a lady can feel down to her knickers around a shirtless man, no matter how genteel he is, but this and dining on roasted frog would soon prove to be the least of our troubles. Our worries began turning to unbridled concern when upon the fifth day, the doctor had still not yet returned, and our food supplies ran out. We had stopped working long enough to sit around listlessly, conserving energy and daydreaming, and it was during this reflection and brain-slowing when it occurred to me that a hat—a single, wide-brimmed sunhat—still hung upon a hook in the doctor's quarters. Would the doctor not have taken his hat into the field with him in this unabashed wasteland of sun?

When I mentioned this to Mr. Wilhelm after his unfortunate encounter with a baby hog who narrowly escaped becoming our lunch, he grew distressed and accused me of causing alarm. He used me as Exhibit A to reason why women should not be allowed in the realm of rational thinkers and angrily contended that female emotion bore no place in the scientific field. My dear Adelaide, I had not so much as shed a tear in the five days before Mr. Wilhelm exploded into misplaced hysterics. He spent the rest of the day grumbling and designing traps to catch our next meal, another failure that made me question his attested skills. Still, I kept my composure, all the while internalizing that we might soon perish if Dr. Atkinson did not return with supplies and transportation. The whole time, his hat upon the hook mocked me, suggesting a different version of the mystery.

If not for the fresh water with which the very land seemed to be soaked, we would not have persisted an entire week, and though Mr. Wilhelm kept insisting we should wait one more day for Dr. Atkinson to return, I knew by now that the good doctor had likely been consumed, swallowed whole, and eliminated by an alligator, shoes and all. My bag was packed and ready by my bungalow door to return to Boston. In the morning, I would begin trekking the miles back to the train depot, calculating that it should take me twenty or so hours to walk.

Only at night, in the privacy of my own quarters, did I allow myself to cry ever so quietly, for if Mr. Wilhelm had seen me do so, he might have been inclined to use me as bait for his traps. All through the night, I watched the trees shift, their shadows encroaching on our encampment. In my exhausted state, I thought I heard them talk to each other, conspire in hushed tones, agree to rid their land of their viral invaders. Through hisses and pops, I imagined them emitting chemical signals of protection from those who might raze them to make way for modern civilization, and though that was not our purpose there, I do not believe the cypress with the large trumpet flowers cared one way or another. In the morning, my suspicions were confirmed when I found they had seemed to double in both size and quantity overnight. How was that possible? Even the fastest-growing trees required time to reproduce. They arched inward, creating a tight canopy that even the tropical sunlight could not penetrate, but most peculiar of all was the fruit, the single offering per tree, that had grown in mere hours as we slept.

Before I could examine it, Mr. Wilhelm was already searching for his knife to cut down the massive bounty sprouting from the center of one trumpet flower. The fruit was yellow and green, brown in spots, resembling an overripe papaya larger than a dog's head, and when my colleague climbed on the roof of the outpost, cut it down, and impaled it with his knife, it let out a hissy breath of fumes. Sweet, tangy, with a touch of retribution. Nervous to challenge a man who had admonished me for "causing alarm" a day earlier, I hesitated to impart my opinion that we should leave it alone. For one, I had never, in all my years of research, seen a piece of fruit grow so quickly and so large, and two, we knew nothing about this species. Nothing at all. Least of all did I tell him that I believed the trees had communicated, conspired in the night as we slept.

But before I could test if my instincts were right, Mr. Wilhelm was already slicing up the fruit whose center pit was so large and misshapen, and if it weren't for my years of study to inform me better, closely resembled a dried human heart. Sustenance! He proclaimed joyfully, almost maniacally, as he ripped into the orangey flesh with his desperate teeth, tearing off juicy chunks of dripping pulp with his knife and shoving them between his thick lips. Watching him, I could tell the fruit was sweet and delicious, the perfect refreshment for a parched throat and empty digestive system, and I would be lying if I said I didn't want to join in his revelry of the unexpected treat. The towering trees themselves seemed to whisper their encouragement, their flexible branches reaching down in the hot breeze, their flowers singing ancient melodies designed to invoke appreciation.

Scientific method be damned, I was hungry.

I reached out to swipe a piece for myself when suddenly, Mr. Wilhelm stopped moving, a piece of stringy flesh dangling from his lips, as he stared straight at me. For a moment, I thought I had offended him again. Perhaps women should also not be allowed to consume fruit directly from the source until a man had sampled it first? In spite of myself, I was prepared to utter apologies for not minding my manners when my colleague's brown eyes glossed over, and he began to convulse. From his mouth began to spew a frothy white foam, tinged with streaks of pink and red. Amid his whimpers, the foam overflowed from his mouth, cascaded down his chin, and dripped toward the ground where its acid caused the foliage to sizzle and smoke.

My dear Adelaide, this is the part where the nurses here shake their heads, and the doctors mumble that I will not be leaving under any circumstances. The orderlies carry me to the isolated room with the cushioned walls, but I assure you and maintain that everything I am telling you is real. As I watched in revulsion, the swallowing passage of Mr. Wilhelm's body, his esophagus, as it is known, was expelled from his mouth, slipped and tumbled to the ground like volcanic lava, followed by his bloated stomach. Foot after bleeding foot of bowels continued to stream out, coiling at his feet like snakes. Even then, I did not scream, for I could only watch in detached horror, as my colleague slumped to the ground, as his fingers grasped and clutched at the earth then hardened into thickened roots, finally snaking into the soil to find footing.

All the while the fruit's toxicity overcame Mr. Wilhelm, he watched me with bulging, pleading orbs that melted into their very hollows. I believe I may have tried to help him then, reached for his hand and tugged on it to help him stand, but at this point, the whole length of his legs had doubled in size and burst from his trousers, brownish purple bruising spreading along his fair skin, and his limbs exploded from within by a spiraling, expanding tree root. Moments later, the trunk of a new cypress rose out of Mr. Wilhelm's abdomen and chest, shredding both apart, and it soared to new heights in the forest. A new tree had formed, the bulk of it absorbing what was left of Mr. Wilhelm's body, and his head snapped off like heavy fruit, rolled away, and became caught in the massive tangle of roots.

Anyone witnessing would have heard the silence.

Not a sound but the flap of heron wings, rustle of leaves, and swishing sawgrass for miles and miles. The drip of Mr. Wilhelm's fluids seeping into the ground, watering his new flesh-infused silhouette. But to the discerning botanist, there was music—a divine, monstrous melody of nature protecting herself. Dr. Atkinson never did return, and I never did taste the fruit of that devil tree's trumpet, but I did sit at its base for hours upon hours, rocking and singing to myself, observing, learning, taking mental notes of this marvelous, intelligent creature. In the night wind, I heard the call of panthers, the hiss of alligators, and the croak of tree snakes, but not once more was I afraid of the fauna.

Not once.

My dearest sister, this letter has gone on long enough, and now I must leave you. The nurse has brought my tea—made, she says, from the dried flesh of local fruit similar to the papaya. I am the first patient at Orangewood Sanitarium for Women to sample it, she says, a real opportunity. Aren't I lucky? When she set it down in front of these pages, I caught a whiff. Sweet, tangy, with a touch of retribution. On second thought, there is no need to help with discharge, for I know I will never leave this place. Perhaps that is for the best. In a few minutes, they will all witness my mysterious disappearance, a new, unclassified specimen in my place. My most significant contribution to science.

Soon we will all be trees, the women here.

Perhaps they will finally name us.

Be well, dear sister.

THE PIKE

PRIS SEARS

MARIA NEEDED to get off the road. It was doing things to her judgment. She felt it pulling at that mental lever marked "casual cruelty" that she'd been trying not to touch. Some days made it hard.

She had just arrived at Barkey's, one of the bigger truck stops in North Carolina. She had been tracking what she mentally referred to as "the Pike" for two years now. She didn't drive herself anymore. Not since she started sensing the Pike. She hitched rides instead, mostly with truckers. She'd gotten adept at passing herself off as an itinerant researcher of highway phenomena. Animal migration, crash statistics, driving behavior. Whatever she thought would appeal to her next prospective host. Generally not too far from what she did in her life before.

The Pike swelled in the east and then north as the season turned warmer.

BARKEY'S WAS A NO-NONSENSE trucking facility. It didn't boast tourist tchotchkes or displays that would attract civilians. Maria had enough of a bankroll to stay holed up in the hotel attached to Barkey's for a couple of days. Months, if she had to, but she didn't think she had that long. She was looking for the right driver heading north.

She didn't mind hanging around for a while. Picking the wrong ride could be disastrous. Her last ride had been close to ideal. Linda, a cheerful middle-aged woman, picked her up when they met at a truck stop in Jackson, Mississippi. Maria told Linda she was researching raptor populations along the coasts. They had driven from Jackson to Jacksonville, Florida, then to North Carolina. Maria played DJ and read the news out loud from the internet when Linda asked. She heated up food, fetched drinks, and generally made herself useful.

Maria had long stretches of quiet on the highway to watch for Pike signs—an unblemished guardrail curled into a nautilus spiral. A bright smear of blood three lanes wide and a quarter mile long, no flesh or fur left behind. The blackened husk of a school bus on the shoulder, windowless. The conflagration had burned so fiercely it left no trace of yellow. The pavement below the bus was clean and gray. No glass glittered in the weeds. She entered them in her database, making corresponding marks on the master map on her tablet. She pointed out hawks to Linda if she spotted any during periods of quiet traffic and pretended to mark her map for those, too.

Linda hadn't been in the trucking business long. She didn't have much of a Pike-light at all, just a slight gray shimmer. Maria had first become aware of the Pike when she started seeing dark auras around places she was working on the roads. Poorly designed intersections where terrible crashes had happened. Trailers where dozens of people had died of heat and exhaustion. She found herself drawn back to such places. When she encountered people responsible, she saw they, too, shone with the dark Pike-light.

Studying the Pike and its light wove a connection over time. The link was growing deeper. She had been able to feel the Pike in her mind for the last year, incoherent yearning and hunger.

The trailer Linda's big truck pulled was thick with Pike-light—a ragged black fog clinging to the length of the long metal box. There was a shiny metal bill box on the trailer's bulkhead behind the truck's cab. It had a little padlock on it, preventing Maria from sneaking a peek at the trailer's paperwork. She never saw Linda open the trailer or bill box. Maria noted the trailer number and originating company. She didn't try to pry into what could have been a volatile subject with her gracious host. Did Linda have any idea what she was hauling, that she was feeding the Pike? Would she care? Should Maria show her?

After Greensboro, Linda was heading west to Johnson City. Maria could feel the Pike was more active to the north. Was it finally going to surface? Maria gathered up her gear and made her goodbyes when Linda stopped at Barkey's for fuel and snacks.

On her own and wide awake even though it was past midnight, Maria bought a shower. Under the hot spray, she could feel the Pike rumble in her mind like the faint vibration of the big trucks on the highway in the distance. It had fed so well for so long, supping quietly and growing below the highways. Now it was moving, turning, kicking.

Maria toweled her hair dry in the well-appointed adjoining restroom. She brushed her teeth, put on shorts and her jacket over a tank top. Leaving the showers, she passed the general store. A small gaming arcade chattered to itself in the quiet wee hours. Machines in the empty coin laundry provided what she needed to wash her jeans, shirts, underwear, and sleeping bag.

Waiting for the dryer, she read up on the freight company that owned Linda's cargo but only hit dead ends. She changed back into her hot, clean, jeans in a bathroom stall and headed for the all-night-diner part of the truck stop.

As soon as she walked in, Lou and Ernie greeted her like old friends in the empty late-night restaurant. They were in a booth in front of a large window facing the parking lot, the only customers at the moment.

"No need to eat alone!" Lou called, voice echoing in the quiet space. "We haven't even ordered yet."

Lou got up and gave her a gallant wave. He slid in next to Ernie, leaving a vinyl-upholstered bench seat empty for Maria. Myrtle, the tired waitress, rolled her eyes but made no comment as she delivered coffee and menus.

The red vinyl seats squeaked, taut and slippery. Embellished with little glittering flecks, they sparkled like metal flake under the fluorescent lights. The worn Formica table top was clean, a sickly green with a pattern of little black and white lines and arcs. It stood sturdily on a central metal post bolted to the floor.

Maria took the vacated bench, still a little warm from Lou's body. She could see Pike-light swirling around his head as he grinned at her and jostled Ernie. The smoky haze telegraphed his unpleasant whims. Lou introduced himself and Ernie as a driver team from Ohio. She got the impression that Ernie hadn't been in the business long and Lou was still trying to sell him on it. Lou seemed like the type that was always trying to sell somebody something.

"OHIO's the best place you could want for a home base. We can take jobs in either direction and still be home for the game on Sunday!" Lou enthused. He was a middle-aged man with blue eyes, a round belly, and a short gray mustache. His unbuttoned plaid shirt revealed a black-on-orange Cincinnati Bengals t-shirt below.

Myrtle returned, refilled their coffees, and took their orders. Chicken and waffles and pancakes for Lou and Ernie, grilled cheese and tomato soup for Maria. Both men's heads swiveled to watch Myrtle as she trudged back to the kitchen.

The Pike-light around Lou's head darkened as they waited for their food. Maria acted distracted, gazing out the window at a truck pulling in as Lou chattered. She kept a close eye on his reflection. It was easy to spot it when he reached over for a napkin and dropped something in her coffee.

Even if she hadn't caught his furtive movement in the window, his flushed, smug, face would have given away that he'd done something. Not to mention the Pike-light that spiked high enough around his groin to see it poking above the tabletop. Maria forced herself not to show her dismay at his attempt to drug her, or her revulsion at his excited Pike-light. She pretended to sip her coffee, finally pushing it away when Myrtle brought their food.

Ernie was a younger man, reserved compared to Lou. Pale skin, shoulder-length stringy brown hair, a fuzz of beard, he could have been as young as 18 or as old as 30. He must be brand new to the road. He hadn't developed a visible Pike-light yet. He had been yawning and not paying much attention to Lou or his well-worn trucking recruitment patter. Maria switched cups with Ernie when both men turned to gawk at Myrtle walking away again.

They ate in silence, Lou stealing glances at Maria as he sawed on his breaded chicken. He figured out something had gone wrong when Ernie slumped into the corner of the booth and let out a messy snore, mouth still full of pancakes.

Glaring at Maria, Lou started to maneuver out of the booth. She reached under the table and snatched the Pike-light still spiking above Lou's crotch. She stretched and wound it tight around the table's metal central support. Her booted foot pressed firmly against the loops of captured Pike-light as she leaned back.

Lou didn't know exactly what was happening. What part of him was her boot's tread digging into? It felt like naked flesh clamped with jumper cables and dunked in gasoline. He froze in his seat.

"I'm not going to hurt you, even though you wanted to hurt me," Maria said.

She pulled paper napkins from the chrome dispenser and wiped both her hands. She hadn't touched someone else's Pike-light like that before, didn't know she could. It had compressed but held together under her grip, stretching like slimy taffy.

She peered at him from gray eyes shadowed deep with sudden fatigue.

"But I'm tired and you need to stop. So I'm going to *show* you."

Black tarry tendrils, swirled through with nacreous smears, issued from her fingers. They squirmed and stretched toward Lou. No longer amped with the raucous energy of one looking forward to some simple savage fun, Lou quivered.

She reached across the table. Lou's eyes rolled with panic. His butt clenched tight on the sparkly red vinyl bench. Maria's wide eyes filled with a fractaling black as she stretched her arms out. Thick sticky extrusions of eager Pike-light caressed Lou's sweating forehead.

He slumped back, eyes bulging as he fell through a cataract of death and pain. Lou's mind buckled under the weight of every worm smashed under speeding tires. He felt every precious life-minute stolen on every road and driveway. He saw a silvery light sparkling away from the inattentive, the inebriated, the selfish, and the uninformed.

Lou felt his essential self slide out of his eyes, through pores in the plate glass window into a pothole in the parking lot. He trickled down through the oily grit into cracks in the compacted layers below. His meat body remained rigid in the diner booth. He was drowning in wasted life force. It pooled in measureless sticky black reservoirs under the highways. It ran everywhere, branching across, enmeshing the continent.

The suffocating black congealment of wasted lives was shot through with shimmering scraps of the vital fluid of tarnished morality. Confettied shreds of superego pared away from oblivious perpetrators. Flayed ribbons of the precious substance unwittingly tossed away, crushed under the never-ending wheels. The silver flakes swirled into the black lagoon, dim stars spangling a lightless void.

All that sacrifice has to feed something. Lou could feel it moving down there. Some well-fed thing was rising, raging against Lou and all its stuporous parents. The Pike was clamoring to know its purpose. To know why it was being born alone. To know why it *was*.

Maria looked Lou over. His body was still motionless. His eyes were regaining some presence amid the onslaught. He was being remade by his baptism in the secret ocean that crisscrossed the continent. Ernie drooled next to him, torpid and blind to the proceedings thanks to Lou's secret sauce.

The black smears Maria had left on Lou's forehead gradually disappeared, dissolving into his flesh. The tendrils retreated into her fingers, leaving them smooth and blank. Her eyes were a determined gray.

"All that ceaseless, thoughtless, loss leaves marks, Lou," she said. "It digs deep and plants seeds. All that blood ground into the asphalt, all those creatures great and small. All that waste so humans can get somewhere fast. All those breaths black with smog have exhaled together to give life to something greater. Somebody needs to be there when it's born. At least we owe it that."

Lou gave a hesitant nod.

Maria drained what had been Ernie's coffee cup, stood, and dropped some bills on the table. She added an extra twenty for Myrtle. Her hands were clean but Lou could see it now. A dense black ring circled above her head, sparkling with pearly gray flakes.

"Come on, Lou," she said. "I think Ernie can make his own way home. We need to be heading north."

Acknowledgements

Douglas Gwilym...

To the nearly 800 talented folks who sent us monster tales from around the world, THANK YOU. You are the stars in this mad constellation, and I will always brag about you.

To the twenty-four amazing creators whose work appears in these pages, your imagination and professionalism blew us away. May your monsters live forever, rising always to feast on the willing.

To my editorial partner in crime, Mr. Ken MacGregor, thanks for the laughs, the relentless attention to detail, the snorts, the reasonable resolutions of conflict, and, always, your hard work and enthusiasm in these here monster-infested story mines. Proud to be on your team.

To Michael Cieslak and Dragon's Roost Press, BIG thanks for providing the perfect, supportive home for our specially-proportioned monster baby.

To my very favorite artist (and mind, and human) Debra Tomson Williams and my girl hero Zelia (known in some circles as "the Creature"), everything is possible because of you two.

To my greater Pittsburgh writer besties and spooky gang, and to all my wonderful writing and music-making pals everywhere, you freak me out, and make me think, and make me laugh. And sometimes even scare me. Keep it up!

Ken MacGregor...

First and foremost, to Douglas Gwilym, for being excited about this project from the beginning, and for the endless conversations, the many laughs, the professionalism and patience, and the months of slogging through the slush pile to find gold. What started as "Hey, what do you think of..." has turned into a pretty amazing book. It's been a hell of a ride, and I'm proud to be working with you.

To the authors who trusted us with your work, both the twenty-two whose stories appear in these pages, and the nearly 800 who submitted to the open call. So many incredible monster stories! It was no easy task to narrow it down to the book in your hand.

To Trevor Henderson, who is not only a spectacularly talented artist, but also a heck of a nice guy.

To Jamie Flanagan, whose work we absolutely adore, for taking the time to write our introduction, which we also adore.

To Dragon's Roost Press, and the man at the helm, Michael Cieslak: I've been with the press since they began, and this is my fifth book with them. When we conceived of The Midnight Zone, I knew DRP was the place to help make it a reality.

To my live-in monster fans, Elise and Milo MacGregor: Hey, kids... I know I've been crazy busy for the past several months, and I'm sorry about that, but... Hey! I have another book!

To Liz Thomas, who has a deep and abiding love for things dark and strange, which apparently extends to me. Thank you for your enthusiastic support for my creative endeavors. There are many foot-pedal moments in this book.

Thank You To All Of Our
Kickstarter Backers

Thank you to all of the wonderful people who backed the Kickstarter campaign.

Patrick Andersson, Juan Aquino, Robert Arber, Michael Axe, Alan Stephen Bailey, Stephen Barerra, Noah Bowles, Bridget Brave, Jennifer Briggs, Melanie Briggs, Lissa Brooks, Earl Corey Brown, Sarah Brunner, Dan Bugbee, Brian P Burgoyne, Carolyn Canterman, Scott Casey, Jeremy Capelotti, Amanda Cavanaugh, James Chambers, Ryan Clark, Kelly Clarke, Greg Clumpner, Jon Conley, Joseph Connell, Amy Cook, T.J. Corona, Barbara Cottrell, Kaitlyn Cottrell, Sam Cowan, Beatrice Crampton, Kanoe Mackenzie Creech, Tim Cuzmar, Lauren Elise Daniels, Tom Deady, Ron Dickie, Erin Dorgan, Marlene Dorgan, Sydney Dunstan, Samantha Eaton-Roberts, Brian Edwards, Chad J Ellis, John Ellis, Rebecca Elliott, Jessica Enfante, Timons Esaias, Jason Ezra, Colleen Feeney, Christina Fernandez, Rob Field, Zachary Fissel, Andrew Foxx, Adam Gainsley, Tiffany George, Philip Giles, Sietel Gill, Elizabeth Goss, Linda Gould, Catherine Green, Lizzie Green, Jon Gregerson, Mindy Gudmundson, Peter Guenther, Heather Hall, Mitchell Hall, Richard Hebson, Jenna Henkel, Christina Heron, Douglas Blake Huffman, Hailey Claire Hull, Larry Ivkovich, Ryan James, Chris Jarocha-Ernst, Susan Jessen, Jeremy C Justus, Jonathan,

Stephenie Kelly, Shad Kelly, Kaden Koba, Windi LaBounta, Jamie Lackey, Algie Lane, Michelle Renee Lane, Adeline LeStrange, Frank Lewis, Janna Liggan, Gerald Loiselle, Lotte Lomholt, Rex Long, Michael W Lucas, Tim Mack, Joshua Maestas, Nicolas Mandujano III, Erik Mann, Mike Mann, Madeleine Marie-Rose, Anthony Matosic, Susan Maze, Paul D McDaniel, Karat McFall, Joshua McGinnis, Kathryn McLeer, Sirrah Medeiros, Jennifer Medicapps, Kristina Meschi, Scotty Milder, Cary Miller, Kirby Miller, Donna J. W. Munro, Poom Namvol, Conor Neilson, Erin C Nickerson, Richard O'Shea, Niko Oinas, Cheryl Orosz, Kevin Parma, Brandy Pastore, Steven Pattee, David Perlmutter, Chris Phillips, Isaiah Badger Pittman, Matthew Plank, Ryan Power, Eric Priehs, Joseph Procopio, Chris Michael Pullen, Jason Ramer, Nathaniel Rebosa, Tynan Reddoch, Louise Richardson, Ernie Ridley, Michael Riesenman, William E. Riggs, Giusy Rippa, Solomon Stone Romney, Joe Rossomanno, Emily Rousell, Corto Rudant, Dr. Casey J Rudkin, Chelsea Russell, Robert Russell, Chris Ryan, Will Sampson, Robert Saenz, Mario Santos, Pris Sears, Jeffrey Paul Sinclair, Josh Singeltary, William Slade, Christopher J Smith, Michelle Steiner, Nicholas Stephenson, Adam Stevens, Kelly Snyder, Josh Strnad, David Swisher, Andrew Thomas, Kevin Thomas, Tonel, Patrick Toner, Paul Trinies, Nelson Truong, Knick Umstead, Matthew Urick, James Van Horn, April Vukelic, Regina Weber, Kalyn Williams, Mark Williams, Laine Wilson, Heather Wiscarson, Tim Woolworth, Andrew Wright, and Skip Zepeda.

Your support allowed us to put together this amazing anthology. Without you, this would not have been possible.

BIOGRAPHIES

Bram Stoker Award-nominated short story author and editor **Douglas Gwilym** (editor) has also been known to compose a weird fiction rock opera or two. His short story "Poppy's Poppy" was a finalist for a Stoker and is being taught as part of the University of Pittsburgh curriculum. His story "Year Six" was recommended by "the venerable queen of horror anthologies" Ellen Datlow for *The Best Horror of the Year volume 14*. He wants to read to you. See him perform 35 hours of classic Victorian and Edwardian Weird on YouTube, and read his own work on *Galactic Terrors* and elsewhere. It was his very great pleasure to teach at Alpha Young Writers (a professional writing workshop for teens) with N.K. Jemison and Mary Robinette Kowal, and to introduce his beloved home city as moderator of the opening panel of StokerCon 2023, *You Can't Get There From Here: Tales of Weird Pittsburgh*. He's edited four of the *Triangulation* anthologies: *Beneath the Surface, Appetites, Harmony & Dissonance,* and *Dark Skies,* and is co-editor of The Midnight Zone, including issue 1, *Novus Monstrum,* which you hold in your hand. He lives with the visual artist Debra Tomson Williams and their daughter, The Creature, in an undisclosed location in the inner-city woods of Pittsburgh, Pennsylvania. Read his work in *LampLight, Lucent Dreaming, Dark Horses, Penumbric Speculative,* and *Tales from* *the Moonlit Path,* or listen at Bloody Disgusting's *CREEPY* podcast or *Tales to Terrify.*

Ken MacGregor (editor) has written three story collections, an award-winning young adult novella (*Devil's Bane*), and has co-authored a novel (*Headcase*). He is a member of the Great Lakes Association of Horror Writers and an active member of the Horror Writers Association. He's also written TV and radio commercials, sketch comedy, a music video, a one-act play, a scattering of poems, and a zombie movie. Ken has curated two original anthologies, one of which (*Stitched Lips*) was a finalist for the Shirley Jackson Award. This, his third anthology, *Novus Monstrum,* was co-edited with Douglas Gwilym. It is the first installment in the Midnight Zone series for Dragon's Roost Press. Ken is also a part-time literary assassin: he will write you into an original short story and kill you for money.

Ken drives the bookmobile and lives with his kids, two cats, and the ashes of his wife.

He can be found at www.kenmacgregor.com.

Trevor Henderson (Cover Art) is a writer and illustrator, and the creator of the internet horror character Siren Head. His love of monsters, cryptids, ghosts, and other horrible entities is enduring and vast. He wrote and drew a middle-grade horror book for Scholastic called *Scarewaves.* When he is not drawing or writing horrible things, he is thinking about the unknowable and hostile forces working against all of humanity, and playing with his cat, who is named Boo. He is available for illustration work!

http://www.trevorhenderson.com/

Jamie Flanagan (Introduction) is an American writer and actor. Screenwriting credits include *The Haunting of Bly Manor, Midnight Mass, The Midnight Club,* and upcoming releases *The Fall of the House of Usher* (Netflix), *Creepshow: Season 4* (AMC Shudder), and Peacock's *Hysteria!*

Joshua Bartolome (Mother Ship) is a Filipino-Canadian writer living in Calgary, Alberta. His prose poem, "The Cadaver," was shortlisted for the Montreal Poetry Prize, while in 2017, his screenplay, "The Red Death," won the Silver Screamfest award for best horror script. "Aswang," a tale of poverty, misery and violence, was published in the anthology *Tales of Blood and Squalor.* Another short story, "The Last Confession of Dottore Gepetto," was published in the *We Shall be Monsters* anthology, and his cosmic horror story, "Barker, Alberta," was included in *Postcards From the Void*, an anthology by the Darkwater Syndicate. In late 2019, his horror screenplay, "The Crossing," became a semifinalist in the Academy Nicholl Competition.

A mass of tentacles and rose vines masquerading as a person, **Amanda M. Blake** (Sight Unseen) is the author of such horror titles as *Deep Down* and *Out of Curiosity and Hunger,* dark poetry collection *Dead Ends,* and the *Thorns* fairy tale mash-up series. For more, visit www.amandamblake.com.

Matt Brandenburg (First Day Jitters at Slappy's) is a horror writer living next to a moldy pumpkin patch in Kalamazoo Michigan. He has a novella coming out with *Unnerving Books.* You can find his work in *34 Orchard, The Dark Corner Zine,* and *Tales to Terrify.* He is also a cohost on the podcast *Staring Into The Abyss.* When he's not writing cartoonish horror, he is usually listening to horror movie scores, watching goofy movies, or playing with Lego. Find him on *X* and *Bluesky* under his name.

Author of *Corporate Body, Words Made of Flesh,* and too many stories about things that crawl into you, Shirley Jackson Award-winning author **R.A. Busby** (Catfish) spends her spare time running in the desert with her dog, hiking through forests, and finding weird things to write about.

The *Oxford Companion to English Literature* describes **Ramsey Campbell** (The Assembled) as "Britain's most respected living horror writer". He has been given more awards than any other writer in the field, including the Grand Master Award of the World Horror Convention, the Lifetime Achievement Award of the Horror Writers Association, the Living Legend Award of the International Horror Guild and the World Fantasy Lifetime Achievement Award. In 2015 he was made an Honorary Fellow of Liverpool John Moores University for outstanding services to literature. Among his novels are *The Face That Must Die*, *Incarnate*, *Midnight Sun*, *The Count of Eleven*, *The Darkest Part of the Woods*, *The Overnight*, *Secret Story*, *The Grin of the Dark*, *Thieving Fear*, *Creatures of the Pool*, *The Seven Days of Cain*, *Ghosts Know*, *The Kind Folk*, *Think Yourself Lucky*, *Thirteen Days by Sunset Beach*, *The Wise Friend*, *Somebody's Voice*, *Fellstones* and *The Lonely Lands*. His Brichester Mythos trilogy consists of *The Searching Dead*, *Born to the Dark* and *The Way of the Worm*. His collections include *Waking Nightmares*, *Ghosts and Grisly Things*, *Told by the Dead*, *Just Behind You*, *Holes for Faces*, *By the Light of My Skull*, *Fearful Implications*, and a two-volume retrospective roundup (*Phantasmagorical Stories*) as well as *The Village Killings and Other Novellas*. His non-fiction is collected as *Ramsey Campbell, Probably* and *Ramsey Campbell, Certainly*, while *Ramsey's Rambles* collects his video reviews, and *Six Stooges and Counting* is a book-length study of the Three Stooges. *Limericks of the Alarming and Phantasmal* is a history of horror fiction in the form of fifty limericks. His novels *The Nameless*, *Pact of the Fathers* and *The Influence* have been filmed in Spain, where a television series based on *The Nameless* is in development. He is the President of the Society of Fantastic Films.

Ramsey Campbell was born in Liverpool in 1946 and still lives on Merseyside with his wife Jenny. His pleasures include classical music, good food and wine. His web site is at www.ramseycampbell.com.

Marco Cultrera (I Clean the Monster that Killed My Husband Every Morning) was born in Rome, Italy, and lives in Ottawa, Canada. After a start as a theoretical physicist, he built a decade-long career as a video game writer, creative director, and game designer, punctuated by a bout as stay-at-home dad of three daughters and, more recently, four cats.

E.C. Dorgan (Bloomer) is an emerging Métis writer from Alberta, Canada. She has stories forthcoming in *The Dread Machine* and *Metaphorosis,* but this is her first publication.

Born in England and raised in Toronto, Canada, **Gemma Files** (The Corpse-Door) has been an award-winning horror author for almost thirty years. She is probably best-known for her novel *Experimental Film,* for which she won both the Shirley Jackson Award and the Sunburst Award, and her Bram Stoker Award-winning short story collection In *That Endlessness, Our End.* Her latest collections are *Dark Is Better* (Trepidatio) and *Blood From the Air* (Grimscribe Press).

Douglas Ford's (Wonce Was A Woman) short fiction has appeared in a variety of anthologies, magazines, and podcasts, as well as two collections, *Ape in the Ring and Other Tales of the Macabre and Uncanny* and *The Infection Party and Other Stories of Dis-Ease.* His longer works include *The Beasts of Vissaria County* and *The Trick*, his newest from Madness Heart Press. His novella, *Little Lugosi (A Love Story)*, won the Literary Nastie award for best long fiction in 2023. He lives on the west coast of Florida.

Sarah Hans (A Grace of Finer Form) is an award-winning writer, editor, and teacher whose stories have appeared in more than 40 publications, including *Apex Magazine* and *Pseudopod.* She is the author of the horror novel *Entomophobia,* the short story collection *Dead Girls Don't Love,* and the novella *An Ideal Vessel.* You can find her on Twitter, Instagram, and TikTok under the handle @witchwithabook, where she loves to talk about what she's reading. She lives in Ohio with her partner, the best stepkids in the galaxy, and a small circus of pets.

Gabino Iglesias (Are Monsters Real?) is a writer, editor, literary critic, and professor living in Austin. He is the author of *The Devil Takes You Home, Coyote Songs,* and *Zero Saints.* His work has won the Bram Stoker Award, the Shirley Jackson Award, and the Wonderland Book Award, and has been nominated for the Edgar, Locus, Anthony, Reading the

West, and other awards. He teaches creative writing at SNHU's online MFA and at the UCR Palm Desert low-residency MFA.

Gwendolyn Kiste (The Sea Witch of the World's Fair) is the three-time Bram Stoker Award-winning author of *The Rust Maidens, Reluctant Immortals, Boneset & Feathers, Pretty Marys All in a Row*, and *The Haunting of Velkwood*. Her short fiction and nonfiction have appeared in outlets including *Lit Hub, Nightmare, Best American Science Fiction and Fantasy, Vastarien, Tor Nightfire, Titan Books*, and *The Dark*. She's a Lambda Literary Award winner, and her fiction has also received the This Is Horror award for Novel of the Year as well as nominations for the Premios Kelvin and Ignotus awards. Originally from Ohio, she now resides on an abandoned horse farm outside of Pittsburgh with her husband, their excitable calico cat, and not nearly enough ghosts. Find her online at www.gwendolynkiste.com.

Jamie Lackey (Unsubscribe Bird Facts) lives in Pittsburgh with her husband and their cats. She's had over 170 short stories published in places like *Daily Science Fiction, Beneath Ceaseless Skies*, and *Apex Magazine*. She has a novella and two short story collections available from Air and Nothingness Press, and her new collection of weird fantasy stories, *Shadows on Glass and Other Stories,* is out now! In addition to writing, she spends her time reading, playing tabletop RPGs, baking, and hiking. You can find her online at www.jamielackey.com.

Joe R. Lansdale (Lizard War) is the author of fifty novels and four hundred shorter works, including stories, essays, reviews, film and TV scripts, introductions and magazine articles, as well as a book of poetry.

His work has been made into films, *Bubba Hotep, Cold In July,* as well as the acclaimed TV show, *Hap and Leonard*. He has also had works adapted to *Masters of Horror* on Showtime, Netflix's *Love Death + Robots*, Shudder's *Creepshow*. He has written scripts for *Batman: The Animated Series,* and *Superman: The Animated Series*. He scripted a special *Jonah Hex* animated short, as well as the animated Batman film, *Son of Batman*. He has also written scripts for John Irvin, John Wells, and Ridley Scott, as well as for the Sundance TV show based on his work, *Hap and Leonard.*

His novel, *The Thicket,* is set to film in the near future, and will star Peter Dinklage. Many of his works have been optioned for film multiple times, and many continue to be under option at the moment.

He has received numerous recognitions for his work. Among them the Edgar, for his crime novel *The Bottoms,* the Spur, for his historical western *Paradise Sky,* as well as ten Bram Stoker Awards for his horror works. He has also received the Grandmaster Award and the Lifetime Achievement Award from The Horror Writers Association. He has been recognized for his contributions to comics with the Inkpot Life Achievement Award, and has received the British Fantasy Award, and has had two New York Times Notable Books. He has been honored with the Italian Grinzane Cavour Prize, the Sugar Pulp Prize for Fiction, and the Raymond Chandler Lifetime Achievement Award. *The Edge of Dark Water* was listed by Booklist as an Editor's Choice, and The American Library Association chose *The Thicket* for Adult Books for Young Adults. Library Journal voted *The Thicket* as one of the Best Historical Novels of the Year.

He has also received an American Mystery Award, The Horror Critics Award, and the Shot in the Dark International Crime Writer's Award. He was recognized for his contributions to the legacy of Edgar Rice Burroughs with The Golden Lion Award. He is a member of The Texas Institute of Literature and has been inducted into the Texas Literary Hall of Fame and is Writer in Residence at Stephen F. Austin State University.

His work has also been nominated multiple times for The World Fantasy Award, and numerous Bram Stoker Awards, the McCavity Award, as well as The Dashiell Hammett Award, and others.

He has been inducted into the International Martial Arts Hall of Fame, as well as the United States Martial Arts Hall of Fame and is the founder of the Shen Chuan martial arts system.

His books and stories have been translated into a number of languages.

He lives in Nacogdoches, Texas with his wife, Karen.

Jonathan Maberry (Critical Mass) is a New York Times bestselling author, 5-time Bram Stoker Award-winner, 4-time Scribe Award winner, Inkpot Award winner, anthology editor, writing teacher, and comic book writer. His vampire apocalypse book series, *V-Wars,* was a Netflix original series starring Ian Somerhalder. He writes in multiple genres including suspense, thriller, horror, science fiction, epic fantasy, and action; and he writes for adults, teens and middle grade. His works include the *Joe Ledger* thrillers, *Kagen the Damned, Ink, Glimpse,* the *Rot & Ruin* series, the *Dead of Night* series, *The Wolfman, X-Files Origins: Devil's Advocate, The Sleepers War* (with Weston Ochse), *NectroTek, Mars One,* and many others. Several of his works are in development for film and TV. He is the editor of high-profile anthologies including *The X-Files, Aliens: Bug Hunt, Out of Tune, Don't Turn out the Lights: A Tribute to Scary Stories to Tell in the Dark, Baker Street Irregulars, Nights of the Living Dead,* and others. His comics include *Black Panther: Doom War, The Punisher: Naked Kills,* and *Bad Blood.* He is the author or co-author of several nonfiction books on supernatural folklore: *The Vampire Slayers Field Guide to the Undead* (writing as Shane MacDougall), *Vampire Universe, The Cryptopedia* (co-written with David F. Kramer), *They Bite* (co-written with David F. Kramer), *Wanted Undead or Alive* (co-written with Janice Gable Bashman), and *Zombie CSU: The Forensic Science of the Living Dead.* His *Rot & Ruin* young adult novel was adapted into the #1 horror comic on Webtoon and is being developed for film by Alcon Entertainment. He is the president of the International Association of Media Tie-in Writers, and the editor of *Weird Tales Magazine.* He lives in San Diego, California. Find him online at www.jonathanmaberry.com.

Donna J. W. Munro's (Brother Bone) pieces are published in *Nothing's Sacred Magazine IV* and *V, Corvid Queen, Hazard Yet Forward* (2012), *Enter the Apocalypse* (2017), *Beautiful Lies, Painful Truths II* (2018), *Terror Politico* (2019), *It Calls from the Forest* (2020), *Gray Sisters Vol 1* (2020), *Borderlands Vol 7 (2020), Pseudopod 752 (2021),* and others. Check out her first novel, *Revelation: Poppet Cycle Book 1.* Contact her at www.donnajwmunro.com or @DonnaJWMunro on Twitter.

Frank Oreto (God Damn You to Hell, John Glenn!) is a writer of weird fiction living in the wilds of Pittsburgh, Pennsylvania. His short stories have haunted the pages of the *Magazine of Fantasy and Science Fiction, Pseudopod,* and *The Year's Best Hardcore Horror.* When not writing, Frank can be found concocting elaborate meals for his wife and ever-hungering children.

Tim Pieraccini (The Thirsty) lives on the South Coast of the UK, with 3,500 books and a similar number of DVDs. When not writing (which is too often) or attempting to reduce his TBR pile (which is too big for that), he can be found videoing performing arts students and editing the results. He has been published by *Flame Tree,* the *Triangulation* anthology series, and *Doctor Who Magazine.* The *Triangulation* story, *F Sharp 4,* featured in *The Best of British Science Fiction 2018.*

Pris Sears (The Pike) lives with her husband, artist Knic Umstead, near their families in Virginia. They make up two-thirds of local band *Your Thing.* Sears is an amateur horticulturist, professional IT geek, and shows metal and mixed media art. She has written newspaper columns and magazine articles in her home state. "The Pike" is her first published fiction.

Lucy A. Snyder (madOdyssey) is the Bram Stoker Award-winning and Shirley Jackson Award-nominated author of 15 books and over 100 published short stories. Her most recent titles are the apocalyptic horror novel *Sister, Maiden, Monster* and the collections *Halloween Season* and *Exposed Nerves.* She lives near Columbus, Ohio with a jungle of houseplants, a clowder of cats, and an insomnia of housemates. Learn more at www.lucysnyder.com.

Jeffrey Thomas (The Path of Skulls) is the author of such novels as *Deadstock* (Solaris Books), *Blue War* (Solaris Books), and *The American* (JournalStone). His short story collections include *Punktown* (Prime Books), *The Unnamed Country* (Word Horde), and *Haunted Worlds* (Hippocampus Press). He has been a finalist for the Bram Stoker Award and the John W. Campbell Award, and his stories have been reprinted in

The Year's Best Horror Stories XXII (editor, Karl Edward Wagner), *The Year's Best Fantasy and Horror* #14 (editors, Ellen Datlow and Terri Windling), and *Year's Best Weird Fiction* #1 (editors, Laird Barron and Michael Kelly). Thomas lives in Massachusetts.

Gaby Triana (Song of the Devil Trumpet) is the Cuban-American author of 22 books for adults and teens, including *Moon Child, Island of Bones, River of Ghosts, City of Spells, Wake the Hollow, Cubanita,* and *Summer of Yesterday.* Her short stories have appeared in *Classic Monsters Unleashed, A Tribute to Alvin Schwartz's Scary Stories to Tell in the Dark, A Conjuring for All Seasons, Novus Monstrum,* and *Weird Tales Magazine.* She has co-authored ghosthunters Sam & Colby's horror novel, *Paradise Island,* and edited the ghost anthology series, *Literally Dead* (*Tales of Halloween Hauntings; Tales of Holiday Hauntings*).

As a ghostwriter, Gaby has penned 50+ novels for bestselling authors in every genre. Her own books have won the IRA Teen Choice Award, ALA Best Paperback, and Hispanic Magazine's Good Reads Awards, and she writes under several pen names, including Gabrielle Keyes for her paranormal women's fiction. She lives in Miami with her family and the four-legged creatures they serve.

Dragon's Roost Press

Dragon's Roost Press is the fever dream brainchild of dark speculative fiction author Michael Cieslak. Since 2014, their goal has been to find the best speculative fiction authors and share their work with the public. For more information about Dragon's Roost Press and their publications, please visit:

http://www.thedragonsroost.biz